THE LAST
SAFE
PLACE

THE LAST SAFE PLACE

By

NINIE HAMMON

BAY FOREST

Copyright © 2012
Ninie Hammon

Cover Illustration by Dogeared Design
Interior Design by Bookmasters

All rights reserved. No part of this publication may be reproduced, stored in a retrieval system, or transmitted in any form or by any means—electronic, mechanical, photocopying, recording, or otherwise—without the prior written permission of the publisher and copyright owners.

Published by Bay Forest Books
An Imprint of Kingstone Media Group
P.O. Box 491600
Leesburg, FL 34749-1600
www.bayforestbooks.com

Printed in the United States of America by Bay Forest Books

Library of Congress Cataloging-in-Publication information is on file.
ISBN 978-1-61328-076-8

For Tom, my rock and inspiration always.

Acknowledgments

I'd like to thank Young Life and the staff of Frontier Ranch, the Young Life camp located in a 9,500-foot hanging valley on the side of Mount Princeton, for granting me access to the *real* chalet in the *real* bristlecone pine forest above the camp at 12,000 feet. Standing there in the cold wind after a summer storm, I stared across the valley at Mount Antero and this story was born.

OTHER BOOKS
BY NINIE HAMMON

God Said Yes
Sudan
The Memory Closet
Home Grown
Five Days in May
Black Sunshine

CHAPTER 1

When Gabriella Carmichael's eyes suddenly popped open, pain and blood were still several minutes away, tucked securely into the glove box of the future, snug as a map of Idaho.

She shook her head fiercely to dislodge the tattered, gauzy remnants of sleep so she could focus. That's when she sensed his presence, maybe even smelled him—a sickly sweet aroma like decay.

Yesheb is here! *In the house!*

A clap of thunder rumbled brutally loud and she jumped, uttered a little peep of a scream. She scooted to the edge of the bed and stared out her bedroom window where writhing lightning torched the night sky behind the silver worms of rain squiggling down the glass.

No! It's not supposed to storm tonight!

Gabriella had checked and rechecked the forecast—cloudy, just *cloudy*—but had propped herself up on pillows to stare into the darkness until dawn anyway. She'd done the same thing when she couldn't sleep the night before. And the night before that.

How could she possibly have drifted off *now?* Dropped her guard like that *tonight!?*

With her heart banging against the walls of her chest like a sperm whale in a fish tank, Gabriella struggled to look at every square inch of the room at the same time. Was he actually here ... maybe even in the bedroom? She began to tremble so violently she was afraid the bedsprings would squeak from the movement, and she had to be quiet!

As her eyes darted from the empty doorway to the shadowed dressing table to the hulking armoire in a herky-jerky motion that made seeing anything all but impossible, a voice from that maddeningly reasonable part of her mind began to plead its case before the High Court of Common Sense.

« 1 »

How could Yesheb possibly be in the house? There was an armed guard patrolling the property—*with a pit bull!* And a brand new security system. Besides that, P.D. was right across the hall. He might be a golden retriever, but he'd at least bark to *welcome* an intruder.

She let out the breath she'd been holding and almost giggled in the flood of sweet relief that washed over her. She'd trust Puppy Dog's nose over technology any day. He would—*P.D. wasn't here!* He'd gone to the guest house with Ty to spend the night with Theo.

Rationality still refused to budge.

Yesheb had obeyed the restraining order, had remained obediently one hundred feet away from her at all times, and the man had never done anything as drastic as this, as breaking into her house!

And that's a valid argument? He isn't here now because he's never been here before?

Come on, Gabriella. You're just overreact—

It's after Good Friday. It's a full moon. It's storming outside. He's here!

She gasped, the intake of air so abrupt and urgent she almost started coughing. Instead, she stopped breathing altogether. Between the lightning flashes and accompanying rumbles … underneath the silence that thundered in heartbeat bursts in her ears … was a noise. A small sound, really, but a noise even one of those mindless idiots in horror movies would consider sinister. Gabriella certainly did since she'd made a Note to Self only a few hours earlier that she needed to get the handyman to put a new brass kick plate on the bottom of the door that led from the side entrance of the house into the kitchen. Something—or some*body*, probably Ty—had bent the edge of the plate and now it dragged across the Moroccan tiles with a scraping sound that she could hear *right now.*

Only that was absurd. She couldn't possibly hear that door scrape way up here on the second floor. She held her breath, strained to hear with every ounce of concentration—

There is it was again! The scraping sound. But the sound wasn't coming from downstairs. It was coming from across the hall, from her son's bedroom. That made no sense at all because the floor in Ty's room was carpeted.

Air exploded out of her lungs and she bit down so hard to stifle the accompanying scream that she tasted blood in her mouth.

THE LAST SAFE PLACE

The old baby monitor!

Ty had found it in the back of his closet and she had been pretending for days she didn't know the boy was using it to eavesdrop on conversations all over the house. She'd spotted the sending unit hidden behind the sugar canister on the kitchen counter before supper tonight.

He must have left the receiving unit turned on in his bedroom!

She grabbed the telephone on the nightstand beside the bed, wrestled the receiver off the cradle with shaking hands and put it to her ear. No dial tone. She stifled a small sob and felt around for her iPhone in the slot in her Bose SoundDock speakers where she'd set it last night to blast out rap music—she *hated* rap music—to keep her awake. She located it—whimpering now—picked it up and then fumbled it in her shaking hands. It fell into her rumpled sheets and she dug around frantically trying to find it in the dark. Wanting to scream. Knowing she couldn't.

Run!

No, hide!

Which?

T HE SCRAPING SOUND stops Yesheb in his tracks. He waits, his breathing even and steady. But he is committed now, halfway through the door. It will scrape again no matter which way he moves it, so he pushes it forward and steps silently into the kitchen. Then he pauses to listen.

Yesheb hears the scuttling cockroaches in the wall behind the kitchen sink—evolutionary perfection, creatures of his realm. He hears the squeak of the air conditioner fan in the basement HVAC unit and the movement of the air through the ductwork. He hears the flutter of an owl's wings in the tree by the porch, the whisper of spiders spinning webs behind the couch and … that sound, beating at the edge of his hearing. Could that be the mad, terrified, thumping of Zara's heart? Does she know he's here?

He hopes so!

Yesheb throws back his head and laughs uproariously without making a sound.

Then he follows the scent of her fear, moving as silently as a daddy long-legs across the kitchen, through the dining room to the living room. His shoes cleave the lush pile of the carpet and the sound purrs softly in his ears.

He has never been inside her house, and the essence of her all around him is almost overwhelming. He can sense her everywhere, the way a bloodhound can still smell a person long after they have left the room. He pauses to breathe her in and his heart responds to her nearness, begins to beat faster. He continues across the darkened room, bumps a table in his haste and reaches out with feline grace to catch a blown glass vase before it hits the floor. The vase shimmers in the sudden white glow of lightning from the window, either black or blood red, impossible to tell without turning on the lights. Yesheb could do that, of course; he does not fear detection. But darkness is always preferable to light. Its sensuous warmth caresses his skin, oils it as he glides in and out of puddles of shadow.

Yesheb draws power from fear, the spawn of darkness, and he feels his strength building. Zara is afraid of him. Her terror pulses off her, disturbs the air around her. Of course, she *wants* him! Every woman wants him. But she's afraid he'll hurt her—and she has every right to be. The thought of her delicious screams shoots through his body like a low-power electric shock. Oh, he will not cause her so much pain that enduring it makes her strong. No, just enough, a sweet agony tart as lemon juice, an ever-present debilitating, demoralizing torment. Just enough so she cowers in his presence and cringes when he draws near her.

He does not want her love; he wants her fear. That will bind his bride to him forever.

GABRIELLA KNEW SHE had only seconds to decide what to do, no margin for error, no mulligans. Her bed was unmade, her sheets still warm. He'd know she'd just left—hiding was futile. She had to run.

She flew to the door of her room in bare feet with her long, white nightgown whipping around her legs. Lightning shattered like bright mirrors into sharp silver fragments outside her window; thunder rattled the glass. She couldn't think with her heart hammering in her ears louder than the thunder.

Calm down.

Yesheb didn't know which bedroom was hers; he'd have to look in them all and hers was the last one, at the end of the hall across from the back staircase. If she could get to the back stairs before he appeared in the hallway from the front stairs ...

THE LAST SAFE PLACE

She peeked around the door jamb.

The night light at the base of the stairs cast a pale yellow glow up the steps—backlighting a grotesquely pointed shadow moving slowly up the wall, its edges as jagged as a shard of glass. She watched, spellbound, like a mouse staring into the eyes of a cobra, as the shadow reached the top step and spread out thick as tar on the hallway floor. She knew the man who owned it was only a step or two behind.

The fine down of blond hair on her arms instantly stood on end, popped upright by goose bumps. She flattened herself against the wall by the door, panting, her face wet. Was she crying? No, it was sweat, fear sweat! She heard a faint squeak, the familiar, carpet-muffled cry of the top stair tread. She pressed herself tighter against the wall and held her breath, afraid Yesheb could hear her ragged, shuddery breathing.

He'd search each room as he came to it, wouldn't he? He'd stop first at the room at the top of the stairs. It was the only one of the six upstairs bedrooms where the furniture was arranged so the bed was not visible from the doorway. He'd have to take two or three steps into the room to see the bed was empty. That was all the time she'd have to dash across the hall and disappear down the back stairs.

She visualized where he must be. Top of the stairs now. Crossing the hall. She counted the seconds—one Mississippi, two Mississippi, three Mississippi. He should be inside the room ... *now*.

Gabriella leapt out the door.

And slammed into Yesheb's chest.

She screamed, the sound of fabric ripping into two shredded pieces. Then she fell back from him and banged her head painfully on the wall behind her.

"Again," he cried, his eyes wild. "Scream again!"

She shrieked louder, a cry of horror more than fear. Yesheb standing in the shadowy hallway, huge, dressed in black, his face twisted in that smirking smile was the single most monstrous sight she had ever seen—her recurring nightmare come to life.

"One more, Zara?"

I'm not Zara!

But she had no air to give voice to the words even if she'd dared. Yesheb's presence had sucked all the oxygen out of the hallway.

"Go ahead, make all the noise you want, get it out of your system. Or are you finished? You might need that voice to cry out for some other reason later on so I'd hate for you to lose it now in a ..." He reached into his jacket and withdrew a vicious-looking dagger from an ornate leather scabbard. Its shiny blade was dulled by some dark liquid. Yesheb wiped some of it onto his finger and licked it off slowly as he continued, "... futile effort to rouse your guard. Or his useless mutt."

She stared at the knife and it dawned on her ponderously, like picking up something huge, that there was no one to rescue her.

"You knew I'd come for you." His voice had the rounded, modulated tones of a television news anchor. Somehow oily, though—greasy. She could imagine his words slathered with slime.

It wasn't a question, so she didn't answer it. But she *had* known. Had been dreading his arrival since April 2. Good Friday. That's when the hourglass of providence had been turned and the sand began to slide silently into the empty sphere below. That's when the four-full-moons countdown clock had started ticking. She'd known then he would come. She'd done everything she could to guard against him but somehow she'd known all along it wouldn't be enough.

"It is time!" A bolt of lightning slashed across the sky, trailing a rumble of thunder as an exclamation point on the end of his sentence. "You can see, my lovely Zara, that the heavens eagerly await our union and our reign. Now, which room is the boy's?"

"Ty? What do you want with—?"

He slapped her. Hard, but casually, like flicking a piece of lint off his shoulder. Her head snapped to the side; she grunted and staggered but didn't fall. With her cheek aflame, she felt a trickle of blood begin to slide down her upper lip.

"Get the boy. I need him."

She looked up into his face to plead for him not to drag her little boy into this nightmare. But the words died on her lips. Though the light was poor, she could see his eyes were the eyes of a shark cruising dark waters in a night sea. Empty, but not lifeless, they were aglow with a sentient brutality barely held in check. She knew him better than he knew himself because she had shaped and formed him, and the message in his ice-blue eyes was unmistakable: There was absolutely *nothing* this man wouldn't do, no evil of which he was incapable.

THE LAST SAFE PLACE

"Ty's not home," she stammered and watched his face darken, his eyebrows draw together like the clouds gathered in the storm outside the window. "That's his room, see for yourself. He's spending the night with … a friend. Joey Thompson, from his school."

Yesheb grabbed her by her upper arm, yanked her across the hallway and through the open door into Ty's room where a fire truck wallpaper border was the last remnant of the "little-kid" decor she was scrambling to obliterate because it had become "just-shoot-me" embarrassing to him. The fire truck bed was already gone, replaced by a double bed with a Pittsburgh Steelers bedspread. Giant posters of Troy Polamalu and Ben Roethlisberger now hung where paintings of fire hydrants, ladder trucks and firemen had marched along the wall above his bed. The room was in its usual state of chaos. Wrinkled clothes were casually strewn everywhere; it smelled of dirty gym socks. But the bed was made; it was clear it hadn't been slept in tonight.

Yesheb was still suspicious. "This is a school night. You wouldn't let him stay overnight at a friend's on a school night."

He was right. She wouldn't. Ty wasn't at a friend's house; he was sound asleep on the far side of the back yard. At least he better be asleep. She'd agreed to allow Ty to stay in the guest house with his grandfather—*if* he was in bed by nine o'clock.

"Ty and Joey are working on a science project together. It's due tomorrow and they needed to work late to finish it." She could feel Yesheb's mounting rage in the fingers that dug into her upper arm. He pointed to the pile of books and the open backpack on the desk.

"Why didn't he take his books with him?"

"He doesn't need the books for the project," she said, fabricating a story as the words fell out of her mouth. "The boys are … building a geodesic dome out of sugar cubes. Mrs. Thompson's bringing Ty home later tonight." He squeezed her arm tighter, glared at her. "When he and Joey are finished, she'll drop him off." Yesheb's pinching grip on her arm had cut off all circulation to her hand.

"What time will he be back?"

"I said he had to be home by eleven o'clock."

Yesheb said nothing. Either he'd believe her or he wouldn't. She had no idea what she would do either way.

"Eleven o'clock. That will leave us enough time."

He let go of her arm and as she rubbed it to get the circulation back, sheet lightning danced across the night sky and he studied her in the splashes of light that spilled in through Ty's curtainless window. She felt horribly exposed in the white cotton nightgown. Her long hair—natural blond but colored jet black—hung around her shoulders in a tangle of curls. The curls were natural, too; she had to use all manner of appliances and goo to achieve a straight-as-a-broom-handle, parted-in-the-middle look.

He moved a step closer.

Here it comes.

Some calm voice inside her informed Gabriella that she was about to be raped. Apparently, she was already disassociating because the voice wasn't even her own. But she recognized it. It was the laboriously cheery voice at the airport that warned: "Do not leave baggage unattended at any time while in the terminal as it may be removed in accordance with TSA regulations."

When he reached out his hand, she shrank back from him. That actually seemed to please him.

"My seed in your womb will produce … perfection." He was breathing hard now. She could smell garlic and mint mouthwash. His voice was thick. "Our union will be a mating like none other the world has ever known." She could feel heat pulse off his body. Every other time she'd been near him he'd felt as cold as death. "I will take you as no man—"

He stopped abruptly, as if he had literally grabbed hold of his own arm. Then she watched him drag himself back from the edge. "But not yet." His voice was breathy. "Not until we have performed all the rituals."

Then he touched her cheek, tenderly caressed the thick expanse of twisted scar tissue that covered the right side of her face that puckered the skin from below the corner of her eye to the bottom of her jaw.

"Beautiful, my dear," he crooned, as if he was talking about the scar and not her face. And maybe he was. He leaned toward her, as if to kiss the scar. She felt his cheek next to hers, his breath on her neck. She cringed away. He began to nibble on her ear—

A lightning bolt of pain stabbed into the side of Gabriella's head and she shrieked. She lurched back and saw blood on Yesheb's mouth and he was chewing …

She reached up, confused, and grabbed her ear, on fire with agony. It was wet—she was bleeding—and there was a ragged …

THE LAST SAFE PLACE

He had bitten off her ear lobe! *That's what he'd been chew ...*

The room began to whirl around and around. The pain dimmed. The light grayed out. The world went black.

When Gabriella came to, she was lying on her bed. The pain in her ear fired her instantly alert. Blood had soaked the top right side of her nightgown and was smeared on the sheets around her. But when she reached up she found a bandage on her ear—crude, made with gauze and some surgical tape Yesheb must have found in the cabinet in the bathroom. She sat up and saw that her gown was hiked up above her knees, twisted around her. She grabbed it, yanked it down, scooted back against the headboard and pulled the covers up around her the best she could.

Yesheb stood rigid in the doorway staring at her. The fire of hunger in his eyes was so fierce she could feel the heat all the way across the room.

"Your skin is soft," he purred. "Smooth beneath my hand." He stopped, took a deep breath and let it out slowly. "But ... I did not, I *would not* dishonor you, my precious Zara."

She stared at him, unblinking, didn't move. Maybe she was going into shock. No, she was already in shock. Reality was wrapped in cotton; everything felt muted, muffled.

"We will be joined together," he rasped through clenched teeth, "only when it is time."

Apparently unaccustomed to reigning in his passions, he turned abruptly, stepped out into the hallway and began to close her door behind him. "I will wait for that time here."

It was obvious he could barely hold his need in check. Maybe he couldn't manage it in the same room with her.

Gabriella burst into tears and didn't know why. Perhaps the menace of his passion was unbearable. But that didn't make her feel like *crying*. Running, yes, but not crying. Sobs wracked her whole body anyway, without the advice and consent of her mind. If this intensity kept up, she'd soon be hysterical. But maybe this was hysteria.

Yesheb seemed to approve of the tears.

Her sobbing ramped up a notch, and still she felt like a spectator to it.

Then he said something that would have been tender from a normal man. "I will be right outside your door, my precious Zara. When you have cried yourself to sleep, I will come in and sit with you in the darkness and watch over you." His next words were spoken in a voice deep and booming, the sound bouncing off the insides of an oil drum. "When the boy comes, we will perform the sacrifice and then *we shall be one!*"

She stopped crying in mid-sob, sucked in a ragged gasp as understanding dawned.

The *sacrifice?* Ty!

Yesheb closed the door behind him as Gabriella fell over in the bed sobbing. But this time her horrified mind had joined her body in hysteria.

He stands in the hallway outside her room and listens to her cry. It is a haunting sound, lost and lonely and lovely, one he yearns to hear often. It rises and falls in something like a melody, a song of fear and horror that goes on and on.

Yesheb hears it while his mind processes dozens of other sensations at the same time. He read once that autistic children are unable to differentiate among all the stimuli assaulting their senses, unable to tune anything out, so for them, life is a cacophonous cauldron of unintelligible sounds and smells, sights and feelings.

Yesheb's mind is more like an autistic mind than a normal one. But rather than being unable to differentiate among the stimuli around him, he is able to attend to all of it at once. He stands in the maelstrom of it now, tastes the salty flavor of blood and tissue, hears the sobbing as part of a symphony of his own breathing whishing in and out and his heart's rhythmic thump-whoosh, thump-whoosh. He smells fear sweat—hers—and arousal sweat—his—and feels the compression of his feet into shoes, his body into clothing and sees…

All the color is gone.

He balls his hands into fists so tight his fingernails dig into his palms. No blue sky, green grass, red lips. No color in anything. Black, white and shades of gray.

He can't think about that now! Will *not* think about it! He maintains absolute control over his mind and body and can remove thoughts from—

Why is the color gone? Where did it go? Is it a punishment?

What have I done to anger The Voice?

The thump-whoosh, thump-whoosh of his heart kicks into a gallop. Horrid little doubts roar around in his head. Ugly bikers on custom Harleys, they race faster and faster as something like panic rises up with a taste of vomit in his throat.

THE LAST SAFE PLACE

And for a long time he stands as if in a trance while huge battles are waged in his soul. Emotions attack in swarms but he fights them off, grapples to regain control. All the upheaval is painted on the background of sobbing. His bride, crying behind the closed door. The princess he has found against all odds, among all the women in the world.

After a while, the image of her begins to steady him. Once she is his, the planets will align properly. Yes. And he will see color again then. Yes!

But if something goes wrong and he cannot have her, will his other senses go away too, stop functioning? Leave him deaf or totally blind, unable to smell or feel?

An ice pick of dread stabs into his belly so powerfully he actually grunts from the pain of it.

"*No!*" he whispers aloud. "My bride and I will be one!"

When his essence is again totally present in the hallway—bloody and battered from contests unseen on the human plane, but triumphant—he listens to the music of Gabriella's tears. How he loves that sound. He could listen to it for—

She has been crying a long time. It's amazing she hasn't exhausted herself by now, sobbing that hard. Yet she continues to cry with the same abandon as when he left her.

A cold fist grabs his guts and squeezes. It is *not* fear! Yesheb has mastered fear!

Even so, he turns with the speed of a striking black mamba, flings the door open and switches on the light. The bed is empty. The window is open; rain has soaked the curtains and drips off the sill into a puddle on the shiny wood floor. On the nightstand, Gabriella's iPhone rests in a slot on a black speaker box. The microphone icon of the Voice Memo app shines on the screen and the sound of her sobbing issues through the speakers.

Gabriella is gone.

Yesheb lets out a cry, a wailing howl of rage and frustration, then turns and bolts down the stairs after her.

"Ty, wake up!"

Gabriella shook her son roughly. He was usually hard to awaken but his hazel eyes popped open instantly and he looked up confused.

"Mom, wha—?"

"Get up, we're leaving."

She threw back the covers and yanked the boy to a sitting position. She'd carry him if she could, but he was too big for that now. The golden retriever at the foot of Ty's bed had gotten to his feet as soon as she lurched into the room, panting and dripping, and stood beside her now, wagging his tail.

"Where are we go—?"

"Just come on!"

The boy picked up his glasses from the bedside table and fumbled them onto his face, then looked at the floor in a daze, searching for his slippers. She grabbed his arm and pulled him to his feet. "No time for shoes. Let's *go!*"

She heard movement behind her and the overhead light flicked on, momentarily blinding her. She turned in slow motion to face the man standing in the doorway, then grunted in relief, took two steps and slapped the light switch back off.

"What in the world—?" Theo began.

In the brief splash of light Gabriella had seen the shock on the old black man's face. She must look a fright. Her hair plastered to her skull, her nightgown soaked and ripped—she'd caught it on something as she climbed off the sun porch roof—with blood dripping from her ear. The bandage had slipped off during her nightmare flight across the yard, her white gown glowing like the tail of a comet in the flashes of lightning, so bright she feared the light would shine in the upstairs windows and Yesheb would see.

"Ty and I have to get out of here." She moved to drag the still sleepy child around him, but the old man stood firm, blocking the door.

"You not gone run outta here in the middle of the night 'less you tell me what—"

"There's a man in the house," she said. "A … stalker."

"A what?"

"A *stalker!*"

"How'd he get past that guard, that rent-a-cop Ridley?"

Gabriella had hired Thomas Ridley after the police refused to listen to any more of her complaints that she was being watched. She didn't have time now to tell Theo about the bloody dagger.

"Just *believe* me," she said. "A dangerous man is after …" She cut her eyes meaningfully to the boy, "… *us.*"

THE LAST SAFE PLACE

The old man's protest broke off as clean as a dry stick. "Then let's git!" He pulled his robe around him and started his peculiar hobble down the hallway leading to the door between the guest house and the garage.

"*You're* not going—" Gabriella began.

"So you gone leave me behind to make nice with Mr. Personality when he find out you not here?" he said over his shoulder without turning around.

Theo was right, of course. He wouldn't be safe here either.

They all hurried barefoot down the hall with P.D. close on their heels. They had just stepped into the garage when Gabriella heard it. The wind bore it into the guest house through the back door she had left open. It was a cry—savage, guttural, more feral than human. The cry of a beast.

Gabriella was weak with relief when she leapt in behind the steering wheel of her Lincoln Town Car and found the keys dangling in the ignition. The keys to the other two cars in the garage—the Mercedes and the Porsche—were in her purse on the dressing table in her bedroom. She'd been *almost* certain she'd left the keys in the Lincoln, but what if …?

As Theo slammed the back door behind P.D. and Ty and jumped into the passenger seat, she cranked the engine, flipped on the headlights and hit the button for the automatic garage door opener. Yesheb would be able to see the garage door opening from the house. The driveway curved around so the doors faced the back yard. He'd know where she was.

The door seemed to take a hundred years to crank up. Gabriella didn't wait until it was fully raised. As soon as it was high enough so the top of the car would clear it, Gabriella slammed the transmission into reverse and the big car charged backwards into the driveway. Thunder clattered like heavy boots on wooden stairs; sudden raindrops rattled like volleys of buckshot against the windshield. They were out in the open now, completely exposed. And she could feel his eyes on them, feel his rage. The most dangerous point was now, when she had to stop and put the car in drive, turn around in the oval and head for the street. If he came now …

Yesheb appeared in the rain-freckled glow of headlights. An apparition, a black ghost. She hadn't seen him coming, he was just there, his face frozen in a mighty contortion of rage, his handsome features so distorted he was hardly recognizable.

She screamed. The hood ornament was centered on his chest like the crosshairs of a rifle and she shoved the gearshift into drive and hit the accelerator, mashed it all the way to the floorboard. The car leaped at Yesheb.

Gabriella tensed for the impact, the horrible thumping sound he would make as the front grill hit him and threw him backward or under the wheels, or up over the hood and the top of the car.

But the car flew forward into empty air. Yesheb was gone. Had she only imagined he was there? Nobody could move *that* fast! She felt only a little bump, as if the back wheel had run over something small.

As the speeding car careened onto the street, Gabriella glanced in the rearview mirror. For only a moment, she saw him. A hulking shape of deeper darkness in the shadow cast by the garage as lightning torched the night sky. He was hunkered down low, like a lion preparing to spring forward, and she had the irrational fear that he could jump that far, that he could leap off the ground and land on the top of the car or crash through the back window.

And then the driveway with its shadowy figure vanished as they sped down the street. Gabriella thought it odd that all the street lights had double halos around them until she realized she was looking at them through both the water on the windshield and the pools of unshed tears in her eyes. She heard a strange, whining cry, but until Theo patted her leg comfortingly she didn't realize she was the one making the sound. She ground her teeth together and swallowed the cry and pressed her foot down harder on the accelerator.

Yesheb hadn't *walked* to her house. He had a vehicle hidden somewhere. Within minutes, he would cleave the night with his rage in mad pursuit.

The hunt was on.

CHAPTER 2

Theo reached over and patted Gabriella's leg when she started to make a whining sound in her throat that sounded like a cat got its tail caught in a lawn mower. The woman was driving through the rain like a bat outta hell and if she got the hysterics she'd ram the car into a tree.

"You doin' jes fine," he told her, but he didn't think she heard him. She was concentrating so hard on watching the road ahead through the windshield and looking in the rearview mirror at the same time that he didn't say nothing else for fear he'd distract her and then she'd ram the car into a tree for sure.

The odds of the three of them making it to wherever it was Gabriella was high-tailing it to wasn't looking real good right now, so he best keep his hands to himself and his mouth shut. And pray.

God, could you please keep this poor, scared white woman from killing us all? I'm a old man, gone be standin' at them pearly gates before long, but the boy here—he got a lot of living to do yet. And Gabriella—she deserve a chance to have a better life than that good-for-nothing son of mine give her. I know you see us and what a fix we in. Any help you got, send it our way. Amen.

Theo shot a glance into the backseat where he could see Ty's eyes magnified by his glasses, open so wide the whites was glowing like dice that come up snake eyes.

"You got your seatbelt buckled?" he asked.

"Yes sir." Theo barely caught his whisper.

Gabriella careened around a corner, hydroplaned for a moment then regained control. P.D. clawed at the seat and would have pitched over onto the floorboard if Ty hadn't grabbed hold of him.

"You hang onto Puppy Dog good and tight, hear."

Theo didn't care about the furball on legs, but that boy needed something to hold onto. "We gone be there real soon now."

Theo had no idea where *there* might be or how far away it was, but if ever was a boy needed reassuring, it was the one with a stranglehold on a golden retriever in the backseat of this car.

Theo was the only one of the three of them who wasn't afraid. Once you'd done your living, played the parts you's assigned, wasn't no reason to be afraid. And scared would wear you out! Life didn't have nothing to hold over your head when it had done took everything that mattered. Well, except the boy. He was another thing altogether. Much as Theo didn't want to admit it, Ty was the source of a ball of cold lard that had settled down deep in the pit of Theo's stomach. If some crazy fool done something to that little boy …

Gabriella made another sliding turn, this time onto Washington Road. They were in Upper St. Clair now, which was a couple of pegs down the pretentiousness ladder from where she and Ty lived in Mt. Lebanon. Now Theo knew where they were going. He'd been to a schmooze-with-the-celebrities party at Bernie Phelps's house once with Smokey and the band.

Smokey. Theo waited for a stab of pain at the thought of his dead son. He felt absolutely nothing at all.

Only thing Theo remembered about Bernie Phelps was that his squeaky little voice sounded like Joe Pesci and his round, bald head sat on his long skinny neck like a golf ball on a tee. Smokey'd said the man'd been married like eight times and Theo couldn't figure out how he got even one woman to say yes. Had to be the money. Even though he had gambling debts all over town, Bernie lived like a king at the end of a cul-de-sac on a street lined with huge oak trees. Gabriella screeched to a halt in the driveway that curved in front of the house.

"I'll go," Theo told her. "You stay here, leave the engine running in case he not home and we got to keep goin.'"

Theo hobbled fast as he could up the steps to the porch with huge, white pillars and rang the doorbell, holding the button in so it would keep ringing. He wanted to pound on the door with his fists and holler, "Let us in, quick! They's a crazy man after us!" But he didn't. Wouldn't do nobody no good to wake the whole neighborhood.

Seemed like he stood there an hour before he saw a sudden puddle of light on the lawn shining out through the rain from an upstairs window. Then the hall light glowed through the stained glass panels on both sides of the door. An eyeball appeared at the peephole and Theo heard the deadbolt snap free. Bernie opened the door but hid behind it like a woman got caught in her nightgown by the UPS man.

The Barney-Fife-nervous little man's whole face was a question mark. "What …?"

Theo didn't answer, just turned and motioned for the others, urging them on with a stage-whispered, "Hurry up!" Gabriella, Ty and P.D. rushed up the steps and scuttled past Bernie and into the house. Gabriella slammed the door behind them and leaned against it, panting and half sobbing.

"What …?" Bernie tried again.

Gabriella ignored him.

"Theo," she gasped. "There's a phone on the table at the end of the couch in there." She pointed into the darkened study. "Call the—"

"The law, yeah, I know."

Before he hobbled out of the entryway, Theo took off his robe and wrapped it around Gabriella's shoulders. She looked surprised, then grateful. Standing there shivering in the bright light in that wet cotton nightgown, she looked like the winner of a wet t-shirt contest. She needed something to cover herself and Bernie wasn't falling all over himself to help her out.

"What are you doing here?" Bernie's voice sounded like he'd just inhaled helium.

"Running for our lives," Gabriella told him.

"I got you a new security system. The thing cost more than the gross national product of most Third World countries."

"Fat lot of good it done if anybody with opposable thumbs can disarm it," Theo said. "Where's the dad-gum light switch?"

"Theo, please," Gabriella said. "Hurry!"

"This *is* hurryin'." He felt around on the wall, mumbling under his breath, "I move fast for a old man. If I's gone live long enough for a walker, I'd need one with a airbag." He found the light switch, then the phone and punched in 911.

Gabriella turned to Bernie. "Have you got a gun?"

"What?"

"A gun in the house?"

"No."

"A hunting knife, an ax, anything?"

"Of course not!"

"Then you better hope the police get here before he does."

"He who?"

"Who do you think—Yesheb. He broke into the house! And you wouldn't believe me that he was dangerous."

Theo put his hand over the mouthpiece of the receiver and spit at Bernie, "You ain't 'xactly doing a bang-up job looking after Gabriella—you know that, don't you? And without her, how you figure to finance all them alimony payments?"

A female voice spoke into Theo's ear. "Alimony payments? This is the 911 dispatch. Do you have an emerg—?"

"Yes, I got an emergency!" Theo turned his attention back to the phone in his hand. "We in Upper St. Clair and you need to send the po-lice 'fore that maniac shows up and kills us all." The Upper St. Clair part'd build a fire under them. Tell the law you was in the Hill District or Homewood Brushton and they wouldn't show up 'til the dead bodies started to stink.

Gabriella rushed over and yanked the receiver out of his hand. "I'm sorry," she said. "I'm calling from 2811 Ft. Couch Road. My son and I and my father-in-law came here, ran here because a man broke into my house and …" He saw her fire a glance at Ty and edit whatever she was planning to say. "… and now he's after us."

She answered a couple more questions, then hung up. Bernie was babbling but didn't make no sense, something about selling Gabriella's new book. Making money was the only thing Theo'd ever heard him talk about. Theo and Gabriella both ignored him.

Soon as she hung up the phone, Gabriella shoved her arms into the sleeves of Theo's robe and pulled the belt tight round her waist. Her eyes swept the room—the dark corners, the doors, the windows—like a prison searchlight. Her gaze passed over Ty and then yanked back to him. The boy was on his knees on the cold tile floor with his arm around P.D. His eyes were still huge, his face pale. She crossed to him and got down on one knee in front of him.

"Hey champ," she said. Her voice was trembly, but she got control of it. "You okay?" She reached out and ruffled his black curls. Theo figured Ty hated that. Most boys did at that age, but tonight, he leaned into her. It was clear Gabriella'd done somethin' to bring a world of hurt down around both they heads. Theo didn't know what it was but he was certain she hadn't meant to put that boy in danger.

"Who was that man, the one we almost ran over?" Ty asked. "Is he the same man we saw at the park and at the grocery store and in Florida? The one who's always sending you black roses?"

Gabriella nodded.

"Did he hurt you?"

The boy pushed the big, round glasses up on his nose, was all the time doing that—more often when he was upset. But he didn't need those big glasses to see the blood on his mother's ear and soaked white nightgown.

"Actually, I hurt myself. Got hung up when I was trying to get away from him."

Theo didn't believe that for a minute.

Gabriella pulled Ty into her arms, held him tight against her. "The man you saw is crazy, that's all. Crazy people do crazy things. But we're fine now, Sweetheart. We're safe here."

Theo didn't believe that either. From the look on her face, neither did Gabriella.

Ty didn't believe a word his mother said. They weren't fine and they weren't safe—here or anywhere else. He was certain they weren't because he knew what none of the rest of them did. He knew *why* the man in black was after them. He also knew the man wasn't after *them* at all. He was only after Ty.

The boy felt cold, a freezing in his veins like crystals forming in the little river of water that flowed across the roof tile outside his window. He'd watched it happen last winter, fascinated by how the cold could turn the clear water milky, sluggish and then still and dead.

The cold expanded all through him, freezing the rest of him as it slowly dawned on him that he had put everyone he loved in danger. His mother and Grandpa Slappy could be struck down along with him.

Ty's mother let go her crushing hug, sat back and looked down at him. Ty stared up into her eyes, locked onto her gaze and held on. He'd heard her tell Grandpa Slappy a couple of days ago that she'd never seen a child as intense as he was, who looked you right in the eye, never blinked or looked away. What his mother didn't know was that Ty always looked dead into her eyes to avoid looking at the rest of her face. He couldn't stand to see it, the ugly scarred horror that had melted away her beauty and turned her into a freak people gawked at and whispered about behind her back.

But her eyes were still beautiful, still the same hazel green—exactly the same color as the eyes that looked back at him in shame when he looked into the mirror.

"I love you, Champ," she said, and he could tell she was about to cry.

And that was his fault, too. Her tears were *his fault*. Everything was, all of it. He was the reason they were being hunted, chased out of their beds in the middle of the night.

Oh, how he yearned to tell her that, to blurt out in a rush how he'd been hunkered down, waiting for this for a long time. How he ached to tell her that the man in black, the Boogie Man, had come for him, not her. But, of course, she was in danger, too, would continue to be as long as she was …

Ty stopped breathing.

… as long as she was near him.

His mother got to her feet when she heard the wail of a distant siren, but Ty stayed where he was on his knees beside Puppy Dog.

Mom and Grandpa Slappy would never be safe until … until Ty was not there to draw the attention of the man who was after him. It was suddenly clear to Ty what he had to do. He had to leave, had to put as much distance as he possibly could between him and everyone he loved in the world. He had to run away.

A TEAM OF police officers rolled up with siren wailing and lights flashing. Gabriella met them at the door. One was a fat, red-headed man with a round face and chipmunk cheeks. The other officer was a hulking black man who stared openly at the scar on her face and asked blunt, borderline-hostile questions. While Theo took Ty into the kitchen in search of Mountain Dew, and Bernie barricaded himself in the den making telephone calls, Gabriella described what had happened to her and how she had escaped.

She didn't fill in all the details—how she'd collapsed sobbing on top of her iPhone in the bed, picked it up and tried to figure how she could use it to call the police without Yesheb hearing her. With her trembling hands, she'd accidentally touched the voice memo icon and watched the needle jump as it recorded her sobs. That's when the desperate plan formed in her mind. She'd forced herself to record ten full minutes of crying, fearing that any second Yesheb would open the door and catch her. Then she set her iPhone in the slot on her SoundDock speaker deck, touched the playback icon and made her escape.

But she did tell them in detail what Yesheb had done to her and described the bloody knife he'd shown her. At that point, Rude Cop spoke into the microphone attached to a clip on his shoulder and before long five more officers appeared, conferred with the first two and then left. She had just completed her account of trying to run Yesheb down with her car when one of them came back into the room and spoke into Fat Cop's ear.

Fat Cop nodded, then gestured toward Gabriella. The other officer gawked at her—he'd figured out she was the famous novelist Rebecca Nightshade—and didn't pick up that he was supposed to tell her what he'd found out until Fat Cop elbowed him in the side.

"Ma am, we looked and there wasn't … I mean, we couldn't find the guard, Ridley, any trace of him," Bumbling Cop said. "Searched all around the buildings and the grounds and didn't find a thing out of the ordinary. No blood, no signs of a struggle. And no vehicle. Did he drive to work?"

"You think a rent-a-cop and an attack dog took a cab?"

Bumbling Cop actually considered the question for a moment before he realized it was sarcasm. "There's no blood in the house, either, Ma'am. None on the sheets—"

"Then Yesheb changed the sheets!"

"Why would he do a thing like that?" Rude Cop asked.

To make it look like I'm the one who's crazy.

But she said nothing because she could already see where this was going. The same way all the other complaints had gone.

"In fact, all the beds in the upstairs bedrooms were made, no evidence anybody'd slept in them," Bumbling Cop continued. "And the windows were closed, too. No blood in the hallway where he … where you say he …"

"Bit off my earlobe? What—you don't believe me? Look at this!" Gabriella turned her head and thrust her bloody ear toward them. "You think I was attacked by killer pinking shears?"

"No, no, I didn't mean that, ma'am … Ms. Nightshade. I'm just saying the house was locked up tight." He held up the car keys she'd left in the ignition of the Town Car parked out front. "Had to use the door key on this ring to get in." He placed the keys on the coffee table. "And the alarm went off as soon as we opened the door. Liked to never got that thing shut down. The phone line worked fine, too."

About half an hour after that, another officer came in and had another whispered conversation with Fat Cop.

The round-faced policeman looked sheepish when he spoke to her, like he was embarrassed for her that she'd been caught in such an obvious fabrication. He'd recognized her by now, too. And had likely been told she was nuttier than a jar of Planters, filed complaints about being watched and followed all the time.

"Ms. Nightshade, we found Officer Ridley's car at his house in his driveway—no dog, though. He lives alone and he wasn't there, but a neighbor said he sometimes goes off, stays gone for days." The officer lowered his voice. "Said he had a drinking problem."

Gabriella just looked at him.

A security guard walks off the job in the middle of the night to go have a beer with his pit bull—that seem reasonable to you?

"And we checked on this Al Tobbanoft guy, the one you have a restraining order against. His butler said he's in the hospital with a broken foot—"

"*That's* what I ran over—his foot!"

"He broke it three days ago, Ma'am. That's what the doctor …"

"What hospital?"

"Stonybrook, a private hospital."

"Do you know who owns it?" she asked, then answered her own question. "I'd say the safe money's on the Al Tobbanoft family. But you might have to trace back through half a dozen corporations … which you can't, and I'm sure you wouldn't even if you could." She let out a long sigh. "Forget it. Just forget it."

The officer assured her they would continue to look into the incident and to check up on Thomas Ridley, who would no doubt show up unharmed after sleeping off a drunk somewhere. He said they hadn't dusted for prints in the house, but would be glad to if she requested it.

Fat Cop had become ingratiating. Any minute now he'd ask for her autograph.

But why look for fingerprints? If Yesheb had been careful enough to haul off the bloody sheets, he wouldn't likely leave any fingerprints behind.

There was no point in investigating further. Fat, Rude, Bumbling—and the other four dwarves—had no idea who they were up against. But she did. The report on Yesheb and his family from the private investigation agency she'd hired to check up on him—the same agency that had sent Ridley to guard her house—had been painstakingly thorough. Ridley had delivered it personally.

"He's a head case," Ridley had told her. The ex-police officer/security guard had gum in his mouth and popped it as he spoke. "Sophisticated, well-mannered, good looking—but a wacko. It was like yanking a redwood tree up by the roots, by the way, to drag information out of people. Everybody who's ever met him is scared of him. All I got was bits and pieces, but it looks like this guy has yo-yoed in and out of mental institutions since he was a kid. Hears voices, hallucinates, delusions of grandeur—one of those guys who thinks he's Attila the Hun one day and the Jolly Green Giant the next. Couldn't nail a diagnosis, but I figure he's at least bipolar and my money's on psychopath. Don't guess the label matters—all you need to know is the guy's insane."

Oh, and there was one other thing she needed to know. The man was also *rich*. Gabriella Carmichael was a wealthy woman; Yesheb Al Tobbanoft was Arab oil sheik rich. Affluent on a scale normal human beings couldn't comprehend. He had the kind of obscene wealth that meant you could do anything you wanted and get away with it.

F ROM THE GUEST bedroom on the second floor of Bernie Phelps's house, Gabriella watched the sun bleach the night out of the sky over Pittsburgh, saw the city stretch, yawn and reach for its morning coffee. She was sitting up in bed, her back against the headboard and her arms wrapped around her knees with Ty snuggled up next to her. He hadn't wanted to sleep by himself.

As gray dawn light slowly chased shadows into the corners of the room, her reflection gradually appeared in the ornate mirror above the dressing table across from the bed. Any time she caught sight of herself in a mirror, she automatically turned her head so only the left side was visible. Her good side. But she no longer had a good side. Her left eye was swollen partially shut where Yesheb had slapped her and a deep purple bruise puddled below it.

Black eye and bruised cheek or scar and mangled earlobe. Pick your poison.

Ty stirred and moaned in his sleep. She stroked his hair. It wasn't kinky—just big, shiny black curls that she probably let get a little shaggy because the curls were so adorable. Of course, if he knew that …

Gradually, the pinched look left his face and he relaxed. Probably a nightmare. Gabriella didn't have to go to sleep to have those anymore. They broke into her house and bit off her earlobe while she was wide awake.

She reached up and touched the tender flesh. One more challenge for her plastic surgeon, and she'd already financed Harvard educations for all three of his kids. Her face was the best reconstruction money could buy, and it was still a work in progress. But it would never look like it had before. The doctor told her that as soon as she woke up, before he gave her drugs that barely took the edge off the searing agony. She'd have to recalibrate her view of normal—that's how he'd put it. She closed her eyes and tried to remember what normal had looked like. Not a beautiful face, but pretty. Definitely pretty. High forehead, dark feathers of eyebrow above large hazel eyes, ho-hum nose, mouth too big, heart-shaped smile and a lone dimple on her right cheek, charmingly asymmetrical. That was gone now, of course. The acid had chewed through the dimple as it ate a hole in the side of her face all the way to the bone.

Bernie loved her scar, but then, Bernie would have loved leprosy if it made him a buck. He leveraged the disfigurement—a face scarred just like the heroine in her book—and created a marketing strategy around it that helped catapult *The Bride of the Beast* to the top of the *New York Times* best-sellers list. Her "Zara signature," along with a wardrobe of "costumes," straight black hair with bangs cut into a sharp triangle with the point at the bridge of her nose and blood-red fingernails combined to form an indelible trademark. Rebecca Nightshade, Gabriella's pen name and alter ego, was a franchise.

Ty wiggled, his brow furrowed and he rolled over onto his side, then over onto his back again. Another nightmare. Or perhaps a sequel to the first one. He looked achingly vulnerable in his sleep, but maybe even more so when he was awake. He'd insisted on big, round frames for his glasses that made him look like a baby owl.

THE LAST SAFE PLACE

She gulped back tears. For the past eight hours, she'd refused to allow her mind to process the greatest outrage of the night, because if she'd thought about it while she was trying to get away, she might have frozen solid from the horror of it, stood like a pillar of salt. But she couldn't dodge the reality any longer.

Yesheb had intended to use Ty *as a sacrifice!* Planned to stab her precious little boy in the chest and drain his life out as a blood offering!

She bleated a single sob, a little snort that roused Ty. So she clamped her hand over her mouth and merely shook silently as she cried. The sacrifice of an innocent had been *her* idea, like all the rest of it, the whole sick, ghoulish tale that had caught the fancy of millions of readers. And one of them used it to create his own distorted delusion, an insane fantasy that could very well get her son killed.

She cried for a long time silently, tears streaming down both cheeks and dripping off her chin. She rubbed Ty's back as she cried, smoothed his hair, kissed his forehead lightly so she wouldn't disturb him. Finally exhausted, she eased down from her sitting position and slid into the bed beside him. She slipped her arm under his neck and he rolled to her, his head on her shoulder. She inhaled the precious little-boy smell of him, lay back on the pillows and closed her eyes. She couldn't possibly fall asleep, of course, but she could at least rest for a little while.

The light is golden and warm.
Or is the warmth golden and bright?
Gabriella often wonders that or something like it whenever she is transported to the place she calls The Cleft. She doesn't know why she calls it that. Perhaps she knew once, but not anymore. The children who stepped into the snow of Narnia from out the back of a wardrobe were in a world that already had a name, and maybe The Cleft has a name, too, and she just doesn't know what it is. Or perhaps The Cleft is its name. She always has a sense that there is so much more to know about the warm golden world of solace and refuge than she can remember, that the place itself is as old as time and her history with it is far more complicated than she's ever tried to discover. She suspects the place is magical beyond her wildest dreams and more powerful than any force she's ever encountered.

« 25 »

But she doesn't really care. It's not important to her to know. She is content to stay here in the warm, golden glow because it is above all else profoundly good. And safe. Here no harm can come to her and that in itself is all the mystery and power Gabriella has ever needed.

She was only a child when she first came here. She has come dozens of times in the years since and the place has changed in those years. Or perhaps it is that Gabriella has changed and the ancient place of safety has remained exactly the same.

At the very least, her perceptions of it have changed because in the beginning it was a much more specific, detailed, real-life place, with real world attributes. Dirt on the ground. The smell of pine in the air. Cold stone, bright lights and a distant rumbling sound like a bowling alley next door. Now it has taken on that blurred-around-the-edges quality of dreams and fantasies with nothing at all that is substantial or earthly.

But one thing that hasn't changed over time is the beauty of the glow itself, the golden light that is the color of the amber stones in the room in the house where precious treasures were kept when she was a child in cabinets she wasn't allowed to touch. The glow shifts through amber, caramel and yellow like the colors in a kaleidoscope, and grants her brother's pale face the hue of a brown-toast suntan.

Garrett smiles at her. He has no front teeth and the gap-toothed grin is indescribably endearing. He speaks, but she doesn't hear. Either the distant booming drowns his words or the glow itself absorbs them because here there is no need for language.

Drumma du, Gabriella. Twin speak for I love you. Maybe Garrett says it, or maybe he doesn't but she hears the truth of it all the same.

Drumma du, too, Garrett.

Sometimes it's Ty's face instead of Garrett's.

But it's never Grant's face. Grant's dead and it is her fault. Hers and Garrett's. She understands that and what it means with a profound despair that is far beyond a child's ability to process.

And with that thought the sense of goodness, hope and safety fades and the glow dims like a dying candle and goes out.

By then, Gabriella was asleep.

When she awoke, a wisp of the golden-glow fantasy/dream blew through her mind like a tiny cloud driven before a mighty wind. Then it was gone. The room was no longer filled with morning sunshine. The sun was on the other side of the house now; it was early afternoon. The space beside her was vacant, the sheets cold.

She raised up on one elbow. Her mouth tasted like old tennis shoes and her eyes were gravelly. She was rested, though. Perhaps she'd gone to The Cleft. She suspected she'd dreamed of it again because she felt calm and relaxed as she always did when she awoke after dreaming about it. But more than that, she felt a sense of purpose now. At some point during the night—or during the dream—she had made a decision. She knew what she had to do—whether Bernie liked it or not. And he definitely wouldn't like it. Whether Ty or Theo liked it or not, and she couldn't predict how the two of them might respond.

There was a knock at the door.

"Who is it?"

"I left you something to wear," Bernie called through the door. "On the chair."

Gabriella rolled off the bed and got to her feet. She was dressed in a t-shirt Bernie had given her last night to replace the bloody white nightgown she'd arrived in. The dress draped over the chair was black—of course—and floor-length, made of satin. It had long sleeves flared at the ends and scalloped—like a bat's wings—with black lace at the neck and around the hem. She recognized it as one of the rejects. Bernie had provided dozens of costumes like this for her appearances at events and book signings and this was one of several she'd refused to wear. It was too low cut, showed too much cleavage.

She sighed. The dress was better than wrapping herself in a sheet.

She was tugging upward on the lace in front a few minutes later, trying to pull it up to her chin, when there was another knock at the door.

"It's me, Gabby." Bernie again.

Bernie was the only person in her life who called her Gabby. She hated it. But that was the least of the bones she had to pick with her ever-offensive literary agent who raked his 15 percent off the top, spoke for her and about her but only rarely to her. Smokey had talked her into hiring Bernie to sell her book during that period in their marriage when she would have done just about anything to keep the peace. It was a painless concession. She knew that book didn't have a turkey's chance at Thanksgiving of getting published, and even if it did, nobody would buy it. She was wrong on both counts. After

Shock Jock Howard Stern raved about *The Bride of the Beast* on his Sirius Satellite Radio show the week it was released, a clandestine video of her interview with him went viral on YouTube. The book was an instant best seller.

Gabriella always wondered what kind of people wanted to read about demons and darkness and evil. Which begged a more important question: What did it say about her that she'd written it?

"Are you decent?" he asked. "If you're not, get decent. And hurry up. It's time."

Time for what? She didn't like the sound of that.

If Han Solo were here, he'd be saying, "I've got a bad feeling about this, Luke."

Bernie was dressed in a suit and tie. He checked her out and nodded his approval.

"Excellent. You look worn out and beat up. That's good. And I like that dress. Shows some v-v-v-vooom."

"I look worn out and beat up because that's what I am. I'm really not into vooming right now, Bernie. What do you want?"

"You know what I want and you're late. Come on."

With that, he turned and hurried down the stairs and she followed reluctantly behind. His was one of those winding staircases—the kind designed for grand entrances.

She was halfway down the staircase before her mind registered the sound below. Low murmuring. The sound of a crowd. They suddenly came pouring out of the den with Bernie in front like he was leading his team onto the field.

Cameras flashed, blinding her. Reporters shoved microphones at her as if they were offering her snow cones.

"... tell us what happ—"

"... you attacked ...?"

"... a crazed fan ...?"

"... Ms. Nightshade, rumor has it you're writing a sequel to *The Bride of the Beast*—is this part of the publicity—?"

She answered that one.

"This has nothing to do with selling some stupid book!" She shot Bernie a look with enough venom to paralyze a walrus. "A man, Yesheb Al Tobbanoft, a crazy fan, broke into my house last night."

"Is that where you got that shiner?"

"Yes, he assaulted me."

"Will you file charges against him?"

"If the police cooperate, I will."

"A reliable source inside the police department says they found no evidence of an assault when they searched your house—is that true?"

"I wasn't there when they searched my house. I don't know what they found. But regardless of what they—"

"And that the man you claimed was your assailant was in the hospital at the time of the attack."

"He *said* he was in the hospital."

"His *doctor* said he was in the hospital."

"The doctor lied!"

"Why would he do that?"

"He was paid off, I guess." Gabriella was getting rattled. "I don't know. All I do know is—"

"My source says you have a restraining order against Mr. Al Tobbanoft and you've filed numerous other bogus complaints against him."

"They weren't bogus!"

"But you couldn't manage to make headlines until you claimed he assaulted you—is that right?"

"I don't decide what makes headlines, you do!"

"You're the one who called this press conference."

"I did not!" But, of course, she did. Bernie spoke with her voice.

"There are lots of ways to fake a shiner. Do you have any other *proof* that you were assaulted?"

"You think I bit off my own earlobe?" She was instantly sorry she'd said that. Nobody had noticed her injured ear. Now they came at her like Medusa, with dozens of spitting heads.

"You're saying this Al Tobbanoft guy *bit your earlobe off*?"

"Is that part of the plot of the sequel? Does The Beast bite—?"

"No, of course not."

"Then you *are* writing a sequel."

"I didn't say that!"

"Why would a crazed fan bite your—?"

"I don't know!" Gabriella finally lost it. "I don't have any idea. But he did." She sounded hysterical, but she couldn't stop herself. "I don't care whether you believe me or not. It happened. Just like I said it did. And it doesn't matter what the police or the hospital or the doctor—" She literally clamped her hand over her mouth to shut herself up. Then she turned, raced back up the stairs to the guestroom and slammed the door shut behind her.

She was sitting on the edge of the bed shaking when Bernie burst into the room a few minutes later. He was jubilant.

"You were absolutely glorious!" he gushed. "Saying he bit your earlobe off—that was *brilliant*. I want to get some pictures to mail out with a press release to—"

Gabriella leapt to her feet and slapped him as hard as she could. The blow staggered him, knocked him backward a few steps and caused his eyes to water.

"You slimy, bottom-feeding, lowlife …" Words failed her. "Now the police will believe that everything I say is a publicity stunt. Do you know what you've done? That monster intends to *murder* my son. Plans to sacrifice …"

She could see on his face he didn't believe her. Or didn't care.

"Get out! Get out of here *now*."

"Just a minute here, Sweet Cheeks. This *my* house and I—"

"Fine! Give me my car keys. And get out of my way."

CHAPTER 3

Gabriella sat on the big overstuffed chair in the motel room waiting for Ty to finish brushing his teeth so she could put him to bed and outline her plan for Theo. She'd moved them into adjoining rooms in a motel after leaving Bernie's. Even though Yesheb was injured, in the hospital, she couldn't face going home yet so she'd purchased three sets of clothes to replace the pajamas they'd been wearing when they escaped, along with a few necessary toiletries at Walmart. She'd made quite a stir pushing a cart up and down the aisles dressed like the Wicked Witch of the West.

If she understood Yesheb's mindset and motivation as well as she thought she did—and she should; she'd personally designed his depravity in excruciating detail—she was safe now, relatively speaking. But that was only true until the earth rotated through another lunar cycle.

"I've got a surprise for you, Champ," she said to Ty as she tucked him in bed. "We're going to New York." They often did that to see Broadway shows. It was a special treat that Ty loved. "I bought show tickets online, but we're not really—"

"Whatever." He rolled over to face the wall. She stood for a moment staring at his back, then leaned over and kissed his cheek, left the bathroom light on because he hated the dark and closed the door between the rooms behind her.

"I've made a decision," she told Theo as she settled herself back down into the big chair. "If I can figure out a way to shake Yesheb's bloodhounds, Ty and I are going into hiding until he stops looking for us."

"What you gone run for?" Theo asked.

"Because the fight-or-flight reflex doesn't offer a wide variety of options!"

"You could stand up to that crazy man, hire a bodyguard and—"

"I called the agency. Nobody has seen or heard from Thomas Ridley." She was sure nobody would ever hear from him again.

"Then hire a whole herd of bodyguards, make yo house into a fortress and then dare that fool to come and get you!"

The old man's blustering was maddening. "We'll go home and collect our things tomorrow. Now's our chance. Yesheb can't try anything for a while, not with a broken foot. And the full moon has passed."

"What the moon got to do with it?"

All the air whooshed out of Gabriella. She was so tired of all this.

"It's about what happens in the book, *The Bride of the Beast*. I wrote it in first person, from the point of view of the character Zara, and Yesheb thinks he …" She stopped. She'd never said it out loud before and it sounded so absurd. "He thinks he's a character in the book—the main character, The Beast of Babylon. I've been terrified for months that he might … and after last night, I *know* he …" She stopped again, gathered herself and spit it out. "Yesheb Al Tobbanoft intends to do *exactly* what the Beast does in the book."

"And that is?"

"Marry Zara—me." She whispered the rest because she didn't have the air to say it out loud. "And … sacrifice Ty. *Kill* him."

If a black man could turn pale, Theo did.

"You telling me that fool is play-acting some story!"

"He's not acting. To him, it's absolutely real."

Gabriella laid out for Theo the script that was the roadmap for Yesheb's behavior.

The Bride of the Beast was a bleak horror story about a lost kingdom of demons. According to the novel's plot, Yesheb would be crowned ruler of the Endless Black Beyond when he found the missing Princess Zara and took her as his bride. Smokey had called it Cinderella meets Darth Vader. The Beast must offer a sacrifice of "innocent blood" and mate with Princess Zara to produce a son and heir—all during the twenty-four-hour cycle of a full moon. Oh, and it had to be after "searing light rips open the canopy of heaven," too. In other words, after a thunderstorm.

Gabriella shook her head.

"*Now* do you see why nobody will believe me?"

That, boys and girls, is certifiably nuts!

If she hadn't seen it last night she wouldn't have believed it herself! Blood sacrifice … full moon … violent storm. Geeze Louise!

Gabriella shook her head again. Things like this didn't happen to real people and she was so ordinary. She bought food processor gadgets advertised on television at 3 a.m., for crying out loud! She'd been on a diet to lose five pounds her whole adult life. She watched Monday Night Football—go Steelers!—shopped with her Giant Eagle Discount Card and drooled over Mark Harmon on NCIS. (The white hair only made him sexier.) This was *crazy!*

Correction: Yesheb Al Tobbanoft was crazy. The rest of them were just along for the ride.

When Theo finally realized there was no way he could talk her out of running, he grudgingly agreed to help her. She hoped she'd light a fire in Ty's eyes when she told him where they were really going. When she told Theo, he looked like he'd been gut-shot.

T HEO LAY ON his back on the big queen-sized bed with sheets that smelled like bleach and had been ironed so stiff you could cut yourself on them if you rolled over wrong.

He didn't waste no time trying to make sense out of the past twenty-four hours because he already knew how he'd got his self tangled up in all of it. You had to be real careful what you prayed for.

Lord, I asked you for a gentle little breeze and you done give me Katrina!

When I said I wanted a chance to spend a little time with the boy, be a better grandfather than I was a father, I had in mind something like playing catch! Okay, maybe not throwin' a ball at him, but talking to him. Listening to him. Teaching him some jokes or how to make a saxophone sing. I didn't plan on gettin' chased out of my bed in the middle of the night by the poster boy for Nuts R Us. Now, Gabriella's sayin' they gone run off and crawl into some hidey hole—did you hear where she say they was goin'! For two months!

Now, what am I gone do? I don't have no more idea than a spook how I's supposed to fit into all this. You gone have to make it so clear a old man like me can't miss it. Like … write it in the sky.

In purple.

In Hebrew!

Amen.

Theo did know two things for certain, though. One was that the hearing was completely gone in his left ear. He'd had to concentrate real hard to understand what Gabriella'd been saying earlier. And he suspected that this time the hearing loss wasn't temporary, figured he'd ought to kiss that one goodbye. And the second thing he knew for sure was that something was eating at Ty that didn't have nothing to do with that crazy fool who wasn't no more The Beast of Babylon than he was the Tooth Fairy. He looked over at the boy in the next bed. Ty was sleeping soundly, not like last night.

Theo had been awake, in his robe and house shoes, when Gabriella came for Ty because he hadn't been able to go back to sleep after the boy woke him up screaming. Ty was fighting the covers, crying out how he was sorry and he didn't mean for it to happen, saying crazy stuff about killing his father. *Stoney'd died in prison!* When Theo shook Ty awake, the boy had curled up in a ball in the bed and told Theo to leave him alone. And all that was *before* the Ghost of Christmas Past showed up. Theo was planning to talk to Gabriella about it, but that conversation got hijacked—and might never happen now that they was leaving.

This wasn't what I had planned, Lord. Just so you know.

Ty stared at the puke green motel room wall as he listened to the rise and fall of voices in the next room. He couldn't understand what they were saying but figured it had something to do with their trip to New York to see a Broadway show.

Who cared about some dumb play! The only thing Ty wanted was to vanish quickly and quietly so the Boogie Man wouldn't come looking for him again and hurt his mother. Now, he'd have to wait until they got back home from—

Wait a minute. New York City. Millions of people. He could run away *there!* Just get up to go to the bathroom during the show and never come back. New York City was full of homeless people; nobody'd notice one more stray kid.

And after he ran away he would … what? Get a job washing dishes or sweeping floors, he supposed. That's what he'd seen orphans do in the movies. He didn't know how long the $300 he had saved would last, but he didn't think it would be long enough. When it was gone … well, he'd figure that out when the time came.

* * * *

Gabriella, Theo and Ty sat dawdling over dessert in the TGI Friday's in the Pittsburgh International Airport, killing time before their flight to JFK in New York.

"This coffee tastes like rat puke," Theo said.

"There's a Starbucks in the food court, Grandpa Slappy," Ty said. "I could get you a—"

"I'm a gone get me some coffee from that Starbucks I seen in the food court!"

"I just said I'd—" Ty started but Theo ignored him again and started to rise. Gabriella touched his arm and cut her eyes to P.D., lying peacefully on the floor at his feet. "Take Puppy Dog with you. You're supposed to be visually impaired, remember."

The big golden retriever—almost 85 pounds of him—was a trained assistance and service dog. When Ty was five years old, their busybody neighbor had convinced Smokey the boy needed a puppy. Since Smokey hated dogs, he'd been a soft sell when the lady proposed they volunteer to raise a puppy and then give the dog to an agency when he was 18 months old for training and placement with a handicapped person. It had sounded good on paper—no dog, just a puppy. It didn't occur to anyone—Smokey included—how attached they'd all become to the animal in a year and a half. When they had to give him up, the whole family went into a meltdown. Smokey held out for six months before he tracked the animal down through the agency and paid the owner $20,000—double the cost of a service dog—to get him back.

But P.D.'s training carried a bonus they hadn't considered at the time. Being a service dog meant he could go along with them wherever they went. Put his harness and sign on him and he was welcome anywhere.

"I don't want that animal nowhere near me," Theo said. He pointed down at the blond glaze of dog hair on the leg of his black trousers. "If I's to collect all the hair that fur factory has left on my clothes I'd have enough for a whole new dog."

Theo hobbled away and Ty stuck his ear buds in and cranked up his iPod while Gabriella called to confirm their reservations at the Warwick New York Hotel. Gabriella could hear the earphone music, a small, distant sound. It was Withered Soul, of course. His father's band. And Garrett's.

A sudden lump in her throat made it hard to swallow and her eyes filled with tears. She didn't mourn Smokey, who'd been the bass player in her brother's grunge metal band. But Garrett … the pain of her twin brother's death still took her breath away.

The melody and pounding rhythm was all she could catch from Ty's ear buds. But she knew the lyrics of *Night Screams,* the song that had propelled the *Vast Abyss* album to gold, because she had written them. And all the other lyrics for the band's music. She and Garrett had been a team, different sides of the same coin.

Gabriella could look back now and see how dark their collaboration eventually became, that together the two of them tapped into a great well of despair and hopelessness that neither one of them could have found alone. But there was a difference between them she didn't understand now any better than she ever had. Gabriella could walk away and leave it; Garrett's whole life existed on the barren plains his wailing laments sang about.

Some critics hailed the loneliness, desperation and anger of Withered Soul. Others deplored it. But none ever found fault with the quality of the music, the complexity of the chord structure, the haunting melody, Garrett's piercing tenor voice and amazing keyboard performance. It was genius. *He* was genius. Beginning the moment he walked into Trombinos Music Store in the Galleria Mall in the South Hills of Pittsburgh two days after his eighth birthday, climbed up on a bench in front of the first piano he'd ever seen and started to play, his incredible talent was a fiery meteor that burned exquisitely bright. Then flamed out.

Gabriella squeezed her eyes shut and tears slid down her cheeks. All the horror and fear of the past few days had ripped the scabs off so many childhood wounds. But not everything that bubbled up out of her childhood was horrible. The sweet, cleansing aroma of pine swirled around her. She could feel a damp mist on her face and a warm, golden glow shone through her closed eyelids. If she opened her eyes, she'd see Garrett's gap-toothed grin. She'd hear his silly giggle and a rumble like—

"Mom?" Ty's voice. "Are you crying?"

She reached up hurriedly and wiped her wet cheeks.

"No, Honey. Not crying, just …" Ty's face swam in the wash of tears, his features pinched, his brow wrinkled with concern. "I didn't get a whole lot of sleep last night and my eyes are tired, watery."

She knew he didn't believe her. What was it doing to the boy's trust that she constantly lied to him and he knew it?

"You know how much they charged me for this piddly little cup of Joe?" Theo eased himself into the chair facing her. "Three bucks! You b'lieve that? Just cause you in a airport and can't go no place else, they allowed to mug you. Might as well club you brains out with a roll of quarters in a tube sock!"

Gabriella opened her mouth to launch into her familiar refrain—that Starbucks coffee was always overpriced, no matter where you got it. That coffee was coffee. Adding a bunch of cheaper ingredients like milk and ice and sugar ought to make the brew cost less, not more. That you were paying for advertising and—

She didn't say any of those things, however, because she caught sight of a young black man with a Pirates baseball cap turned sideways on his head and full sleeves of tattoos all the way up both arms making his way to their table. He was decked out in full bore hip-hop. Baggy shirt, pants belted tight ten inches below his waist so the crotch hung down between his knees and his plaid underwear was plainly visible. He had an earring in his left ear the size of the Hope Diamond, a teardrop tattooed on his right cheek and a silver stud in his tongue. And he held a copy of *The Bride of the Beast* in his hand, glancing down at the picture on the back cover as he approached.

Gabriella was surprised she'd been recognized with her black hair in a neat bun, her pointed bangs pulled back under a headband and her scar hidden beneath a thick layer of makeup. She sighed. In a few minutes, this fan would likely be very sorry he'd spotted her. The poor boy had no idea what getting that book autographed was about to cost him.

"This is you—right?" the young man asked.

"And who you think you be, fool?" Theo said before she could answer. He glared at the stranger through the steam rising out of his Starbucks cup.

Theo wasn't a big man—five-eight maybe, with rounded shoulders and a paunch—but he had an intimidating presence Gabriella could only acknowledge, but not define or explain. Maybe it was all those years on stage playing to hostile crowds or fielding the jabs of hecklers. His thick mat of hair—slicked back in a mass of waves that resolved into curls at the back of his head—was the dark gray of a pipe wrench, his eyebrows and beard stubble as silver as a new quarter, and the fire in his yellowed, chocolate-drop eyes could burn a hole through boot leather.

"You think you Jay Z or Snoop Dogg? 50 Cent, maybe? Why don't you ask one of yo pimp homies what it mean in the iron house to walk 'round with yo pants on the ground like that."

The young man looked remarkably unruffled by Theo's verbal assault.

Theo turned to Ty. "I ever catch you dressed like that, Tyrone, I rip yo arm off and beat you to death with the bloody stump." He turned back to the young man. "Pull you pants up, boy!" He reached out and plucked the ball cap off the stranger's head. "And take off yo hat when you talking to a lady."

Gabriella stepped in quickly before Theo had a chance to launch into his tattoo speech or his body-piercing speech.

"Yes, that's me," she said. "What can I do for you?"

The young man's smile went totally flatline. He reached into the hip pocket of his baggy pants and pulled out a sealed envelope.

"You can take this," he said and handed Gabriella the envelope. "Gabriella Carmichael, aka Rebecca Nightshade, you've been served."

"What? What is this?"

"What's it look like—it's a summons." The young man turned to Theo. "You can keep the cap, Pops. Have a nice day." He turned and strutted out of the restaurant. Theo threw the cap at him, but missed.

Gabriella stared unbelieving at the envelope in her hand.

"How that process server get in here?" Theo boomed. "You got to go through security, got to have a boarding pass. How …?" He noticed that Gabriella hadn't moved. "Well, don't just sit there sucking on a prune pit—open that thing up and let's see what's in it."

She slid her finger under the flap and pulled out the single piece of paper inside.

Words leapt off the page and smacked her hard in the face.

Slander.

… made false and defamatory statements to the press …

… damaged the reputation and good name of …

Yesheb Al Tobbanoft!

She couldn't breathe. Theo snatched the paper out of her hand and scanned down it.

"He claiming you *slandered* him?" he said.

"What does slander mean?" Ty asked, looking from his mother to Theo and back to her.

Gabriella's head was spinning. Why would he …?

"This summons gone put a hitch in your git-along," Theo said and tossed the paper down on the table in front of him. "Says here you got to appear in court at 9 a.m. on June 26—here in Pittsburgh."

That was why! June 26 was the date of the next full moon.

The waitress materialized at Gabriella's elbow. She was absurdly basketball-player tall, six-feet-three and skinny as a shoe lace. The ingratiating, adoring look on her face told Gabriella the girl had recognized her, too.

"Excuse me, but … could I have … would yinz sign dis?" The girl said, her accent decidedly Pittsburgh. She held out a napkin. "It's all I could find, but it's all right, heh? For an autograph, I mean."

"Sure," Gabriella said, and switched to autopilot. She fixed a smile on her face like putting on a surgeon's mask and fished around in her purse until she found a pen.

"Could you make it 'To Louise Yurkovich … from *The Bride of the Beast*?'" Gabriella took the paper napkin and the girl continued to gush. "I can't believe I seen yinz here today—right here, in my very own restaurant. Your book is like my favorite book *ever!* The way you write, it's … poetry—only it ain't. I got to ask—how'd yinz ever come up with somethin' that … real?"

Because the pain that spawned it was real. And poetry was the voice of Gabriella's soul. She'd been a rising-star poet when she walked away from her blossoming career to put into words the feelings her twin brother could only express musically.

And suddenly, he was *gone*.

The way Garrett died and the reason he died had combined to rip Gabriella's heart right out of her chest.

She couldn't breathe, couldn't think or move or … *be* without him. Born three minutes before she was, he had always been there, every second of her life. They had their own language no one else spoke. How could there be life without him? Her husband and son faded into a background world where their voices were muted, like people shouting in a soundproofed room and what you hear through the closed door is muffled.

In the end, both her marriage and Garrett's band disintegrated without him. The band fell apart because of the absence of his presence; her marriage fell apart because of the presence of his absence. The rest of her life crumbled while she mourned his death, poured out her anguish and anger the only way she knew how—by tacking words onto it. But her hurt was too ugly for the delicate sensibilities of lyric verse. To release that putridness onto the page required the sturdier genre of fiction.

Gabriella wrote what the girl had asked, handed the napkin back and said "We'd like our check, please."

"Oh, yinz don't owe me nothing. Your check's already been paid." The girl leaned closer. "The tip, too. A twenty-dollar bill!"

"Already paid?"

"Yes ma'am. That's how I knew. But soon's he said your name … *The Bride of the Beast* was the first book I read all the way through since I was—"

"As soon as *who* said my name?" Gabriella felt an empty, hollowness in her chest that made it hard to talk.

"The man who paid for your lunch." The waitress turned and pointed to a man sitting alone at a table beside the door. He hadn't been there when Gabriella came into the restaurant. Nobody had been sitting there when Theo left to go to the food court for coffee. She was sure of it. But he was there now. A man dressed in black—shirt, pants, tie and coat. With pale blonde hair, ice blue eyes and the perfect Germanic features of a Nazi SS officer. He faced them, smiling at her with a sneering, crooked smile. There were crutches leaned against the empty chair on the other side of the table and he had a splint of some kind from his left foot halfway up his leg.

Gabriella's heart began to knock so hard in her chest her vision pulsed; the arteries in her neck thumped like jolts of electricity were firing through them. She got to her feet, though she did not will her body to rise, and walked slowly toward him, her eyes manacled to his, such a brilliant blue she could see the color from all the way across the restaurant.

The closer she got, the colder she felt, as if she were approaching a glacier. She stopped in front of him and expected to see her breath frost in the air.

"Going on a trip, I see," he said. "The Warwick offers a great location but I consider the accommodations in such an old hotel lackluster at best.

I can get you the presidential suite in any five-star hotel in the city with a single phone call. And about those show tickets. I—"

"Stop ..." she whispered. As soon as she saw him, fear had expanded in her chest like an inflatable life raft and now it was so huge she could barely speak. "Stop following me."

"I'm not following you," he said pleasantly, his smile as thin as a filleting knife. "I'm not going anywhere." He glanced down at his injured foot and a murderous look flashed across his features like a puff of wind scattering dry leaves. The leaves settled back into place as he lifted his eyes to lock into hers again. "As you can see, I'm not up to traveling right now. But it was certainly worth the price of two plane tickets to ..." He pulled a boarding pass out of his pocket and noted the destination. "... ah yes, Cleveland, to watch my man hand-deliver your little invitation to court. And there's more where that came from. I—"

"Can't you ... *please* ... leave me and my family ..." Her words struck the hard surface of his demeanor—splat, a rotten tomato on a window pane—and slid off it to the floor.

An armed TSA air marshal appeared in the concourse a few feet away and as he walked past them a tiny flame from the furnace of anger in Gabriella's heart began to warm her. Hard to find a safer place than an airport. You couldn't slip so much as a pair of fingernail clippers through security and the corridors were patrolled by guys carrying automatic weapons.

"*Leave us alone!*" She heard the words leap out of her mouth before she could grab hold of them. Emboldened by the environment, she went on. "It's not real, none of it. Can't you see that? You're not The Beast of Babylon. *I made him up!* Go away—"

He struck like a pit viper, grabbed her wrist, twisted it and yanked her down toward him with such force she almost toppled into his lap. "You will not speak to me like that when I rule—"

The murderous growl of an angry wolf froze Yesheb like an ice sculpture. He released his hold on Gabriella in surprise and turned slowly to see P.D. poised to pounce, only inches from his face. Teeth bared, canines glistening, the ever-affable golden retriever had been transformed into eighty-five pounds of savage beast that would go for Yesheb's throat if the man so much as blinked. Gabriella allowed herself a tiny smile. She'd managed to pack a weapon through security after all!

She straightened up, turned and motioned for Ty and Theo.

"You two go on to the gate," she said, amazed that her voice was level. "I'll be right there."

Theo took a step toward Yesheb, his hands balled into fists at his sides.

"I need you to look after Ty. Please, get him away from here."

Ty's face was ashen, his eyes huge. He stared at Yesheb with the look of a rabbit caught in the talons of an eagle.

Theo scowled at Yesheb, but nodded and shoved Ty in front of him out toward the crowded concourse. The old man paused as he passed Yesheb, though, leaned close and said quietly, "Some days you the big dog and some days … you the *hydrant*." Then he limped away.

Alone with Yesheb, Gabriella's fear returned, rose up in her throat like vomit.

Yesheb spoke without moving, his eyes fastened on the growling, menacing P.D. "I will kill this dog. Give me time and I will devise an appropriately brutal way to dispatch him." He remained rigid, but moved his eyes up to Gabriella's face. "I will stomp the old man, crush his brittle bones, leave him to die slowly. And I will kill the boy, your son, rip his heart out of his chest while it is still beating and offer it as a sacrifice to join us together for all eternity."

The ice in Yesheb's eyes flowed out of them and into Gabriella's heart. She reached down a trembling hand and took the handle of P.D.'s harness. He was still growling, the hackles standing up on the back of his neck. The dog had never done anything even remotely like this. Had he merely reacted to a threat to his master? Maybe. Or was it more than that? Could it be that his animal senses responded to the presence of evil?

"Heel, P.D.," she said, and the dog immediately turned away from Yesheb and moved to a spot beside her right leg. Though no longer growling, P.D. never took his eyes off Yesheb.

"See you in court on June 26," Yesheb purred. "I'll pray for rain. And I wouldn't plan any more little trips if I were you. I've convinced the prosecutor—he and several of the circuit judges were dear friends of my father's—that you didn't just assault me. You tried to kill me."

She stepped around Yesheb out into the flow of human traffic in the concourse, didn't turn when he called out to her.

"When that attempted murder charge is filed against you, my sweet Zara, you'll be stuck right here until I come for you."

Y ESHEB'S CALM IS only skin deep. Below it is a fury as finely tuned as an ice pick, a single, clear high note of rage that he could focus on her back and stab through sinew and tissue and bone right into her heart. He could kill her with his anger alone. He does not need the kind of weapon they look for here with their X-rays and scanners.

He can't do that, of course. She is his bride, his beloved. He cannot kill her. But he can make her pay. He will extract a high price for all that she has done to him, a high price indeed.

He'd been fantasizing about it in the hospital, lying in bed in agony because he had refused pain killers. He could not allow his senses to be dulled even for a moment. He is accountable. He is being watched.

As he lay sweating on the crisp, white sheets, gritting his teeth to keep from moaning, he had occupied his mind by considering what would be a fit punishment. Many came to mind—all of them involving tools like bolt cutters and tin snips. Disfigurement arouses him in ways beauty never can. Many more would surface, brought to mind by the heartbeat throbbing of his broken bones held in place by temporary splints. Though the fracture had not been displaced—the bones had not moved—his foot was so badly swollen the orthopedist said it would be a week before the splint applied in the emergency room could be replaced by a cast.

"I do a good job?"

Yesheb looks up into the face of the grinning hip-hop process server.

"Splendid."

"When she saw what it was in her hand she 'bout had a cat." The young man continues to babble, pumped about sneaking into an airport to deliver a summons. "That old man, his eyes was this big." He pauses. "Say, he wasn't that boy's *daddy* was he? The kid was mixed, but surely ..."

Mixed.

That's what his family had thought Yesheb was. Among other things. When he was born—a blonde, blue-eyed child to Iranian parents—it seemed obvious that his mother had shamed his father by bearing a son who could not possibly have been his. A son about whom there were whispers and dark rumors even before he was born, a son who engendered terror—even as a tiny baby.

Yesheb's whole family had been long dead before he understood it all. He learned the truth from an old servant who confessed to eavesdropping on a conversation between Anwar Al Tobbanoft and his wife's doctor while Yesheb was still in his mother's womb.

Serena Al Tobbanoft had been carrying twins—two distinct heartbeats. And then there was only one heartbeat. The doctor told his father that one of the twins was dead.

"How did my son die?" his father demanded—certain that his firstborn would be a son and heir.

"One of the twins … *absorbed* the other."

"Absorbed the other? What does that mean?"

"It means," the doctor told him quietly, "that one of your unborn sons has *eaten* his brother."

Though the old servant feared retribution for eavesdropping, and even worse punishment for the awful news he had delivered to Yesheb, he'd been surprised when his master responded with uproarious laughter.

Yesheb's cell phone rings and he dismisses the hip-hop moron with a wave of his hand.

"Mr. Al Tobbanoft, the surveillance team is in position to pick up the subjects at the baggage claim in JFK."

"You understand the importance of continuous contact?"

"It's a crack, four-man team, sir. The subjects will never even know they're being watched. We're also tracking them electronically, of course. They couldn't possibly shake my men."

"Are you willing to bet your life on that?"

There is a heartbeat pause.

"Yes sir."

Yesheb hangs up and acid-tasting bile rises in this throat. He has let her slip out of his grasp! He had been injured, hadn't been thinking clearly. After he'd summoned help and a team to do cleanup at her residence, it had taken a few hours to find her again. She had left the monitoring chips planted in her wallet, the heel of her shoe and her cell phone case behind when she ran. He hadn't moved fast enough with the summons and the criminal charges and she had slipped through his net. Oh, how he wished he could simply kidnap her and hold her hostage until it was time. But he couldn't do that. It must take place precisely as it was foretold. He must go to her alone, unaided, crush her resistance and take her.

Yesheb feels a shiver of doubt run down his spine.

After a millennia of looking for her, he has finally found her. Now the clock that allows him three opportunities to become one with her is ticking. Their joining will grant him unfathomable power; it will usher in the reign of The Beast of Babylon as the sovereign ruler of the abyss. But ancient decrees require precise timing. The first full moon after Good Friday, the day of death, was for preparation. He'd fasted and precisely performed the prescribed rituals and self-flagellation—beat himself with a whip tipped with broken glass and pieces of metal until he was barely conscious. After that, there remained three lunar cycles. He must mate with her during one of them and she had gotten away from him this month! She must *not* escape again!

He rises slowly, in some ways relishing the agony in his foot because it keeps him hyper alert, on a razor's edge. He picks up his crutches and hobbles on them out into the concourse. He briefly considers going to their gate and waiting there with them until their flight takes off. But there would be plenty of time for intimidation—and payback—later. Revenge is, indeed, a dish best served cold.

CHAPTER 4

Theo had to hand it to Gabriella. She had orchestrated their disappearing act in New York City like they was characters in a television spy show—not that Theo watched such things, of course. The only time his television was on was so he could watch the news or sports. And that didn't count as watching television.

Course he didn't have no television now. Didn't have nothing. They'd left everything they owned behind. Well, except that rock, Gabriella's crystal rock. Wasn't no way she was gonna go anywhere without *that!*

Gabriella had launched what she called the Great Escape as soon as they got to New York. They checked into the Warwick Hotel, then went directly to the Bank of New York on East 45th Street where Gabriella had a private conversation in the manager's office and cleaned out all her accounts, walked out with all the cash she could lay her hands on, a little over $75,000. From there they went to Macy's, where they purchased a whole new set of clothes each—from the underwear out. Socks, shoes, trousers—the works. Gabriella was certain Yesheb had somebody watching them every minute. But she suspected he might also be keeping tabs on them with some kind of electronic tracking device. In their clothes, their shoes, their luggage, somewhere. So they'd bought new everything, all the way down to their birthday suits. Theo picked himself out a bright red button-up sweater. Gabriella picked him out a fedora to go with it. He hadn't never worn a hat, told her it made him look like one of the Blues Brothers in blackface, but he knew it was part of the plan.

After that, they went directly to Mama Rosina's in Little Italy for dinner before the show, dressed in their new duds with their old clothes in Macy's sacks. Mama's was a family-run Italian restaurant with lots of atmosphere, which meant it was dark as an old maid's underwear drawer, lit only by candles on the tables that had dripped mountains of wax down the sides of their wine-bottle holders. The place instantly made Theo uncomfortable because it looked just like the restaurant in the first *Godfather* movie where Mikey Corleone shot the crooked cop and the drug dealer Sollozzo. Which maybe was what had given Gabriella the idea.

Halfway through the salad, Theo got up and excused himself and went to the restroom—just like in the movie, only not to pick up a gun hidden behind the toilet tank. The restrooms were in a small hallway off the kitchen with a back door at the end leading to the alley. A red sign on the door warned: "Emergency exit. Do not open. Alarm will sound."

He came back to the table a short time later, his gimpy limp a little more pronounced than usual, as the pasta was being served. They all ate, talked, didn't laugh though. They couldn't pull that off. Right after the main course, Ty started to get sick. Within minutes Gabriella had to rush him to the bathroom so he wouldn't puke on the table, with P.D. only a step behind, of course. They stayed there a long time, didn't return for the rest of dinner or the tiramisu dessert.

Theo figured if you'd been hired to keep track of the folks who'd gone to the bathroom, you'd have to be a special kind of stupid not to notice they never came back out. There was likely a lot of yelling going on somewhere on the subject. But by that time, Gabriella, Theo, Ty and P.D. were driving through the Holland tunnel into New Jersey in a bunged-up, five-year-old Honda Accord with so much mud on the license plate you couldn't read the number.

After the meal, the old black man seated at their table used his napkin to discretely wipe off his silverware, glass and the two, crisp $100-bills he used to pay for the meal—told the waiter to keep the change. He gathered up all the Macy's bags, pulled his red sweater close around him against the chill in the air and took a cab to the Warwick Hotel. He got in the elevator, punched every button so it stopped on every floor all the way up. When the doors finally opened on the 38th floor, the only thing inside the elevator was a pile of Macy's bags.

Three hours later, the afternoon shift maintenance crew supervisor, an old fellow who'd been called Drumstick back in the day, punched out on the time clock in the hotel basement like he'd done just about every day for the past thirty-seven years. Dressed in his blue jumpsuit uniform, the old, bald black man with coke-bottle-thick glasses made his way down the hall past the garbage chute that was the final resting place for the tiny, snipped-up pieces of a fedora and a red sweater and went out through the Sixth Avenue staff entrance. He walked the two blocks to the subway entrance on Seventh Avenue and Fifty-Third Street and took the D train home to Harlem—with $5,000 in crisp, hundred-dollar bills tucked snug in his hip pocket.

Least that's the way he and Theo had planned it and Theo assumed that's the way it'd worked, prayed that it had.

The man who'd played drums in Theo's band forty years ago had exchanged the keys to the Honda for Theo's red sweater, his hat and a 30-second demonstration of Theo's limp in the bathroom of Mama Rosina's. Folks had joked back in the day that they was twins separated at birth and even after all these years they were still the spittin' image of each other. Except Drumstick didn't have a hair on his head anymore. And he could barely see. Hated contact lenses, though, only wore them to Mass on Sundays, weddings, funerals … and other special occasions. Drumstick arranged for the car to be parked outside the restaurant's back door—between two dumpsters that blocked the view from both ends of the alley.

The alarm on the back door in Mama Rosina's hadn't worked since the Eisenhower administration.

Soon as Gabriella, Ty and P.D. hopped into the car, they laid over in the seats and Theo covered them up with blankets. He had already gotten that crazy wig situated on his head with the dreadlocks hanging halfway down his back and put on the mirror sunglasses that made him look like a pimp.

Only thing Gabriella said was: "Did your friend get what I asked for?"

Theo wordlessly nodded to the glove box and she opened it. Inside was a .38 revolver. Serial number filed off. Untraceable. The whole transaction had cost $20,000.

Once they got away from the restaurant, Gabriella took the wheel and the others remained covered up with blankets for the next two hours. Theo had spent most of that time praying—that the "watchers" hadn't spotted them and that Gabriella'd stop soon so he could go to the bathroom before he wet himself. She drove through the night, getting off the expressway every thirty or forty miles, watching the exit ramps to see if any suspicious vehicles got off, too. Nothing. Maybe that didn't prove they weren't being followed, but it was all she could do.

They was eating McDonald's big breakfasts in the car in Salisbury, North Carolina, when Gabriella asked Theo where he wanted her to drop him off now that his part in this wild ride was over. She apologized for dragging him into her nightmare, thanked him for his help and said she'd give him plenty of money to get by on—because they both knew he was in Yesheb's gunsights now, too, and he'd have to vanish his own self for the next couple of months.

Theo shoved a syrup-slathered hunk of pancake into his mouth and said, "I ain't goin' nowhere 'cept with you."

Her look of shock would have been comical if her face wasn't all puckered up on one side—Smokey's handiwork.

"You're going with us, Grandpa Slappy?" The instant of pure joy on that boy's face made Theo's throat draw up so tight he couldn't swallow his own spit.

"Oh no, he's not!" Gabriella said.

"How you figure to do this if I don't? Face like yours ain't 'xactly gone blend into a crowd. Every time you check into a motel, or go in some convenience store to pay for gasoline, or buy a box of fried chicken at a drive-in window—somebody gone see you. Anybody ask 'em later, they gone remember."

Gabriella couldn't argue that.

"But a old black man ... don't matter what they say, most white folks still think all black people look alike. And ain't nobody looking for a old *bald* black man. Under all this nappy cotton, I bet I look just like Denzel Washington."

"Theo, this is ... dangerous."

"Ya think?"

"You won't like where we're going."

"I don't like where we been! You ever notice how many fat women they is in the South?"

"Theo, I'm serious."

"So am I. That woman over there, she got so much flab on her arms she look like a flying squirrel."

Ty tried unsuccessfully to stifle a giggle.

"And them spandex pants. They's stretched so tight over them thunder thighs, she try to run, her legs gone rub together and start a fire."

Ty lost it then, laughed so hard he spilled his syrup and Gabriella used cleaning up his mess as an excuse to drop the subject. She didn't bring it up again.

They stopped at a Walmart in Charlotte and bought suitcases, toiletries and bare-essential clothing—they had to travel light. Made it as far as the suburbs of Atlanta before Gabriella crashed. Next day, they went into the city and got Gabriella a laptop and Ty a Nintendo 3DS and just about every video game ever invented. They drove to Nashville then and spent the rest of the afternoon and most of the next day going from one music store to another until Theo found what he was looking for—a vintage Selmer Mark VI tenor saxophone. Wasn't no way he planned to spend eight weeks in exile without a sax to keep him company.

That's what it was supposed to be. Two months. Gabriella said if she could hide from him through two more full moons, the Beast would be screwed and Yesheb wouldn't be after them no more.

Theo figured that Yesheb giving up the chase was about as likely as successfully milking a chicken. He hadn't known a whole lot of madmen in his life, but the ones he had known didn't take losing real well. Yesheb might not be able to marry her two months from now, but that wouldn't keep him from killing her. Would make it even more likely, from where Theo sat. He didn't say that out loud, of course. He didn't have to; Gabriella wasn't no fool.

※ ※ ※ ※

All the color drains out of Yesheb's face.

"Say that again, slowly," he says into his cell phone. His modulated, television-announcer voice quakes, his hand grips the small device so tight it might shatter.

"Sir ... I have teams out, more than a dozen men sniffing for her trail—we'll find it. Our techies have hacked into her credit cards, we'll know as soon as she uses one. We—"

"Explain to me how you *lost* a scar-faced woman, an old man, a little kid and a dog!"

"We had tracking devices in their luggage, which they left in the hotel room. We had one in the heel of the woman's shoe and one in the boy's ... but she bought new shoes and left the old ones—"

"How did they *get away?*"

"We had eyes on the subjects every minute. They went for dinner at an Italian restaurant and the team leader posted a man in front of the restaurant, one inside and two more out back—one at each end of the alley."

Yesheb listens with rising fury as the man explains the bathroom fiasco.

"They must have slipped out the back door. Employees of all the shops on the street park in the alley, but only four cars left during the time the subjects were in the restaurant—no passengers in any of them. We photographed them all, standard procedure and we'll pull license plate numbers—"

"The old man, the grandfather!"

"Had a team waiting in his hotel room prepared to extract the location of the woman and boy with a minimum of noise and blood. But … our man followed the old man into a crowded elevator in the lobby and just as the doors were closing, the old man managed to slip out—"

"He's a gimpy old man!"

"We're searching the building for him now, sir, have operatives on every exit. *Nobody* will get past them! We will wait him out. Eventually, he'll make a break for it and we'll have him."

Yesheb speaks two words through gritted teeth before he breaks the connection.

"Find her!"

He pauses, then places another call. He instructs the person on the other end of the line to arrange for the man he had just spoken with to meet with a tragic and untimely death. Suicide. A swan dive off one of the balconies of the Warwick Hotel.

* * * *

For a moment, Gabriella didn't recognize her own reflection in the polished metal mirror in the rest stop bathroom on Interstate 70 west of Ellis, Kansas. Oh, it wasn't just the bilious light from the flickering fluorescent bulb overhead—the kind that'd make the winner of the Boston Marathon look like he was dying of pancreatic cancer. Gabriella's hair was curly now, forming a yellow cloud of ringlets on the top of her head. The curl was natural; the butter color wasn't. It was L'Oréal Honey Blonde, because she was worth it, but it wouldn't be long before her natural blonde grew out enough to blend with the color out of the bottle. The short style was courtesy of the not-too-shabby haircut Theo had given her right before he shaved his head.

When he'd finished both jobs, he'd turned to Ty and asked, "You know the difference 'tween a man with a bad haircut and a woman with a bad haircut?"

Here it comes.

Theo didn't wait for an answer, of course.

"Six weeks." Theo paused; timing was everything. "A man with a bad haircut thinks, 'In six weeks it'll grow out.' Now a woman … she get a bad haircut, she be calling Judge Judy. She be going into therapy!"

From there it was one small step into Dueling Groaners.

"Know where you find a one-legged dog?" he asked Ty.

"Wherever you left it," Ty said, and fired back instantly, "Knock, knock."

"Who's there?"

"Dwayne."

"Dwayne who?"

"Dwayne the bathtub, I'm dwowning."

"Know how to prevent diseases caused by biting insects?" Theo's volley.

"Don't bite any insects."

Gabriella was sure that by the time they reached their destination, Ty would be able to repeat the whole trouble-in-River-City sequence from the *Music Man* in under a minute and burp the melody of the *Star Spangled Banner.*

And who knew what else he might learn from his Grandpa Slappy, aka Theodosius X. Carmichael. Theo never told her what the X stood for, if, indeed, it stood for anything at all. He did tell her, the first time he showed up unannounced after she and Smokey were married, that "with a name like Theodosius, you learn to fight early and dirty." He also told her he was likely the only man she'd ever meet who had a nickname for his nickname. As a jazz saxophone player for half a century, he'd been known as Slap Yo Mama Carmichael. That was shortened to Slappy when he added stand-up comedy to his act. After a while, everyone in his life called him Slappy. Except Gabriella. She called him Theo. It seemed respectful. She could tell he appreciated it, too, though torture and the threat of imminent death wouldn't have forced him to admit it.

THE LAST SAFE PLACE

The old man had never come around much. Ty's father had hated him. The train wreck of Smokey's life was rooted in his childhood—a mother who died when he was a toddler and a father who crawled into a bottle in his grief and didn't return for twenty years. Gabriella still had no idea why Theo had suddenly appeared out of nowhere. All he'd said was, "I only got me a little while 'fore I got to be somewhere important. I'll be moving on in a day or two."

He'd been in residence at the guest house almost two weeks when Yesheb showed up.

"Did you hear about the parrot that walked into a bar," Theo began, "and said to the bartender—?"

"Ding! Ding! Ding!" Gabriella had reached her limit. "That sound you hear is the Corny Joke Alarm. Evacuate the building!"

It was feast or famine with Theo. He often ignored what was said to him, acted like he didn't hear it. And other than an occasional dribble of the conversational ball, the old man had only spoken in monosyllabic grunts since they turned west from Evansville, Indiana, and headed out into the flatlands.

The three fugitives had taken the name Underhill, like Frodo Baggins when he was on the run. But unlike Frodo, they were not taking a direct route to their destination. In the beginning, the zigzagging was about the pursuit Gabriella constantly strained to see behind her in the rearview mirror. She did everything she could think of to leave no trail. Theo always checked them into motels—small ones in out-of-the-way-places, paying cash so nobody'd ask for identification. Paid cash for their meals in truck stops, mom-and-pop cafes and interstate fast-food restaurants. Paid cash for gasoline. And kept going, a moving target—through seventeen states so far.

But in repeated nightmares, Gabriella saw a trail she couldn't erase—the heart-prints of her terror. Each frantic beat gave off a puff of pale fluorescent blue, sparkly, like snowflakes. The heart-prints hung in the air behind her as she ran away from Yesheb through a dark forest of dead trees. And no matter how fast she ran or how well she hid, he followed the floating puffs of blue and found her. Sometimes, when she looked in the rearview mirror on some lonely road at night, she fancied she saw puffs of sparkling blue hanging in the air behind the car.

As the days stacked up on days, the trip itself, the act of moving on became symbolic of just that—moving on. Every day, she put more distance between her and a life that had become increasingly hollow and meaningless. Leaving that behind became the shedding of a skin—tight at first, but looser as it dried out, disconnected from the lifeblood. And as she crawled out of that skin a little further every day, she felt a newness that was at once freeing and frightening. The new being had not the tough skin she had grown over time to protect it. It was vulnerable, tender and fragile, but it looked at the world with eyes that saw possibility in the peril. Her new freedom made her exquisitely aware of how captive she had become. A prisoner of her idiot agent, of the role she played to market her books and of the madman who chased her.

Oh, she understood her freedom now was limited—not only by the threat behind but by her own soul, still entangled in the tentacles of the past. It would take much more than a cross-country road trip to set her free from the pain of all those years.

She left the rest stop bathroom, got back behind the wheel and drove for another couple of hours before Theo finally spoke up. "Tell me somethin'. Outside of *Blazing Saddles*, you ever see a black man in a cowboy movie?"

Gabriella sighed. "You didn't have to come, Theo. Nobody held a gun to your head."

"If I'd stayed, somebody'd a held a gun to my head—and pulled the trigger!"

He was probably right about that.

"Speaking of guns to the head …" Theo was quiet for a moment, then began to tick things off with his fingers. "Way I see it, you 'bout to ignore a court-ordered summons for slander—that's one. You running away from an attempted murder charge—that's two. And you got an illegal firearm in your glove box—three."

"What's your point?"

"My point is—if that man show up and you go to the police for help— they gone bust *you* 'stead of him."

"Take a look around, Theo." She gestured toward the world outside the car windows. Theo had been reading a newspaper for the past couple of hours, conspicuously avoiding the grandeur around him. "You think you can dial 911 out here and a cop will show up at your door in five minutes with a SWAT team?"

THE LAST SAFE PLACE

The bigness they drove through now didn't feel like the big empty prairie and plains they'd left behind in Kansas and Nebraska. This was not empty bigness. This was majesty. The land had been steadily rising, undulating as they drove west. Beneath a gigantic blue sky with puffy clouds hanging like white dirigibles high above their heads, the road in front of them was visible for miles, a gray ribbon with yellow stripes stretched tight across open grassland dotted with clumps of cedar trees and mesquite bushes. The highway was deserted, not another vehicle of any kind in sight. Specks of houses in the distance were tethered to the highway with winding dirt roads, but all the works of man—highways, roads, fences, buildings—were so dwarfed by the land and sky they seemed utterly insignificant. The darker green of forested hills edged the horizon on both sides of the highway to the north and south. But the green, fenced pastures ahead were stitched to the blue sky with a jagged line of mountains. *Purple* mountains. Even from this distance, you could see a powdered sugar dusting of snow on the peaks.

A green sign with white lettering flew by the window and Ty announced, "Next stop, Colorado Springs."

"In case you're interested," Gabriella said, "I've read that the city's sometimes called the Protestant Vatican. More than 100 Christian organizations—all the big ones—have headquarters there. Focus on the Family, the Navigators, Young Life—."

"Six Flags Over Jesus," Theo muttered.

"The U.S. Air Force Academy's there, too," she said.

"Sounds like a great place to live, but I wouldn't want to visit there." Theo said. "Tell me we not staying."

"We're not staying."

"Where *are* we staying?" Ty asked.

Gabriella hadn't been explicit about their exact destination. Partly because when they bolted from New York, she thought Theo would soon head out on his own and she didn't want him to know specifics about where she and Ty were going, just in case ... Besides, the one word "Colorado" had been so overwhelming—to Ty because he was ecstatic and to Theo because he was appalled—that neither had asked for a more specific destination.

When her response formed in her head, Gabriella realized she hadn't said the words out loud in almost thirty years.

"We're staying in St. Elmo's Fire." She felt an exquisite thrill of excitement that popped goose bumps out on her arms. "It's a cabin in a hanging valley eleven thousand feet up on the side of Mount Antero."

If ever there was a shock-and-awe statement, that was it. The stunned silence that followed was so thick you could have spread it on toast.

"We'll stop in Bueny first for supplies."

"Booney?" Ty asked.

"Bueny—rhymes with puny. Buena Vista. It's a little town in the Arkansas River Valley at the foot of Mount Princeton. That's where we'll rent a jeep."

"A *jeep!*" Theo said.

"You have to have four-wheel drive to climb the trail up the side of the mountain to the cabin."

Ty's jaw dropped open; Theo looked like he was about to vomit.

Gabriella threw back her head and laughed out loud because … well, just because.

T<small>Y STARED AT</small> his mother and couldn't believe what he saw. She didn't look the same with short, curly blonde hair, of course, but that's not what he meant. She looked … *different* in some other way, too. In a way he didn't know the words to describe.

In the past few days it had begun to sink in that she had done it. She'd gotten them away from the guy dressed in black who had hurt her in his effort to get at Ty. The boy had his own plan to run away all mapped out when suddenly his mother, grandfather and dog had run away with him! They'd all left the scary man behind and escaped. Ty had been so frightened he hadn't dared believe it at first. When his mother told him they were going to Colorado, he hadn't dared hope that it was actually true.

But here they were!

This was a place so huge the bad man would never find them. Ty understood, of course, that this was kind of like a parole, not a Get-Out-of-Jail-Free card, that even if the Boogie Man didn't find him, one day he would have to pay for the unspeakable crime he had committed. You didn't do what he'd done and get away with it! Sooner or later … But he put that thought firmly out of his mind. For today, he and everybody he loved were safe and that was good enough. And it wasn't even *all*.

THE LAST SAFE PLACE

Ty took a deep breath and let the words sink in. A cabin on the side of a mountain. That you had to get to by jeep!

THEO TOOK A deep breath and let the words sink in. A cabin on the side of a mountain. That you had to get to by jeep!

For a moment he was afraid he was going to puke. He closed his eyes, needed to have his self a serious, sit-down talk with God.

You've known me since way before my baby face was puckered up tighter than the drawstring end of a black laundry bag. And don't none of what's happening right now come as a surprise to you. But Lord ... a cabin on a mountainside?

I don't hate much in life, but me and mountains is not on good terms. As you is well aware—I don't do high and I don't do deep. You know why. You was there. If you hadn't been there, *I wouldn't be* here.

All these years since that day, I stayed away from oceans, never even went to the beach. Kept my distance from lakes. Rivers, too, of course. And other than airplanes—they don't count 'less you look out the window and I got better sense—I can't get higher than a stepladder without getting the trembles.

Now, we talking a mountain!

I get up there, I might die of pure fright, and I got to stay on this earth to see to the boy.

Ain't it supposed to get easier as you gettin' down to the end of it—life, I mean? For the record, this is not easier. Just something to consider is all I'm saying. You gone do whatever you gone do. Amen.

He paused, then added,

I appreciate you getting us away from that man. He got a stink like meat gone bad only it ain't something you can smell with your nose. He evil. I ask for your protection from him and his schemes.

He paused again.

And about this mountain thing ... if it was good enough for Moses, I s'pose Theodosius X. Carmichael got no right to complain.

GABRIELLA HAD NO idea she would respond so profoundly to the sight of Mount Princeton. The southernmost mountain among the Collegiate peaks of the Sawatch Range, it was one of Colorado's 54 "fourteeners," rising 14,197 feet out of the Arkansas River Valley into the crisp mountain air.

When the mountain appeared above the rock outcrops on the foothills that had blocked its view, Gabriella pulled off on the side of the road, got out of the car and stared up at it, shading her eyes with her hand.

"Oh, Garrett," she whispered under her breath. "Look at this!" Their word for beautiful leapt into her mind. "It's bleeg, Garrett, just like I remember it."

Ty got out and came to stand wordlessly beside her. Theo sat in the car, studiously reading his newspaper.

Because the tallest of its three peaks was in the center and the two on either side were about the same size and shape, Mount Princeton's aesthetic balance made it arguably the most picturesque mountain in all the Colorado Rockies.

"Is that Mount Antero?" Ty asked.

"No, that's Mount Princeton. Mount Antero is behind it. You have to drive around the base of Princeton and then up Chalk Creek Canyon beside it to get to the road up Antero. Of course, the roads may be different now. I haven't been here in …" she stopped to think. "In more than a quarter of a century."

Gabriella didn't remember the first time she ever saw Mount Antero but she did remember the last, staring up at it out the rear window of the car with the sound of her mother's hysterical sobbing in her ears and Garrett beside her, whimpering like a lost kitten.

Her family had come to the cabin that summer when she was seven going on eight for the same reason her parents traveled all over the country every summer—hauling first one, then three children along with them. Phillip and Natalie Griffith were rockhounds. Glass-front display cases exhibiting their finds filled one whole room in their house in Whitehall, a suburb of Pittsburgh. Shimmering, iridescent hematite and tomato-red mica from Virginia, quartz crystals the size of hotdogs and emerald green cat-eye from Arkansas, pink fluorite crystals as delicate as hand-made lace from Tennessee, honey-colored calcite from Missouri and a rainbow of colored geodes from Kentucky, Indiana and Iowa.

The couple had dedicated the whole summer of 1982 to adding aquamarine to their collection and had rented a cabin on Colorado's Mount

THE LAST SAFE PLACE

Antero because it was the best aquamarine site in the whole country. But the mountain was renowned for more than its gemstones. Mount Antero's high iron content turned it into a gigantic lightning rod and during the sudden summer storms that sprang up almost every afternoon, lightning writhed in the sky around the peak like sparks off a blown transformer. No place in the Rocky Mountains was more dangerous during a thunderstorm than Mount Antero.

The image of flashing light and the rumble of thunder skittered on little rat feet across Gabriella's memory and she shuddered.

"This cabin we're going to, why's it called St. Elmo's Fire?" Ty asked.

"Don't know. I guess because whoever built it saw St. Elmo's fire there."

She saw his next question coming. "And I don't know a whole lot more than that about St. Elmo's fire, either. It's some kind of weird weather thing. A bright blue or violet glow appears on tall, pointed things like lightning rods or the masts of ships, even leaves or grass or the tips of a cow's horns. Garrett and I called it firesies and we wanted to see it so bad we stuck a broken fishing pole in the ground for it to land on."

Where did that *come from? Garrett and I never—*

But they *did!* She didn't remember it until she heard herself say it. Gabriella felt a sudden chill so dramatic she looked up to see if a cloud had passed in front of the sun. The image of the "firesies-stick" the two of them had erected with a little pile of rocks took up her whole mind, shoved every other thought and idea and feeling to the side and glowed there in quiet brilliance. The hair on her arms stood up, like it had done that day from the static electricity in the air. Thunder rumbled, but they'd ignored it until it was too late and—

The thought stopped there. Beyond was a walled-off place, a bunker sealed tight. She never went there, never got anywhere near it, knew that locked inside was the single worst thing that had ever happened to her.

And the best thing, too.

Gabriella froze. Yes, the best thing! But what was it? She had no idea. You always paid a price when you built a wall and hid life behind it. When she locked up the dark memories in a bunker she'd locked up that memory, too. In fact, right now, standing here looking up at Mount Princeton, was the first time she had gotten near enough to the bunker to recall there was more locked inside than horror.

She had known all along that was one of the risks in coming back here. That by being in the place where it had happened, she would somehow break the seal on the bunker and all the awful would flow out of it in a putrid stench. She'd told herself that was the chance she had to take because this was the only place she could think of that she believed her family would be safe. But standing here, looking up at Mount Princeton, she realized that perhaps that wasn't the only reason she'd come. Perhaps she wanted to be here because some part of her yearned to know what else lay in the bunker in her mind besides the nightmare, wanted to set the enchanted memory free.

Oh, how she hoped Ty could make some enchanted memories of his own here. He was certainly entitled to beauty and freedom. He had earned a reprieve from the sentence of darkness surrounding his parents and what had happened between them.

She reached up and ran her hand over the scar on her cheek, then saw that Ty was watching her with an odd look on his face and she jerked her hand away. Maybe that was his bunker memory—hiding under his bed while his father had made good on his threat to Gabriella to "make yo outsides look like yo insides."

CHAPTER 5

A FLEA WITH A PET ELEPHANT. THAT WAS BUENA VISTA, COLORADO. The mammoth, hulking presence of Mount Princeton towered more than six thousand feet above the little town, dwarfed everything to insignificance, cast a gigantic shadow across the valley floor that grew bigger as the sun progressed down the western sky.

Bueny was a typical Colorado small town with wide streets, neat houses, crisp, clean air and lots of pickup trucks. What had changed since Gabriella last saw it was the artsy, touristy flavor of the place. It seemed there were galleries, RV parks and an outdoor outfitting store every five feet.

When she drove slowly down the town's main street, taking it all in, the juxtaposition of cultures was jarring. A leather-faced man wearing scuffed cowboy boots and a sweat-ringed Stetson ... next to a yuppie in the latest trendy hiking gear, featuring pants with a dozen zippered pockets and a jacket with a hole for the cord of her iPod ear-phones ... beside a shaggy college kid who carried everything he owned in a gigantic backpack and very likely smelled of campfire smoke and marijuana.

Theo, of course, kept up a running commentary of disparaging remarks: "Check out that bowlegged cowboy. Stand him up next to a knock-kneed woman and they'd spell OX. They start dancing, it look like a egg-beater."

Gabriella stopped at the BP station on US Route 285 so Theo could do his business. The car motor had begun to knock sometime late yesterday afternoon and the sound had gotten so much louder today that turning off the ignition felt uncomfortably like a mercy killing.

As she stood beside the ailing Honda waiting for Theo, she allowed the feel of this hauntingly familiar place to settle over her again. She had gotten an odd sunburn the first few days of the summer she'd spent in the mountains years ago. Dressed in jeans and a jacket—it was cold at 11,000 feet!—the

Pittsburgh-white skin of her hands and face had gotten fried. Cool air, hot sun—like being in two different climates at the same time.

She'd repeatedly warned Theo and Ty—mostly Theo with his bare-as-a-baby's-butt head—about the sun. And that they might have headaches in the higher elevation, usually a result of dehydration.

"You need to drink lots of liquid. And it'll take a week, maybe longer, to get used to the air with less oxygen. Don't overexert yourselves."

"So you sayin' if a bear come running out the woods after me, I's supposed to walk away slowly?"

"Are there bears?" Ty's eyes were huge.

"Yep, black bears. You leave them alone, they'll leave you alone—just don't get between a mama bear and her cub."

"Are there mountain lions?" the boy asked.

"Probably. They keep to themselves, won't come anywhere near the cabin. You didn't ask about fish—the finest mountain trout in the whole world! And an ice-cold stream where you can fish for them."

Ty was ready to jump out of his skin with excitement. She could barely get him to eat his enchiladas at the Coyote Cantina even by bribing him with honey-filled sapodillas for dessert. Theo didn't eat but a bite or two of his tacos, scowled at the waitress when his complaint about the heat in Colorado was greeted with the standard response: "Oh, it's not so bad—it's a *dry* heat."

But his poor appetite might have been more than his dismay over their geography. Gabriella had noticed he didn't look right, couldn't put her finger on exactly what it was, though. It appeared he'd lost some weight, too, got around slower. She supposed that was to be expected when your age was pushing three quarters of a century. Maybe it hadn't been such a good idea to bring him here. Maybe …

Then it banged into her mind why they'd come. For a moment, she'd forgotten about the specter that stalked them. They weren't here on vacation. They'd come to a refuge; they were running for their lives.

Sticking to her cross-country strategy of staying, shopping in small, out-of-the-way places, she found a small jeep rental dealership in the shadow of a big one. Twenty minutes later, she walked out with a set of keys. For an additional fee, the owner had agreed to allow her to leave her car parked out back until the end of the summer. It took half an hour to pare their few belongings down to what they could jam into the jeep and still have room for passengers and supplies. The rest they stored in the trunk of the Honda.

Ty called shotgun. Theo sat like a puddleglum in the back with P.D. and the luggage. Gabriella tried to look a whole lot more self-assured than she actually felt when she slid in behind the wheel. Oh, she could drive the thing. The whole time she was at Carnegie Mellon she'd dated a guy whose hobby was four-wheeling and she'd piloted many an excursion in the mountains of West Virginia to explore the surface-of-the-moon terrain of strip mines. Still, the mountain they were about to tackle was another thing altogether.

"Buckle up," she said.

"And make sure yo seats and tray tables is in they upright and locked position," Theo said.

The jeep lurched forward a little awkwardly and then they were off toward the cabin that Theo had launched a last-ditch argument against while he moved his uneaten tacos around on his plate at lunch.

"Why we goin' to a place Mr. Gestapo Wannabe might be able to connect to you? Don't it make more sense to throw a dart at a map, pick somewhere you ain't never been, rent a house and lock ourselves inside? How he gone find us if we done that?"

Gabriella explained yet again that there was no possible way for Yesheb to connect her to the house in the mountains, but she had to grant that it certainly wasn't as anonymous as picking a random house in some arbitrary city. What she was doing didn't make as much logical sense as Theo's suggestion, but for reasons she couldn't explain she was certain that her family's safety rested in something more than mere anonymity.

They headed south out of Buena Vista on US 285. When they passed a collection of buildings encircled by a tall fence on the outskirts of town, Gabriella answered Theo's unasked question.

"Uh huh, that's a prison. The Buena Vista Correctional Facility—houses about nine hundred medium security inmates."

She shouted because the crisp, fresh air that whipped through the topless vehicle on the open road carried her words away. She wasn't sure Theo heard her.

"The wind's blowing your hair, Mom," Ty didn't quite have deadpan down but he was close to pulling it off. "Maybe you should roll up the window."

The freshly scrubbed breeze on her face and the laughter of her son in her ears vanished. That's what Yesheb had said—*exactly* what Yesheb had said—that day when he appeared out of nowhere on a street corner in Orlando and leaned into her rented convertible while she sat helpless at a stop light.

The remark had been the tipping point. The moment when she saw with chilling clarity that under the trappings of intelligence and good manners resided a being that was neither rational nor civil. That simple attempt at humor had exposed him.

Because he couldn't pull it off! It was so clearly a rehearsed behavior, like a windup toy. He couldn't do humor because humor is the exclusive domain of human beings and Yesheb didn't believe he was human. And maybe he was right.

Gabriella is cold and uncomfortable, seated in a high-backed wooden chair with no cushion in a room that with only minor alterations could function as a meat locker. But Bernie is in charge and concern for Gabriella's comfort never makes it to the higher centers of his brain. All his calculations are focused on the most efficient way to shuttle readers past Gabriella in a freight-train rush.

"Just sign and move them through," he tells her. "No small talk. It spoils the image and the image sells books. All your readers think you're some kind of mythical creature—and a being from the Endless Black Beyond wouldn't exchange recipes for bean dip with a fan. Keep your mouth shut and the line moving."

The signing is in a little store called Twice Told Tales on Atwood Street in the Oakland section of Pittsburgh. It's a lovely bookstore, smells of old paper and stale pipe tobacco, a nurturing environment where patrons can browse, sit in overstuffed chairs, read poetry, discuss universal themes or existentialism or Stephen King's latest best seller over a cup of Earl Grey that has tiny flakes of tea in the bottom.

Gabriella is "in costume"—witch-black dress, long straight hair, pointed bangs, claw-like fingernails and cherry red lips on deathly pale skin. And the scar, of course, revealed in all its glory—no makeup. The combined effect of the author and the atmosphere is conducive to fantasy, so it's easy for the fans to suspend disbelief and buy into the illusion that it's all real.

THE LAST SAFE PLACE

Cult fanatics have been camped outside the bookstore since early the evening before because the cramped space will limit the number of people who can get their books autographed, though Bernie does everything short of using a cattle prod to keep the crowd moving past Gabriella so their signed copies can be rung up at the old-fashioned cash register in the corner, the kind with buttons that really does ring out "cha-ching" with every purchase.

Gabriella's back hurts, her hand is cramped and her butt is numb. She glances at the grandfather clock in the corner and groans. Two more hours before she can go home and get out of this Halloween get-up, make SpaghettiOs for Ty and help him with his homework before bed.

"... was so scared I had to sleep with the lights on for a month," says a small, white-haired woman who resembles Tweety Bird's grandmother. Gabriella merely nods, does not connect or respond. She has gone mercifully brain dead, has vanished into a kind of eyes-open coma where she's only vaguely aware of the herd of readers passing in front of her.

Then she spots him. He is tall, six three or four, and stands ramrod straight, dressed in black—turtleneck, sports coat and pants—with a small silver pentagram on a chain around his neck. His hair is pale blonde, his features patrician perfect, his eyes a shade of blue that seems to shift as she looks into them, from light ice blue to the turgid gray-blue of a stormy sea.

A smile that reveals perfect teeth appears on his face as soon as she makes eye contact. It is a crooked smile, though, odd looking, like he's taken lessons, worked really hard to learn all the muscle groups he must employ to pull his lips back in a particular fashion that's defined as "smiling." But he hasn't got it quite right so one side of his mouth draws back farther than the other. There is no warmth in that smile. No warmth in him, either. In fact, as he steps up to her table he seems to bring cold with him, as a door left open on a blustery day allows a chill wind to blow through.

And darkness, too, only that's crazy. How can a man give off darkness like a candle gives off light? She senses something predatory, too, a subtle new pressure, the way the air feels before a violent thunderstorm.

"Good day, my dear Zara," he says, totally deadpan. That surprises her. He doesn't strike her as the kind of man who indulges in illusion.

"I'm not Zara." For some reason, it is important to her to make the distinction between reality and fiction. "I'm Rebecca Nightshade." Which, of course, isn't really true, either. "Zara is a character I made up." She tries to make light

of it. "Me Rebecca …" She taps the top book on the stack. "Her Zara. Me real, her fantasy."

He stands perfectly still, in quiet confidence—only for some reason it feels like the poised stillness before a pounce, the breathlessness of a coiled snake.

"Your name isn't Rebecca Nightshade." His voice sounds like it comes from the bottom of an oil drum or some other deep, dark, echoing place. And there is a certainty in his tone that is unnerving. She had worked hard to keep the shield of the pseudonym between her and the prying public. "And Zara is no fantasy. She is as real as the beauty of my beloved Babylon and as old as the Endless Black Beyond, a kingdom she will rule with her mate by her side."

Gabriella catches sight of Bernie at the edge of her vision. He is grinning.

"You got that right," she says to the man standing before her, but she looks pointedly and defiantly at Bernie. "Zara is as real as Babylon and we both know how real *that* is." She turns back to the tall, blonde stranger. "We've already opened the twenty-first century, taken the tag off and everything. Don't you think it's a little late to send it back?"

Out of the corner of her eye she sees Bernie scowl. He doesn't like her humor. It makes her human and real and neither characteristic appeals to him personally nor satisfies his purposes. Bernie doesn't like for her to break character. That's the main reason she does it.

But the man before her never blinks. There is something chilling about his astonishing good looks. His features are too well-defined, as sharp as a hatchet, poster boy for the Hitler Youth.

"Sweet Zara, you're even more lively than I pictured, with even more sparkle. A bit untamed to be sure, but that spirit can be bridled." He manages to make "bridled" sound menacing. "I've been looking for you for millennia. Now, our time has come."

Okay, this guy is definitely certifiable. Gorgeous, but crackers.

Gabriella picks up a copy of *The Bride of the Beast* and opens it to the cover page in the front. She reaches for a pen and says formally, "I'm sorry, sir, but you're holding up the line. Do you want me to write something in particular or just sign it?"

He leans down close and she smells a hint of garlic his breath mint can't disguise, a fresh lime aftershave and some other scent that eludes her. It is an earthy smell, like fresh plowed sod or damp leaves, but unpleasant. Moldy leaves, perhaps. And dirt from an open—

THE LAST SAFE PLACE

"Write: 'To my Master and Lord. I will honor you, serve you, obey you and bear you a son. We will reign together, the Beast and his Bride.'"

His voice is thick and clotted with urgency; his breathing labored. The cold he emanates chills Gabriella to the bone and she begins to tremble. She drops her pen, yanks her hand away from the book and looks up into his face. That's a mistake. His eyes seize hers and lock on. She falls into their frigid depths, deeper and deeper into the blue that darkens through purple to black.

His eyes hold her captive. She is only set free when he drops his gaze—like she'd seized an electric cable and couldn't let go until the juice was turned off. She slumps back in her chair gasping.

"I will see you soon, my Love," he says. "I will come for you when it is time." He straightens up, turns and walks away—leaving the un-autographed book lying beneath her trembling hands.

Gabriella feels tears well in her eyes and spill soundlessly down her cheeks as she watches him go. She has never been so frightened in her life. Needlessly frightened. The man did absolutely nothing menacing, yet everything was menacing. An image blooms of the hobbits, Frodo, Sam, Merry and Pippin, crouching against the embankment as the Black Rider sniffs for them on the road above. Sick, mindless fear. How could anything human possibly be so innocently terrifying?

To Bernie's vast dismay, she lurches to her feet and retreats to the ladies room and refuses to come out until he clears the bookstore. Then she sneaks furtively out the back door and into a waiting limousine to go home.

The day after the book signing, three dozen black roses were delivered to her house. That's when she learned his name. Yesheb Al Tobbanoft. From that moment forward, his unrelenting attention became the canvas on which every day was painted. Over the course of the next eight months, he sent her flowers, presents, cards and letters—she refused delivery on all of them. Then he began to show up wherever she was. How did he know she was taking Ty to the museum, that she was going to the dentist or to the grocery store? She finally went to court and got a restraining order from a reluctant, unbelieving judge. That didn't make Yesheb leave her alone, it only moved his attentions back a few yards. When she saw him on the sidewalk in front of her house or inside the fence, standing in the trees watching, she called the police. Time and time again. But he was never there when the police arrived and she quickly became the little boy who cried wolf.

After he showed up at the intersection in Orlando, where she had sneaked away to take Ty to Disneyland, she employed a private detective who documented his family's fabulous wealth—and the tragic deaths that befell one family member after another until Yesheb was the only man standing. After Good Friday, she'd lived in constant terror. No one knew better than she the timetable for the Beast to collect his bride. If he failed to seduce her by the full moon in July, he would lose forever his right to rule Babylon.

And Gabriella suspected that never in his life had Yesheb Al Tobbanoft failed to get exactly what he wanted.

* * * *

Yesheb holds the heavy damask drapes back from the window and stares with unseeing eyes into a world colored the cheerless shade of gray peculiar to the south of England in the springtime. The sullen masses of clouds harried by a chill wind have worn thin, but aren't threadbare enough to allow a single shard of sunlight to slice down out of the evening sky.

Though no mist or fog or drizzle is actually visible in the air, it is nonetheless wet. So is every surface in the stone courtyard and the perfectly manicured rose gardens—the blood-red blooms rust-colored in the gray light—that stretch out beneath the high window on the north side of the manor house. Yesheb can just make out the blanket of flowers on the floor of the bluebell wood beyond the stone fence in the rolling hills of Hertfordshire where his sisters played when they were children.

Perhaps an hour of daylight remains before the wet air scrubs away all color and washes darkness down the day, and Yesheb wonders as he has wondered countless times over the years why his Iranian father chose to purchase a sprawling estate here in the unrelenting drear.

He smiles a joyless smile. Ah, but Anwar Al Tobbanoft did not choose. Perhaps he thought he did, in his ignorance, but his father was mistaken. Anwar Al Tobbanoft was *chosen*. It was his honor, and the privilege of his submissive cow of a wife, to bring royalty into the world, and the revelation of Yesheb's regal lineage had occurred here in England.

THE LAST SAFE PLACE

Yesheb drops the curtain and turns back to the ornate desk. He hobbles on his walking cast the few steps to the big leather chair. As he settles his long frame into it, his mind snaps back to his obsession with the force of a stretched-too-tight rubber band.

The Bride. *Where is she?*

His herd of private investigators have scurried around with insectile frenzy searching for her, but have not turned up so much as a hint of her whereabouts. They searched her house but found nothing that suggested her destination. They accessed the contacts list in her computer and were systematically investigating every person named in it. They were checking out every school she ever attended, every classmate, roommate, bunkmate, old friend, old flame and every neighbor every place she ever lived.

They were investigating the old man just as thoroughly, though his history is longer, not as well documented and harder to track.

Zara's sniveling little literary agent—clearly the progeny of a rat bred with a pit viper—had been drawn to Yesheb's power and sucked up to him unashamedly. The man gave Yesheb's investigators every speck of information he had about Zara, which quickly made it clear Phelps hardly knew her at all.

The agent collects her mail and gives it to Yesheb's men. Nothing. The investigators watch for activity on her ISP address. Nothing. She and the old man left their cell phones behind and there is no way to trace a burner—a pre-paid cheapie phone. There has been no activity on her credit cards and her ATM card, but they learned she had withdrawn more than $75,000 in cash from the bank that day in New York two weeks ago. Unless the three of them have forged passports—and why would they?—they have not fled the country. Still, you could go a long way on $75,000.

She and the others—the boy, the old man and the dog—have vanished in a puff of smoke.

Yesheb picks up off the desk one of his father's most prized possessions. The jeweled, enameled Easter egg, the Royal Danish Egg, is one of the eight missing Faberge eggs. Its value is incalculable. He turns it over in his hand, looks at it without really seeing it. Then, in a sudden flash of rage, he hurls it across the room to smash against the bookcase and growls a string of profanities under his breath.

They *will* find her. No one can hide forever from a manhunt as thorough as the one he has launched. She will surface, do something stupid and he will snatch her up like a frog grabs a fly. He has time, he tells himself firmly, trying to calm his frayed nerves. He still has twelve days until the next full moon. And another full moon after that one. He will find her, sacrifice her son, mate with her and plant the seed of his own son in her womb. They will rule together. And he will make her pay for running from him. Oh, my yes. He will make her pay as his father made his mother pay.

Even as a boy, Yesheb knew his father believed his mother had been unfaithful and he couldn't figure out why his father hadn't killed his wife and her newborn baby on the spot. Why had he let them live?

When he grew older he understood: Anwar Al Tobbanoft kept them alive to make them pay!

Other boys were borne away into slumber to the tune of lullabies; Yesheb went to sleep every night to the sound of his mother's screams. His father beat her regularly, broke her nose so many times it was as flat as a prize fighter's, shattered countless other bones over the years, knocked out most of her teeth and blinded her left eye. No one outside the household ever knew, of course. Anwar Al Tobbanoft was an important, respected and *rich* man. He was also a Muslim man, not in belief but for convenience. And it was certainly convenient that he could cover his wife's battered body from head to toe whenever she went out in public with a full burka—the kind that featured only a mesh slit for the eyes.

When Yesheb was about twelve, he found out that shortly after he was born his father had commissioned DNA testing on the blonde, blue-eyed baby boy and discovered that Yesheb had, indeed, come from his seed. So why had his father continued to punish his mother for a crime he knew she did not commit? And why did he visit unspeakable cruelties on his only son as well? It took years for Yesheb to understand it wasn't about making anybody pay. It never had been. It was about the screams, the delicious delight of screams.

Yesheb shivers in anticipation of the sound of Zara's screams and feels power surge through him. There is power in fear and even greater power in domination. But the greatest power of all lies in living while others die at your hands. Power feeds on the screeching cries of their anguish, grows in the fertile soil of death like entangling, choking vines.

THE LAST SAFE PLACE

Yesheb killed for the first time when he was eight years old. It was the day he first heard The Voice. When the growling whisper spoke words into his ear that first time, he had not been frightened. It was almost like he had expected to hear it, like he had been waiting for it, holding his breath in anticipation of it his whole life.

Yesheb. Make an altar and offer a sacrifice to me—your sister's puppy.

"Who are you?" Yesheb had asked out loud. Though he knew. Yesheb had always known. What he learned that he did not know, however, was that The Voice tolerated nothing less than instant, complete, mindless obedience. He learned that lesson as all children learn best—by suffering the consequences of their misdeeds. The Voice rewarded Yesheb's question with agony, detonated a bomb of searing pain inside his head so excruciating he instantly dropped to his knees gasping. He writhed in delirious agony for seven days and seven nights. The finest medical care money could buy offered no relief. Doctors could find no cause for pain so torturous that the boy was literally blinded by it and could only barely hear above the buzz of a million locusts in his ears. The pain left him as abruptly as it had come. He awoke in a hospital. To the astonishment of the medical personnel hovering over him, he sat up, ripped the IV tubes out of his arms and demanded to go home.

Even weak from seven days of lying motionless, he got out of his bed as soon as the rest of the family slept and slipped into his little sister Pasha's room. The German Shepherd puppy she had gotten for her seventh birthday slept in a pillowed bed at the foot of hers. Yesheb picked it up silently. The dog licked his hand and Yesheb felt an ache in his heart for the helpless beast but he did not hesitate or falter.

Years later, he read that crack units of Nazi SS officers had been given puppies to raise and train, and on the day they graduated, they were ordered to slit the dogs' throats. Any officer who failed to respond instantly to the command was dismissed from the unit.

Yesheb would have passed the test. He sneaked into the kitchen for the sharpest knife he could find and then out the back door to do as The Voice had commanded.

He never questioned The Voice again.

Sometimes, there are other voices in his head. Some speak Arabic, others speak English, French or Italian. One is a sultry woman's voice; another is a child. The voices tell him things he could not possibly know, warn him of impending danger, soothe him sometimes and inflame his anger at other times. Those voices often tell him what to do, but the ultimate authority always rests with The Voice.

The Voice revealed Yesheb's true identity two years after the boy killed his sister's puppy. He was a day student at Haileybury, the prestigious British boarding school peopled by the children of the rich and famous from around the world. Located on Hertford Heath twenty miles north of central London, the school boasted a quad touted as the largest academic quadrangle in the world, and that spring the Kipling House, one of the boys' dormitories, used soapstone to construct a scale model of Stonehenge in the center of it.

Although Yesheb's striking good looks, his maturity and his air of authority had made him an instant leader when his father enrolled him, the boy disdained leadership, made no friends and kept to himself. After the other students fell victim to his caustic tongue, hair-trigger temper and vicious, mean streak, they cut a wide path around him. Left him alone, though none of the insipid fools realized he was never alone. The Voice and the minions of The Voice were always with him.

As Yesheb watched construction of the scale model of rocks one day after class, his mind was inexorably drawn to thoughts of destruction and desecration and it occurred to him that it would be entertaining to defile the stones like the graffiti-slathered walls in London's tube stations and bus shelters.

His fellow students were intent on their work and paid no attention to his feigned interest as he sauntered around behind the largest carved stone. He sat down in the grass beside it and ran his hand over the smooth, almost greasy surface of the soapstone. As soon as he was certain no one was watching, he withdrew a felt-tip marker from his pocket and scrawled YESHEB AL TOBBANOFT on the base of the rock, down low where the tall grass would cover over his handiwork from the casual observer. Then he stood and stared up at the stone, wondering how long it would take his classmates to discover that he'd made their precious work of art as ordinary and mundane as a bridge abutment where some brainless lover had scrawled ShaMika Loves LaRon 4-Ever.

As he smiled at his desecration, The Voice displayed its power, came to Yesheb in a mighty vision and revealed to the still tender boy his identity, his royal place among the powers of the universe.

THE LAST SAFE PLACE

Yesheb's ears began to ring with a thousand tiny bells and The Voice spoke rumbling, powerful words inside his head in a language the boy had never heard before and Yesheb has never heard since. The world all around him grew too bright and he had to squint to keep his eyes from watering. Then a searing light focused on the rock in front of him and left everything else in pale shadow. The light grew brighter and brighter until Yesheb could barely stand to look at it. Then, out of the light, burning gold letters began to appear one at a time on the stone, as if a giant invisible pen were inscribing each one. Yesheb stood transfixed as words began to appear slowly, one letter at a time, until the stone stood like a mighty doorpost with a name inscribed in burning gold letters upon it.

THE BEAST OF BABYLON.

Yesheb had no idea who or what The Beast of Babylon might be, but stared at the flaming letters in awe and wonder. Then the most amazing thing of all happened. The small, black marker-inscribed letters of Yesheb's name lifted off the bottom of the rock one at a time, floated up into the air and grew larger and larger until they were the size of the flaming letters written by the invisible pen. Then each letter from his name was inserted into the words on the stone. When his black letter covered a flaming letter, it blocked out the light—like placing a lid over a candle—there was a sizzling sound and smoke rose up all around it.

The Y of YESHEB became the Y in *BABYLON*. The E in YESHEB became the E of *BEAST*. And so it went, one letter after another until all the letters of Yesheb's name had been used and all the flaming letters had been capped in black. There on the stone, with smoke rising up around each letter, were the words THE BEAST OF BABYLON—spelled with the letters of Yesheb's name. The Beast of Babylon and Yesheb Al Tobbanoft were one and the same. Yesheb had learned his true identity.

Of course, it was years before he understood the future laid out for The Beast of Babylon. He learned that in the pages of Zara's book—her diary disguised as fiction, her prophesies set down in the form of fantasy.

Only Yesheb understands that it is neither fiction nor fantasy. After a millennium of searching, the identity of the Bride has been revealed. And the path they must travel to their destiny has been laid out. Follow that path and the throne of a mighty kingdom in The Endless Black Beyond will be his, ushering in a Dark Age of demonic rule on the heels of their apocalyptic victory over the forces of light.

But he must follow the path. He cannot stray from it. Everything has to happen as it has been prophesied. His world, his kingdom and his life depend upon it.

Yesheb gets to his feet and hobbles back to the window. He stares into the deepening gray shadows of evening, concentrates, wills his mind to reach out and connect with the mind of his beloved Zara. For an instant it seems he almost does, he imagines he smells something—a hint of pine or cedar—but it is gone in a heartbeat. Wherever Zara is at this moment, her mind is closed to him.

CHAPTER 6

The aroma of pine and cedar filled every breath and Gabriella sucked in great lungfuls of it as she followed the winding road into the mountains. The air was a feast of crispness; it smelled so clean it must have been scrubbed with lye soap and hung out on the line to dry.

U.S. 285 had led her along the valley floor in front of Mount Princeton for eight miles to Nathrop, where HWY 162 peeled off to the right and began to wind up through Chalk Creek Canyon between Mount Princeton and Mount Antero. As the road curved along beside the creek, massive chalk cliffs reared up on the south side of Princeton, towering 1,500 feet into the cloudless sky.

"Those are called Moon Cliffs," Gabriella told Ty, shouting so he could hear her above the wind in the open jeep. "You can read a newspaper outside from the reflected glow off them when the moon's full."

A full moon. Twelve days away.

The road followed the creek higher and higher up the canyon. Mount Antero reared up above the road on the left and filled the whole sky, bald and snowcapped above the tree line.

After a 45-minute gradual climb, they rounded a curve and came upon the little town of St. Elmo. Named a National Historic Site, the resurrected ghost town rested at an elevation of 10,000 feet. It had been a mining camp in the late 1800s and its buildings were authentic period structures, wood frame, with raised wooden sidewalks that stretched for four blocks along both sides of Chalk Creek Canyon Road, which formed the town's main, and only paved, street.

Gabriella could see houses down a handful of side streets—small adobe structures mostly, with dirt yards. She was surprised that anybody actually lived here full-time. By September, the upper reaches of Princeton and Antero were snow-clogged and many valleys like this one were impassable.

Skiers didn't come here, though. The resorts and striking Colorado slopes were on the other side of the Mount Massive Wilderness Area—an hour and a half north in Vail or three hours away in Aspen.

There were cars, pickup trucks and SUVs parked in front of businesses, along with several jeeps she suspected were rentals and other battered, mud-splattered jeeps she was certain weren't. Some of the vehicles obviously carried tourists, easy to spot with their cameras and binoculars dangling around their necks, or holding cell phones out at arm's length to frame and capture digital images. But the locals were easy to spot, too. Hispanic, many of them, some Native American, they chatted, two or three together here and there, dressed in not-a-fashion-statement frayed jeans, well-used Stetsons and scuffed and muddy cowboy boots.

Gabriella pulled her jeep to a stop in front of a building flanked on one side by the dry goods store and on the other by the apothecary. A hand-painted sign on the front proclaimed St. Elmo's Mercantile, Established 1885. The proprietor, a man named Pedro Rodriguez, was the man Gabriella had driven more than a thousand miles across seventeen states to see. He held the key—literally—to her future. If what James Benninger had said in every Christmas card in the past five years was true, the owner would welcome Gabriella and her family, supply them what they needed and give them directions, maybe even a hand-drawn map to direct them to St. Elmo's Fire, snuggled in a hanging valley on Mount Antero 11,673 feet above sea level.

Gabriella opened the jeep door and got out, then turned to help Theo clamber out of the backseat. But he stepped down unaided and shook off the hand she'd placed on his elbow.

"You'll know I need help standing up when you see me falling down. And you'll know I's ready for the Reaper when I stay down there cause I like the view."

"A little grumpy, aren't we? You're just afraid I might find out you've got a heart of gold."

"So does a hard-boiled egg."

Ty and P.D. had already bounded up the steps to the wide wooden sidewalk in front of the Mercantile. Gabriella couldn't remember the last time she'd seen the boy's eyes lit with so much joy. He must feel like he'd left the real world to take up residence in a cowboy movie. She and Theo joined him and pushed open the door and set the bell above it jingling. P.D. didn't have his guide dog sign hung around his neck but Gabriella suspected this was a place where animals were as welcome as people.

The interior of the store was dim and shadowy, the array of merchandise on the shelves an eclectic hodgepodge of items. What appeared to be a well-stocked small supermarket filled the whole left side. Theo headed that way, likely searching for licorice. In the center was a Southwest souvenir shop like those they'd passed every fifty miles since they crossed the Oklahoma border into Colorado. Ty had pleaded with her to stop at Injun Joe's Wampum or Crazy Harry's Rattlesnake Ranch or the one with a twenty-foot-tall purple Tyrannosaurus Rex out front that advertised Indian rugs, turquoise jewelry, pizza and Chinese carry-out.

The Mercantile's souvenirs included the classics: T-shirts that proclaimed I HEART Colorado or My Parents Went to Colorado and All I Got Was This Stupid Shirt. Rubber tomahawks, Indian bows with stoppers instead of arrowheads on the arrows, cap guns, slingshots, Indian drums topped with stretched rubber instead of animal hides and Indian headdresses made from dyed chicken feathers. For the more discerning shopper, the back wall featured turquoise and silver jewelry, genuine handmade Indian pottery and rugs and Pendleton blankets.

And a huge section of rocks.

Gabriella was instantly drawn there. She gazed at the kinds of minerals she'd grown up with, housed in cases and on shelves in a special room in her childhood home. Glittering pyrite—fool's gold; deep purple fluorite octahedrons; flaky, milk-colored mica that looked like shaved glass; dense blue apatite; shiny black squares of galena and slices as big as a saucers of quarter-inch-thick granite, striped with black and reddish brown veins, polished to a finish as smooth as a granite countertop.

And of course, blue, white and purple aquamarine—some polished into semi-precious stones and others in the natural, crystalline state her parents had found on the mountain.

"Mom, come look at this," Ty called. He was standing with P.D. at the counter of a small post office on the far wall of the Mercantile next to a bank of post office boxes and a small array of mailing paraphernalia—first class envelopes, small boxes and brown wrapping paper. A mini laundromat—three washers and three dryers—occupied the wall on one side of the post office and on the other side stood swinging doors like those in an Old West saloon. Gabriella could see what appeared to be a family room beyond the doors, likely the living quarters of the proprietor.

Ty was talking to a rugged Hispanic man with a thick black mustache who stood behind the post office cash register. A dark-haired girl was down on her knees petting P.D.

"Check that out, Mom." Ty pointed behind the counter to a life-sized poster beside a collage of snapshots under the banner Wall of Honor. The snapshots were of grinning fishermen displaying trout of every variety—rainbow, brown, cutthroat—and every size.

Gabriella smiled at the poster. It showed Napoleon Dynamite—one of Ty's all-time favorite movie characters—with his hair a curly red fuzz-ball and his arm draped around the shoulder of a smaller, dark-haired boy on whose upper lip sprouted something that approached a mustache. Both wore t-shirts that proclaimed "Pedro for President."

So did the man behind the counter.

"His name is Pedro, too," Ty said, and nodded to the man, who extended his hand.

"Pedro Rodriguez. I'm happy to meet you, ma'am."

Pedro was tall, broad-shouldered and barrel-chested, a sturdy man whose unibrow shaded direct brown eyes. The bright smile that lit his face like a halogen bulb revealed perfect teeth beneath the black broom of mustache. His features were craggy, not traditionally handsome but rugged and strong. Gabriella was embarrassed to discover that if she'd had to describe him in one word, that word would have been "sexy."

He looked her dead in the eye when he shook her hand, took in her face as a whole rather than a collection of pieces with one side slathered in makeup that camouflaged but didn't completely hide her deformity.

"This is my daughter, Anza—Esperanza," he said. "In Spanish, that is Hope."

"I'm Gabriella … Underhill." She didn't think he picked up on the pause. Even after using it for two weeks, the fake name didn't flow easily off her tongue and she was always afraid Theo and Ty would forget it altogether.

The girl stood and Gabriella got a good look at her as they shook hands. Her hand was small and soft, but her handshake was firm—no dead fish on a stick.

"Your boy tells me you're going to be spending the summer at St. Elmo's Fire," Pedro said.

"Mister Rodriguez says—"

"Pedro ees fine, son." The man's Spanish accent was the musical kind where every word is linked to the next in a melodious daisy chain.

"*Pedro* says that St. Elmo's Fire is the only cabin on the whole mountain, Mom! On the only road on the whole mountain. And there's a creek there with a waterfall and trout and at night the moon shines on the chalk cliffs, which aren't really made out of chalk and—"

"Breathe in there somewhere, Ty," Gabriella said, "before you pass out."

At that moment, she was acutely aware of Ty's *little boyness*. As evidenced by his exuberance, of course, but more apparent by what failed to light a fire under him than what did. Ty paid no attention at all to the young woman smiling beside her father. And any male human being who didn't stare at the girl slack-jawed was clearly pre-pubescent. Or a blind eunuch.

Though voluptuous in a peasant blouse, Esperanza Rodriguez was modest and demure, with a head of glossy black curls, a china-doll face, and warm, brown skin as clear as morning light. She had the kind of plump, moist mouth men grow stupid about, pouty lips that were red without lipstick and brown, doe eyes with obscenely long eyelashes. Beside a girl so strikingly beautiful, Gabriella felt like a troll under a bridge.

"Not the only road, son, the only *jeep trail*. There's a road up the other side of the mountain for prospectors. Folks have staked claims to about every square inch of that side of the mountain to mine the aquamarine."

Gabriella found her voice and hoped she hadn't been caught gawking.

"You have the key to the cabin—right?"

"Not just the key but a warm welcome to go with it for Jim's mystery guests."

Gabriella's gut clenched into a knot and she had to struggle to make her question seem more surprised/bemused than desperate/frightened.

"Mystery guests? So what's Jim been telling you about me?"

"Oh, he didn't call you that. It was … I … a few years ago, five or six I guess, he said he'd invited someone to stay at the cabin whose family spent a summer there back in the 80s."

"We were here when I was seven … almost eight years old."

"He talked about it a time or two after that, never mentioned your name though, and I …" Pedro grinned and Gabriella noticed how comfortably a smile fit on his face. "Well, I got to thinking of you as his 'mystery guests.' Before he left for Sudan, he called and said he'd invited you to stay the whole summer and if you showed up, to give you my spare key to the cabin and the gate, and to play host for him, make sure you have everything you need." His smile grew wider. "As I'm sure you know, Jim"—pronounced with a long "e" sound in the middle—"may be a little … scattered … but he ees an amazingly gracious man!"

Gabriella felt the knot in her stomach slowly relax. This was the last hurdle. She had no idea how much Jim Benninger knew about her. He obviously knew her name and her parents' names, but did he put it together with the famous Garrett Griffith, or somehow link it to Rebecca Nightshade? And how much had he shared about her and her family's connection to St. Elmo's Fire with the person who kept the key? If Jim had given out her identity, poured out her whole story, maybe—at least as much of it as he knew—it would have been too dangerous for her to stay here. She'd have been forced to move on and find another hiding place, take Theo's advice and throw a dart at the map.

She first heard from the Rev. James Benninger in a Christmas card in 2005—the first Christmas after Garrett's death. Getting that card was the only thing she could remember clearly about that Christmas. It shone like a single, bright star in the black depths of her grief.

She'd never sent out cards, thought it was crassly commercial, and over the years most folks had marked her name off their Christmas card lists, too. She remembered the envelope lying by itself on the table by the front door, addressed to Gabriella Griffith in care of Phillip and Natalie Griffith at her parents' old address on Old Boston Road in the Whitehall neighborhood of Pittsburgh. The family had lived there until Grant's death and then moved away. But years later, Garrett bought the house—said it was the only place they'd ever lived that felt like home. He could have afforded a mansion, but he lived for years in that modest house. Died there, too. After his death, she couldn't bear to sell it, just left it empty. Mail delivered there was forwarded to her address.

She'd only opened the envelope because of the address. She remembered sinking down to the floor and staring at the picture on the front of the Christmas card—a stunning photograph of St. Elmo's Fire. Not the simple, rustic cabin she remembered but freshly painted and beautiful with the unchanging rise of mountain behind it and the waterfall in the background.

Written inside the card in a fluid script not usual in a man's handwriting, was a message:

You don't know me, Gabriella. My name is Rev. James Benninger and I pastor St. Stephen's Presbyterian Church in Biloxi, Mississippi. I purchased St. Elmo's Fire in Colorado ten years ago and have gradually been renovating it ever since.

The next line kicked her heartbeat into a loping gallop.

When the carpenters tore off the roof to add a second floor, they found a box of items in the crawl space of the attic that had belonged to previous owners or tenants. One of the things in the box was a bunged-up family Bible in which a little girl named Gabriella Griffith wrote a diary and drew pictures during the summer of 1982. The final entry sent me digging into your family's connection to St. Elmo's Fire and I learned about the horrible tragedy that occurred at the end of that summer. I am so sorry for your loss.

I hope I am not invading your privacy by contacting you. But given the significance the cabin has in your life, and the obvious strong feelings you must have about the time you spent there, I thought you might like to visit sometime, and I want you to know you are welcome to stay at St. Elmo's Fire anytime you would like.

This is my address and phone number. (I got your address from a blank check in the Bible. I hope someone in your family still lives there to forward this on to you.) Give me a call to arrange a time when the cabin is free.

And may the blessings of this special season soothe your heart and restore your soul.

God bless,
Jim Benninger

She'd certainly needed a soothed heart and restored soul that Christmas, but it would have taken more than a Christmas card—however kind and sincere—to assuage her pain. She'd stared at the photo through her tears, then threw the card away and never thought about it again.

Another card arrived the next Christmas, and every Christmas after that. The message in each of them was different, but they all contained the same offer to visit St. Elmo's Fire. She had thrown every card away, never wrote down Rev. Benninger's address or phone number or made any effort to get in touch with him. But she had grown to anticipate and enjoy his cards—seeing the changes in the cabin—the new second-floor deck, new wraparound porch, the trees in the aspen forest taller.

The card this past Christmas varied from the usual message, however. Rev. Benninger said that he and his family would be working at a refugee camp in Sudan from March until October, 2010.

"We won't get to enjoy St. Elmo's Fire at all next year," he wrote. "So there's no need for you to schedule a time to visit. In fact, the cabin is yours for the whole summer if you want it. I've asked my good friend Pedro Rodriguez at St. Elmo's Mercantile to give you a key. If you are able to come, he will take good care of you and your family!"

He also ended his message differently.

"Ever since the first of November, you have been in my thoughts often. I have learned over the years not to question it when the Lord places someone on my heart. Perhaps you have some need I don't know about, some need St. Elmo's Fire might meet. I urge you to take advantage of my offer and spend time there. The beauty of creation all around cannot help but draw you closer to the Creator."

Since the first of November … Yesheb had shown up in her life on Halloween.

When she decided to run, to hide, she instantly thought of the cabin, as if it had been waiting in the back of her mind for her to summon it. She had never made any connection to Rev. Benninger. She'd never mentioned him to anyone and had thrown away all his correspondence to her, including the card last Christmas. Her family had traveled the country like gypsies every summer of her childhood. There was no record of where they'd gone, no possible way to connect her to a single cabin where they'd stayed once *almost 30 years ago*. St. Elmo's Fire might be … an answer to prayer.

"We'll need directions, too," Gabriella said. "I'm not sure I could still … find it. Maybe you could draw us a map."

"You will not need a map. Head down Chalk Creek Canyon Road for another four miles until you come to a big house on the left. It ees not your typical mountain cabin, it looks like … well, you will see for yourself. Steve Calloway, *Dr.* Steve Calloway, lives there—a retired GP—and the trail up the mountain runs right beside his place. You can't get lost on the trail because like I told the boy,"—he reached out casually and ruffled Ty's curls, and Ty didn't seem to mind a bit!—"the trail doesn't even show up on maps, except the most detailed ones for hikers."

"People hike up the trail?" Gabriella didn't mean to sound so alarmed but she could tell Pedro picked up on it.

"Not that I know of. There's nothing on this side of the mountain to hike to."

"But, the aquamarine …"

"Years ago people looked for aquamarine up there, but that was before they found huge deposits of it on the other side of the mountain. And prospectors can't take a jeep up the trail to St. Elmo's Fire—there's a gate on it that's locked when Jim's not here and I've got the only key."

Pedro smiled again, such an engaging infectious smile, Gabriella found herself smiling back. "I'm the St. Elmo's Fire gatekeeper/custodian/maintenance man/tour guide/service department/technical support and concierge. Mostly I check on the place, keep it in good repair and make sure it's stocked with supplies for Jim when he comes."

Before Gabriella could say anything else, Pedro's eyes turned to a woman approaching the counter with a handful of mostly wilted wildflowers.

"Hóla, Contessa," Pedro said. "What have you got there?"

The woman had salt-and-pepper hair in a windblown frizz and wore a man's suit jacket over an Indian-design long skirt. With sparkly bangles of jewelry hanging off her everywhere she could dangle something, she looked like a gypsy fortune teller. Or a Christmas tree. If Gabriella had met her on the streets of Pittsburgh, she'd have thought she was a bag lady.

As soon as the woman spotted P.D. she issued a little squeal of delight and got down on her knees in front of him. He endured her "oh-what-a-pretty-doggie-you-are!" stoically. His guide-dog training had disciplined him to sit quietly under the gushing ministrations of dog-loving humans.

The woman straightened up finally and answered Pedro's question.

"Just painting out in the meadow above Buffalo Creek—still life." Gabriella noticed paint smears in various hues on the woman's hands and clothing. "Larkspur and loco weed—blue and purple—and a touch of red king's crown."

The woman noticed Gabriella for the first time and gave her a silly little wave that animated the bracelets on her arm in a jingling, clattering dance.

"Oh, excuse me—I didn't mean to interrupt," she said, then flashed a be-friendly-to-tourists smile. "Hope you enjoy our mountains." She turned her attention back to Pedro as Theo hobbled toward them. "And when I saw these golden asters and blanket flowers—oh, Pedro! The yellows and rusts must have been blended by angels from a celestial pallet …"

Theo leaned toward Gabriella.

"Couldn't find no licorice," he muttered, then whispered into her ear. "Bet the only angels that screwball knows is Hark and Herald."

Gabriella flashed him a *behave!* look.

"… and I had to stop and pick a bunch for Angelina," the woman continued. "She seemed to like the smell of the Indian paintbrushes I brought her last week."

"Gracías. I am sure she weel enjoy them."

"Why don't you put them on her pillow," Anza said, and turned toward the double saloon doors with the paint-splattered artist in tow. When the doors swung open briefly to admit them, Gabriella caught a glimpse of an elderly Hispanic woman working at a long table in what appeared to be a large living room-kitchen combination. Something else in the room caught her eye, but then the doors swung back shut.

"I apologize for the interruption," Pedro said. "You were asking about hikers and I was assuring you there were none. Anything else you would like to know?"

"Just us!" Ty said to Theo. "There's nobody but us on the whole mountain, Grandpa Slappy!"

Gabriella cringed. They'd agreed to leave references to their past life—like Slap Yo Mama Carmichael—behind them.

But Theo was quicker on the uptake than she expected. Extending his hand to Pedro, he said, "Name's Theodosius X. Slapinheimer."

Gabriella burped out a giggle she managed to disguise as a cough. Theo's face remained expressionless.

"Growing up with a name like that, I just mailed my milk money to the school bully."

Gabriella was grateful for the rumble of Pedro's laughter so she could let go of her own.

"My friends call me Slappy," Theo said, still deadpan. "You can call me Mr. Slapinheimer."

"Theo!"

The whole exchange blew right by Ty. The boy had other things on his mind.

"And the cabin is waaay up on the side of the mountain, Grandpa Slappy—and the only way to get to it's a rutted jeep trail!"

"Goody," Theo said.

"As you can see, Ty's grandfather is less than thrilled to be here." Gabriella struggled to keep a straight face. *Slapinheimer?* "He's never been in the mountains."

Pedro didn't patronize him.

"The mountains aren't for everybody; some people hate it here. As for me ..." The halogen smile lit his face again. "This ees as close to heaven as I will ever be on earth—literally as well as figuratively. My mother used to tell me God had to work nights and weekends to create the Rockies."

Theo softened a little.

"Maybe that's why He brought us here—so He could show off."

"Maybe so." Then Pedro turned back to Gabriella. "I am not going to lie to you, Mrs. Underhill. That jeep trail, it ees a bear. Seven switchbacks and lots of overhangs and drop-offs." He fixed her with a pointed, anxious look. "You sure you can handle it?"

What choice did she have?

"Bring it on."

Pedro studied her for a moment, then continued. "I keep the cabin stocked with the essential nonperishables—canned goods, salt, pepper, sugar and bottled water." He stopped, turned to Theo. "About water. Be sure to—"

"One more person tell me 'drink lots of water,' or 'yeah, but it's a dry heat,' I gone smack 'em!"

"Same go for 'the air ees very thin up here'?"

Theo nodded.

Pedro addressed Gabriella. "Just a reminder for *you*, then." With that thick mustache, she could see a full-on smile, but a mischievous little grin was harder. "Do not expect to do what you always do. You will tire out quickly. Sit down and rest or we will be sending a medevac helicopter to pluck you off the mountain."

"They can do that, can they?" Theo asked. "Come get you off the mountain?" Pedro nodded. "Good. If I die up there, I don't fancy being a snack for the bears, a little dark meat to vary they diets."

Pedro laughed again and Gabriella watched Theo thaw to something like room temperature. The old man loved it when people laughed at his jokes. She suspected Pedro had figured that out.

Reaching into his pocket, Pedro fished out a key ring. Gabriella noticed that every key was meticulously labeled and Pedro saw that she noticed.

"I am only a leetle OCD," he said. "Not enough so I label my sock drawer or arrange the soup cans in the cabinet in alphabetical order." He removed a key from the ring and handed it to her. "This key unlocks the gate as well as the cabin. If I were you, I would get on the road as soon as possible. There ees a thunderstorm almost every afternoon this time of year. They do not usually last long, but they can be fierce—lightning, hail and enough rain to make the roads slippery. And that trail ees hard enough to get up dry."

Gabriella purchased a few basic perishables—bread, milk, lunchmeat and Lucky Charms for Ty. Ty bounced out the door like he was riding a column of turbulent air. His feet only touched the ground a time or two between the store and the jeep. Theo had retreated to his perpetual state of ill humor; Gabriella was sobered. And … okay, admit it, concerned. Pedro's warnings awakened her gnawing anxiety about Theo. He was stronger than most men his age, but he was seventy-four years old. Would the thin air bring on heart problems? Would the ride up the mountain scramble his internal organs?

"Theo," she said before she started the jeep's engine. "You don't have to go with us. I can give you some money and you can vanish wherever you—"

"We done been over this. You two goin' up that mountain, Theo goin' up that mountain. So let's get to it—you heard what Pancho Villa said. There ain't no top on this thing and I done took me a shower today."

As they headed down Chalk Creek Canyon Road toward the trail up the mountain Gabriella noticed white and gray clouds moving in over the mountaintops to the west.

THE LAST SAFE PLACE

Theo sat in the backseat with P.D., who was snapping at the wind that flapped his ears. The old man had placed two sacks of groceries between him and the animal and hoped the breeze would blow off some of the dog hair the walking fur machine had slimed on his shirt on the ride to St. Elmo.

He sighed, closed his eyes and had a brief but intense conversation with God.

Are you sure you thought this one all the way through, Lord?

Far be it from me to tell you how to run the universe, but Theodosius X. Carmichael climbing up the side of a mountain … that sound right to you?

I know it's not like you asking me to leap over the Snake River Gorge on a jet-propelled motorcycle, but just so we clear on this—I would rather face down a serial killer with a sinus infection and poison ivy on his privates than ride up a hiking trail in this jeep!

Amen.

Oh … and I hope you was plannin' on lookin' after us 'cause I gone keep my eyes squeezed shut the whole way.

When they spotted the house set back from Chalk Creek Canyon Road in a grove of aspen trees, Gabriella understood why Pedro said it wasn't a typical mountain cabin. Actually, it was more a compound than either a house or a cabin, a collection of half a dozen small buildings surrounding a big one. All the buildings were made of red stone and shaped like Indian cliff dwellings. Painted in yellow below all the windows were Hopi Sun designs, a circle with three uneven lines—two short and one long one in the middle—extending out from the top, bottom and sides. A sign proclaiming "Heartbreak Hotel" formed an archway in a stacked-board fence that zigzagged out of sight into twin aspen groves on the sides of the gravel driveway leading to the big building.

A tall, white-haired man with a hatchet-thin face and wire-rimmed glasses stood beside the gate as if he were expecting them, and with a sweeping gesture of his Stetson invited them into the compound. There was no way to ignore the invitation without being rude, so Gabriella turned down the driveway and parked next to a battered vehicle with "Lotions, Potions & Deadly Elixirs" printed on the side. It looked like the Libyan terrorist van from *Back to the Future.*

P.D. hopped out the window onto a well-tended lawn—must water it every day for it to be so green—framed by a rock garden, yucca plants and flowering cacti. The dog dashed from one new scent to another, in doggie heaven from all the olfactory delights. The three humans climbed down out of the jeep as the man walked from the gate to greet them.

"Pedro called and said you were coming," the man said. His tousled white hair fell across his forehead into eyes magnified into big, blue marbles by his glasses, and he wore old jeans and scuffed cowboy boots. "I'm Steve Calloway. I hear we're going to be neighbors this summer."

"Looks that way," Gabriella said. She introduced herself, Ty and Theo uneasily, eager to disengage from the conversation and be on her way. She'd seen the doctor give her scar a quick once-over and knew he wasn't likely to forget it.

Ty pointed to the van.

"What's an e-lix …?"

"Elixir. Old-fashioned medicine that made well people sick, sick people sicker and killed more people than it cured," Steve said. "Some folks in St. Elmo painted that on the side of the van once when I was out of town— because it's kind of a traveling drug store/first aid station. I don't have a shingle hanging on my door, but it's a hike from here out to Buena Vista for folks with medical problems."

Theo gestured toward the buildings. "This a hospital?"

Steve laughed. "No, it's more an old-folks camp. All my retired friends come here to go fly fishing. A bunch of city boys descend on the mountain every summer, strip it of vegetation and all other life forms, leave it a barren wasteland and fly back east. I'm from Cleveland. Where are you from?"

"Pittsburgh," Ty said, though their cover story had them hailing from Salt Lake City. "You a Browns fan?"

"You mean a fan of the greatest football team that ever put on pads?"

"The *Browns?*" Ty shot a glance at Theo, who nodded almost imperceptibly and the boy went for it. "You know why the Browns are like a possum?" He didn't wait for an answer. "Because they play dead at home and get killed on the road. You know why they're not like a dollar bill? Because you can get four good quarters from a dollar."

Dr. Calloway staggered backward in mock pain, holding onto his chest. "You're killing me, boy! You're killing me. Bury me with the oldest of the old up above St. Elmo's Fire."

"Where?" Ty asked.

"There's a forest of bristlecone pine trees in a boulder field between the cabin and the peak," the doctor said. "Bristlecone pines are the oldest living organisms on earth."

"So there might be a tree up there that poked out of the ground the year Grampa Slappy was born?"

"That's some serious old, boy," Theo said.

"Actually, there might be a tree up there that sprouted from a pine cone when Julius Caesar became the emperor of Rome. A bristlecone pine tree can live up to 4,800 years."

Even Theo was impressed by that.

"When my granddaughter was little, she called them Jesus trees. There might be a tree up there that …"

Gabriella wasn't listening anymore. At the mention of the bristlecone pines, her mind flashed on golden light. A sudden hum filled her head like the sound an old refrigerator makes when the compressor kicks on, and she was at once in two worlds. The childhood fantasy world of The Cleft was a golden overlay on reality, coloring trees, the sky, Dr. Calloway, Ty and Theo in rich amber shades, golds and different hues of warm brown. The Cleft's golden light was brighter than she had ever seen it, a blazing sun so brilliant her mind squinted in the glow. The sense of peace was more profound, too, a joyous bubbling in her soul that was like exhaling a breath long held, unclenching fingers long squeezed into a fist, allowing cleansing tears to flow in sweet relief. A long, gentle *ahh* in her heart.

With the sensation of a final puzzle piece slipping effortlessly into place, Gabriella suddenly understood. The fantasy was so powerful here because she was closer to its source! She had dreamed it up *here* when she was a little girl! Her Wonderland, her Narnia, the fanciful creation of a sad little girl to make herself feel better—The Cleft. It was created here on this mountain!

"Mom!" Ty waved his hand in front of his mother's eyes. "Earth to Mom. Do you read me?"

She focused and flashed a smile that was warm and sweet, wafted upward from the dying embers of the golden glow in her mind.

"Read you loud and clear, Mr. Spock." She held up her hand in the V shape of a Vulcan salute.

"Your face looked blanker than a wino's bank statement," Theo said. "If we gone do this, we best get at it, 'less you can get Scottie to beam us up to that cabin."

"Maybe not Scottie …" Dr. Calloway said. He looked toward Chalk Creek Canyon Road. "At the risk of mixing TV show metaphors, will Speedy Gonzales do?"

They all followed his gaze. The rumble of the approaching jeep clearly indicated it needed a new muffler. Pedro was at the wheel, wearing a straw cowboy hat pulled down low over his brow. He turned off the highway onto the trail but didn't drive into the compound, just stopped and called out to them.

"I told Steve to stall you while I got someone to watch the store," he said. "Thought I would tag along if you (pronounced "choo") don't mind. I want to make sure everything is all set at the cabin."

No, you don't. You want to make sure we make it up this trail to the cabin alive.

CHAPTER 7

Ty rode in the backseat so he could keep a firm hold on P.D., positioned on the floorboard between his knees. Pedro invited Theo to ride with him because the front bucket seats in his jeep had more padding than the rental's.

The road wound through the trees beyond Dr. Calloway's for a quarter of a mile, then it made a sharp right turn and immediately began to climb. And to deteriorate. In less than half a mile, Gabriella had to shift into four-wheel drive to claw her way up what had become a narrow pothole-strewn, boulder-blocked trail.

Pedro had explained that the serpentine trail climbed the mountain by traversing it, back and forth, higher and higher, each level of trail tied to the next by a hairpin switchback. Gabriella had just slammed down into a pothole the size of a washtub and then bounced up over a huge, gnarled tree root when she spotted the first switchback out in front of Pedro's jeep.

The sight of it rendered her momentarily mute and airless. The strip mine where she had gotten experience in negotiating a jeep off-road had not prepared her for anything like this. The hairpin turn fastened the steep trail on which she was traveling north to its equally steep twin going back south. But the northbound lane of her interstate rested at least fifteen feet lower on the slope than the trail going south. The rutted, bumpy hairpin turn that joined the two together was carved out of solid rock. From where Gabriella sat, it appeared to be more a retaining wall than a turn, the grade so steep that nothing but momentum and centrifugal force would fasten the jeep to it. Hit the turn too slow and the jeep would slide sideways, maybe even tumble over on its side. Hit it too fast and you'd lose control and … all bets would be off.

But that was not all, said a voice in her head that sounded eerily like *The Cat in the Hat*. Oh, no, that was not all.

At the point where the top part of the curve joined the upper road, a metal gate stretched across the trail. The posts on both sides were sunk in concrete that had been poured into holes drilled into bedrock.

Pedro pulled to a stop well short of the switchback, got out and clambered uphill to the gate.

"Besides the one in your pocket, I have the only other key that fits this lock," he called out, indicating the deadbolt mechanism that held the big metal gate to the post on the uphill side. He unlocked the gate and pushed it open.

"You couldn't blast that out of the ground with a bazooka," Gabriella said, secretly thrilled. "Why such an imposing gate? Seems a little … excessive. Was the good reverend expecting terrorists?"

Pedro laughed. "Oh, he was not trying to keep out the meanies. Most of the time when Jim is here, he does not lock eet. The gate posts were sunk in concrete because that is the only way to keep the gate from washing out."

Pedro made his way back down the steep incline, got into his jeep and cranked the engine. It rumbled in muffler-less abandon. Gabriella's heart began to pound. Her mouth went dry. Her hands were instantly so sweaty it was hard to hold the steering wheel. She watched Pedro give his jeep gas, hit the smoothest part of the angled turn, which was the more-or-less unrutted top side, and roar around it using a kind of slingshot effect to fire him up onto the higher road. He drove forward well past the open gate and stopped to wait for her, turning around in his seat. He smiled and gave her a thumbs-up. Swell. The only thing that could possibly have made this ordeal worse was an audience.

She knew if she sat and looked at it she'd freeze and they'd all have to walk back down the mountain. So she swallowed hard, told Ty to hold tight to P.D. and gunned it.

Somewhere out there in the world beyond the mountains, people were listening to music, getting their eyebrows waxed, buying a used car or planting chrysanthemums. But here on Mount Antero, a crazed woman was risking her life and the life of her child and his dog in a wild, bumping, tires-spinning, scrambling charge up the high side of a switchback turn.

Gabriella was that woman.

And the crazed woman was screaming, a ferocious yowl that sounded like a gut-shot yak.

THE LAST SAFE PLACE

Gabriella was that woman, too.

Her jeep bounced over the final hump and skidded to a stop behind Pedro.

"Muy bíen!" His admiration was real.

"Piece of cake."

The two jeeps continued up the rutted, bone-jarring trail. Each of the switchbacks presented its own individual challenge. The second one was a right turn. Gratefully, the smoothest route was on the low side. That was fortunate because ten feet beyond the high side was empty air, a drop-off. The fall could have been five feet. Or a thousand. Gabriella had neither the time nor the inclination to look back over her shoulder after she had negotiated it to determine which.

She had assumed it would get easier as she went along. It didn't. Her proficiency increased, but her fear did not lessen. As she started into the fourth switchback, she caught sight of her reflection when an errant tree limb whacked the adjustable side mirror. And she realized with a shock how nakedly her fright was revealed on her face. But being scared was the price of doing business. Though she had to admit that if she'd known how "challenging" it would be, she might never have attempted it, the ability to traverse this trail was a life skill she had to master to survive.

The trail was scary; Yesheb was infinitely scarier.

She also grasped as she bumped and scraped along, that she'd never have made it through the first switchback if Pedro hadn't been there to show her how it was done, though he never gave her a word of instruction or advice and pretended not to notice that she went to school on his every move. By the time they came around the fifth curve, she understood that he'd known all along she'd never make it without him.

About fifty yards beyond the seventh switchback, Pedro made an abrupt turn to the left and began to climb what appeared to be a dry creek bed. He followed the wash up about sixty yards before his jeep disappeared over a crest. Gabriella struggled after him, taking care to go fast enough to keep sufficient momentum to make it to the top but not so fast that her back tires broke traction and spun out in the dry, crumbly rock.

Her heart had shifted back into high gear again, banging in her chest as she roared up over the crest behind Pedro. The dust from his ascent still hung in the air and it was a second or two before she could see clearly.

A rock wall appeared on the right and she edged along between it and a sharp descent on the left.

The air cleared as she passed the forward edge of the rock outcrop and she found herself in … Narnia, without the snow—a world so foreign to the one she'd just left that the transition was jarring. That much hadn't changed. The abrupt entrance into the hanging valley at 11,670 feet still packed the emotional wallop it always had. After clawing up the rocky, dusty trail and the dry wash, the struggle was over and the jeep purred into an aspen grove along barely discernible double worn tracks in a ground cover of small green ferns, rocks covered with gray-green lichen and fallen leaves. The aspens stood at attention, their white trunks straight and tall. The trees grew so close together they looked like cigarettes in a pack; their leaves trembled even though there appeared to be no breeze at all. Tall, lacy ferns grew in profusion among the trees. Blanket flowers—bright yellow blossoms with red centers colored like Indian blankets—painted the small clearings among the trees. The trail wound through the aspens, then spilled the jeep out into the open space beyond.

The pale shadows of Gabriella's childhood memories were instantly filled with life and color—only brighter and crisper. The scene was hauntingly familiar but new, novel and strange at the same time. It looked just like she remembered … except it wasn't really anything at all like she'd thought it would be.

Stretched out before her was a bowl-shaped hanging valley—about half a mile wide and maybe three-quarters of a mile deep—carved out of the mountain as if a giant had gouged a hole in the solid rock with an ice cream scoop. The land dropped away on the east side in a sheer cliff, offering a breathtaking, panoramic view of the whole Arkansas River valley 6,500 feet below.

The aspen grove she'd driven through on the north side of the valley gave way to a forest of stately ponderosa pine, Douglas fir and lodgepole pine trees standing sentinel above a carpet of brown pine needles. The woods, sprinkled with blue spruce and Rocky Mountain maples, circled around the back side of the bowl and down the south side to the cliff drop-off.

The back wall of the valley behind the forest was a rocky slope that climbed two hundred feet up the mountainside, topped by a boulder field and the bristlecone pine forest Dr. Calloway had talked about. In the back right corner of the valley was a trail that led up the slope to the boulder field. In the back left corner, Piddley Creek flowed out of the bristlecone pine forest, down the slope, over a pile of rocks and dropped fifty feet into the stream bed in the bowl, forming a small, gurgling waterfall. She didn't know what the Benningers had called it, but her father had dubbed it Notmuchava Waterfall because in August the creek had gone almost dry and the waterfall had been reduced to barely a trickle.

The stream below the waterfall wound among the trees and down out of the valley along the steep incline next to the cliff face. Between the aspen grove on the north and the pine forest on the west and south sides of the valley was a meadow of wildflowers. On the eastern edge of that meadow, looking out over the cliff to the panorama of the valley beyond, sat St. Elmo's Fire.

When the images settled, solidified out of the realm of memory into reality in Gabriella's mind, she realized that the hanging valley itself had not changed since she last saw it almost thirty years ago. Oh, the trees were taller, the aspen grove denser, the meadow more colorfully painted with all manner of mountain wildflowers. But the cabin had changed dramatically. She'd seen the changes over the past few years in Jim's Christmas cards, but somehow that hadn't prepared her for the reality. Even from the outside, it was apparent that Jim Benninger had completely remodeled the structure. What had been a simple, rustic cabin in Gabriella's childhood had been transformed into an alpine lodge with a wraparound porch and second-floor decks on the front and back. Stretching the whole length of the cliff edge in front of the cabin was a three-foot-tall creek-rock fence.

Pedro pulled up beside the lodge and she stopped next to him and turned off the engine. Ty and P.D were out of the jeep before she even had time to unfasten her own seatbelt. The two of them bolted around the back of the cabin and into the meadow beyond where P.D. smelled every stem of grass and every flower, jumped and danced and snapped at butterflies. If dogs could laugh, it would be a sound like P.D's joyous barking now. Ty made a beeline across the meadow toward the stream, hollering over his shoulder, "Look—a waterfall!" Apparently, Ty thought it was Moreava Waterfall than her father had. The boy's jubilant cry was borne on a wind that had set the trembling aspens to jitter in anxious, nervous anticipation of the coming storm.

"Don't go too far," Gabriella called after him.

She climbed out of the jeep and found Pedro at her side, his eyes following the progress of the boy and the dog.

"They never even looked at the view," she said with a sigh, as she turned and walked slowly, almost in a trance, toward the rock wall in front of the cabin.

"Sometimes Steve's friends bring their sons to fish with them, teenage boys from the city who've never stood on anything taller than a skyscraper." Pedro gestured toward the Arkansas River Valley below them with US 285 stretched across it like a strand of spaghetti and Buena Vista a toy town in the distance to the left. The view encompassed hundreds of square miles. "And you know what they look at when they're in the mountains?"

He answered his own question. "Their shoes. In the presence of all this stunning beauty, they're staring at their Reeboks or Converse."

"If those boys are staring at their shoes when they're in your store there's something seriously, seriously wrong with their hormones. Anza is a knock-out."

Pedro smiled. "Both of my girls are muy bonita. Angelina is almost seven. My little angel ees so beautiful she takes your breath away."

He said the child's name with something like reverence, as if speaking it was almost a sacred act. But there was something else in his voice, too, that she couldn't define.

"My son, Joaquin is sixteen. His name means 'established by God.' The boy is tall, much bigger than his father. And everything is still growing, like a sapling. It is hard to tell what the tree will look like."

He didn't mention a wife. Gabriella stole a glance at his left hand. No wedding ring.

Danger, danger, danger Will Robinson!

Gabriella heeded the robot's warning and quickly slammed shut an emotional door that had eased open a crack—but not before her heart bleated out a single, "yippee!"

Theo got down out of the jeep carefully and didn't look toward the view either, just watched Ty and P.D. race across the meadow toward Piddley Creek. Gabriella saw his head tilt backward as his eyes traced the ascent of the remaining 2,600 feet of mountain to a rock crest that towered 14,269 feet tall. Antero was only two hundred seventy-one feet shorter than Mount Elbert, the tallest mountain in Colorado.

"So, how did Theo do on the trip?" she asked Pedro quietly.

Pedro laughed. "You mean other than complaining about every rock, hole, bump and jolt the whole way up the mountain? He was true to his word, though. He said he planned to keep his eyes closed and he did not open them a single time from the moment we left Steve's until I told him we had arrived." He leaned over and whispered conspiratorially, "Never had a four-year-old ask me any more often, 'Are we there yet?'"

"Did you enjoy the ride?" Gabriella called out to Theo.

"*Hide?* There wasn't no place to hide. If there had been, I'd a found it. All that bouncing around—I'd rather clean dog poop off my shoe." He turned and crossed slowly to the cabin's front porch. He kept his head down as he walked as if he found the ground at his feet positively fascinating.

A sudden crack and rumble of thunder announced that the storm that'd been tuning its instruments as they climbed the mountain was about to strike the opening bars of its performance.

"Ty!" Gabriella, called instantly terrified. What was she thinking to allow him to run off like that with a storm looming! The lack of oxygen must have muddied her thinking. She rushed around to the back of the cabin and called out for him again. "Ty, come back here. The storm's coming."

He'd obviously heard the thunder, but either didn't hear her call or pretended not to.

"Ty, now!"

As if to reinforce her words, lightning flashed, followed by a grumble on the mountaintop.

"Beep! Beep!"

She jumped when Pedro sounded the horn on his jeep. Ty heard that, turned and came running back across the meadow with P.D. at his heels.

He and the dog almost made it to the cabin before a fine mist swept down off the peak and across the valley, followed by a torrential downpour that formed a curtain of water between the cabin and the cliff face, scrubbing away the view with a gray eraser of water.

Pedro herded them all up onto the front porch under the second-floor deck. A rustic sign proclaiming "St. Elmo's Fire" hung by two chains above the porch steps and it whipped back and forth in the rising wind. Thunder cracked and rumbled around them. Gabriella had forgotten how quickly storms came up in the mountains. Five minutes ago, there'd been a handful of gray clouds; now the sky bubbled and boiled, rain lashed the sides of the cabin and the cold wind blew the water up under the decking.

Pedro produced his own key quicker than Gabriella could lay hands on hers, unlocked the door and shoved it open. "I'll get your stuff in before it's soaked."

Ty commanded "Shake!" and P.D. performed his amazing, all-body spasm, sending most of the water flying off his coat before he went inside.

When Gabriella stepped through the doorway, she recognized only one thing from the simple cabin of her childhood. Covering the whole wall of the living room between it and the kitchen was a huge stone fireplace. A massive structure, the stones built it up two feet off the floor; the creek-rock facing stretched up to the ceiling and the fireplace also opened up as large into the kitchen on the other side. She and Garrett had played on the hearth as children, used rocks to build forts there for the stick soldiers they'd made.

Pedro burst through the door, drenched, carrying luggage. He deposited his load of suitcases on the floor and turned to rush back out into the rain for the supplies.

Lightning flashed bright nearby and thunder boomed.

"No," Gabriella said, grabbed Pedro's arm and wouldn't let go. "The lightning's too close." She didn't mean to sound so frightened but that's how it came out. "Stay inside. The bags are plastic; the rain won't hurt the groceries."

Either Pedro decided he agreed with her or merely acquiesced to the superiority of her emotion because he turned and closed the door behind him, took off his hat, slapped it against his leg to knock the water off and hung it on a hook by the door.

"Ty, go get Pedro a towel to dry off on. The bathroom's right over … at least it used to be and … well, I guess there are towels."

"Towels in the bathroom, sheets on the beds, canned goods in the cabinets, a refrigerator full of the basics and a freezer full of meat—from hot dogs to sirloins."

"A refrigerator and freezer. Then there must be …" she looked around, spotted a switch, stepped to it and flipped it. A big chandelier made of elk antlers burst to life. "… *electricity*."

"You mean tell me you thought we was gone stay up here in the dark?" Theo said. He was striving for grumpy, but didn't quite get there. He didn't look good and he was breathing hard, almost panting.

THE LAST SAFE PLACE

"Jim put in electricity right after he bought the place," Pedro said. "He ran a line up from Steve's. Cost him ... well, probably more than I make in a year. Jim inherited a lot of money when his parents died—said once that when he told them he was going to seminary, they wrote him out of the will. So he was stunned when he got the whole estate. Last I heard, he had given about all of it away. In fact, the only money he spent on himself was fixing up this cabin. Oh, how that man loves the mountains."

Ty arrived with the towel as thunder shook the house again.

"Guess storms sound worse here 'cause you so close to the sky you got to lean over so you don't bump your head on it," Theo said.

"No, storms sound worse here because they *are* worse here," Gabriella said, her voice tight. Though she'd already told them how Antero actually attracted lightning, it was a warning worth repeating. "Storms come out of nowhere. You can't see them building on the other side of the mountain until they pop up over it like a target in a penny arcade. One minute the sky's clear and the next minute lightning ... And *you're* the target. In any open space—the meadow out back, the boulder field, the bristlecone forest, above the tree line. If you're the tallest thing around, you're warm and you're moving, lightning will take a bead on you and ..." She had raised the drawbridge between those memories and her mind a long time ago, but now they were swimming the moat.

She didn't even realize she'd started to cry until Ty came and put his arms around her waist. His shirt was wet. She needed to tell him to go put on a dry one, only she couldn't find her voice.

"What's wrong, Mom?"

She reached up and quickly wiped the tears off her face, embarrassed by her sudden display of emotion and the awkward silence that followed.

"I'm sorry. It's just ... I'm fine." She cleared her throat and then announced too cheerily, "Check this out!" She looked around at the kitchen in genuine awe. "New everything. New cabinets and stove. And there's a microwave. New flooring—it's oak, gorgeous. It's all changed, everything's better."

Once she pulled back from the edge and recovered her emotional equilibrium, she didn't have to manufacture excitement about the cabin's transformation.

The small windows she remembered on the front had been replaced by a huge picture window that provided an unobstructed, panoramic view of the whole Arkansas River Valley. The décor was typically Southwest, tastefully done. A big cow skull with massive horns hung on a piece of tanned rawhide over the mantle in the living room. A leather couch with a matching loveseat and recliner were made cozy with colorful Indian blankets and rugs on the hardwood floors. On one wall was an oil painting of the Chalk Cliffs on Mount Princeton; on another was an abstract watercolor of what appeared to be the meadow behind the cabin—with red, purple, yellow and white wildflowers as big as trees.

A small office opened off the kitchen, as did a mudroom in front of the back door. There was one bedroom off the living room with an adjoining bath that could be accessed from the living room as well. In the open doorway next to the bathroom was a staircase to the second floor.

Ty and Gabriella went upstairs and found two additional bedrooms and a single bath. A doorway on the far end of the landing in front of the stairs opened onto a deck that overlooked the view. The front upstairs bedroom also had a door leading to the deck and Gabriella claimed it as her own and assigned Ty the other upstairs bedroom—which had a door leading to a smaller deck on the back of the house facing the mountain. That left the bedroom on the ground floor for Theo. All the beds had four-poster oak frames with hand-carved designs on the footboards—a wagon train on Gabriella's, a cattle drive on Ty's and a herd of wild mustangs on Theo's.

Gabriella and Ty came downstairs and Ty grabbed his suitcase and headed back up to his room to unpack. P.D padded along one step behind him. She passed Theo on his way to lie down. He had not once cast so much as a glance out the big picture window.

"That doctor we met has a slow leak," Theo mumbled.

"Has a slow— ?"

"I don't have no idea what he was talking about, but that's what Pedro said. You figure it out."

She found Pedro in the kitchen opening cabinets and drawers, checking on the supplies. The rain still battered the roof, but the lightning and thunder were moving away across the valley.

"What did you say to Theo about Steve?" she asked.

"I told Mr. Slapinheimer—"

Gabriella barely choked off a laugh. "You can call him Slappy. He was only kidding. Or Theo."

« 100 »

THE LAST SAFE PLACE

"Theo maybe ... eet ees hard to call a grown man Slappy." He opened the empty bread box. "You got bread, right?" She nodded and he turned to the pantry. "I just told *Theo* that Steve was the speaker at a fly-fishing class at the Chalk Creek Canyon Lodge on Saturday. Thought maybe he would want to learn."

He turned to face her. "Why?"

Gabriella thought for a moment, then burst out laughing.

"What?"

"You said Dr. Calloway *has to go speak*, didn't you?"

"Uh huh."

"Theo said you told him Dr. Calloway *has a slow leak*."

"He's losing his hearing, isn't he?"

"You know when you text, how your phone fills in the rest of the word after you type only a few letters—that must be what Theo's brain does with sounds. Only sometimes the sounds it fills in aren't the right ones. He told Ty the day before ... once, that I said we'd have roaches in the kitchen all winter when what I'd really said was we were having roasted chicken for dinner."

Gabriella leaned against the kitchen doorframe for a moment studying the kitchen, then asked, "How'd he do it?"

"He who do what?"

"He Jim Benninger. Do ... *this*." She made an all-encompassing gesture. "It was all I could do to get myself and a rented jeep up that road. How did Jim Benninger get all this furniture—a stove, refrigerator, couches, a recliner—up here?"

Pedro closed the pantry door, checked out the array of cereal boxes in the cupboard and turned to face her.

"He brought most of it up here by helicopter, landed in the meadow out back."

"A helicopter?" Gabriella felt an empty sensation below her rib cage. She'd thought this place was totally inaccessible, but if a helicopter could ...

"It took some doing, negotiating a chopper in these mountain wind currents. Could only come up on a still morning and they had to unload quick so the helicopter could get out of here before the afternoon storms."

"So if it was storming ..."

"A chopper would get blown right off the mountain."

Gabriella let out a breath she hadn't realized she'd been holding and remembered her manners. "Please sit down. Would you like something to drink? I bought some Diet Pepsi—but you know that because you sold it to me. Or I guess I could make coffee. Do you know if there's a coffee maker?"

"In there," Pedro pointed to a cabinet beside the stove. "It's one with all the bells and whistles, grinds coffee beans I have to special order from Denver and makes a sound like an F18 Hornet taking off the deck of an aircraft carrier." He said that with the authority of a man who had actually heard a fighter jet take off an aircraft carrier.

Pedro settled his large frame into one of the six chairs around the oval oak table that had a bowl in the center piled high with miniature cowboy boots. "I only tried to make coffee with it one time and the result would have eaten the chrome off a trailer hitch. A glass of water is fine with me. It's pumped here from the creek and then purified. The refrigerator has an ice maker."

Gabriella shook her head as she searched the cabinets, found two glasses and filled them with ice water. "A refrigerator with an ice maker. We had ice in a cooler—until it melted, then we put Daddy's Coors in the creek to keep them cool."

She sat down across from Pedro at the table.

"Yes, but roughing it makes great memories. I bet your family had a wonderful time vacationing in this cabin." He must have seen the look of surprise and pain on her face. "Forgive me, por favor, I did not mean to pry, I just—"

Might as well tell him the truth, at least part of it.

"It was only one summer and it wasn't exactly a vacation. The aquamarine drew my parents here. And then there was a family tragedy, a death."

"I am sorry for your loss," he said, and sounded like he meant it.

"After that, we never came back."

"And now?" he asked quietly. She wasn't expecting the question.

"Now … Ty, Theo and I need to … get away from the world for a while."

Pedro set his water glass down on the table.

"Speaking of getting away from the world, I think I have been away from mine long enough."

"But it's still raining." Actually, it was only sprinkling. "You can't go down that trail in the mud."

"It has good drainage—water doesn't puddle. And it is easier going down. Besides, if I did not travel on wet roads in these mountains I would never go anywhere."

He stopped then, and looked at her. The silence thrived, full and heavy.

"If you need anything, anything at all, Mrs. Underhill, I—"

"No way. You can balk at Slappy, but I'm Gabriella."

He nodded. "I am right down the mountain. I would give you a phone number to call, but cell phone service up here is hit and miss—mostly miss—and Jim never saw the need for a land line. But I weel check on you—often."

Gabriella was unexpectedly embarrassed by his solicitousness. It had been so long since anyone had been kind to her she didn't quite know how to respond.

He seemed to sense that, too, because he backed off, gave her emotional space.

"Thank you, Pedro. If you hadn't 'tagged along' I wouldn't have made it."

"That is true, you would not have made eet," he said with disarming honesty. "But you figured it out. You will be fine now. Except … you need to know. Going down takes a whole different skill set than coming up." He didn't have to be intuitive to see her obvious dismay. "Please do not worry. St. Elmo's Mercantile delivers—at least to this cabin. Jim needed twice-weekly supplies so we worked it out that he would come down to the store on Tuesdays and I would bring supplies up on Saturdays. Of course, that was just an excuse for me to come up here, enjoy the view and spend time with Jim." He smiled and got to his feet. "Jim Benninger is an amazing man."

Then the smile faded and he added, his accent more pronounced, "The kind of friend who weel stand by you no matter what choo have done." The moment passed. "Do you know him well?"

Gabriella shifted uncomfortably in her seat. "Actually, I never met the man."

She could tell her answer surprised and intrigued Pedro, but he didn't ask about it. All he said was, "I will be back in a couple of days. You can follow me down the mountain and I will show you how it is done. You are a quick study."

He lifted his hat off the peg by the door, called up the stairs to Ty, "Adiós, muchacho," and left.

Pedro Rodriguez had been up and down the trail to St. Elmo's Fire dozens of times. But he still could not put it on autopilot. Lose your focus, daydream on this trail and you could run right off a cliff.

This was one of the most dangerous jeep trails in the mountains. Of course, he did not tell Mrs. ... did not tell *Gabriella* that. Though he suspected she would have climbed up the mountain if there had been no trail at all. She looked that determined. That desperate. Maybe even that afraid.

When Pedro joined the Marine Corps out of high school he discovered he could predict with uncanny accuracy which recruit would make it and which would wash out, could tell who was going to freeze when shots started flying, who was going to take crazy chances, who had something to prove and whose wife had told him she had a headache last night.

He had always been able to read people. Even before his own heart, his whole soul had been ripped out of his chest and stomped into a bloody lump at his feet. Even before he understood emotional pain on a personal, visceral level so intense he would be forever sensitized to it in everyone he met.

And all those heightened sensitivities told him Gabriella Underhill was one hurting woman.

He did not allow himself to picture what must have happened to her that put a scar on her face so disfiguring even a quarter-inch blanket of makeup couldn't hide it. It had to be a moment-to-moment torment to know people were staring at it or trying not to. Obviously, a bad burn. But what kind and how it happened—he did not like where his mind wandered when he considered the possibilities, so he shifted gears altogether, thought about the curly-haired little boy with oversized Gandhi glasses. The boy had a kind of lost look, too, or maybe Pedro was just imagining it. He certainly wasn't imagining the old man's gaunt face, his scarecrow-thin frame and the ashy gray tint to his skin. Just old maybe. Or sick. Pedro's money was on Door Number Two.

And Gabriella had never even met Jim Benninger! Oh, how Pedro wanted to call Jim and ask him about her. Could not do that though, even if he had been convinced checking up on the people at St. Elmo's Fire was a good idea—which he was not. Jim was unreachable, off being a missionary in the wilds of Sudan. Serving and helping, that was Jim. He had invited these people to spend the summer at St. Elmo's Fire for a reason, though it was possible, even likely, Jim did not know what the reason was.

Pedro owed Jim a debt he would never be able to repay. All he could do was pass on what Jim had given to him to somebody else, and as he bumped over rocks and down into potholes, he suspected the intended recipient of some act of kindness on his part was sitting up there on the mountainside trying to start a fire in the fireplace with wet wood. Of course, she would figure out how to do that on her own. But maybe there were other things she would not be able to figure out without a little help.

CHAPTER 8

Theo had found a rocking chair on the back porch that suited him and sank down into it now with a grateful sigh. He shivered like P.D. shaking rainwater out of his fur and pulled the Indian blanket he'd gotten off the couch up around his neck. Should have bought a hat to cover up his naked skull! Theo hadn't been able to get really comfortable since he got here, didn't have a speck of meat left on his boney backside for padding when he sat down and sure didn't have enough antifreeze in his veins for the wind that felt like it'd blowed right off a glacier—and maybe it had.

That jeep ride up the mountain three days ago had just about done him in. He shuddered at the thought of it, bouncing and banging around, holding on for dear life with his eyes squeezed so tight shut even the scared tears he was crying couldn't slip through. Got to the top and that storm hit and he feared he was going to ride a lightning bolt into the presence of his maker. And when that didn't happen, he was certain he'd close his eyes that first night and not never wake up, that his brain needed way more oxygen than he was sucking in, panting like P.D. chasing a rabbit.

That didn't happen, neither. He just kept on going like the Energizer Bunny. No, more like one of them Timex watches that takes a licking and keeps on ticking.

Theo heard Ty holler and watched P.D. bound across the meadow. The two of them had adjusted easily to the altitude, far quicker than Theo or Gabriella. Theo paused about every three steps to catch his breath; Gabriella fared better, but after a couple of trips up and down the stairs, she was panting, too.

The dog dived into Piddley Creek and splashed water all over Ty. The creek was only two or three feet deep but the snow-melt-off water had to be frigid. Which didn't appear to bother Ty any more than it did P.D. That spot in the back corner of the valley had become the boy's home-away-from-home since the moment he hopped down out of the jeep here. He'd already captured a couple of frogs and brought them back to the house, claimed he could see trout in the water, swimming around with the minnows—though Theo doubted there was fish that big in such a small creek. But then, how would *he* know? He'd lived his whole life in cities. The only trout he'd ever seen was on a plate, covered in cornmeal and fried up with hushpuppies and … but maybe he was thinking of catfish.

Lord, your ways is strange ways. You said that, mind, I didn't. 'Fore we got here, I's beginning to think that boy had plum forgot how to smile. What'd he have to smile about? But now, you couldn't scrub the grin off his face with steel wool. Maybe you bringing us here … wasn't such a bad thing. They's less tightness around Gabriella's mouth, too, so I s'pose you did think this through better than it looked to me like you did at first. I might a been wrong. Maybe. Amen

Theo allowed his eyes to travel up the mountainside behind the hanging valley, up, up, up past the boulder field and the bristlecone pine forest all the way to the snow-dusted rocks at the summit and the dry wash that extended down from it on the east side, facing the chalk cliffs of Mount Princeton. He'd been practicing. Was able to look up at the top now without feeling dizzy hardly at all. Now, the front of the cabin, looking down from it to the valley floor—that was another thing altogether. Every time he so much as glanced out one of them front windows, the world started to spin and he had to swallow hard not to upchuck on the hardwood floor. What a sense of humor God had, putting Theodosius X. Carmichael up on the side of a mountain. Theo almost laughed out loud at the absurdity of it.

He wiggled around a little on the chair cushion, which was the only thing between the bones on his backside and the solid oak of the rocker seat.

"Ain't got enough meat on my butt for even one good cheek."

And since he'd gotten sick, he'd probably lost fifteen pounds; all his clothes had got baggy and he'd caught Gabriella looking at him sometimes like maybe she could tell. He hadn't planned on hanging around long enough for her to figure things out. It being cold enough up here he could wear sweaters in June—that'd help for a little while. But eventually … Well, he'd worry about eventually when eventually got here. No sense fretting about it now.

Gabriella came out the back door through the mudroom and sat down in the rocker next to Theo's and he saw Ty and the dog turn and head down the creek through the woods. She was wearing jeans and an untucked plain chambray shirt, and had her short, curly blonde hair tucked back behind her ears. She looked ten years younger without that long black hair and those pointed bangs, and dressed normal, not in that black gothic stuff. Pretty, even. Except for the scar on her face. The sight of the uncovered scar sickened Theo. Oh, not because it was ugly—which it certainly was—but because of what it meant, because of who was responsible. It had cost Gabriella her looks and Smokey his life.

"You know, the view is a whole lot prettier out front," she said.

"Yeah, way up here in East Jabib ain't the end of the world, but I bet you can see it from that front porch."

She smiled and looked more relaxed than he'd seen her in … maybe than he'd ever seen her. This place was sucking the tension out of Gabriella just like it was Ty. Oh, how Theo wished he didn't hate it here as much as the two of them loved it.

"I'd rather look up the mountain than down it. Any crime in that?"

"Theo, are you afraid of heights?"

"What you talkin' 'bout, woman! Theodosius X. Carmichael ain't 'fraid of nothin'. A piddling little old mountain, why …" Why was he ashamed to admit it? Maybe the good Lord brought him up here to beat some of that stubborn pride out of him, wanted to humble him so he wouldn't be strutting around heaven like some banty rooster. Theo sighed. "Not afraid, 'xactly. More like … scared spitless. I look down into that valley out there, it's all I can do not to spew my breakfast all over my shoes."

"Theo, why didn't you tell me? What else are you scared of you didn't tell me?"

"Water." It just popped out. He bristled instantly at the incredulity on Gabriella's face. "Now, don't look like you ain't never heard nothing so pitiful in all your life. I ain't scared of water like bathwater or rainwater, puddles, creeks, things like that. Just … deep water."

"Heights and deep water. You fall off a cliff into a lake?"

"Not a lake. And didn't nobody *fall*."

"Somebody pushed you—who?"

"You the wrong color for us to be talking 'bout a thing like that." Oops. Probably shouldn't have said that.

Gabriella was so shocked it took her a moment or two to respond—long enough for Theo to figure out there was no "probably" about it. He absolutely should *not* have said that. Soon as she caught a breath she went off like a bottle rocket.

"What's *that* supposed to mean? Don't you dare play the race card with me! Why'd you come with us if me being white—?"

"I shouldn't a said that—okay? I …" He couldn't say he was sorry, never had been able to say that. So instead he told her, "Don't get your panties in a wad. My son marrying a white woman … I ain't gonna lie—I advised him against it." He held up his hands before she could jump on him. "I'm just telling it like it is. I thought it was a bad idea because I knew it would cause trouble for the both of you—and don't you tell me it didn't. Or that it ain't hard on Ty sometimes, too."

She didn't argue with him.

"You a fine woman." He couldn't believe he'd said that! Was being sick making him soft, or was that what happened to you when you brain wasn't getting enough oxygen? "Ty's a good boy. I ain't much of a grandfather, but I'm the only one he got and for whatever time I got left—"

"Whatever time you … are you all right? You … don't look good. Are you sick?"

Stepped in it again.

"I'm seventy-four years old. I traveled a lot of miles in my life, girlie, and most of them roads wasn't paved."

The details of his issues were private. Might not ever have to explain nothing, might be like that doctor said, that he'd just drop over dead one day.

He'd finally given in and gone to a doctor after he got where he was afraid to drive. Sometimes he'd go completely blind for two or three seconds. His hearing came and went, too, like some little kid was playing with the volume knob. And every now and then he got so dizzy he'd swear he'd downed a whole bottle of Boone's Farm in one gulp—when hadn't *a single drop* of alcohol passed his lips in ten years. Had the AA chip to prove it!

Them doctors had poked and prodded him, took scans and X-rays and way more blood than he figured he had to spare. Then that doctor said it flat out. A little Asian man who could barely speak English, looked like the moon-faced Chinaman who sold tickets for a nickel to ride the Jack Rabbit at Kennywood Amusement Park when Theo was a boy.

"Mr. Carmichael," the doctor said. "You have …" and then he said a word so long it used up almost a whole breath.

"You mind chopping what you just said into bite-sized pieces so I can gum it—left my dentures in my other suit."

Blank look.

Before the doctor could point out that Theo had all his own teeth, he told the little man, "No mayonnaise talk, okay?" Theo didn't waste his time with folks who used words that had more letters in them than mayonnaise.

Blanker look.

"Small words … like in a fortune cookie?"

Big smile.

"Ah, yes sir. A brain tumor. Cancer. You are fortunate man. It is operable. We remove it, you be good as new. You have surgery very soon, though. You wait, too late."

"And if I don't want you to cut my head open?"

"You die slowly, maybe. Or you drop over dead. Hard to say."

That'd been a conversation stopper. Oh, you didn't get to be seventy-four years old without wondering what was going to get you—because *something* was, and somewhere around sixty-five your odds of dodging whatever it was got worse with every breath you took. But when your wait your whole life to find out a thing, kind of takes your breath away when you finally do.

So there was a tumor growing up there in his brain that could kill him. He thought for a moment. He'd call it … Cornelius. Always did hate that name. A thing as important in your life as what could kill you had ought to have a name but no sense wasting a good one on it.

Then the Asian doctor wanted to schedule his surgery—in three days! But there was something Theo had to do first—just in case Cornelius didn't fancy getting evicted and decided to blow up the building. He had to see Ty, spend some time with the boy. A few days, maybe a week, that was all. After that, he'd let them take an ax to his head. 'Course, he didn't have no idea then he was gone get shanghaied! This wasn't the first time ole Slappy'd played long odds, but these was getting longer every day.

He couldn't tell Gabriella none of it. If she knew, that woman'd grab him by the ear, haul him off this mountain and drop him on the doorstep of the nearest brain surgeon. Besides, she had enough on her mind already. He looked up at the mountain behind the meadow and purposefully yanked the conversation away from his health.

"Them trees right up there," Theo pointed to the mountainside that rose up above the valley. "The ones that look all shrunk, twisted up. Them the Jesus trees? You ever seem one up close?"

Ty wished Joey was here. Joey Thompson was his best friend, or at least he had been before they left Pittsburgh. Didn't have a chance to tell him goodbye, though. Ty hoped Joey wasn't mad at him about that because he couldn't wait to tell Joey about the green snake when they got home.

Home. How could Ty ever go home again? How—?

He forced himself to focus on the snake, which he certainly couldn't tell Mom about! She'd totally freak out. He'd brought a worm in the house once and she about went postal! Girls were like that, didn't like dirty things and for sure didn't like snakes.

Joey would love the snake, though. It was the color of lime sherbet. Ty had seen it two times by the big rock down from the waterfall. He'd tried to catch it, of course, but it slithered away before he had a chance. And he hadn't really tried all that hard because he wasn't completely sure it wasn't dangerous, poisonous or something. He didn't think there were any poisonous snakes in North America except rattlesnakes and water moccasins, but he wasn't sure. He should have listened better when they were studying reptiles in science class. But that was when his father had—

He stopped right there. Had gotten pretty good at that in the past couple of years, of grabbing hold of thoughts before he had a chance to think them, thoughts that would take him *there*. He visualized that the ugly, scary, guilty thoughts were green slimy things like the stuff he coughed up that time he had bronchitis. And when they'd come sliding into his mind through a door cracked open in the dark place—all infected, ready to make him sick—he'd grab them with one of the hairclips mom used that had teeth like a dog biting down. And he'd open the door into the dark place where all the ugliness in his soul was stored and toss the green things in and slam the door back shut real quick. He'd lock it, too. But it never stayed locked.

He picked up the slimy green thought, but it hollered before he could get it to the door. *You did it! Your father's dead and it's your—!*

Bam! He banged the door shut, then took a deep, trembling breath. It was easier here to get past the shakes he always got when he had to handle one of the slimy things. This place was so different from everywhere he had ever been that it was almost like he was on a different planet, like all that had happened to him, what he'd done, was in another whole galaxy. And maybe … *maybe* it didn't even count here!

He didn't really believe that, but even lying to himself was easier here than it was back home.

The green snake wasn't the only wildlife Ty had seen in the past three days. There were squirrels in those tall, straight trees—Mom said they were lodgepole pines, or ponderosa pines. He called them rusty trees because they sounded like a door opening on a rusty hinge, like they needed an oil can as bad as that tin man in *The Wizard of Oz*, which was Mom's all-time favorite movie ever. Ty thought it was okay if you liked singing but the special effects sucked—you could totally see the wires on those flying monkey things. Some of the squirrels in the rusty trees looked like the ones back home but others were gray with real bushy tails and great big ears that stood up on the tops of their heads.

He'd heard owls hoot in the woods and woodpeckers pecking but hadn't seen any. There were lots of other birds and Mom knew their names. He never dreamed his mother knew so much cool stuff. She'd pointed out bluebirds and birds as yellow as lemons he couldn't remember the name of. The big ones with black stripes on their wings were called tanagers, the little fat ones were warblers. And you could see hawks circling in the sky and maybe eagles and falcons, too—they were too far away to tell. Mom said golden eagles could spot a rabbit from two miles away! And that an owl's round face acted like a satellite dish to capture sound. Yesterday, she put sugar water in this glass thing on the back porch and this morning there were hummingbirds around it—tiny things green as pickles, with wings moving so fast you couldn't even see them.

P.D. bounded up to him, wet on his underside where he'd been splashing around in the creek. The dog raced around him in circles a time or two until Ty held up his hand, palm out toward the dog and P.D. instantly sat. Ty made a fist and moved it in a downward motion and P.D. obeyed by lying down in front of him. Then Ty got down on one knee to pet the dog, who promptly rolled over onto his back so Ty could scratch his wet belly.

"Good dog, good boy, good Puppy Dog!" Ty said, scratching furiously. He loved to watch P.D.'s left rear leg paw the air in rhythm with his scratching.

P.D. hadn't been with him either time he'd seen the snake; he had been running around in the meadow chasing butterflies. It was a good thing, too, because P.D. would have caught the snake for sure, would have killed it. But what if the snake was poisonous?

Pedro would know. He knew all about these mountains. Ty liked Pedro, liked that his eyes were kind, that he talked soft and didn't say mean things and laughed easy. And when he smiled—the way it looked like he'd lifted a broom up off his teeth made Ty want to laugh out loud.

Something moved in the damp undergrowth about ten feet away and P.D. was on his feet and after it faster than Ty could follow. Maybe it was the green snake. Then Ty saw a flash of it, dark and splotchy looking. P.D. snapped at it and missed then pawed at the spot where it had slipped away into the rocks covered with lichen. Whatever it was popped out the top of the rocks, P.D. lunged, caught it in his mouth and Ty cried, "Drop it!"

The dog instantly dropped whatever it was at Ty's feet. It wasn't hurt, and before it could get away again, Ty scooped it off the ground. He pushed his glasses up on his nose and looked at it in wonder. It wasn't a snake—it had legs—so Ty knew it wasn't poisonous. The only poisonous lizards in the United States were Gila monsters, and those lived in the desert. He did remember that from science class.

But this thing might not be a lizard. It was fatter than a lizard, with a round nose. He couldn't see any teeth in its mouth. Its skin was skin—not scales like a lizard and it had yellow spots on it.

"Joey's never gonna believe *this*," Ty told the dog, who cocked his head to one side as if he understood every word. "I'm going to keep it, as a pet."

P.D. barked once in agreement.

Ty turned toward the house. His grandfather was sitting in the rocker on the back porch and his mother had just stepped out the back door to join him. Ty headed down the creek instead of across the meadow, so he could go past the house and in the front door without being seen. P.D. padded along right beside him.

G<small>ABRIELLA THOUGHT SHE</small> heard something on the deck above their heads, almost sounded like the door opened. But then Theo asked her about the Jesus trees and her mind went in an entirely different direction.

"You ever seen one up close?"

Gabriella looked up at the mountain stretching above them, the sight so achingly familiar she could almost believe she was a kid again, seeing it fresh and new every morning.

"There's a chalet up there in the bristlecone forest—at 12,500 feet," she said. "I don't think my parents even knew it was there when they rented this cabin. I can see why it wouldn't have been listed on the lease. It was more a glorified cave than a building, snuggled among the boulders with a wood frame and rock walls sealed with grout, one big room that had wooden platforms for sleeping bags, some cabinets and shelves and a big stone fireplace, bigger than the one here, covered the whole back wall. There was a picnic table, too, where Grant carved three interconnected G's—Grant, Garrett and Gabriella."

Gabriella's mind created the scene in the air in front of her as real as the golden aster, the blue larkspurs and red Indian paintbrushes that splashed color on the meadow.

"That summer, we all went up to the chalet almost every day, the whole family, took supplies and spent the night sometimes. And if you think *this place* without electricity was rustic!"

She pointed to the bare rock near the mountain's peak. "Up there, above the tree line past the bristlecones, that's where my parents and older brother looked for aquamarine. They also found gem-quality smoky quartz, blue beryl, calcite and chalcedony, too, beautiful rocks, but their best specimens were aquamarine."

"That where you got that crystal rock you wasn't 'bout to leave behind in Pittsburgh?"

"I don't remember where I got that one. But I wouldn't leave it behind because it was the only one left. All the rocks we had around the house when I was a kid—they're all gone except that one."

Theo squinted up at the forest above the back wall of the hanging valley. "And your whole family stayed *up there?*"

"We were just kids, didn't mind the hard beds and the cold. We'd get up every morning and Mom would fix a big breakfast over an open fire in the fireplace—eggs and bacon or sausage we hauled up there in backpacks. Made coffee in an old metal coffee pot where you put the grounds in the water. Then they'd take Grant and climb up above the tree line looking for rocks and leave us behind in the chalet. We had this arruga horn we could use to call if we needed them; they weren't more than half a mile or so away." She laughed. "Child Protective Services would snatch your kids and never give them back if you did something like that today—left twin seven-year-olds alone for three or four hours at a time on the top of a mountain! But it seemed perfectly normal to us."

Actually, that wasn't entirely true. She had been frightened, though it hadn't bothered Garrett in the slightest. He liked being on his own.

"They'd always be back by noon. The storms came in the late afternoon and we'd be long gone before that."

"What'd you and Garrett do in that chalet all by yourselves for hours?"

The same thing they did in the cabin—amused *themselves.* Twin seven-year-olds on the side of a mountain and their parents didn't bring a single toy or activity from home for the children to play with. Which had come back to bite them severely the first time it rained for three days in a row and they were stuck inside St. Elmo's Fire all together. Her mother had been about to lose her mind when she stumbled upon the Bible in the back of a bookcase. It was huge, the big Family Bible variety, probably twelve inches wide by eighteen inches long and three inches thick. But it was clearly not somebody's treasured heirloom. The white leather cover was stained and torn and no longer attached to the pages, which were tattered and dirty themselves. The top right corner of the thick slab of pages had been chewed on by some animal with exceedingly sharp teeth.

"Here," her mother had told her. "Use this for paper and draw me a picture." While Garrett played with a make-believe train he'd constructed out of broken pieces of fireplace stones, Gabriella wrote and drew pictures on the pages of the Bible—which was conveniently designed with wide white margins and small-print text set in a block in the middle of the page like a picture framed by a large mat. Over the course of the summer, the book became a picture diary, an image journal that told the tale of Gabriella's mountain adventure recorded with three broken crayons—red, blue and green—and a ballpoint pen.

In Exodus, she drew pictures of the cabin. In the book called Numbers—she could read that word without Grant's help—she drew stick figures of the family. She and Garrett wore identical overalls, her mother had red, curly hair and an apron, her father wore a tie and Grant … he was identified by his huge smile. In First and Second Samuel, she drew the creek and Notmuchava Waterfall. Through the Psalms and Proverbs were pictures of the Chalk Cliffs. When they went to the chalet, she'd tear out pages to take with her, then folded the pictures neatly and slid them back into the Bible when she returned. She also had folded napkins with pictures she'd drawn in restaurants—even a blank check her mother had ripped out of her checkbook in frustration once to give her something to doodle on.

Gabriella remembered the first thing she put in the book, too, on the blank page opposite Genesis 1. Below a huge drawing of Mount Antero she'd printed: "I love you, Mount Anero! Your friend, Gabriella Griffith."

Her last picture, in the back of the book, the last page, was an angry scrawl of black lines, made with a ball point pen applied with such force it tore the thin paper. Back and forth, she had scratched until the page and the back cover beneath it were torn. In small, block letters on the tattered bottom, she'd written, "I hate you!"

That Bible was the book Jim Benninger had found. Gabriella shrugged off the image of the torn page and focused on Theo's question.

"What did we do while our parents and Grant were up on the mountaintop? Well, we were supposed to figure out some way to entertain ourselves—and *stay inside* the chalet."

She paused.

"But, of course, we never did."

Images formed in the air in front of her. Images she hadn't looked at in thirty years.

Gabriella and Garrett wave at their parents and Grant and watch them until they are out of sight. Then they wait five more minutes. That's the rule, five minutes. In case somebody forgets something and has to come back—though nobody ever has. But they're careful anyway. They time the minutes on the big clock on the wall, stare at the second hand as it goes around and around and around.

And when it comes up to the twelve for the fifth time, they are free!

Out the door they scoot to play in the boulder field and the bristlecone pine forest. Each tree is unique, bent over, warped and deformed, twisted by the constant wind in summer and blizzards in the wintertime, growing in the rocky soil that has no grass cover—only gray-green lichen and tiny white and purple wildflowers. But since the trees are short and dense like shrubs, with wide spaces between them, the forest is a huge fairyland maze the children have learned over time to negotiate, branching out farther and farther from the chalet as they explore. Sometimes they stop in a clearing to gaze out over the Arkansas River Valley spread out seven thousand feet below them.

They play hide and seek and treasure hunt, leave trails of broken sticks for each other to follow, or pretend Garrett is Indiana Jones and they're looking for the Arc of the Covenant in the forest. But no matter what the game, they almost always wind up at the same place. It seems like a long way from the chalet, on the mountainside where the boulders are huge, big as cars, and the bristlecone pine forest is thinned out. Garrett is the one who spotted it. He's always the most adventurous of the two, always wants to go farther and farther away from the chalet when Gabriella is ready to go back so they won't get caught.

In fact, she'd been telling Garrett they should go back but he went forward instead, out where even their parents wouldn't go—beneath the overhang! A big rock juts out from a crest high above. It looks like the thing the doctor sticks in your mouth and tells you to say "ahh." It's so big and tall you can see it from the chalet and their father had pointed it out one day. Said it looked to him like that rock was barely hanging on, like it was ready to let go in a landslide that would take out everything below. To which her mother had said that he was being silly. That the rock had been there for thousands of years and just because he thought it was barely hanging on didn't mean it was going to come loose if he walked under it and topple down on top of him. It was always like that. Their father was always cautious and their mother poked fun at him for it. She liked to explore, take chances, live more ... her father called it "on the edge."

Grant was like their father, looked like him, too. Both parents adored him, doted on him, talked to him like he was a grown-up. When they talked about

Grant, they had special looks on their faces they never got about the twins, and Gabriella sometimes thought that maybe her parents didn't mean to have any more children and suddenly there they were—two of them. She wasn't at all clear where babies came from, so she supposed it was possible for them to show up even when their parents didn't want them.

Garrett was as much like their mother as Grant was like their father. Gabriella didn't know which one of them she was like; it wasn't as obvious as with her brothers. Garrett was always pushing the limits, wanted to go farther, do more. Since Gabriella didn't, maybe that meant she was like Grant and her father.

She'd actually been wondering about that when Garrett was so determined to go out under the overhang that day. He didn't care that it was a dangerous place, with those rocks above ready to tip over and fall down right on top of him. He didn't care that they weren't supposed to go there—ever. In fact, that's probably why Garrett wanted to go in the first place.

"Must really be somethin' to stand right up next to trees was alive same time Jesus was walking around on the other side of the planet. Your folks spend much time there?"

His voice brought her back abruptly from where she'd gone. The scene fell out of the air in front her and she imagined she could hear it shatter into small, shiny pieces on the ground.

"We all went through the bristlecones on the way to and from the chalet, but nobody except Garrett and I spent any time there. If you got caught out there in a storm, you might as well paint a bull's-eye on your chest." She glanced at one of the half dozen lightning rods that protected St. Elmo's Fire. "My dad must have put a dozen lightning rods around that chalet. Garrett and I called them zagga sticks."

"Twin language?"

She nodded. "Grant said when we were little, we'd babble away at each other and nobody could understand a word we were saying. But by the time we came here, we only used a few words." She paused. "Special words."

"It still there, the chalet?"

"I suppose so. But odds are the overhang didn't survive thirty years of snow and ice." She told Theo about the balanced rocks, how Garrett had wanted to go there and explore. Something in the telling created an itch in her mind, but scratching it might edge her too close to images she'd been avoiding for three decades.

She shivered, but not from the chill in the breeze, then deftly redirected the conversation.

"We had a whole lot more fun playing in the creek and Notmuchava Waterfall. We saw a bobcat there once." She didn't mention they also watched a black bear amble across the meadow one evening, too. She didn't imagine Theo was up to stories about bears. Or cougars, which they'd never seen anywhere near the cabin, but twice had heard their cry. "And we caught all kinds of critters there. At least Garrett did. I wasn't into slimy, dirty things. Garrett put a bucket full of tadpoles in the sink once, brought frogs and lizards into the house. Even caught a green snake."

Theo looked alarmed.

"Oh, they're harmless, but Dad made him take it back where he found it and let it go. And he must have caught half a dozen tiger salamanders—dark brown lizard-looking things with yellow spots. He didn't tell our parents about those. Tried to make pets out of them. He'd hide them under his bed—our room and Grant's was where the stairwell, the office and the mudroom are now. He'd put them in shoeboxes and poke holes in the tops so they could breathe."

She sighed.

"Apparently salamanders don't fare too well in captivity, though. At least, Garrett's didn't. I can't remember a single one that even made it through the first night. And when they died they smelled worse than a dead rat under a porch."

TY SAT STILL on the deck floor directly above his mother, looking at the shoe box with a lid he'd just cut holes into. He could hear the creature he'd captured at the creek scratching around inside.

Well, he'd just have to take the salamander back to the rocks beneath the waterfall and let it go. No sense keeping it if it was going to die.

He'd have been a lot more disappointed if he hadn't had other, more exciting things to think about than some stupid spotted salamander. A chalet!

Up there in the Jesus tree forest! Tomorrow, he and P.D. would go find it. And go explore under that overhang thing, too, if it was still there. Just like his Uncle Garrett.

* * * *

Yesheb has escaped the bonds of living flesh, has died to mortality, risen from the pathetic shell of skin and soars now, prince of an ancient, unseen order that is powerful beyond understanding—a brotherhood with savage hungers and black intent.

He is master; legions bow to him. He is heir apparent to—

And then he is falling, falling, falling into an abyss deeper than time, darker than blindness, home to the essence of agony and isolation whose heart is still and cold.

Yesheb!

The word stabs into his head with such force his ears bleed black blood down his neck.

Time grows short.

The Voice melts the skin off his bones and it drips into a puddle around his feet. The profound dark gobbles up his agonized cries.

Do. Not. Fail.

A sliver of icy terror frozen into a glistening dagger punctures the right side of his chest and slices through him slowly. His heart beats frantically, like the wings of a fettered bird, as the ice inches closer, freezing everything it touches. His heart shrinks away, squeezes backward from the advancing needle as a man might back away from a hissing cobra.

When there is no more room in his chest, nowhere for his cowering heart to run, the ice skewers it, impales it, a fish stuck on a pike, flopping frantically. There is an odd crunching sound as the ice stabs deeper and deeper.

His skewered heart still beats in frantic agony but it pumps no blood, merely quakes, shivers and grows weaker and weaker. Until finally, the pounding heart stops. But the pain does not. It grows with every second of silence, festers until finally it—

Yesheb bolts upright in tangled sheets soaked with sweat and shatters the crust of the vision. The shell falls away and leaves him there like a wet, trembling baby bird with bulging blind eyes.

He sucks air into his straining lungs in ragged gasps that so sear his throat he begins to cough. Pulling himself free of the twisted bed covers, he leaps up, groans at the sudden weight on his injured foot, staggers to the window and shoves it open. He leans out into the cool, pre-dawn air and drags in great, heaping gulps of it.

The tears in his eyes from his coughing paint fuzzy circles around the lights of the city far below. It is a live thing. He can feel its dank breath on his face, hear its heartbeat of blaring car horns and wailing sirens. The city that never sleeps. How he loathes New York.

When he can finally breathe evenly again, he pulls back inside, closes the window, leans his back against the wall and then slides down it until he is on the floor with his arms wrapped around his knees.

He tries to think about what he has seen. It was not a nightmare, of course. The insipid conjuring of their own imaginations were the products of pathetic mortal minds. Yesheb's was a vision. No, a *visitation*. Though his mind yanks back from it the way your hand instinctively jerks away from a flame, he must force himself to breathe slowly and deeply, to recall every detail of this melding of the world beyond darkness, examine it, listen to it, learn from it. *Obey* it.

Time is short.

That's what The Voice said. As if Yesheb needs reminding. The hourglass is a fixture on the edge of his vision, a thing that moves if you try to look at it, but is never gone. The sands in that hourglass slip silently through the hole, pile higher and higher in the bottom half, golden grains in a pointed hill like a volcano. And sink lower and lower in the top glass, sucked down a vortex of swirling sand the way his soul is sucked ever downward by the circumstances of his life. The sand shifts beneath him and then falls away, dumps him into a whirlpool that will soon pull him out of this world, back into the other world where he will receive his reward. Or his punishment.

The full moon in June is only nine days away. Nine days! And he has no more idea now where his bride is than he did the day she gave the surveillance team the slip here in New York. His army of investigators eventually managed to pick up her trail at the restaurant in Little Italy. A background check of every guest in the Warwick Hotel the day the old man disappeared there revealed nothing. A check of the hotel employees netted them

Eli Jackson, aka Drumstick, who had once played in a band with Theo Carmichael. With very little persuasion, Mr. Jackson divulged his involvement with the escape plan. The $5,000 he'd earned for his services wouldn't likely cover the cost of his funeral. Yesheb's investigators "purchased" toll booth camera footage that placed the Honda Accord with Gabriella at the wheel in New Jersey but after that the trail went cold. Before he drew his final, painful breath, Mr. Jackson had also described in detail the pistol he'd left in the glove box of the Honda.

Did Gabriella honestly think she could stop him with a gun?

The Voice suddenly roars in Yesheb's head: *Time is short!*

His mind is struck so violently by the force of the words that it jackknifes, the front end slams into the back, the past into the present in a sideways slide toward oblivion.

He is six years old, crouched naked in a gilded birdcage that is not tall enough to stand in and not big enough around to sit down. The cage is suspended five feet off the floor in the corner of the huge dining room where the remaining members of his family, his father, mother, and three younger sisters are seated at the table.

They are having dinner. It is formal and tense. His father wears a blue satin disha dasha with pearls inlaid in a design around the neck and sleeves. His long hair is slicked back from his face in a stylish ponytail. The females wear black hijabs and abayas. No child dares speak. His mother certainly has better sense than to open her mouth. His father has not yet had enough wine to pontificate about anything so the silence is broken only by the scraping of forks and spoons on plates.

Yesheb can smell the food; the aromas seek him out like streams of water running toward a drain.

His mouth would water if he weren't so thirsty his tongue was stuck to the roof of his mouth like a piece of dried meat to the paper it is wrapped in. He has had nothing to eat in three days and only a cup of water each day and that was this morning.

No one may speak to him or acknowledge his presence. Make eye contact with him and you will join him.

This is Yesheb's punishment for wetting his bed.

THE LAST SAFE PLACE

His three days in the cage will end at midnight unless he dares to foul himself before a servant hands him a can through the bars later tonight. If he cannot wait, he will remain in the cage for another three days.

When his sisters are punished, they are beaten. He often hears their cries and yearns to watch his father whip them. Someday, he will have his own whip and his own women.

Someday he will be too big and too strong to force into a birdcage!

The Voice speaks again the words it spoke in the vision: Do Not Fail.

The words are eerily familiar, of course. The last words his father ever said to him. Almost.

Yesheb has been summoned to his father's bathroom. While his father relaxes in a just-installed whirlpool tub, the twelve-year-old boy must answer his questions. History. Science. Mathematics. His tutors have taught him well because they fear the wrath of his father as much as he does. They will be beaten if Yesheb makes a mistake. Yesheb will be punished, too, of course. His father will shove a sewing needle under his fingernail if he answers incorrectly. Yesheb can see a packet of them on the top of the marble steps leading to the tub. He will shove the needle deeper if Yesheb fails to answer the next question instantly and will insert a second needle under another fingernail if the boy is wrong a third time. When his father first imposed this particular torture, Yesheb was so distracted by the pain, he couldn't think, and ended the question session with needles under every fingernail on both hands. But he quickly taught himself to wall off the pain, close the door on it and will it out of existence.

"Answer me correctly," his father tells him, his eyes pools of menace and threat, the greasy dark brown color of shallow water in which something has drowned. "Do not fail."

His father reaches over and pushes the button on the side of the tub and the bath water instantly begins to froth and foam as if full of piranhas in a feeding frenzy. He smiles, groans in pleasure and stretches his feet out to the end of the tub.

"Tell me who ruled Persia in 2580 BC," he says and leans his head back.

"The Unnamed King of Awan," Yesheb replies confidently. His father had been unable to trip him up about Babylonian kings a week ago—which angered him. Yesheb suspected he would change tactics this week and in anticipation of the change, he has memorized the names and dates of every known ruler of the Persian Empire since 2700 BC, beginning with In-Su-Kush-Sir-anna, as well as the rulers of Mesopotamia, of course, and of—

All at once his father's head vanishes under water; his arms and legs begin to splash frantically.

The boy takes a tentative step forward, tries to figure out what—

His father's face barely breaks the frothing surface long enough for him to gasp, "Turn it off!" before he is sucked back under.

Yesheb understands now. Anwar's long hair has caught in the water intake of the new tub!

By arching his back and pulling with all his strength, Anwar is able to lift his nose and mouth above the water again.

"The tub switch—off!" he yells.

Yesheb doesn't move. His father's voice seems to come from a great distance, as if he is shouting up from the bottom of a well. That's because the other voice that speaks to Yesheb is so loud, clear and powerful it drowns out all other sound.

"Yesheb. Do nothing," The Voice instructs.

The boy doesn't move, merely looks at his father, watches him strain with all his strength to keep his nose out of the water.

"Yesheb," his father gasps, and in opening his mouth he swallows water and almost strangles. "Off," he commands. "Turn the tub off."

"Your time has come," The Voice says. "Watch. Enjoy!"

"Now!" His father is gurgling, coughing. The commanding, demanding tone is gone. "Yesheb, my son …" It is the first time in Yesheb's life his father has ever called him that. "… turn it—"

The boy starts to laugh. He throws his head back and roars. The more he laughs, the more the laughter takes control until he could not stop even if he wanted to. Which he doesn't. He wants to laugh. He wants his laughter to be the last sound his father ever hears.

Even after his father chokes, strangles, finally stops thrashing spastically and floats still in the water, Yesheb continues to laugh. He howls until his sides hurt so bad tears run down his face.

THE LAST SAFE PLACE

When he is finally able to control himself, he steps to the tub and picks up the packet of sewing needles. He lifts his father's limp, still-warm hand out of the bubbling water and carefully shoves a needle under each fingernail. Though it punches holes in the skin of his own thumb so deep they bleed, he pushes each needle all the way in until it is invisible. When he has used ten of the dozen needles in the packet, he pockets the remaining two—mementos of the occasion. He leans over and spits into the water, then turns and walks out of the room.

The Voice seemed benevolent when he was a boy. It was his only friend. Over the years that changed. That all changed.

Yesheb hugs his knees tighter; the words ring in his ears.

Do not fail.

What can he do that he isn't already doing? Should he hire another hundred private investigators? Another thousand?

The ones he has now are tripping over each other. What possible good could it do to pay more …?

His head snaps up. That's it. That's what he should do. *Pay more!* Not hire more people. Pay the ones he already has more money! Offer a reward.

He leaps up, ignores the pain in his foot at the sudden movement and hobbles to his cell phone on the night table. He hits a speed dial number. The man at the other end picks up on the first ring.

"Tell your men I will pay five million dollars cash to the one who finds my Zara!"

CHAPTER 9

Gabriella sat propped up with pillows on her bed staring at the empty screen of her new laptop. The curser mocked her—blink, blink, blinking on the blank Word document. What in the world had made her think she could still do it? Poetry came from a place in your soul that was pure, and nowhere inside her was pure anymore. The core of who she was lay slathered with filth and reeked of sulfur. She reached up and touched the scar on her cheek—*her outside matched her inside.*

Words appeared on the page and she wasn't even conscious of typing them.

Insides and outsides, ugliness all.
No mirror reflects, no nostril detects
wretchedness reeking, forgiveness seeking
a glimmer of hope however small.

It was awful, of course. Totally lame. So were the other words that lined up behind the first ones, leaping unbidden from her fingers. Tortured structure, painfully awkward, forced and clumsy and … burn-it-when-I-die bad.

Gabriella kept typing anyway, on and on. Words filled the white expanse of screen, lined up like cadets for inspection, neat and tidy. She didn't stop until she heard music. Then she sat still and listened.

She'd always thought it was beautiful, eerie, haunting and way too complex for her to understand. Oh, she grasped the incredible skill it took to produce it, was awed by the musicians' ability to improvise something that complicated, make it up as they went along.

But unfortunately, when she added all her responses to jazz together, the total still came up just short of liking it.

THE LAST SAFE PLACE

Smokey loved jazz! Loved to hear his father play, told her that before his father had bailed out on him when he was a kid he would sit for hours as the old man made his tenor saxophone sing, wail, cry, laugh—created sounds on the instrument Gabriella suspected it was never designed to produce.

Slap Yo Mama Carmichael was never more at home, in his element, than when he was playing. And today, that home was St. Elmo's Fire.

The Tony Lama boots she'd purchased from Pedro on her first solo trip down the mountain three days ago were not broken in yet so they felt stiff and uncomfortable, but she leapt down the stairs in them nonetheless. She'd driven into Buena Vista that day and returned with some of the belongings they'd left in the trunk of their getaway car. It would take several trips to ferry everything up to the cabin, but she'd prioritized—first things first: Ty's Nintendo and video games, her laptop and Theo's vintage Selmer saxophone. And now Theo was playing it!

She found Ty sitting with his legs crossed Indian style in front of Theo on the back porch with P.D. lying beside him, his chin resting on Theo's fleece-lined leather moccasins. The old man wore a flannel shirt, a heavy sweater *and* a denim jacket. Ty was dressed in a western shirt and jeans. Even in the I Heart Oklahoma sweatshirt she'd bought in Tishomingo, Gabriella was cool. Little boys had different thermostats altogether, she thought, and remembered how Garrett and Grant spent the summer in short sleeves—their arms turned a lovely caramel brown in tacky trucker's tans by the surprisingly hot, high-altitude sunshine.

Theo sat in his favorite rocker and cradled his new saxophone tenderly in his lap, his eyes closed, his mind transported to that place jazz musicians go, a country far distant from this Colorado mountainside.

She closed the back door softly behind her, didn't want to break some kind of spell, though Smokey said that when his father got into a zone you could switch on a food processor full of quarters next to his ear and he wouldn't drop a beat.

She also didn't want to intrude on the endearing scene. The boy and his dog at the feet of the old black musician, absorbing every sound, every nuance. She wondered if Ty would become a musician someday and shuddered at the thought. The lives of almost every musician she'd ever met were marked by hairline cracks—in response to life or to art, she didn't know which. And the cracks never healed, just got bigger and deeper until the artists could only hold their fragmented lives together by medicating. Drugs. Booze. She could write the names of those who had survived to see their thirty-fifth birthdays on the back of a gum wrapper—Dentyne at that. Sooner or later, most of the musicians she knew fell into the fissures in their own souls and died in the dark there, alone.

Except Theo, of course. A faith from his distant childhood had somehow sustained him, kept his head above water while most everyone he loved slipped below the surface and was gone.

Ty put his finger to his lips. Clearly, he didn't want her to break the mood either. So she stopped, leaned against the porch railing and tried to go to the place jazz transported those who loved it.

She didn't know how long Theo had been playing before she heard a jeep on the trail through the aspen forest. Even though she clearly recognized the rumble of Pedro's muffler-free engine, the sound of an approaching vehicle instantly dried up all the spit in her mouth. She turned and watched the spot where the trail emerged from the trees until Pedro's jeep bumped out into the open, dragging a thin plume of dust behind it.

He waved, almost like he knew she needed reassuring. Surely the man wasn't really as tuned in to her feelings as her imagination led her to believe.

He pulled up beside the cabin and killed the engine but didn't get out of the jeep, and Gabriella realized he was listening to Theo, too. When Theo's music abruptly stopped a few minutes later, Pedro opened the door and stepped down to the ground.

"I did not mean to interrupt," he said.

Ty leapt to his feet, barreled down the porch steps and skidded to a stop in front of Pedro.

"I found something in the creek. I'll show you." He turned and bounded off across the meadow with P.D. on his heels.

Theo stood, holding his saxophone, and fixed Pedro with a steely stare. "Don't ask," he said. "All I've done since I got here is drink water and make wee."

"I was at Heartbreak Hotel talking to Steve," Pedro said, "and we heard this sound. It was you. We could hear you playing all the way down the mountain."

"Sound carries that far?"

"The wind distorted it, gave it an eerie wail that freaked out his grandchildren. They didn't know what it was."

"What'd he tell them?"

"That Bigfoot plays a mountain goat's horn when he ees hungry—and he ees *not* a vegetarian. Steve will not have to worry about the kids sneaking out after lights-out tonight."

"A furball honking a goat horn, huh? I s'pect I do sound like that. Don't have the wind up here to get it right. Think I'll go lie down."

He turned and shuffled across the porch. Gabriella watched him anxiously.

"It takes longer with some people," Pedro said. "Getting used to the thin air is harder the older you get."

"Did you come all the way up here to listen to Theo play?"

"No." But he didn't say why he did come. "You figured out how to make coffee yet with the jet engine?"

"As a matter of fact, I made a fresh pot for breakfast. Have a seat and I'll get you a cup."

"Just black, strong enough to trot a squirrel across."

When she took his coffee out to him, she found him sitting on the top porch step, not in one of the two rockers. He had hung his hat on the post on the porch railing and she noticed what she hadn't seen before. There were streaks of gray in his thick black hair. She sat down beside him, on his right side, so her scar would be facing away from him. Ty stood on the ground in front of him with a wiggling tiger salamander in his grubby hands.

"These things don't live long in captivity," he told Pedro knowingly, "or I'd keep it for a pet."

"You don't say." Gabriella leaned back away from the creature and wrinkled her nose as if it reeked—which it didn't. "Take it back to the creek and let it go."

"I was going to, Mom. I just wanted to show Pedro." To Pedro, he said, "You ever seen a green snake? There's one that lives under a rock by the creek."

"Not that I recall."

"I'll try to catch it and show you!" Ty turned back to his mother. "They're harmless, you know. You'd like to see one, wouldn't you Mom?"

"Sounds wonderful."

She made a shooing gesture and the boy turned and bolted for the creek.

"Did you say 'sound's wonderful' or 'I just smashed my thumb in a car door,' because it was hard to tell from my end?"

"And you've never seen a green snake?"

Pedro shrugged.

"I like animals that have fur on them and legs—no more than four. I don't do creepy crawlies."

"Neither does my sister." He pronounced the word "see-ster." "But that's because her older brother, who shall remain nameless, put a wet frog down the back of her shirt when she was a kid. Something like that happen to you?"

"Goodness no! Grant would never do a thing like that. He was perfect."

She was astonished to hear the word drop out of her mouth. How ridiculous. Of course, her older brother wasn't per … Yes, he was. Grant *was* perfect. At least he was from the viewpoint of a little girl who tried to emulate his every move, every gesture, his lazy smile and that laugh of his that was so infectious everybody laughed with him when they heard it, even if they had no idea what was funny.

She never allowed herself to think about Grant. Never let the image of his face form in her head. But she did now, maybe because she couldn't help it, being here, so close to where she last saw him. Or maybe just because it was time.

Her mind served up snapshot images, like black-and-white photos on the front page of a newspaper.

Snap-snap.

Grant punching Mikey Zambino in the nose for putting bubble gum in her hair on the school bus.

Snap-snap.

Grant lifting up the covers in the midnight dark so she could get in bed with him when she had a bad dream.

Snap-snap.

Grant answering her questions about rocks or salamanders or why Pamela Wolenski didn't want to be her best friend anymore. Or explaining how aspen trees grew close together because all their roots were connected. Or reassuring her that Mom and Dad were just busy; that's why they told her to "hush and go play" all the time.

Snap-snap.

The silver box that held Grant's body. Her father said he was in there and she knew her father was telling the truth because she'd seen ... but she kept looking for Grant at the funeral home anyway, expected to see him leaning against the back wall or standing in the doorway with his grin warming up that awful cold room that smelled like her mother's Jungle Gardenia perfume. The room where everybody cried and her parents didn't even know she was there and she couldn't take her patent leather shoes off even though they'd been too small for her since Christmas but Mom never got around to buying her new ones.

"My little sister could probably come up with a lot of words to describe me, but I do not think perfect would be on the list," Pedro said.

Gabriella's mind had one foot in today, the other in yesterday, and she hopped frantically back and forth, trying to make it across the bed of hot coals in between without getting burned.

Grant told her once that the aspen trees dropped leaves on the ground in the fall that looked like scales shed by a golden dragon. He said rubies and sapphires were the same stone. Sapphires were blue rubies; rubies were red sapphires. He said—

"You know, having a conversation with you is a little like being on hold without any music," Pedro said. "After a while, it ees hard to tell if you are still connected."

Gabriella returned to the porch, to the smell of fresh coffee, the murmur of the aspens and the feel of the hard porch slats on her butt.

"I'm sorry. I haven't thought about Grant in ... He died up here when he was fourteen. Struck by lightning."

She never mentioned Grant's death, not to anybody. Pedro said nothing, but somehow his silence didn't feel awkward.

Then he said softly, "Do you want to talk about it?"

Nobody had ever asked her that! Not her parents, her grandparents, her friends or teachers. Not even Garrett. Not once in the twenty-eight years since Grant was killed had anybody ever wanted to know how *she* felt about it.

Gabriella had to use a crowbar to pry open the locked door in her mind and then walked tentatively into the bunker. The first sight she saw there plowed into her chest like a runaway train.

"I got to him first, to his body after it happened. I found him."

"How old were you?"

"It was my eighth birthday."

Pedro groaned like somebody'd punched him in the belly. Then he reached out wordlessly and placed his hand over hers. It felt warm. The warmth spread up her arm to her chest and neck, thawed the words frozen in her throat so she could speak.

"I remember it smelled like the time a sparkler singed my hair on the Fourth of July. Only a thousand times stronger. And I didn't know at first what it ... what *he* was."

The ground is wet, the rocks slick, but she runs anyway, slips in a puddle, goes down hard in it and soaks the leg of her jeans, skins her knee. She gets back up and keeps running. The raindrops dangling off the needles of the bristlecone pines sparkle like Christmas tree lights in a shaft of sun beaming through the clouds. She stumbles and brushes up against a branch and the whole left side of her shirt is instantly wet, but she doesn't care about that either, just keeps running.

Grant is looking for her! She's certain of it. Maybe she even heard him call her name, but she's not sure about that part. Sometimes she hears his voice in her head when he's not even talking to her and maybe this was one of those times.

She has left Garrett behind; she can run faster than he can. And he's not as scared as she is so maybe she did only hear Grant's voice in her head and not out loud.

The storm that just passed didn't wait until afternoon, had popped up out of nowhere from the other side of the mountain. She and Garrett didn't even have time—

She races around a boulder so big she can't see over it and finds something lying on the ground ahead of her on a bare spot encircled by stubby bristlecone pines. She has no idea what it might be. It is black and little trails of smoke rise off it into the damp air. But she doesn't have time to gawk at weird things right now. She has to get back to the chalet. If Grant has been calling her, that means her parents have returned early from rock hunting! Which means she and Garrett are in big, big trouble.

As she gets closer, she catches a whiff of the black thing. It smells like burned hair. And it looks burned, too. Blackened like a hot dog. That's what it looks like, a blackened hot—

THE LAST SAFE PLACE

The world slows as Gabriella slows. The black thing isn't a hot dog. It's a giant doll. A doll bigger than she is! A burned-up doll. Now she can see the form of legs and body and … the clothes are stretched tight on it, like the doll's a balloon that's been blown up too big.

She stumbles over a shoe on the ground. Blackened and smoldering. It's an Air Jordan like Grant's.

She stops running there, at the shoe. And her eyes are dragged to the doll's bare feet, so puffed up they're round on the bottom and she thinks, "Why did they make a doll's feet like that? You'd never be able to get it to stand up on round feet." Her eyes travel from the round feet up the too-tight, burned jeans—split open they're so tight. And so's the shirt and jacket. A red jacket like—

The doll's face is a ruin. The skin is charred black. Not skin! It's just a doll. Dolls don't have skin.

Gabriella starts to scream, to shriek. She puts her hands over her ears so she can't hear. And screams and screams.

There's the sudden smell of vomit. She didn't hear it happen because her hands are over her ears and because she's screaming, but she feels Garrett next to her and knows he's throwing up.

Then she sees her mother come running down the trail on the other side of the burned doll. She stops so abruptly when she sees it that Gabriella's father runs into her from behind. She stands totally still, staring, her eyes so huge you can see white all the way around. And then she shrieks, but it's not a wail like Gabriella's. It's a word. It's the word Gabriella doesn't want to hear. That's why she put her hands over her ears, so she couldn't hear her own mind screaming it. But she can't not hear her mother. Her mother's voice is too loud and the word gets into Gabriella's head in between her fingers.

"Grant!"

The rest of it was only fragments of memories. The world shattered into a million shiny pieces when she saw him lying there. Every time she tried to pick one up to remember it, the sharp edges cut her hands. So she stopped trying a long time ago.

Gabriella turned and looked at Pedro. Tears were welled in his chocolate-brown eyes and the sight of his response to her pain lessened it somehow. She dropped her gaze again, stared at a spot on the ground where a lone Indian paintbrush grew, the petals blood red dangling from a green stem. Then she pushed ahead. For some reason, it had become terribly important that she finish it. That the first time she had ever spoken about what happened on this mountain almost three decades ago she would tell it *all*.

As Smokey used to say about playing football, she would leave nothing on the field.

She knew—without understanding how she knew—that her words would land in the same place in Pedro's heart that they'd come from in hers.

"I screamed until my mother slapped me. It didn't hurt. I couldn't feel it at all. It just knocked me sideways and bloodied my nose or my lip. I don't remember which, just that the blood spots were bright red … the color of an Indian paintbrush on my clean white shirt. And I shut up."

"And I remember Dad came over and tried to pull Mom away, but she wouldn't let him, fought him. Clawed him with her fingernails."

She gathered a breath and said it, out loud. It was the truth.

"Mostly, I remember that my mother wailed and my father didn't make a sound. He didn't say anything to Garrett or me, never even looked at us. It was like we didn't exist."

She waited for Pedro to offer some platitude about how upset her father must have been, both her parents must have been. How they'd just lost their son, they'd been in shock, didn't know what they were doing. Those were the things she always said to herself. But she didn't believe them. Apparently, neither did Pedro because he didn't say them.

What he did say was, "Tell me the rest of it."

How did he know there was a "rest of it"?

Gabriella couldn't sit still. She stood abruptly, took two steps down the porch stairs, then stopped and leaned against the railing. Her eyes were pointed at the mountain beyond the meadow, but she saw no further than her own heart.

"There are holes in my memories about that day. I've told you all the actual memories I have of when Grant was killed—everything before I found him and after is gone, blocked out, I guess. Garrett remembered more than I did. But it wasn't until we were older that we realized neither one of us remembered it all. We didn't have the complete picture until each of us put our pieces out there and we fit them together."

"Garrett is …?"

"My twin brother." She almost said, "And he's dead, too." But she didn't. If she went there …

"He remembered Dad didn't speak to us, too, but he also remembered that Mom did. She shrieked at us. He said she didn't slap me because I was hysterical. She slapped me because *she* was hysterical."

They'd been twelve years old when Garrett told her about it, but by then he really didn't have to. He was merely painting words on a reality they both understood intuitively.

She and Garrett had been loading up boxes for one of their many moves. After Grant's death, they moved around like nomads. Moved out of the only home the two of them had ever known because her mother said she couldn't live there, too many memories. They moved again because the second house they picked looked too much like the first. So it went. Eventually, her father lost his job. It was a family law firm; they understood. But after a few years, they had to fill his position. She was sure her father was glad to stay home where he didn't have to put a pretty face on his shattered life.

Garrett bobbles a box full of books and the contents spill out on the floor. Something falls out of one of the books where it had been slipped between the pages. It is a faded snapshot of Grant. Their parents took hundreds of pictures of Grant—the first on the day he was born and the last two days before he died. She and Garrett have stared at all of them, looked longingly into the depths of them again and again over the years until they can see each one with their eyes closed. In fact, sometimes it seems that Gabriella can't really remember Grant at all anymore, only the pictures of him, like his face has been erased from her memory and all that remains are the replicas of him—faded images she looks into, searches, looking for … something, but she doesn't know what.

But this is a photo they've never seen. Nothing other than that is remarkable about the picture—just Grant, probably the summer he died, holding a rock and grinning into the camera. What's unique is that it is a new image, so it's like opening a tiny window into the past and there stands Grant. And in that first instant, he's alive. Like you've looked up and he's standing in the room. Gabriella hasn't stared at this picture so often that repetition has scrubbed Grant's soul out of the face.

In unspoken unison, she and Garrett sink down on the floor together. They sit silent for a while, taking it in.

"While you were screaming that day, did you hear what Mom said?" Garrett asks.

"Just to shut up. She yelled at me to shut up."

"She yelled a lot more than that." Garrett's face fills with so much pain Gabriella is instantly frightened. She knows that whatever is eating away at his heart is about to be unleashed to attack her heart as well.

Over the years since their older brother died, she and Garrett have come to share an intimacy beyond that special bond only achieved by twins. Each is all the other has. Ships adrift in the sea of their parents' indifference, the two of them are set apart from the world by their incredible gifts and knit to each other by their common pain. Whatever hurts Garrett will do the same damage to her, too.

"She screamed that she wished the two of us were dead instead of Grant."

When the storm came up that day, their parents had been much higher on the mountain than Grant. They'd dodged into a protected crevice in the rocks and motioned for Grant to run back to the chalet. When he got there, his little brother and little sister were gone and he went looking for them.

If they hadn't disobeyed, if they'd done what they were supposed to do and hadn't gone off to play in the bristlecone pine forest, Grant would still be alive. They have never spoken of that until now.

But Garrett isn't finished.

"She said she tried to get rid of us, that she would have, but she waited too long and when she went in they wouldn't do it." Garrett pauses. "At the time, I didn't know what an abortion was." He does now. They both do. And now they both also know that if their mother had gotten what she wanted, they would be dead now. And Grant would be alive.

By that point in the telling, Gabriella was crying, though she didn't remember when she started to cry or when Pedro had come to her and put his hand gently on her shoulder.

"Our parents vanished after Grant was killed, were never a part of our lives, mine and Garrett's." Her voice was thick and tear-clotted, her throat tight. "They weren't abusive … just absent. They ignored us. Without ever saying it out loud they let us know in a hundred different ways that they'd ended up with two kids they didn't want and lost the one they did."

The knot of barbed wire in her throat began to shrink.

"Nothing we ever did mattered." She let out a sardonic *humph* sound. "We were *prodigies,* both of us, and that didn't mean a thing. Everyone else in our lives was amazed by us, astonished—aunts, uncles, grandparents, teachers ... but our parents never cared. My mother and father died on this mountain with Grant. Garrett and I raised ourselves."

It was done. She'd said it all. Tacked words onto thoughts and feelings she'd never given voice before. It was both freeing and heartbreaking.

As soon as she no longer had to keep them in check so she could speak, the tears ramped up into great, heaving sobs that wracked her whole body like small, rhythmic seizures.

Pedro turned her and took her into his arms and held her tight against his broad chest. He smelled clean—his neck like soap, his chambray shirt like starch. It felt good there in his arms. Safe. It seemed to take a long time to cry herself out. When the tears finally dissolved into something like the hitched breathing of a little kid after a tantrum, she pulled away from him, stepped back, instantly embarrassed. And for a moment, she felt empty and alone without his arms around her.

She sniffled and reached up to wipe the tears off her cheeks. As soon as her hand touched the scar, she turned it away from him. But Pedro reached out and gently took her chin, turned her face back toward him and wiped the tears off her cheeks with a handkerchief that had appeared in his hand out of nowhere.

That kind of tenderness from such a strong, rugged man left Gabriella breathless.

Gratefully, Ty skidded to a stop in the dirt in front of the porch, panting, before the moment could turn really awkward. But he saw the tears.

"What's wrong?"

"I would tell you," Pedro said, his accent thick, "but theen I would have to shoot choo."

Gabriella burst out laughing. Incipient hysteria.

Ty grinned while she laughed, a little confused, but didn't join in.

"One of Mom's brothers could laugh and it'd make other people laugh, too, even if they didn't know what was funny," he told Pedro. "I don't know which one. But it was Uncle Garrett who caught a green snake down at the creek."

How did Ty know that?

The boy sighed, disappointed. "I tried, but couldn't find it."

"Have you seen the trout in that creek?" Pedro asked. "They are easier to catch than a green snake. They taste better, too. Jim keeps his fishing gear in the closet in the mud room. I could show you how to use it."

"Really!"

The boy started up the steps toward the back door.

"I do not have time to go fishing today," Pedro said.

Gabriella watched Ty's face fall. Smokey was always telling Ty he'd do something with him as soon as he "had time." Pedro picked up on Ty's reaction, too.

"And I do not have my gear with me. I did not come up here today prepared to go fishing. I came to invite your family to a party."

"A party—where?" Ty asked.

"How about I deal with our social calendar and you go inside and wash the creature slime off your hands," Gabriella said. Ty started up the steps and only paused at her final shot. "And no salamanders-under-the-bed-in-shoeboxes, okay? When they die they stink so bad you need a Hazmat suit and a blowtorch to clean the room."

"Ty," Pedro said. Ty turned around.

"I *will* teach you how to fish." Ty smiled, but it was lifeless. Either he didn't believe Pedro, or the promise sparked unpleasant memories.

"I think a body surfaced," she told Pedro when Ty was inside.

Then she explained that Garrett had rented a houseboat on Lake Tionesta one weekend when they were in college. A water patrol boat came by the first night and an officer told them to be on the lookout—that a man had drowned in the lake earlier in the week and his body had not been recovered. The officer explained that it took time for a dead body to bloat and float to the surface.

"Then the officer said, 'he's due up today.'"

Pedro wrinkled his nose.

"The phrase 'a body surfaced' became code between Garrett and me to describe when something caused one of the rotting memories in our storehouse of dead bodies to float up into our minds."

Pedro looked at her with such compassion she quickly looked away and changed the subject. "About that party …"

"It is a birthday party at my house, which is in the back of the store. All three of you are invited, and Puppy Dog, of course. The whole town will be there—which is only slightly more people than you can comfortably shove into a Volkswagen bus."

She couldn't go, of course. The whole point of coming here was isolation. Making friends wasn't part of the game plan. Although the people she'd seen in St. Elmo appeared to be of the Louis L'Amour, Larry McMurtry and *Farmer's Almanac* persuasion—not horror fiction fans. But people surprised you sometimes. If even one of the Tony Lama boot, Stetson hat–wearing citizens of St. Elmo had ever seen her picture on a book jacket …

But she was surprised to discover how badly she wanted to go, how much she wanted to spend time with Pedro. And how she ached to be in the company of normal people—not wacked-out musicians, money-hungry publicists, or weird groupies.

"When's the party?"

"Next Saturday night, 7:30."

Saturday. June 26. A full moon.

That night, Gabriella woke from a sound sleep as if an alarm had gone off in her head. She lay in the dark, stared out the window at stars the size of hockey pucks on the black satin sky and tried to puzzle it out. A fragment of memory, a detail from the horror she'd shared with Pedro that afternoon now itched in her mind like a mosquito bite.

When she told him about finding Grant, she'd described how she slid in a puddle, skinned her knee and soaked the leg of her jeans, how she brushed against a tree limb and drenched the left side of her shirt.

But how could she have been *dry*?

There had been a monstrous storm. Grant had been out in the pouring rain looking for her and Garrett when lightning struck him.

If she and Garrett had been out in the storm, why wasn't she soaked? And if they hadn't been out in the storm … where *had* they been?

CHAPTER 10

Bernie Phelps's mind was always spinning. It had gone around and around from one thing to the next, bang, bang, bang, his whole life. He knew what nobody else knew about that, though. He knew it was the spinning that kept him upright and moving in the right direction. Like the gyroscopic action of the tires on a bicycle, his whirling mind powered him. If he ever calmed down, stopped rushing, making deals, playing the odds—and the ponies—chasing the babes and corralling his golden-egg-laying goose, he was certain he'd fall over dead like a bike that hits a wall.

But his mind was spinning now with the force of a tornado—fast even for Bernie. No, make that a hurricane. His mind was spinning so fast it might just lift up out of his head, unhook from his spinal cord and float up into the sky like those stupid balsa wood helicopter toys you could buy on the street corner in New York with the rubber-band launchers that fired them up into the nearest tree.

And no, he wasn't high on coke. At least, not right this minute. But as soon as the thought entered his mind, he could feel a yearning itch in his bones and longed to suck a line of power and competence up his nose.

Oh, he wasn't an addict. He could stop anytime he wanted to. Anytime. And right now he didn't need cocaine or ecstasy or meth or any of the growing list of recreational drugs with which he entertained himself. He could get stoned for a week on the words in the email on his computer screen.

He glanced at his reflection in the mirror on the wall opposite his desk. Then examined it more closely, ran his hand over the top of a head as perfectly round and smooth as a marble. Maybe he'd get a hair transplant. Why not? He'd be able to afford it. With $5 million, he could afford *anything*.

No, not $5 million. Four million five hundred thousand. The other half million would go to some member of the Rebecca Nightshade Fan Club.

Bernie had it all figured out. His whirring mind had sliced and diced it and come up with a plan half an hour after he learned Yesheb Al Tobbanoft had offered to pay $5 million cash to whoever located Gabby. And Bernie had an edge on all the other guys. He wasn't just *one* investigator. He was thousands of investigators. Hundreds of thousands. Hundreds of thousands of people in big cities and small towns all across America. Rebecca Nightshade's *fans*.

Al Tobbanoft might have financial resources, but Bernie had human resources. He had access to an army of rabid fanatics who would drop whatever they were doing to beat the bushes for their literary heroine. Rebecca Nightshade had a cult following; her fans were like the Grateful Dead's Dead Heads and Star Trek Trekkies. Bernie'd even heard that one of them, some wack-job in Tacoma, had used a razor blade to give himself a forked tongue like the Beast. That was hardcore. When Bernie set them loose, all those fanatic fans would turn America upside down and shake it looking for the Beast's creator. One of them would end up $500,000 richer and Bernie would be set for life.

And that meant he wouldn't have to wait to reap the rewards of the marketing campaign he'd designed to launch a merchandising machine associated with *The Bride of the Beast* to rival *The Lord of the Rings* and *Harry Potter*. He'd been shrewd enough to exclude those rights from her contract with Hampton Books. Zara and The Beast action figure dolls. Replicas of Zara's black heart necklace and her ruby scorpion broach. Gabriella was set to make a fortune—with his 15 percent off the top, of course, just as soon as the sequel was released. Pure genius!

But like so many other geniuses, Bernie was underestimated and undervalued. He knew that. It was impossible to miss Al Tobbanoft's disdain for him. The man would be singing a different tune, though, when he handed Bernie $5 million in exchange for Gabby's whereabouts.

Bernie wondered as he had dozens of times before what a filthy rich, drop-dead gorgeous man like Yesheb Al Tobbanoft—probably in the top ten of most eligible bachelors in the world—saw in a scar-faced woman like Gabby. Oh, she'd been pretty once, but now … What was the man's fascination with her? Bernie didn't buy that the guy was crazy like Gabby claimed he was, that Al Tobbanoft thought he was the *real* Beast of Babylon. You didn't get to be a billionaire oil baron with *that* many screws loose. No, there was something else, some other reason for the man's attraction to Gabby, but for the life of him, Bernie couldn't figure out what it was.

Well, whatever his motive, it was clear he would stop at absolutely nothing to find Zara/Rebecca Nightshade/Gabriella Carmichael.

For a moment, Bernie allowed himself to wonder what Al Tobbanoft intended to do with her once he found her. It certainly didn't seem to Bernie like the man's obsession had anything to do with the slander and murder charges he'd lodged against her. Those were merely ruses to get her back to Pittsburgh. But once he got her here, or went out and found her somewhere else, what did he plan to do with … or *to* her?

Bernie believed that Yesheb had broken into Gabby's house—sailed right past that pricy home security system Bernie'd sprung for to shut Gabby up when the guy first started to get weird. Like Gabby'd said to the police—she didn't bite off her own earlobe.

Which meant Al Tobbanoft did. What did that say about the guy's marbles? And there was the other nagging issue—what happened to that armed guard and Lassie? Neither of them had shown up yet—more than three weeks after they disappeared.

Maybe Bernie was mistaken here. Maybe this Al Tobbanoft guy really was the psycho Gabby claimed.

So what if he was? That wasn't Bernie's problem. He had to look after Number One. Right now, Gabby's legal problems splashed all over the press, coupled with her disappearance, had launched her book sales off the charts. But the public was fickle. Who knew what—

Bernie had a horrifying thought: What if she never came back? Never did any more book promotions? *Never finished the sequel?*

Yes, sir, $4.5 million in the bank was worth a whole herd of books in the bush.

Then his jaw tightened. She'd slapped him. In his own house after he sheltered her family in the middle of the night. Called him a slimy, bottom-feeding lowlife.

"If you're holding your breath waiting for me to feel sorry for you, sweetheart," he said aloud, "you may now resume your regularly scheduled respirations."

He squared his thin shoulders and began to type. It didn't take long to tell the story, not long at all to seal the fate of Rebecca Nightshade. As the administrator of her Facebook fan page, he was the only one who could make changes to its content. He read what he had written another time through before he hit post.

> *Hey there, Rebecca Nightshade fans. Listen up!*
> *How'd you like to win $500,000? CASH!*
> *That's right—half a million bucks. No tricks, no gimmicks. All you have to do is FIND REBECCA NIGHTSHADE.*
> *She'll be introducing a NEW book just in time for Christmas. Yes sir, the rumors are true and you heard it right here first. Rebecca Nightshade is working on a sequel to The Bride of the Beast! That's why she DISAPPEARED!*
> *You've all been wondering what happened to her. Now, you know. She vanished to give her loyal fans a sneak peek into* Apocalypse in Babylon—*because that's what happens in the book—Zara vanishes! I won't tell you any more than that. You'll have to read it to find out.*
> *But you know all you need to know right now—she's gone and if you can find her, you'll win $500,000 in cash. And you'll become a part of her national marketing campaign, too, appear with her on* Good Morning America *and* The Tonight Show, *talk to Ellen DeGeneres and Jerry Springer. You'll get all that if you can FIND REBECCA NIGHTSHADE!*
> *She could be anywhere. She might be the woman who just moved into an apartment down the street from you in Missoula. Maybe she's in that beach house in Hilton Head where you clean the swimming pool. Or in a brownstone in New York where you deliver the mail. She's out there somewhere. And with a face like Rebecca's, she should be easy to spot.*
> *Half a million dollars. Think what you could do with that kind of money—and start LOOKING.*
> *Message me here if you've seen her. Leave a name and phone number where you can be reached. When your sighting is confirmed, we'll turn over the cash.*
> *Happy hunting!*

That should do it. Give these people a few days and they'd flush her out. Bernie hit "post" and got up to get himself a cup of coffee. He noticed his reflection in the mirror again, turned his head from side to side, looked at it from different angles. Yeah, a hair transplant. It'd make a new man out of him.

* * * *

Gabriella sat on the deck outside her bedroom and watched darkness drain out the hole in the sky created by the rising sun. A chill rippled through her, raised the hairs on the back of her neck and she nestled deeper into the Snuggie she'd found in a closet.

Theo had snorted in disdain when he saw one advertised on television when they were in a motel room in Amarillo. Said it was a scam, aimed at the same "witless idiots" who actually paid for water in a bottle.

"I've had a Snuggie all my life," he'd said. "Just didn't give it no advertising department name."

Ty had taken the bait.

"What'd you call it, Grandpa Slappy?"

"Called it Wearin' My Bathrobe Backwards."

Gabriella liked the blanket with arms, especially in the chill of early mornings in the mountains. She shivered again; she never should have come out here in the first place, should have stayed in her bed where it was warm.

And lie there staring into the dark?

No, it was better to watch the sun come up out here than to jump at every little creaking sound in there. Even though she'd placed P.D. on guard downstairs, she could not force herself to close her eyes. Hadn't been able to last night either. The average person couldn't manage two nights without sleep. But then the average person wasn't waiting for a crazy man to show up and bite off her other earlobe—and worse.

The average person wasn't awaiting The Beast on a night when the moon was full.

Thirty days ago, Yesheb had shown up at her house in Pittsburgh. She unconsciously reached up and felt her mauled ear. Hadn't had time to determine if her plastic surgeon could repair it. But really, what was the point? It's not like it was detracting from an otherwise beautiful face.

When the moon cleared the horizon a few hours ago it had filled the valley below with a light bright enough to read the ingredients label on a bottle of aspirin. And the Moon Cliffs on Mount Princeton to the north had glowed like the banks of stadium lights at Heinz Field.

When the sun that was coming up now began to set ten or twelve hours from now, the *full* moon would rise and shine even brighter. More beautiful. And infinitely scarier. The maddeningly rational voice in her head tried to convince her she was safe, of course, that she'd found the perfect hiding place, but she still expected to see Yesheb bopping up the jeep trail in his Mercedes.

Her heart slugged away in her chest, fear a cold sludge in her belly that sloshed when she moved, made her nauseous.

The sun slowly climbed up the sky behind the mountains on the other side of the valley, sending beams of brilliance over the peaks. As the light struck Gabriella, a beam of clarity did, too. She was so tired she couldn't fight it anymore; all her defenses collapsed. Staring out over the valley in the gray light between night and day she faced what she'd been dodging for so long.

The truth still in the husk was chilling: She was afraid of *way more* than Yesheb Al Tobbanoft. The terror she felt right now was far beyond a reasonable fear of what Yesheb could do to her, what he planned to do to her and to her son. All of those things, any one of those things, was reason enough to be terrified. But she knew her fear was bigger than that.

She finally shook hands with the reality that she was reacting in some visceral way to the presence of evil itself, an evil she had created. Or had called forth from some great source of evil. One or the other; she didn't know which. Did it matter?

What is it they say—when you realize you're in a pit, the first thing you should do is stop digging. But she hadn't stopped digging. Garrett's death had knocked her off the world and down into a deep place that was below the planes of the universe, a place where the usual laws of reality didn't apply. And she sat down in the muck at the bottom of that pit and kept digging, deeper and deeper, until she found herself staring into the bottomless dead eyes of total Despair. It spoke to her in a voice like the hiss of serpents and the cries of dying children and she embraced it, gave it free rein in her heart. The Despair within her spawned images that her immense talent, her great gift, turned into words on a page.

For days unnumbered, she breathed only because it happened without her willing it, ate only because food was set in front of her, connected to nothing and nobody in the real world, survived by going through the motions of life. And then slowly, agonizingly slowly, the motions began to have meaning again. The relentless darkness began to recede, the great open wounds that caused such agony if she touched them scabbed over and she started to heal.

Maybe she would have continued to heal until she became a normal human being again. But the thing, the evil she had created—or encountered or somehow *awakened*— lived and breathed in the pages of her book. Even before Yesheb, she feared it. He gave it human form, but the fear of what loomed in the shadows beyond Yesheb—not fear for her life and her son's life but the mindless terror of evil incarnate—*that* overwhelmed her.

That was the real Boogie Man.

Gabriella took a deep, trembling breath. There was something freeing about facing reality at last, however awful. She sank back into the chair, temporarily at peace. Pulling the Snuggie up to her chin, she closed her eyes.

She awoke with a start, momentarily disoriented, in the chair on the deck. The sun had cleared the mountains across the valley and rode high in the sky. It had to be ten or eleven o'clock at least. Theo and Ty had let her sleep.

She got to her feet and stumbled into the house to take a shower. When she passed her dresser, she stopped, captured by the beauty of the rock that rested on top of it, the lone possession she had brought with her from Pittsburgh. She picked it up and gazed at its crystals. Surely there was no rock anywhere on the planet as stunning as this one. It was perfect. That's what the old jeweler had said, too. Perfect and utterly impossible. And she wondered as she had wondered for almost as long as she could remember where the rock had come from and what had happened to the other half of it.

After a quick shower, she toweled her butter-colored hair dry and shook her head—the natural curl would take over as it dried. It certainly didn't take her long to get dressed here on the mountainside. No long hair to straighten, and she didn't bother to hide her scar behind makeup with no one to see it but Ty and Theo. By the time she was ready to face the day, the image of the rock in her mind had been replaced by a different image. Not a beautiful one. The gun, the .38 Theo's friend had left for her in the glove box of their getaway car. Every day since the day after she arrived at St. Elmo's Fire, she had faithfully practiced with it until the weapon felt as comfortable in her hand as a blow dryer.

By mid-afternoon, Theo was seated in his rocker on the back porch and she stood just beyond it. Ty had drawn a bull's-eye on a shoebox lid—that already had holes in it, *hmm*—and was setting it up in the meadow behind the cabin. Gabriella's accuracy was improving. And though she harbored a totally irrational fear that it would take more than a mere bullet to stop Yesheb, being proficient with the gun made her feel a bit safer.

She'd just finished reloading when she heard Ty cry out. He stood alternately shaking then holding his right hand.

"Mom!" he shouted and started to cry.

Gabriella's heart was in her throat as she raced to him. It couldn't be a poisonous snake! Rattlesnakes didn't venture up this high. But she carried the pistol along with her as she ran, pointed away from her and at the ground. She intended to kill whatever had bitten him!

By the time she got to him, tears were streaming down Ty's face and his eyes were red and swollen. He was crying so hard he could barely catch his breath.

"It hurts!" He held out his hand. She examined it as he hopped around in pain. There was a nasty red welt on the back of it but no puncture wounds. She leaned closer and saw a tiny black hair sticking …

"It was only a bee," she said.

Relieved, she held up the pistol, found the safety and engaged it.

"Come on, Honey, we need to put some ice on …"

When she saw his hand, she stopped. In the few seconds she had looked away, the swelling had traveled down to his fingers and puffed them out like sausages.

She lifted the crying boy's chin and looked at his face. His eyes weren't red and puffy from crying; his lips were swelling, too. And the raspy breathing was getting worse.

"That boy must be allergic to bee stings."

She hadn't even realized Theo had followed her into the meadow until he spoke up at her side, voicing the fear that had expanded as quick and huge as a Navy dinghy in her chest.

Benadryl. If only she had some Benadryl!

"You got to get this boy to a doctor!"

Gabriella dropped the pistol in the grass, scooped Ty off his feet and ran as fast as she could with him in her arms toward the jeep. Theo hobbled awkwardly along behind her.

* * * *

Bernie hadn't bothered to check the Rebecca Nightshade fan page in three days. What was the point? It was patently obvious his magnificent plan had blown up in his face.

What had he been thinking? If he'd reasoned it out instead of leaping in with both feet, it might have occurred to him that half a million dollars was the tiniest bit excessive. He'd have been a whole lot better off if he'd offered say … $100,000 instead. But even that was enough money to drive most people bonkers. And the half mil offer he'd posted had chucked thousands of fools completely over the edge.

He'd gotten more than 250 messages in the first half hour after he posted the reward offer.

Rebecca Nightshade was absolutely working as a short order cook in a diner in San Francisco.

Oh, no, no, no. Rebecca Nightshade was dating a shrimp boat captain in Louisiana.

Oops, wrong again. The *real* Rebecca Nightshade was on a tourist bus in the Catskills.

And the messages kept coming.

The most exasperating part was that Bernie was absolutely convinced a genuine Gabriella sighting was hiding in there *somewhere* in the herd. Somebody really had seen her and had sent in her location like a good little doobie. But the sighting had been lost in the avalanche of people who were either sincerely mistaken or con artists trying to milk the system.

He glanced over at the computer screen. Knowing she was in there somewhere and he couldn't get to her made him want to pull all his hair out. If he'd had any hair.

So much for a transplant. Lean over and kiss the "new man" goodbye, Mr. Phelps. Sayonara, Sucker.

Gabriella flew down the jeep trail with such reckless abandon she could barely keep the vehicle on the road. Theo sat in the backseat cradling a gasping Ty in his arms. They'd ignored P.D. and the dog was too well-behaved to hop into the jeep uninvited. But nobody told him to stay, either, and Gabriella saw him in a side mirror, running behind the jeep. He raced around the switchbacks or cut through the trees between the higher and lower roads. At one point, he scrambled out of the brush just as the jeep passed and came close to getting crushed under the tires. She had no time to stop for him, and there was nobody to hold him in the bouncing jeep if she had. The vehicle leapt into the air when she hit rocks and tree stumps and slammed down into potholes with teeth-jarring force. She made herself keep her eyes on the road, only occasionally snatched quick glances at Ty in the backseat. The boy's eyes were so swollen she was sure he couldn't see. He gasped for every breath.

She roared under the sign into Heartbreak Hotel with her hand on the horn to announce her presence. The lotions, potions and elixirs van was nowhere in sight. Two teenage girls, a blonde and a redhead, stood on the porch of the large building. The blonde had her phone out taking pictures of the redhead posed on the porch railing.

Gabriella skidded to a stop in a spray of dirt, killed the engine, leapt out of the jeep and was two steps up the sidewalk before the blonde girl said. "If you're looking for Grandpa, he's not here."

"Where is he?"

"In St. Elmo at a birthday party."

Gabriella turned, ran back to the jeep and jumped in. As she cranked the engine, she spotted P.D. standing behind the jeep panting. She made the "get in" hand motion and the dog leapt up into the seat beside Theo. They'd be on smooth road the rest of the way.

T HE REDHEADED GIRL noticed the dog running along behind the jeep before it skidded to a stop. Cheyenne loved golden retrievers. Her little brother back home in Cleveland got one for Christmas—just a puppy. The woman who was driving the jeep jumped out and the girl saw an old, black man in the backseat cradling a little boy about the age of her brother. The kid's whole face was puffy, he had a rash and his breathing was noisy and labored. His eyes were swollen, but not shut. He looked terrified. She knew instantly that the little boy had—

When Mary Beth said their grandfather wasn't home, Cheyenne dragged her gaze momentarily away from the choking little boy and noticed the woman who'd gotten out of the jeep—saw her face. Saw the *scar*.

After the woman ran back to the jeep, Mary Beth turned and gestured for Cheyenne to lean back against the railing again, but Cheyenne reached out and snatched the phone from her cousin's hand.

"What are you do—?"

"I need this," Cheyenne said, focused and intense. "I have to do this *right now!*"

The woman in the jeep motioned for the dog to get in. When she did, she turned her face momentarily toward where the girls were standing. The huge scar on the right side of it was plainly visible.

Cheyenne raised Mary Beth's phone and punched a button.

* * * *

Most people didn't consciously think about learning from their mistakes, but Bernie Phelps did. He bobbed and weaved his way through life, went to school on what he did wrong so he'd be more clever next time.

That's why he was sitting at his computer in his underwear and bathrobe on a Saturday afternoon scrolling down the huge list of Gabriella sightings. Not because he actually believed he'd find the needle in the monumental haystack he'd created. He was there as an exercise in self-discipline, using this colossal blunder to teach himself a lesson about going off half-cocked, being impulsive, not considering the possible ramifications of his decisions. This was an expensive lesson. It was going to cost him millions so he wanted it to count.

And there was no better way to do that than to force himself to face the result of his poor judgment.

So he sat and scrolled.

Didn't read the postings, of course. It'd take weeks to read them all! Oh, every now and then he'd spot a word or phrase and he'd pause, see if the comment was unique in any way. Because in addition to teaching himself a lesson, Bernie was doing what he did best—making life's lemons into lemonade.

The idea had come to him at his lowest moment, which is when he sometimes did his best work. And he'd been coming down off a coke, high, too.

All those people out looking for her; Gabby could move the masses when she wasn't even there!

In a flash, he had the perfect advertising campaign for her new book—which she'd better turn in on deadline or he and Hampton Books would sue her for every dime she'd ever made. The campaign would center around the overwhelming response to the contest and how it demonstrated her popularity with her readers.

He planned to—

There was a ding and a new sighting posted. He glanced at it, then stopped and read it. "I've seen her and her dog. I've got a picture to prove it."

… and her dog.

There was no mention of a dog anywhere on Gabriella's fan page or website. She was private about her personal life. Wouldn't allow him or her publisher to use pictures of her family or private information about her. Bernie had made lemonade out of that lemon, too—portrayed her as a mystic, a seer, reclusive and inscrutable.

Oh, he was sure if you wanted to know bad enough, you could find out about P.D. Google was the Wicked Witch of the West's magic ball—it would show you whatever you wanted to see. But it wasn't like Gabby's dog was common knowledge.

He shook his head, then. Yeah, but if he'd been the guy on the other side of this offer looking to make half a million bucks, he'd have found out how many fleas Rebecca Nightshade's dog had!

Still …

So he clicked on the link to a photo website in the message. He expected to see some vague outline of a woman and a golden retriever—as dark and blurry as pictures of Sasquatch or the Loch Ness Monster.

But he didn't. He saw Gabriella. Not P.D., just Gabby. The picture was obviously taken with a cell phone, an older model. The face was angled away from the camera. But the scar! It was perfectly clear and unmistakable. And if anybody knew what that scar looked like, it was Bernie Phelps!

Bernie would never admit it, of course, but he had become morbidly fascinated by Gabriella's injury. In the beginning, when she first got out of the hospital, Bernie had stared at her ugly wound with macabre interest, captivated by how her face had … *dissolved,* the skin and tissue. He was both horrified and mesmerized by how her beauty had melted like candle wax. Over the ensuing months, he'd watched the wound heal, noted the pits and lumps of the resulting scar, its texture, how a thick vein of it pulled up centimeters short of her eyelid. She'd come perilously close to losing an eye! He knew exactly where her eyebrow stopped, burned off.

Bernie Phelps *knew* Gabriella's Carmichael's scar. And he was certain he was looking at it *right now!*

His hands shook as he picked up his phone and dialed the telephone number listed in the message.

* * * *

Yesheb stands perfectly still, looking out over the skyline of Chicago from his penthouse office, and gathers himself, summons his strength, calls forth power from another world to make his mind quicker, more clever. He must act swiftly and decisively and there is no time for error.

And he had come close to making a grievous error, was seconds away from blowing off the sniveling little literary agent's babbling rant about a teenager with a cell phone and a photograph.

But a voice spoke to him, stayed his hand before he could hang up. "Wait," the voice said. Only the one word.

It was a voice he'd never heard before, neither male nor female, with a soft purring sound—cards shuffled in the hands of an expert blackjack dealer.

Yesheb is obedient. He waits, hears Bernie Phelps out. And he is rewarded with a photograph of his darling Zara. Seeing her face—mostly her beautiful deformity—reduces him to speechlessness. He might even be crying—from relief as much as longing—when his mind shifts from celebration to calculation.

He must get to her quickly, before she has a chance to move on. He must find her and then … and then summon the rain.

THE LAST SAFE PLACE

There is a buzz and a voice issues from a black box on his polished cherry desktop.

"The chopper is on the roof, ready to take you to the airport, sir."

"I will be there in two minutes." He picks up his cane and his sunglasses and starts for the door. He barely breaks stride when he pauses to snatch his jacket off a hook by the door. It's hot in Chicago in June but it will likely be chilly in the mountains.

On the way across the city to the airport where his private jet is gassed up and ready for take-off, Yesheb confirms the sequencing his minions have set in motion. He will arrive at Chicago Midway Airport in ten minutes. The flight across four states will take about two and a half hours—that's with all the stops pulled out. Another chopper will be waiting when he lands to take him to a small town at the base of the mountain. By then it will be dark—and stormy weather is in the forecast—so he will travel by car the last half hour from the town up into the mountains to the little berg where he will find Zara.

"I'm still trying to locate a car rental on short notice in a place as small and remote as—"

"Then don't *rent* one." Yesheb's voice is as cold as liquid nitrogen. "*Buy* one. Buy a whole car lot full of cars if you have to. There *will* be one waiting for me when I arrive. *With the engine running!*"

"Yes sir!" Former military. Most of the men Yesheb has hired over the years were once soldiers—who fought a great cause and lost, or who were bloodied in a futile war on some nameless, forgotten battlefield. Evil is the petrie dish in which the cells of war divide and multiply; hatred is the soil in which it grows. Both have fueled battles uncounted in Yesheb's realm, where he has led legions of demons to victory. And one day soon he will rule supreme over a kingdom without end. He and Zara.

"How many operatives will you require, sir? I have my two closest men en route now and six more—"

"Call them off." Yesheb's voice is stern. "There is to be no one else there. Is that understood? I require no assistance. I will do this *alone*."

Yesheb sits tense on the sculpted leather helicopter seat and watches Chicago fly by below him.

A thousand miles away, Gabriella sits tense on the flat leather jeep seat and watches the mountains fly by above her.

CHAPTER 11

Wind that smelled of pine and cedar, damp earth and coming rain slicked Gabriella's short yellow curls back from her face as she roared down Chalk Creek Canyon Road.

A storm. A full moon.

She brushed the thoughts out of her mind like a housewife sweeping dust bunnies out from under a bed. She had far bigger concerns right now than the Lord of the Flies.

She turned for a quick glance into the backseat. The look on Theo's face frightened her almost more than the sight of Ty limp in his arms. The wind bore away the sound of the boy's labored breathing. If he was breathing at all.

She stifled a sob and tried to shove her foot down harder on the accelerator. But the jeep was going full tilt now, as fast as it would go. Gratefully, this remote stretch of road was empty. If anyone had gotten in her way, Gabriella would have run them off into a ditch.

When she rounded the final curve and spotted St. Elmo up ahead, she could see the Mercantile. Dr. Calloway's Libyan terrorist, lotions-and-potions van sat with a handful of other vehicles off to the side but the parking spot in front of the building was vacant. She slid into the empty space and stirred up a cloud of dirt that hit the steps like a spray of snow from a skier stopping at the bottom of a downhill run.

Gabriella jumped out of the jeep and found Steve leaning into the open back of the van.

"Ty got stung, it was a bee, I think," she said. "And he swelled up. He can't—"

She turned to Ty, really looked at him. He was gasping for air but he *was breathing!* His hand where the bee had stung him was puffed up like a boxing glove.

"I have what I need for an allergic reaction," Steve said, then stepped quickly past her and climbed up into the back of the jeep, wordlessly wrapped a rubber tourniquet around the top of Ty's arm and felt around on the inside of his elbow for a vein.

"He got stung once before, last summer, and it swelled up a little bit—" Pedro appeared beside her. "It made a welt, but nothing like …"

She realized she was babbling and clamped her jaws shut. She was vaguely aware that a crowd was gathering on the porch of the Mercantile and that Pedro had put his arm around her shoulder.

"Hey, big guy, you're going to feel better real soon," Steve said. "This will sting a little big, but you need to lie still—okay?"

Steve wiped the skin on the inside of Ty's arm with an alcohol rub and deftly inserted the IV needle. Ty didn't even flinch. Then the doctor reached up and loosened the tourniquet.

"Keep this up above his head," he told Theo and handed him a bag of fluid attached by a coil of plastic tubing to the needle. Holding the needle steady with one hand, Steve pulled a roll of white tape out of his shirt pocket and held it out to Gabriella. "Tear me off two pieces about three inches long."

With trembling hands, she ripped off a piece and Steve stretched it across the needle and around Ty's arm.

"I should have known," Gabriella said as she handed him the second. "When it swelled up the last time, I should have known that—"

Steve cut her off. "There's no way to know a reaction like this is going to happen until it does. Bee sting allergies fire up fast. But you got him here in time." He smiled. "Your boy's going to be just fine now. See?"

Ty's gasping eased with every inhalation; the rasping sound grew less and less hoarse. Inside a minute, he was breathing almost normally again. He took a long, deep breath and let it out in a slow sigh and tried to sit up. Theo held firm.

"You rest here a bit. Doctor says you gone be fine, jess fine."

"I've given him a corticosteroid IV," Steve said. "As you can see, it relieves the symptoms quickly." The doctor turned back to Ty. He put in the ear-tips of a stethoscope and placed the chest piece on Ty's shirt. He listened, moved the silver disc to a different place on Ty's chest, then to the another. Gabriella noticed that the crowd of people on the porch in front of the Mercantile was quiet, as if they were listening, too.

The doctor removed the stethoscope from his ears and hung it around his neck. He patted Ty on the knee. "Feeling better now, son?"

"Uh huh," Ty said, his voice gravelly. "I can breathe."

P.D. barked—just "Woof! Woof!"—but it was so like he understood and was voicing his relief that it broke the spell of silence in the crowd. People let out the collective breath they'd been holding and chuckled, and began to talk among themselves in animated, cheerful voices.

This time when Ty tried to sit up, Theo didn't stop him. With his free hand, the boy reached over and petted Puppy Dog, who grinned back at him with his perpetual golden retriever smile.

Maybe P.D. did understand; you never knew with that dog.

Steve got down out of the jeep and told Gabriella that after the IV bag was empty, he needed to keep an eye on Ty for a while.

"Sometimes after the first dose wears off, the symptoms rebound. I need to watch him for several hours to make sure that doesn't happen."

"Gabriella was planning to spend the evening here anyway." Pedro said. He seemed to become aware for the first time that he had his arm around her shoulders. She was immediately uncomfortable but he wasn't. He just gave her a reassuring squeeze, let go and stepped back. "You *were* planning to come to the party, yes?"

Actually, Gabriella had no intention of attending the party. Not before she came roaring down the mountain and certainly not *now*. She'd just thrown on an old shirt and a pair of jeans when she got up this morning—but she wasn't worried that she was underdressed. What did concern her was that she *wasn't wearing a speck of makeup*. Her scar was naked, exposed!

Pedro picked up on her reluctance.

"Surely, you do not intend to miss the most festive event in the St. Elmo social season. Actually … it is just about the only event in St. Elmo's social season. But what community celebrations here lack in frequency they make up for in intensity." With his thick mustache, it was hard to see the small smile on his lips but you couldn't miss it in his eyes.

"Wouldn't miss it," she said with as much fake enthusiasm as she could muster. She had no choice. She couldn't very well sit out here in her jeep until Steve was sure Ty was going to be all right.

She turned to Steve.

"How can I … thank you, Steve," she said, embarrassed by the emotion in her voice. But he shrugged it off.

"Let's go find this young man somewhere to sit quietly until the IV's done. I'll give you some prednisone—can he take pills?"

She nodded.

"Good. Liquid prednisone is nasty, tastes really bitter. I'll give you a six-day dose pack—gradually decreasing amounts." He gestured toward the store. "I'll tell you all about it over tacos."

He reached up and took the bag from Theo, handed it to Gabriella and helped Ty out of the back of the jeep. Then he extended his hand to Theo, who took it wordlessly and climbed carefully down to the ground.

The doctor held onto Theo's hand, eyed him up and down.

"You okay?" the tone of his voice edged the words out of superficial/perfunctory into semi-clinical.

"Fine, now!" Theo pulled his hand out of the doctor's grasp. "But it's a miracle of God any of us made it off that mountain. That trail has potholes so deep I seen Elvis down in the bottom of one of 'em." He looked around. "I need a bathroom, got to make water—'less my plumbing's been shook so hard the hose is disconnected."

Gabriella had never been past the saloon doors that separated Pedro's home from the store. What lay on the other side was a large room with log walls and a high ceiling. Since all the buildings in St. Elmo were wood frame, with rusted metal roofs, the outside walls must have been built over the original log structure—probably a one-room cabin. The chinking between the logs had been replaced in spots, but most appeared to be original.

The room was windowless, lit in artsy fashion with lanterns and candles on tall stands, and the dim light made Gabriella feel fractionally less exposed. It was definitely better than standing in the bright sunshine outside. There was a long, wood-slat table in the center of the room with benches on both sides instead of chairs. Another table stretched the length of the side wall in front of a huge, unlit fireplace where a gun rack with four rifles hung above the mantle. The aroma of jalapeños rose on ribbons of steam from dishes on the table and a small army of women were assembling tacos as efficiently as a manufacturing plant. Pedro excused himself and disappeared out a door that must have led to the kitchen.

It took Gabriella's eyes a moment to adjust. As the room gradually emerged from shadows, she noticed what was inarguably the most prominent feature of the room. A hospital bed rested against the back wall. An occupied hospital bed with a machine of some kind on a table beside it.

Though no one paid it particular mind, neither did they ignore it. Or the person stretched out on it. The woman Gabriella had seen the first day in Pedro's store, the one who looked like a bag lady, was standing next to the bed chatting with another woman—clearly including the bedridden person in the conversation. A teenage boy—Joaquin, she surmised; he looked like his father—was perched on the end of the bed in a deep, rapid-fire Spanish dialogue with another young man who stood beside it.

When the bag lady shifted position, Gabriella got her first look at the person lying in the bed. She was asleep. No, she was Sleeping Beauty.

Even from a distance, Gabriella knew instantly that the little girl in the hospital bed was Anza's little sister. Her face, expressionless in sleep, had a fragile, haunting quality that left Gabriella breathless. She had believed Pedro's older daughter was the most beautiful girl she'd ever seen, but this precious child was even prettier. Her long black hair lay in a braid that stretched over her right shoulder and all the way down the front of her lacy white nightgown to her waist. It was tied at the end with a red satin bow.

Steve stopped beside her and followed her gaze.

"That's Angelina, Pedro's youngest daughter," he said, then took the IV bag attached to Ty's arm and walked the boy over to a comfortable chair. He continued to chat as he suspended the bag from the edge of a floor lamp next to the chair. "You've met his other daughter, Anza, right? She's the birthday girl."

"Oh, I assumed … I thought it was Pedro's birthday."

"No, he throws a big party every year on his children's birthdays. Anza turns eighteen today. Joaquin's birthday is in the spring. And Angelina …" He turned and looked at the still child lying on the hospital bed. "Angel will be nine on Christmas Eve."

Christmas Eve. That's when Smokey had died.

THE LAST SAFE PLACE

Yesheb has sat motionless for more than two hours staring out the window of the jet at the ground below. It is a featureless expanse dappled with shades of brown and green, bisected by sewing-thread strands of rivers. None of man's precious creations, art or architecture, is visible from this height—a perspective with profound significance, though he doubts that one in a thousand, one in a million of the globe-trotting lemmings racking up frequent flyer miles ever chances to glance out the window, much less understand the import of what he can see.

"Would you care for something to drink, sir?" A voice speaks at his elbow but he doesn't turn, keeps his gaze fixed on a distant nothing out the window. "A cup of coffee? A glass of wine, perhaps? We have a lovely—"

"When do we land?"

"Half an hour, sir."

"And everything will be set up when we get there?"

"Absolutely. The helicopter is waiting."

Yesheb nods approval and dismissal.

They don't get it down there. And they label those who do crazy.

All at once, a single, imprisoned memory makes a break for the fence, with searchlights circling, zeroing in.

The walls of the room are not padded, but of course, they wouldn't be in a facility such as this. A single room here costs more than a whole suite at the Ritz-Carlton in Paris—but without the view. Yesheb will not be here long enough to miss it. The school will have called his grandfather. Yesheb will be set free as soon as they reach the old man—which could be a bit tricky sometimes. The hands-on director of the family's oil fortunes, Yasser Al Tobbanoft is old school, spends most of his time at oil rigs in the desert and pipeline pumping stations. After Anwar Tobbanoft's unfortunate and untimely end in the bathtub, their pathetic mother was certainly incapable of caring for Yesheb and his sisters so the old man assumed responsibility for them—fiscal and moral responsibility, certainly not emotional. He pays others to look after them, packs them off to boarding schools all over the world, sees them infrequently—at Ramadan or other holidays. Some years.

His absence suits Yesheb perfectly. He needs no one to "raise" him. He is directed by the voices. No other authority is necessary nor would be tolerated.

Which has gotten him into the situation he finds himself now. The voices were too loud, shouting in his head. They did that sometimes to torment him, to toughen him. But he was tired. He cried out, answered them, argued with them and they set off bombs of pain in his head in retaliation. Unfortunately, even with a private room, his schoolmates next door heard his voice. They came to check on him, found him writhing in the floor in his own excrement, foaming at the mouth. They called the headmaster and …

Yesheb's grandfather's absences are convenient until his presence is necessary. And it is necessary now. Yesheb can't stay here. This is a place for crazy people and he is infinitely sane, confidently, proudly sane. It is the others, the rest of the herd, whose minds are clouded. But not by insanity, by stupidity.

Then the buzzing starts again in his head, the gnawing sound, like creatures inside are using chainsaws to get out. And he starts to scream again. He can't help it. He screams and screams and …

Yesheb's mind locates the escapee, trains machine guns on the memory and shoots it down. The frothing water of his soul slowly becomes smooth again. Glassy.

He stares undistracted now at the empty expanse below his private jet and understands what mere mortals cannot fathom. He can see the unformed fetus of mankind, deep in the forever dark of the immortal womb. Its eyes are blind. And it yearns to remain eternally sightless. It doesn't want to know. It wants to curl up safe and snug in ignorance, fears the razor edges of truth and the pain of existence.

But inevitably, birth and life demand a choice. Open your eyes, recognize goodness and evil and choose your side. Or keep your eyes closed and see neither. The current state of the world is testimony to the cowardice of the many and the futile courage of the few. Everywhere on the globe, evil thrives in the soil of denial, pruned by cynicism, fertilized by disbelief, watered by inaction.

Yesheb smiles a rueful smile. In the great apocalyptic battle to come, his forces will prevail, of course. He and Zara will reign supreme. But he wonders how many of the others, the shuffling turtles on the other side, will even pick up weapons for the fight.

Yesheb's ears begin to pop. The plane has begun its descent.

"My little Angelina is beautiful, is she not?"

Theo jumped. He hadn't heard Pedro come up beside him as he stood at the foot of the hospital bed. The tumor he'd dubbed "Cornelius" had got shook real good by that jeep ride and it was payback time. His temples throbbed relentlessly. He held onto the railing around the bed because if he let go, the dizziness would turn him upside down and drop him face first on the floor.

"I am sorry. I did not mean to startle you."

"Hearing's about gone, worn out. Just like the rest of me." He taps his chest. "Got a lifetime warranty and it's about up." Theo turned back to consider the angel lying so still before him. "What happened to this chile?"

He saw Pedro flinch. Theo always had been blunt, cut to the chase. Lately, it'd gotten worse, though. When your train was about to pull out of the station, you didn't have time for pussyfooting conversations.

"Brain damage."

"So she not gone wake up for the party."

Again the flinch.

"No."

"She ever gone wake up?"

"… probably not. She has remained a little baby, never grew up, talked, walked or …" There was a heartbeat pause, then Pedro rushed ahead, "Oh, God could perform a miracle. We pray for that every day. We have hope, but …"

"But probably not," Theo finished for him.

Both men were quiet. The sheet that covered the child's thin chest rose and fell in rhythm with the whoosh and hiss of the machine sitting on the table beside the bed. There wasn't a wrinkle in the sheets anywhere. The lace nightgown was as perfect as the outfit on a doll. A clean, white bandage on her throat covered up the opening there for the tube that stretched across the bed to the ventilator.

The old man could hear the hum of conversation around him and music of some kind—a mariachi beat, nothing he cared about. He was beginning to discover that being deaf wasn't an altogether bad thing.

"Because she ees my child, too, just like the others," Pedro said. Theo heard that, turned and looked questioningly at him. "You want to know why she ees right here in the living room, in the middle of everything."

"If I'd wanted to know, I'd have asked."

Pedro smiled a little. At least Theo thought he did. With that broom on his upper lip it was hard to tell. "Yes, I suppose you would have."

"You think she knows she's here, knows what's going on around her?"

Pedro's eyes were suddenly moist, but he didn't blink, looked steadily into eyes that age had yellowed. "I pray every day that when I meet her one day in heaven, she will say she knew, she was aware every minute, she heard every word."

G‌ABRIELLA SAT DOWN on a couch covered with a beautiful Indian blanket—and fell so deep into the cushion it would take a forklift to get her back out. Obviously, the blanket hid a broken spring.

"Should have warned you," Steve said as he eased down next to her. "This old couch is stuck here in the corner for a reason."

Gabriella had elected to sit there for the same reason. Damaged goods had a way of finding each other.

"So finish what you were telling me about the guy with the string tie," she said. For the past couple of hours, all through the taco buffet dinner, Steve had been giving her a running commentary on the various characters in the room—the old Indian with the rheumy eyes, the fat, bald man with a strawberry birthmark on his head. Every one of them had a story.

The string-tie man was middle-aged, with boots a little too polished and the creases in his hat a smidge too perfect. Drugstore cowboy.

"He's pretty tight-lipped but I've got him down to an investment broker on the commodities exchange, a bookie or CIA. The safe money's on bookie."

There was the tall, clean-shaven, pressed-shirt-tucked-in man who'd moved to St. Elmo with his three wives, escaping a crackdown on multiple marriages by the Mormon Church in Utah. The youngest wife had promptly taken up with the man who drove the gasoline delivery truck that serviced the filling station. The other two couldn't get along—not with each other—with *him*. They finally threw him out and lived together now with the seven children in the house he'd moved the herd into. He lived in a trailer set back from the creek down the road.

THE LAST SAFE PLACE

Ty ran in and out of the room now and then as the newest member of the Mormon herd. Or tribe, since it included a couple of native American kids and several young Hispanics.

The boy seemed perfectly fine, but the swelling in his face hadn't gone down as quickly as Steve would have liked. He said if Ty's eyes and lips were still puffy four hours after he finished the IV, he'd give the boy another one.

Steve pointed to a couple of indeterminant age standing near the head of the hospital bed. He had a full-bore Jeremiah Johnson—or John the Baptist—beard and long hair that fell in his face. She looked normal enough—except for the full sleeves of tattoos on both arms and both legs and growing like morning glory vines out the collar of her shirt.

"Albert and Sadie live in the house on the other side of the dry goods store. For five years, they had a line painted down the middle of the floor of their living room and on election day Al couldn't cross that line. Their house is the polling place in St. Elmo and in Colorado a paroled convict can't vote until his parole is up."

He answered her next question before she had a chance to ask it.

"Some kind of drug charges, I think. Using, not selling."

She spotted Theo and Pedro in conversation at the foot of Angelina's bed and allowed her eyes to caress the child's perfect features again.

"That little girl … she's not just asleep, is she?"

"Angelina's in a PVS, permanent vegetative state. She was like that when I bought Heartbreak Hotel five years ago."

"How does Pedro …?" It hadn't escaped her notice that the cooks for the event were Anza and another woman old enough to be the girl's grandmother. "It looks like he's single—"

She was surprised and a more than a little dismayed by how much she was hoping he was, that his wife wasn't just visiting her sister in Omaha. She'd even searched the photographs on the wall, looking for a woman at Pedro's side, but found nothing but pictures of the children.

"His wife left him. Pedro doesn't talk about it much, but apparently she wanted to put Angelina in a nursing home, a permanent care facility, and he wanted to keep her at home so …"

"How does he do it, take care of her all by himself?"

"He has Anza." He gestured to the room. "And all of St. Elmo. I bet Pedro's telling Theo right now about the alarm system."

Steve pointed to the machine that rested on a cart by the hospital bed.

"Angelina can breathe without that ventilator for short periods of time, but not for long. If the machine failed—came unplugged or the electricity went out—Angelina could be in trouble quick so Pedro rigged up an alarm. When it goes off …" He looked at her and grinned. "… the result gives a whole new meaning to close-knit community."

* * * *

Yesheb buckles the seatbelt but he has to wrestle the harness. He motions for the helicopter pilot to lift off anyway—he'll figure it out in the air. He can see the flashes of distant lightning. It's storming in the mountains on the western horizon.

* * * *

There was a sudden crack, followed instantly by a boom of thunder. The sky had turned ugly after Gabriella got to St. Elmo. She'd have to stay here until the storm passed and the rainwater drained off the trail. Even so, she wasn't looking forward to wet rocks in the dark.

Thunder rumbled again.

A storm. And a full moon.

* * * *

Yesheb hops out of the helicopter while it is still a foot off the ground, leans over and races through the hurricane wind of the blades toward the lone car that sits at the far end of the church parking lot where the chopper has been directed to land. The engine in the car is running.

He has kept in constant contact with Bernie throughout the trip, who is in contact with someone yearning to collect half a million dollars in cash for a chance encounter. As of Yesheb's last conversation with the smarmy little agent, the informant remained certain Gabriella was attending a party in a tiny collection of houses high in the mountains that stood as behemoth shadows against the night sky above the valley floor. The information stopped there—no address to feed into a GPS that would display the route with a red arrow using information sucked down from some whirling silver ball of technology in the sky. But Yesheb doesn't need a computer voice to talk him through the journey. Google Earth shows the town to be so small it would be impossible to miss a gathering there of more than two people.

Yesheb isn't worried about finding her. He is a top-of-the-food-chain predator. Once he gets near enough, he'll be able to smell her. He turns out of the parking lot and down the street. The tires squeal when he shoves his foot down on the accelerator, then night folds like the wings of a bat around the car and he disappears.

* * * *

When Gabriella jumped at a sudden boom of thunder, Theo looked at her with compassion. The old man had eased down on the couch beside her after Steve left about half an hour ago and Gabriella wondered if he had remained there because he was comfortable or because he couldn't get up.

Her eyes scanned the room, seeking out Ty to make sure he was all right, was safe. The swelling was almost gone. She didn't think it was likely Steve would have to give him another IV. To look at the boy now, you'd never have guessed he'd brushed up close enough to death to feel its cold breath on his neck. She shuddered, then dragged her thoughts away from Ty's close call to the festivities around her.

The party had not started out loud and boisterous, but it had finally cranked into high gear. Once everyone had eaten, the old woman who'd helped with the tacos—who, it turns out, actually was Anza's grandmother—brought out the birthday cake. The crowd of assorted misfits and miscreants held hands and formed a circle around the bed of a Sleeping Beauty who could not be awakened by a prince's kiss. Pedro said a prayer of gratitude for the gift of Anza, then the group launched into an off-key rendition of Happy Birthday. Some sang in Spanish, others in English.

Afterwards, Pedro pulled out his vintage collection of old rock and roll tapes and actually had a boom box to play them in. Anza dragged him out onto the dance floor and though Pedro was certainly no Michael Jackson, the two of them danced to *Thriller*. Then the whole crowd took to the cleared-out area in the middle of the room, women dancing with women, children with old men, jumping around joyous and uninhibited.

Gabriella watched them, *studied* them with something like awe.

A flash of lightning strobed the darkened interior beyond the swinging doors and Gabriella jumped when the thunder on its tail rumbled.

Then she felt a hand slip over hers. Theo squeezed reassuringly. "You safe here."

Such tenderness from Theo stunned her. Apparently, it stunned him, too, because as soon as it hit him what he'd done, he pulled his hand back like he'd stuck it in a toaster oven.

Gabriella struggled out of the hole in the couch to her feet. "I need to … after that taco, I could use a Tic Tac," she said. "There's some in the jeep."

"Pedro moved it away from where you parked in front of the porch steps, put it down at the far end on the right …" He paused, wrinkled his nose. "… *keys in the ignition.*"

She knew Theo still couldn't wrap his mind around all the unlocked doors and cars. He'd told her, "leave a car unlocked in the neighborhood where I grew up and next morning that car gone be stripped down to a bare metal frame with teeth marks on it."

Gabriella walked through the darkened store and stepped out into the damp night where the rain had been reduced to the dribble and plop of drops off the store roof. She sucked in a lungful of clean, ozone-scented air and let it out slowly. She'd used the Tic Tacs in the jeep as an excuse to escape. The real reason she'd left the party was that she was … what? Overwhelmed. It sounded so trite and corny, but she was blown away by the joy she saw all around her. For the first time in … maybe for the first time *ever* … she was in the presence of simple, happy people. Not her walking-dead parents. Not tweedy college English majors. Not wacked-out musicians or fanatical fans. Just people whose lives, by anybody's standards, were far from perfect.

And *Pedro!* In all their conversations, he had never mentioned his own suffering. She'd dumped a load of her personal sewage on him last week, wailed about the pain in her life and he never said a word about the pain in his.

She had nowhere to put that kind of behavior, nowhere to process it. She probably hadn't lived a day, in total accumulated time, in the peace and relaxed joy that was all around her at that party. It shocked her, engaged her … and frightened her. How ya gonna keep 'em down on the farm after they've seen … How could she not long for that kind of freedom now that she knew it really was out there in the world?

A full moon shone through a crack in the clouds, but Gabriella didn't notice it. Almost frantic to distance herself from the laughing people at the party, she hurried across the porch, down the steps and turned right on the street. The breeze blew wet pine needles along the ground and they tickled her shins as they passed like kittens with milk on their whiskers.

Then she felt a sudden chill. She hadn't thought it was that cold outside.

* * * *

Yesheb drives through the night with all the windows down. The cold wind that smells of spruce and pine trees is refreshing and exhilarating. Far from feeling light-headed in the thin air, he feels complete clarity and laser-sharp focus. His time is drawing near.

He slows when he reaches a collection of old buildings on both sides of the road. He parks in the shadows across from what is clearly the only party in town. He can hear loud music and bursts of laughter every now and then. He is content to stare at the door of the building. Knowing his Zara is beyond that door, so close, fills him with a longing and a need he did not know he could feel.

As a circling lion closes in on its prey, so Yesheb must close in on Zara. He must figure out a way to separate her from the herd of people, isolate her. The others—the boy, the old man and the dog—are totally secondary. What is of paramount importance is that he subdue Zara, strike such terror into her heart that she will offer no resistance, will follow his lead, docile as a baby rabbit. He imagines her eyes full of fear and pain and feels a thrill of such power and passion it is almost too glorious to contain.

The storm has set off fireworks in the sky, fulfilling the prophesy in the holy book. Now it is time for him to claim his bride and—

The door he is staring at opens. Zara steps through it and out into the cool mountain air. For a moment, he is too surprised to move, merely follows her with his eyes. She stands for a moment, staring into the night, then steps down off the porch and begins to walk down the street.

His shock vanishes. He opens his car door slowly; he has already loosened the bulb in the overhead light so it will not shine when he gets out.

He pushes the door closed but does not latch it. Then his senses drink in the darkness, his lair.

Though in human form he can no longer see them, he senses their presence. Demons surround him, all sizes and shapes, their corrupted mouths in drooling smiles. They glide along the cold ground where he places his cane and each footstep carefully, silently. He can almost hear the murmured approval from their pitted throats. They watch him, their leader, their master. They cannot aid him, but they have come because their mere unseen presence grants him the superhuman power he needs. He makes his way through the shadows. She walks in and out of the puddles of light cast by the pitiful little street lights that are nothing more than lanterns hung on poles.

He watches her movement, her grace. Then he wills himself to her, moves through space without limping, without even touching the ground until he is behind her. He reaches out his hand and places it on her shoulder.

She whirls around, the fabric of her garment making a whuffing sound like sheets on a clothesline in the wind, her scar pallid white in the moonlight. She opens her mouth to cry out, but is too stunned, too surprised to make a sound.

So is Yesheb.

CHAPTER 12

Gabriella walked only a short distance before she imagined she heard someone behind her. The sudden realization of what she'd done hit her so hard it stole her breath. She had just dashed off into the night—into the *full-moon* night. *Alone!* What had she been thinking? Her heart went into hyperdrive, hammering a hole in her chest wall. She didn't burst into a run because she knew her legs wouldn't carry her if she tried.

Then, in a reality ripped from her recurring nightmare, she felt a hand on her shoulder. But this was no dream. No overactive imagination.

And in the space between one heartbeat and the next, Gabriella Carmichael decided she was prepared to die—if it was *quick*. She wouldn't let him drag her off somewhere and ... *No!*

It only took a second to whirl around, but by the time she faced him she was determined that the only way Yesheb Al Tobbanoft would get her off this street was to kill her.

She opened her mouth to cry out, but didn't. Just stood there staring.

"I am sorry," Pedro said. "I only wanted ... you looked upset when you left. Are you all right?"

Gabriella couldn't speak. Terror and surprise and relief banged into each other in her head like bumper cars. Her knees felt weak. And she had to strangle back a peal of hysterical laughter.

When she said nothing, Pedro looked more closely and was instantly contrite.

"I really frightened you. I am sorry, I never meant ..." He took her arm and guided her to the porch steps in front of the dry goods store where she plopped down with a decidedly unladylike clunk when her knees collapsed out from under her.

Gabriella finally found her voice. "Don't be ... sorry, I ... overreacted."

"No, you *other* reacted. You thought I was somebody else—who?"

« 169 »

"Pedro, do you believe in evil?"

"That is like asking if I believe in air. Evil *is*. Whether I believe in it or not—whether *anybody* believes in it—does not matter."

"Do you believe in … demons?"

"Same question. Evil is the what; demons are the who."

"So you think demons are real, that they exist here, around us?"

"I think the single best promotion of evil in the history of mankind was when we made it a cartoon and dressed it up in a red suit with horns and a forked tail."

"But how can you tell the difference between real evil and … homicidal insanity? Between someone who is savage and brutal because he's evil and someone who—?"

"If you are on the receiving end of the savage and brutal, it is a distinction without a difference. Is someone trying to hurt you, Gabriella?"

Her voice grew quiet. "The kind of man who delights in hurting other people—is he crazy or evil?

"Both."

* * * *

Yesheb stares dumbfounded at a young woman who looks just like his Zara—but *isn't*. Flowing black gown. Long black hair hanging straight down around her shoulders. Bangs cut to a point on her forehead. Red fingernails, bright red lipstick. And a scar! *The* scar. The *exact* scar that graces the face of his beloved.

"Who are you?" he demands, his voice tightly controlled so she hears no emotion, neither anger nor desperation.

The girl backs up a step. "Who are *you*?" But she appears only startled, not frightened. And then he watches it happen, the shift, sees in her eyes what he has seen in the eyes of countless other women so taken by his good looks they wouldn't notice if he held a severed head in his hand that was dripping blood on their shoes.

"Why are you dressed up like Zara?"

"Zara? Oh, no, not Zara! Though they're certainly quite similar, aren't they." The girl touches the scar on her face and giggles self-consciously. "But in my mind's eye, I see Rebecca Nightshade's appearance as merely suggestive of Zara, like a sketch of the original, an underdeveloped negative. I wrote that in a paper once, the underdeveloped negative part. I got an A minus." She realizes she's babbling, stops and refocuses. "But who knows how much of herself Rebecca Nightshade poured into Zara since she's never granted an interview. That's why we want her to come here."

"Who is 'we'?" He speaks each word individually, for clarity and because his jaw is clenched so tight he can barely speak at all. His blood is beginning to boil. Literally. Rage is a blast furnace in his chest. Every vein, artery and capillary is swelling with over-heated liquid.

"We are The *Live* Poets' Society ... like the movie with Robin Williams, except not 'dead.'"

Yesheb doesn't respond.

"English majors at Plymouth State University."

He still doesn't respond.

"*In Plymouth.*" She is beginning to address him like a three-year-old. "That way." She points toward White Mountain, a gigantic dark smudge on the black New Hampshire sky—where the clouds have cleared away in front of the full moon. "The society is dedicated to *living* authors. We're into nontraditional literature like horror fiction. And the Silver Center for the Arts flicks its intellectual ashes all over 'trade writers,' only invites speakers like Rosanna Warren, Marilyn Nelson, Sharon Olds."

She pauses. "Warren ... Nelson ... Olds ... *poets!*"

Yesheb can tell the grace his good looks purchased for him has about run out. His grace toward her is about gone, too.

* * * *

Gabriella's heart could finally speak each beat clearly again without stuttering. She took a deep, trembling breath and yanked the conversation firmly away from discussions of pain and evil. Even managed a small smile when she asked Pedro about something she'd been wondering all evening.

"When I got here this afternoon with Ty, it was almost like Steve was waiting for us. He came up with that steroid IV out of his van in seconds. How could he possibly have known we were coming?"

"His granddaughter, Cheyenne, called and told us about you. She's the redheaded girl you met when you were looking for Steve. She's allergic to bee stings so she spotted right away what was wrong with Ty." He paused. "Now Steve has an interesting moral dilemma. He'd grounded her—that's why she wasn't here at the party—for running up a $450-and-change cell phone bill, took her phone away and said she couldn't make another cell phone call of any kind all summer. So should he—?"

"He can't punish the kid for trying to help—it wasn't exactly a trivial call."

"Sí, you are right. He would be violating Rule 139."

"Okay, I'll bite. What's Rule 139?"

"Do not sweat the petty stuff and do not pet the sweaty stuff."

* * * *

The young woman standing before Yesheb smiles at him dismissively.

"I really need to go. I left my dog in the car and I—"

"Why are you dressed like Zara?"

"I was picked to make a presentation about being broad-minded, thinking outside narrow paradigms, to the Silver Center this afternoon—before Bartlett's annual June Moon party." She nods toward the lighted house where the music is so loud you can understand the lyrics out on the street. "And I came up with this idea—didn't tell *anybody*—that it would be more effective if I gave the presentation looking like Rebecca Nightshade! My roommate, Ruell—rhymes with spool and tool, it's from the Bible—she's a theatre major and she is a-*ma*-zing at stage makeup. You should have seen the Quasimodo head she did for—" She stops, refocuses again. "Anyway, she made the scar out of latex, used the picture on the book jacket to—"

He hits her in the face with his cane. It is made of hand-carved ebony, a serpent whose head and forked tongue form the handle. He smashes it into the fake scar on her cheek, watches her fly backward in slow motion with blood squirting out of her nose and mouth. Then he takes two steps to where she lies crumpled like a broken doll, the black wig askew, pale blonde hair spread out in a halo in a growing pool of blood. He lifts his foot to slam it down on her face, again and again until every trace of his beloved Zara is gone. But he hears voices; someone's coming. He turns, silently blends into the shadows and is gone.

Gabriella thought they should call the trout "star-spangled fish" since they were caught on the Fourth of July.

"Okay now, stand under the sign and hold that fish up high," Pedro said.

When he was satisfied with Ty's position, he pulled out his cell phone and captured several shots. He'd post the pictures of the boy and the trout he'd caught in Piddley Creek on the Wall of Honor in the Mercantile, in the "first catch" category.

Pedro had arrived early that morning with three days' worth of supplies and his fly fishing gear—to try again. He and Ty had already spent two unsuccessful fishing excursions, traipsing up and down the creek, and today Ty finally landed a trout. Pedro caught two more—enough fish for supper. It was a shame Theo missed the excitement. The old man hadn't gone to the creek with Ty before lunch like he usually did, said, "This thin air done give me a headache again," and had spent the whole day stretched out on his bed.

As soon as Theo had adjusted to the altitude enough that he could walk more than ten yards without gasping, he began to accompany Ty and P.D. across the meadow to the waterfall. He'd come back weak, winded and hobbling painfully. Then he'd get up the next morning and do the same thing again.

Pedro slipped his phone back into his pocket, took the fish from Ty and laid it with the two he'd caught on the natural table formed by a large rock that stuck up out of the ground just beyond the front porch. From a leather scabbard at his waist, he produced a vicious-looking hunting knife, the kind that was no doubt used to field dress a deer, and chopped off the fish heads before he began to clean them.

"Your Uncle Garrett and I used to break rocks on that piece of granite, looking for thunder eggs," Gabriella told Ty.

"What's a thunder egg?"

"It is a rock that looks ordinary on the outside …" Pedro stopped. "No, actually they are particularly *ugly* rocks on the outside, round and kind of lumpy. But there's beauty deep down inside that you can't see."

"Are you talking about a geode? Mom's got the prettiest one you ever saw in your whole life! I'll show you."

Ty raced up the steps and into the cabin.

Pedro stopped cleaning the fish and looked questioningly at her. "You found a geode on Antero?"

"No, but we found them in other places our parents went rock hunting. When I was six, we went to Keokuk, Iowa, and it's known as the geode capital of the world."

"Anza used to stand with her nose pressed to the glass, staring at the geodes in the rock case in the store."

"Oh, they're the perfect kid rock, like Easter eggs you crack open and find candy inside." Gabriella smiled at the memories. "Garrett and I'd sit here in the evening with a hammer, breaking up hunks of granite, certain we'd find a thunder egg if we looked hard enough."

Ty burst out the front door with Gabriella's geode and held it out to Pedro.

"Bet you've never seen anything like *this!*"

Pedro looked at the rock—his hands were too fish slimed to touch it—and Gabriella watched the surprise on his face downshift through wonder into awe. That's how she had always felt about the rock, too—wonder and awe.

The whole geode would have been bigger than a softball. This was only half, like a cantaloupe split down the middle. But instead of seeds in the hollow center, a lone three-inch crystal the size of Gabriella's thumb rose up like the Washington Monument out of a shell carpeted with sparkling white crystalline quartz. The large crystal was as clear as a drop of pure water and its planes refracted the sunlight into colored beams that danced in the air around it. Surrounding the base of the crystal like the petals of some exotic flower were seven smaller crystals the size of two-inch pencils. The seven were identical, the same size and shape, except each was a different color—the colors that sparkled in the air around the clear crystal. The colors of the spectrum. Red, orange, yellow, green, blue, indigo and violet.

"I … I've never seen a geode with …" Pedro stammered. "How can it be …?"

"It can't," Gabriella said. "This rock is a geologic anomaly. Unexplainable. Impossible."

A pale memory formed in Gabriella's mind, thin and transparent, gauzy with the collected dust of time.

She and Garrett are eleven. They live in the little house on Churchview Avenue in Pittsburgh's Baldwin neighborhood, the one that has no rocks, no crystals and no hope. Hard times. Her father doesn't go to work; her mother waits tables.

That evening, her father has brought home an old friend he ran into in a deli, a geologist turned jeweler who appraised Phillip's aquamarine and other gemstones years ago in another life. Natalie is polite to the man, fastens a smile on her face like a Halloween mask, serves him a soft drink, offers him cookies. But her eyes are as dead as they always are except when she is talking about Grant.

The house is small and cramped. Garrett is in the tiny bedroom they share playing Chopin on his keyboard. He has perfect pitch and says not a single key on it is in tune. Gabriella is on the floor beside the couch, playing with her rock collection. Though her parents got rid of all their minerals—the memories were too painful—she still has a small collection of rocks she found herself when her parents were out looking for more impressive specimens. Two shoe boxes full of granite chunks, petrified wood, one fossilized trilobite, some sparkling fool's gold and half a dozen geodes—all different sizes, broken open to reveal the crystals inside.

The jeweler and her father are making small talk, forced and stilted. The man obviously knew about Grant's death but didn't realize until he got here that the wound was still raw and bleeding. Suddenly, the man stops in mid-sentence and stares at the geode Gabriella has in her hand. He is a tallish man, with a long, horse's face, jowls and a large mole on his right cheek below his eye.

He reaches out his boney hand. "May I see that?"

Gabriella gives it to him. It is the largest of her geodes—the prettiest of all her rocks. The prettiest rock she has ever seen, in fact.

The man studies the rock. "Where did you find this geode?"

She shrugs her shoulders. "I don't know. I don't remember."

Her father chimes in then. "I've never seen this rock."

Gabriella had been playing with it the night before, making colored sparkles on the wall as she sat on the floor beside her father's chair. He had never looked down.

"We took the twins with us to Iowa and Georgia, but I imagine this is one she picked up in Kentucky." Her father pulls his glasses down off the top of his head and settles them on his nose. When he focuses on the stone, really sees it, he gasps. He and the jeweler exchange a look.

"It's plain quartz," Gabriella says, looking from one to the other. "Right?" Even Gabriella knows quartz is the most common mineral in the world.

The jeweler nods. "But ... the crystal—six-sided prisms terminating in six-sided pyramids. Flawless. Not milky—as transparent as window glass. Every one of them, all eight crystals, they're perfect."

"The colors," her father stammers. "How did ...? All those different colors are—"

"Utterly impossible," the jeweler finishes for him and shakes his head in wonder. "There's no way it could have happened ... but there it is. It's like—"

And then he says the odd thing that Gabriella never forgets.

"What does nomally mean?" Ty asked and pushed up his glasses. When it was hot, his glasses yo-yoed up and down his sweaty nose.

"Anomaly. Something not normal."

"You mean it's like ... magic?"

" I don't think scientists know for sure how a geode forms, at least they didn't when I was a kid." She looked a question at Pedro and he shrugged. "But the simplest explanation is that water seeps through a crack into the cavity of a rock and whatever mineral is dissolved in the water slowly turns into crystals there."

"Why?"

"I don't know that either; nobody does. But I do know the crystals are usually quartz." Another glance at Pedro.

"I got some for the store once that had agate crystals and there were some that were way too expensive that I didn't get with amethyst crystals. All the rest were quartz."

"And I also know that no matter what mineral forms them, the crystals in a geode are *only one color*. Several shades of the same color, maybe, lighter and darker. And different colors in different geodes." Gabriella shook her head. "But seven *different* colors in *one* geode. The colors of the spectrum—which is a refraction of *light*. It'd be hard to find a darker place than inside a rock! And arranged in order like a rainbow. *No. Possible. Way.*"

"Must be some way," Ty said, "'cause there it is."

"An old jeweler who spotted it in my rock collection said there was only one explanation—it was 'made by the hand of God Himself.' He was so impressed with the rock my father gave it to him."

"But it was yours," Ty said. "You were the one who found it."

"That didn't matter," she said quietly. "*I* didn't matter." She saw the dismay on Ty's face and hurried on. "The jeweler mounted it on black velvet and set it on the counter of his jewelry store. Said it was more rare, more precious than a diamond. Kept it there for years. When my father died, the old man brought the rock to the funeral home and gave it back to me."

"If you don't remember where you found it, how do you know you didn't find it here?" Ty asked.

"Well, I don't. But—"

"It *could* have been here, couldn't it?"

"Anything's possible. But—"

"Me and P.D. are gonna find a thunder egg, too." He leapt to his feet, bounded down the steps and started scouring the ground like someone looking for a lost contact lens.

"Try around the waterfall," Pedro said. He picked up the cleaned fish and started up the steps to take them into the kitchen. "Water washes rocks down from the top of the mountain. That's why the old prospectors used to pan for gold nuggets in creeks."

Ty turned wordlessly and raced off toward the waterfall with P.D. one step behind.

"Why are you encouraging him? You know—"

"I know little boys love to look for buried treasure." He went into the house, came back a few minutes later with his hands smelling like dish soap, and sat down beside Gabriella on the top step of the porch.

"You're right about little boys and buried treasure," she said. "If you'd told Garrett there was a treasure here, he'd have dug up the whole mountain!"

Pedro picked up the geode off the porch and watched the crystals refract light. "Where is your twin brother now?"

Gabriella felt like he had kicked her in the belly.

"He's … dead. Suicide."

Now it was Pedro who looked like he'd been kicked in the belly.

"Both of your brothers. Lightning, then suicide." He set the rock back down on the porch. "It was not you, was it? Tell me you did not …"

"Find him? Yes, it was me."

How did we get here?

She felt her cheeks flush, her eyes fill with tears. But Pedro didn't respond like she expected. Didn't get embarrassed, awkward that he'd obviously opened up a painful wound, didn't try to back pedal or change the subject. He sat quietly beside her, staring out into the valley, tossing the geode up and catching it unconsciously like a pitcher waiting for a sign from the catcher. When she looked over at him, there were tears in his eyes, too.

He felt her gaze. Didn't turn, just continued to stare into the valley thousands of feet below.

"I used to question why God allows suffering," he said. His Spanish accent was very pronounced and it struck her that perhaps he had to concentrate to keep it out of his speech, that it took an effort he didn't, or couldn't, apply when he was upset. "But I do not do that anymore."

"Suffering makes sense to you?"

"No, I do not understand eet. But I do understand that 'why me?' ees not the right question."

"What is the right question?"

"Why *not* me?" He caught the geode and set it down on the porch between them. "Things happen for a reason, but knowing the reason does not change anything." He turned to face her. "It still hurts."

She thought of the beautiful little girl lying as still as a china doll in his living room. She almost asked about the child, but didn't. She wasn't like Pedro. Her own pain hadn't made her reach out to others with compassion. It had isolated her, built walls lined with razor wire that imprisoned her.

Pedro changed the subject then, flipped the switch and turned off the spotlight of painful introspection he must have seen shining out through the cracks in her soul.

"You said you and your twin brother were prodigies, right? What special gifts did God give you?"

She had never looked at it that way—that their talents had been gifts from God. If she'd ever considered it at all—which she couldn't recall ever doing—she believed they were less "special gifts" than door prizes. She and Garrett had walked into the talent store and happened to be the one-millionth customers. During a two-for-the-price-of-one sale.

"Garrett was a musician. The first time he ever saw a piano, he sat down and played—not a song, but chords and harmonies—a little like jazz, with no discernible melody but obviously music."

"How old was he?"

THE LAST SAFE PLACE

"He'd just turned eight. It was in a music store right after Grant was killed."

"And you?"

"I … drum roll please … am a poet."

Her own words surprised her. She wasn't being disingenuous, wasn't consciously trying to mislead him, throw him off the scent so he wouldn't figure out her identity. It had slipped out. Gabriella hadn't thought of herself as a poet since those days years ago when her poignant, insightful, lyric verse earned her the Antivenom Poetry Award and the May Swenson Poetry Award and her first book of published poetry, *The Crystal Pillow*, was on the short list for the prestigious Kingsley Tufts Poetry Award—and its $100,000 prize.

She didn't see herself as a poet when she was writing lyrics for Garrett's music, lyrics that spiraled down into the darkness of her brother's soul. And she certainly didn't see herself as a poet after she wrote *The Bride of the Beast*.

The handful poems she'd written here—the verse stiff and stilted from disuse—did that make her a poet again?

"You look troubled. Is writing poetry painful?"

"I guess you could say that," she picked up the geode and watched the shiny crystal refract sparkles in the air. "You start with pure beauty—like this—and you have to exchange it for mere words. Sometimes it breaks your heart."

"When did you realize that you—?"

"The day Garrett played the piano."

"The *same* day?"

"Does seem odd, doesn't it. Obviously, we'd been born with special talent—you don't instantly acquire it out of nowhere. But I'm with you, I always thought it was strange that we both … The first poem I ever wrote was about the suit we bought that day for Grant to be buried in."

Her mother's face, wild with grief, was still high-def clear in her mind. In a state of unrelenting hysteria, there'd been no reasoning with her, and Gabriella's father had tried. Though he'd been shattered himself, he'd attempted to make his wife understand that there wouldn't be an open casket, not with Grant's body so … damaged. What was the point of a suit and tie? She'd shrieked that she would see him, even if nobody else did. He was her precious baby and she would dress him herself, make him look nice no matter …

So they'd been dispatched to purchase a suit.

"The poem was about the look in my father's eyes when he picked it out, about how Mom's hands shook when she took it from him and carried it into the back room at the funeral home and closed the door behind her."

The poem described Gabriella's fantasy of a strikingly handsome Grant lying in the silk-lined box in the suit, juxtaposed against the reality of what it must have been like for her mother to fit him into it, into any kind of clothing after what had happened to his body. It was a profoundly moving piece because it was so simple, a pen-and-ink sketch of horror—told with powerful, haunting imagery in misspelled words and endearingly clumsy iambic pentameter.

"I wasn't as gifted at writing as my brother was musically, though. Garrett Griffith's music was pure genius."

"Garrett *Griffith*?" Pedro turned to her, his eyes wide. "… *the* Garrett Griffith?"

The geode slipped out of her hand and dropped into her lap. She wanted to rip out her tongue! She'd relaxed, dropped her guard. Pedro was so easy to be with, so easy to talk to. She never should have … but how had a Hispanic man in a dead little Colorado town ever heard of a grunge metal musician like Garrett? Why would Pedro listen to the desperately dark music of Withered Soul?

"How did you … where …?"

"Joaquin and his friends discovered Withered Soul on the internet about a year ago. Most of what they listen to is … is …" He turned to look out over the valley. "Rap ees *not* music!" he said. "Rap ees *chanting!*"

"How do you really feel about it?"

"The *music* of Withered Soul is amazing but the lyrics are … they bothered me."

"They bothered me, too. I wrote them."

"You wrote *Wilted Dreams*?" He paused, then surprised her by repeating the song's chorus, word for word. "Despair rises in us like the tide coming in, the tide coming in, the tide coming in. Hope lies abandoned with the tide going out, next to death, pain and sorrow on the sand."

Gabriella's face flushed. Those lyrics had bubbled up out of the muck of an awful, dark place that had produced all manner of ugliness.

"It wasn't exactly my finest work, but yes, I wrote it. Only that was when …" When she had hitched her wagon to her twin brother's star that became a meteor hurling toward its own destruction—and she had very nearly flamed out with it. How could she make Pedro understand a thing like that? She couldn't. Because she didn't really understand it herself.

All she knew for certain was that there had been a time once when her … "gift" *hadn't* been a dark burden.

"When I was younger, before … things were different. *I* was different. I wrote a poem called *Morning* for a third-grade writing assignment." She closed her eyes and called the words of a stanza to mind.

"The light then scrubs the darkened skies
awakens deer and antelope.
And time breathes life in slow, sweet sighs
perfumed by jasmine, love and hope."

"You wrote *that* at age … what? Nine!" Pedro studied her face. "Light and dark. You are a complicated woman, Gabriella."

She felt her face flush.

"No, I'm not. I'm a simple life form. An amoeba, actually, in a protozoan world."

Ty barreled around the corner of the cabin and skidded to a stop in front of the porch. He had used his shirt as a sack, held the bottom portion of it out in front of him and filled the hollow formed behind it with rocks, all sizes and shapes.

He dumped the pile of them at his mother's feet and asked, panting, "Are any of these geodes?"

Clearly, they weren't. Oh, a few hunks of granite in varying sizes were sort of round and definitely lumpy like geodes. The rest were flat slate.

But Gabriella took her cue from Pedro.

"I don't think so, but anything's possible. The only way to find out for sure is to crack them open and see. There's a hammer in the toolbox in the mudroom. Get a bucket of water and clean the fish slime off that rock first."

T<small>Y DIDN'T FIND</small> any geodes. He used the hammer to crack open all the rocks he'd gathered along the banks of Piddley Creek and near Notmuchava Waterfall where the water was all frothy so maybe it had broken something loose.

Nothing. Every broken rock revealed a solid center. No holes in any of them.

Ty was okay with that, though. He wasn't likely to find a geode down here around the cabin anyway. He'd already figured out his mom probably found hers up there in the Jesus trees when she wasn't supposed to go outside. Tomorrow he'd sneak away again and go to the chalet.

He turned and looked up at the mountaintop rising high into the bright blue sky.

He had first gone to the chalet the day after he overheard his mother tell Grandpa Slappy about it. He and P.D. had gone off to the creek, right after breakfast before his grandfather had his second cup of coffee. Then they sneaked through the forest behind the meadow to the other corner of the hanging valley. There was something like a rock wall about two hundred feet tall behind the meadow; Piddley Creek wound along the south side of it and fell into the creek bed below in Notmuchuva Waterfall. He'd seen what looked like a trail on the north side that had to be the one that led to the chalet.

He tried to hurry up it. He'd be in plain view as he climbed if his mother happened to go behind the cabin and look up toward the peak. But the trail was more challenging than he expected. It was steeper than he thought it'd be even though it angled across the incline. And the rock and gray dirt and gravel were loose underfoot. He slipped twice. When he finally made it, P.D. was waiting for him, wagging his tail.

"Show-off," Ty said.

At the top lay the forest of Jesus trees you could see from the meadow. What you couldn't see from the meadow was how gnarled and twisted they were, all of them leaning in the same direction, the way the wind had blown them for thousands of years. He could totally see why his mother and uncle had wanted to play there. Most of the stubby trees were short enough for grown-ups to see over, but they formed a labyrinth of passageways for children. He wasn't about to get lost in them, though, like those terminally stupid kids you saw in movies or read about in stories who ran mindlessly into the woods without giving any thought to how they were going to find their way back out. He was smarter than that! He'd brought along a sack full of marbles from the Chinese checkers game in the cabin and dropped them at intervals behind him as he explored.

THE LAST SAFE PLACE

The trail was overgrown, barely visible. Just past a big pile of boulders stood the chalet. It was pretty bunged up. Unlike the cabin below that had been redone, nobody had fixed up this building. One of the posts that held up the porch roof lay on the steps and there was a hole in the chalet roof near the chimney. Ty managed to shove the door open and inside was the picnic table his mother had described. It was bunged up, too, but he could see carved into the surface the three G's his mother had talked about.

Pedro's voice interrupted Ty's memory.

"Gotta go," he said, and pulled his hat low on his brow. Ty knew that was so the hat wouldn't blow off, but it still made Pedro look kind of like the bad guy in a cowboy movie. "Remember, you do not cast the fly rod, you—"

"Cast the fly *line*," Ty finished for him. "The rod is an extension of your arm."

"I have taught you well, Grasshopper."

"Huh?"

"Never mind."

As Pedro's muffler-free jeep rumbled away from the cabin, Ty picked up the hammer and cast a final glance at the mountain. Maybe the geodes were farther up, near the aquamarine at the peak. He absolutely, one hundred percent did *not* want to climb up that high. But no, his mother had said that while her parents and older brother went up the mountain, she and her twin played in the forest and that Uncle Garrett had wanted to explore … *under the overhang!*

Mom didn't think the overhang would still be there, but it was. He'd seen it in the distance when he was at the chalet. It was just as his mother described it. Maybe the magic geode had come from there.

* * * *

The Reverend Jim Benninger actually had internet access! For the first time in three months. He and his wife had boarded a steamer a week ago—maybe more than that, the days tended to run together here— and traveled up the White Nile River to Khartoum so Betty Ann could get back on her feet from the virus that had been draining her strength since Easter.

The minister had been going through the backlog of emails in his Yahoo! account and spotted one sent yesterday from Pedro Rodriguez in St. Elmo. When he opened it, a smile spread quickly over his tired, lined face.

The message was short:

Thought you would like to see how much Gabriella's son is enjoying St. Elmo's Fire.

Pedro

So she'd actually come this year!

The attached picture said it all. It showed a little boy on the porch of the cabin holding a smallish trout and grinning so wide the smile almost split his face open! The look on the child's face captured the essence of joy and peace Jim's family always felt when they were in the mountains.

It occurred to the pastor then that he ought to capture that joy for Gabriella to remember. Quickly, because the WiFi in the hotel wasn't reliable, he went on Google and found a store in Pittsburgh called The Frame House that did custom prints and framing. He emailed the photo of the little boy to the store and paid by credit card to have it printed, mounted, framed and delivered to Gabriella's house so it would be waiting there for her when she returned home from Colorado.

He wanted the picture to bring her time in the mountains to a surprise end.

And it did.

CHAPTER 13

Gabriella figured that it must have been indigestion—courtesy of the fried trout she had for dinner. Or maybe it wasn't a memory at all, but a dream. After all, it had come to her in that gray twilight between lying in bed wondering when you will ever go to sleep and the netherworld of disconnected dream images.

Whatever its origin, the night after she and Ty watched the Fourth of July fireworks display in Buena Vista from the front porch of the cabin, Gabriella recalled a memory—or invented a fantasy—about finding the geode full of pure quartz.

It is shadow-day. That's what she and Garrett call it. The rising sun lights up the valley and would wake everybody in the house at dawn if not for the room-darkening blinds. That part is sun-day. But after the sun balances on top of the mountain at lunchtime—you can look at it there if you squeeze your eyes all squinty—then it goes down behind the mountain and the rest of the day is in shadow.

She and Garrett are standing next to the hunk of granite that sticks up out of the ground by the front porch, breaking open the rocks they collected that morning while they were at the chalet. Grant always encourages them to pick up rocks they like and they have their own rock sacks. Of course, their mother and father don't know they found most of the ones they're breaking now while their parents were near the peak of the mountain looking for aquamarine.

They don't find any thunder eggs, though. Grant said there aren't any here, and Gabriella would have stopped looking except Garrett keeps at it. He is sure if they look hard enough, they'll find one. So she goes along, is patient with Garrett's determination to find what he's looking for—even when he sometimes gets so caught up in looking that he forgets they have to get back to the chalet by noon.

Garrett bangs the hammer down on the last of his rocks. A hunk of it breaks off, enough to see it is solid inside instead of hollow.

"I'm gonna go see the aquamarine Grant found," he says, tosses the hammer over into the dirt and starts up the steps.

"I bet he won't show you."

She giggles and he looks back and grins. Tomorrow is their birthday and last year Grant had given each of them a beautiful rock, the prettiest ones he'd found all year. Mother had almost cried because that was such a sweet thing for Grant to do. The gift was precious to Gabriella and Garrett because the family spent every summer rock hunting so their mother never got the twins birthday presents. "You can't go shopping when you're out in the middle of nowhere," she always said.

"I'm going to ask anyway. You coming?"

"In a minute."

She waits for Garrett to go into the cabin and shut the front door before she pulls the lumpy round rock out of her canvas rock sack. Somehow, she just knows this is a geode.

Today, it hadn't been Garrett who almost got them caught in the bristlecone forest. Gabriella had been the one intent on finding a rock. Not just any rock, but the one she had tossed down into the place where they always sit and dangle their feet. They go to the place almost every day, sit on the edge and toss pebbles down into the opening. They've tossed in so many, in fact, that they've used up almost all the small pebbles near the edge.

Then Gabriella had felt the cool of a shadow on her arm. That was their clock. When the shadow of the overhang stretched out to touch them, it was eleven o'clock and they had to get back to the chalet. Garrett got up to leave.

"They might come back early today," he said, and pointed to clouds that were already visible above the other side of the mountain.

Gabriella had picked up a round chunk of granite to put into her rock sack, but instead turned and chucked it into the opening. She watched it hit the ground and then saw it roll—just like a soccer ball—across the ground and disappear like a rabbit into a hole through an opening between the boulders she'd never noticed before. Garrett climbed down off the boulders and headed for the chalet. She climbed down, too, but then turned and went around to the other side of the boulder pile to see if maybe …

Garrett yelled at her, said she was going to get them into trouble, threatened to leave her there and go back without her. He'd already turned to head back up the trail when she found it. Just as she suspected, the opening at the base of the boulders went all the way through to the outside. The rock she'd tossed in from the top was lying there where it had rolled out, and it looked like the opening might be big enough—

Garrett yelled in his "last chance" tone, so she picked the rock up, shoved it into her canvas rock-collecting bag and ran to catch up with him.

She stares at the rock now and feels a tingling sensation of excitement. She places it on the piece of granite and lifts the hammer. You have to be careful. Hit a geode too hard and it will shatter. She bangs the hammer down and the rock splits open like a watermelon hit with an ax.

It is a thunder egg! Gabriella stares at it dumbfounded. Inside the cavity are the most amazing crystals she has ever seen.

"They're … bleeg," she whispers in awe. That's what she and Garrett call beautiful. You can see through the crystals like they were made of glass. The big one is clear; the smaller ones are colored—all different colors!

She leaps up to go show Garrett and then she stops because she knows what she must do with the rock. She will give half of it to Garrett as a birthday present tomorrow and save the other half to give to Grant for Christmas. She and Garrett don't ever get each other gifts, but she's a big girl now—almost eight!—old enough to start doing grown-up things. Then she pauses and a wide smile spreads across her face. Maybe Mother will be as proud of her for giving up her special rock as she was of Grant last year!

She shoves both pieces of the rock back into her rock bag. She'll hide Grant's rock in a really cool secret place she found until they're ready to go back to Pittsburgh. And she'll give Garrett his rock right after supper tomorrow night when there might be a "party." Mother never makes a cake for the twins' birthday like she does for Grant's in October—for the same reason she never buys them presents. But last year, she put candles on matching Hostess Twinkies for her and Garrett and everybody sang Happy Birthday. Gabriella hopes they'll do the same thing again this year, but even if they don't, her rock will be a great birthday surprise.

Gabriella awoke with the image of the geode so clear in her head she could almost touch it. Not the half on top of the dresser but the other half, the *amazing* other half!

She got up and crossed the room to the geode sparkling in the morning sun, watched the refracted colors dance around the center crystal.

"Maybe this belongs to you, Garrett," she whispered softly. "A birthday present you never got."

Was it possible she really did find the geode here, somewhere on this mountain? That was utterly ridiculous, of course. Nobody'd ever found geodes up here.

Surely, she'd only imagined it, conjured up the scene in her head in a dream. But it seemed too real to be a dream, too … ordinary. Details like the feel of the rock in her hand—how it was warm even though it had been lying in the shade on top of the boulder until she threw it down into the hole. There was nothing odd or distorted about the scene, either, the way dreams are fuzzy around the edges. Could it have been … real? And if it was, that, of course, begged a more important question: Where was this "special place" of hers where she'd hidden the other half of the rock?

She thought about it for three days—didn't mention it to Ty, of course, or he'd have dug up the whole mountain. There was a lot of Garrett in his nephew. She couldn't wait for Friday so she could go down to the Mercantile for supplies and tell Pedro about the dream.

Of course, that wasn't the only reason she was anxious to talk to Pedro. She was *always* anxious to talk to Pedro. His gentle voice and kind eyes made her feel … safe. In Gabriella World, that was a precious commodity, indeed.

PEDRO HAD JUST finished unloading a grocery truck and now ice picks of pain stabbed into his lower back. More irritating than the pain was the sense that he must be getting old. He was thinking about that, and other, more unpleasant thoughts, when he sat down on the porch of the Mercantile, took off his hat and wiped his brow on the back of his arm. He sat for a few minutes catching his breath, then replaced his hat and started to rise. That's when he saw Gabriella driving into town.

Seeing her planted an instant smile on his face and he sank back down and waited for her. He looked forward to his trips up the mountain to deliver her supplies, found himself watching the clock on the days she was due to come down. In fact, if he was not careful, he thought about her *a lot*—occasionally even considered making up an excuse to go up the mountain so he could see her, sit with her on the porch and talk. He knew he needed to put the brakes on, that his feelings had already edged out there past friendship. And he'd do that. He would. He wouldn't let it get ... out of hand.

There was no danger of that today, though. He was much too preoccupied to entertain fantasies about the golden-haired woman on the mountain with the sweet smile and sad hazel eyes. He listened to her account of the dream and the geode without comment. When he said nothing after she'd completed her tale, she prodded.

"Well ...?"

"Like I told Ty—anything ees possible."

"Don't give me the anything's possible line. What do you really think?"

"I think anything is possible." Before she could protest, he continued. "I really do believe that we have a much too narrow view of what could happen in our lives—both good and bad. We cruise along on autopilot, assuming that the way things are today will last forever. Only it does not work out that way."

When Gabriella said nothing, he realized how caustic he had sounded. He sighed. He needed to man up and tell her what was really bothering him. And it bothered him even more when he realized he *wanted* her to know, to understand, to ... share what he was struggling with.

"I am sorry. I heard from my ex-wife last night and that is always ... unpleasant."

Just *unpleasant*?

Once a Marine, always a Marine. His sergeant's response to the sight of a recruit parachuting into a tree and bouncing off every branch of it until he hit the ground was a simple: "That'll leave a mark."

Talking to Adriana wasn't unpleasant. It was ... maddening, infuriating, galling and ... He didn't have the right words, at least not in English, to describe it. Talking to her was impossible.

"Adriana has remarried. I met her in San Diego when I was stationed at Camp Pendleton and after the divorce she moved back. She called today— again!—about Anza going to San Diego State in the fall, in their nursing program."

He could feel his anger rising.

"You see, Adriana is the moral authority on everything in life. She knows what ees best for everybody. I bet she stops strangers on the street and tells them where they ought to go to school, who they ought to marry, what they ought to—"

He clamped down hard to shut himself up.

"Sorry. She pushes buttons I never knew I had."

He ground his teeth and stared into the distance. Jim Benninger had once called that look a "thousand-mile stare" and up at St. Elmo's Fire, you could almost believe you could see that far.

"What does Anza want to do?"

"Stay here and help me look after Angelina." He paused, tried to drain all the emotion out of the words. "Her mother does not understand that. She thinks Angelina should be in some kind of facility. A nursing home."

This was the wedge driven between them that had sent an ever-widening crack through the heart of their marriage. Nowhere inside himself could Pedro find a place that understood warehousing their precious daughter. Nowhere inside Adriana could she understand allowing the child's condition to dominate the rest of their lives. Irresistible force meets immovable object.

He took a deep breath, tried to pull back from the darkness he'd edged too close to. He cleared his throat and looked at Gabriella.

"When Anza told her mother she did *not* want to leave St. Elmo, did *not* want to move to San Diego … well, that was gasoline on hot coals—and it *blew up in Anza's face!*"

Gabriella's expression went flatline and her fingers reached up reflexively to cover her scar.

Pedro groaned. What an outrageously thoughtless thing to say.

"Gabriella, I deed not mean … I wass not talking about …" What could he say? "I am sorry. Forgive me, por favor."

PEDRO'S SPANISH ACCENT was thick. She was right. It did become more pronounced when he was upset. And she didn't want him to be. She wanted to find some way to get him off the hook for an offhand remark that meant no harm—and to shift the conversation to some subject that wasn't covered in barbed wire and razor blades.

But she didn't know how, wasn't as adept at sliding effortlessly in and out of pain the way some people could. She wanted to show as much compassion to Pedro as he'd always shown to her, but that wasn't a thing you could manufacture out of thin air. You couldn't give away something you didn't have.

"It wasn't a fire, actually," she found herself saying. "It was acid. My ex, too, although he wasn't an *ex*-husband yet when he threw it in my face."

Pedro actually gasped.

"He said he was going to make it all match—my outside and my inside, make my face as ugly as my soul."

Did I say that out loud?

In the world she had inhabited her whole life, people used rehearsed lines so they could talk to each other and not really say anything. It wasn't like that here. Gabriella had never told anybody—not the police, the prosecutor or the judge—what Smokey'd said to her the day he'd cornered her in the family room. He'd stood there with the acid in a jar, swaying because he was so drunk he could barely stand. And he'd yelled that at her. Those words were the last thing she heard before he punched her in the jaw and knocked her into the wall. She woke up in the hospital two days later with half of her face missing.

When Pedro touched her arm, his hand was shaking.

"Gabriella, please tell me you know that ees not true—what he said about choo." Pedro's accent was so pronounced he could have passed for an undocumented alien. "Please tell me you understand that the one whose soul ees hideous … ees a man who would beat up his wife." How did Pedro know Smokey knocked her around? "And a man who would throw acid in his wife's face …" Pedro ground his teeth; she could see the muscle clench in his jaw. He had gone from compassionate to a barely controlled fury. "… that man has no soul at all!"

His rage was almost more touching and comforting than his tenderness.

But Pedro didn't know what she'd done. All the things she'd done, starting when she was seven years old.

"You don't understand, Pedro. I—"

"No, *you* do not understand if you think you somehow … *deserved* thees." He reached out and actually touched the scar. His hand was still shaking. "If all our outsides matched our insides, everybody—all of us—would look hideous." He stopped, then continued in a voice as devoid of emotion as a metronome. "My scars would be bigger and uglier than—" He paused again, seemed to struggle for words. "Gabriella, scars tell us where we have been, but they do not have to control where we are going."

"*You* didn't create a monster," she said, her voice surprisingly level. "*I* did. And it takes a monster to create one."

She stood up before he could say anything else and walked up the steps to the Mercantile without looking back. He might have called out for her to stop, to wait. She wasn't sure because the only sound she could hear was a great heaving roar in her ears. She opened the door, heard the muted jingle of the bell and lost herself among a tour-busload of morning shoppers.

* * * *

Billy Whitworth stepped back and surveyed his work. It looked pretty good, if he did say so himself. The picture of a kid with owl glasses holding up a fish—looked like a trout—was a garden-variety photograph. Billy'd had to work hard to give the picture some character.

Because the St. Elmo's Fire sign above the kid's head was rustic, Billy had selected faux barn wood for the frame—it was rough-cut and looked like the sun had bleached it to a chalky gray. Then he'd used a red mat, so the kid's red shirt would "pop." All he lacked now was cutting the non-glare glass.

Billy looked at his watch. Though it was only 4:30, today was Friday and he intended to sneak out early. He and some friends were going down the Yough—the Youghiogheny River—tomorrow. It was a two-hour drive and then they had to set up camp. He'd brought his sleeping bag and tent to work with him in the trunk of his car.

Setting the picture off to the side of his workbench, Billy cleaned up the scraps of red mat material. He'd finish the picture Monday morning, take it to UPS by lunchtime. He already had the label ready: Gabriella Griffith, c/o Phillip and Natalie Griffith, 4650 Old Boston Road, Pittsburgh, PA 15227. The boss hadn't said anything about this being a rush job. The picture would be delivered by the middle of next week.

Billy flipped off the light and headed for the back door.

Ty sat on the edge of his bed trembling in the gray light of dawn, his sheets tangled and sweaty. His pillow had flopped on the floor when he jerked upright in bed, screaming. But he must have screamed only in his head, not out loud, because his mom didn't come running. His *real* mom. Not the monster with the melted zombie face.

Ty had to bite his lip to keep from bursting into tears. He wanted to dash into his mother's bedroom, crawl into bed beside her and cuddle up snug and warm, hide from the monster who was after him. Not the real one, the man in black they'd escaped in Pittsburgh, but the dream one who had come to him in South Carolina, Kentucky, Oklahoma and now here in Colorado. *And who would come to him no matter where he went for the rest of his life!* The monster with a ruined face and arms outstretched to grab him and tear him apart, rip him open with its dagger-sharp teeth and—

The boy grabbed hold of the thought, wouldn't let himself go there. He gritted his teeth and held on tight, tears streaming down his face. Gradually, the nightmare images faded and his breathing slowly returned to normal. He picked up his pillow, straightened the sheets and got back into bed. He'd lie there for a little while—didn't dare go back to sleep!—then get up and …

When Ty's eyes popped back open it was mid-morning. The cabin was silent. His mother had already left to go into St. Elmo for supplies.

Ty padded down the stairs and found his grandfather lying on his bed staring at the ceiling.

"Ty?" The old man kept staring at the ceiling, didn't look at him. "Got a headache." It was a weak whisper. "Sound … hurts."

Ty backed out of the room and closed the door quietly. Seemed like Grandpa Slappy'd had a headache every day this week. Must be the altitude.

His mother wouldn't be back until the middle of the afternoon so he had plenty of time to go to the overhang. Not that he intended to stay there all day. He remembered how his mother had said she and his uncle always went back to the chalet before noon because of the afternoon storms and he planned to be all the way back down here to the cabin by then.

He'd gotten seriously scared the first time a really bad storm hit the mountain. It was a couple of days after he got stung by that bee. The wind whistled in the trees, made an awful wailing sound. The rain pounded on the roof. And the lightning! He'd never seen lightning that close; it struck all around the cabin. Ty didn't intend to *ever* be outside in the open when a storm like that came up. He wasn't some bonehead, wasn't terminally stupid.

He and P.D. didn't bother to go to the creek and then angle through the forest along the back side of the meadow. He went straight across the meadow to the path up the mountain and through the bristlecone forest to the chalet. He didn't have to carry colored marbles in his pocket anymore when he came here because he knew the trail well, could find his way around in the maze formed by the trees that surrounded the chalet. In fact, he'd even taught P.D. a game to play there. On the command "hide" the dog would bound off into the bristlecone forest and hunker down under a low limb or beside a rock and not move until Ty came and found him.

But Ty had brought a pocketful of marbles today. He and P.D. were going to venture out beyond the part of the forest he knew. Today, they were going to the overhang to look for geodes.

Technically, he wasn't being disobedient. His mother had never told him he *couldn't* go to the chalet. By the same logic, he wasn't breaking any rules by venturing out under the overhang, either, except the rules of basic common sense. That overhang was mean-looking. One huge flat rock—like it wouldn't fit in his school gymnasium!—stuck out from the mountainside like a popsicle stick. It looked to Ty like the only thing holding it up there was a pile of rocks on the far end—and not a big pile of rocks, either. He remembered the comment his mother said his grandmother had made—that it had been hanging there like a gazillion years so there was no reason to believe it'd suddenly drop. But it sure did *look* like it was about to drop, like it was barely balanced up there at all.

Ty forgot all about the overhang, though, as soon as he got close enough to it to see what lay in the small clearing below it. Not directly under the overhang, but definitely in the flight path of the rock if it ever fell was a pile of boulders the size of Volkswagens. But these boulders weren't like the others he'd seen all over the mountain. For one thing, they were all about the same size and shape and it looked like somebody had set them there on purpose, arranged them to form what looked like a giant igloo. And it also looked like that same somebody had built steps beside the igloo. Rocks formed a natural spiral staircase that wound around the side of the igloo to the top, which was probably twenty feet off the ground.

Before Ty could say a word, P.D. bounded up the steps like a mountain goat, stopped at the top and sat down, like he was looking at something. He turned back toward Ty and barked. A single yap—his happy bark, his come-see-what-I-found bark, and his plume of a tail brushed back and forth across the rocks so furiously you could actually see the dust fly up.

Ty followed P.D. up the steps. When he got to the top he saw that P.D. was sitting beside a crevice, a hole. You couldn't see it from the ground, but the rock pile was hollow. There was an empty space between the boulders. Only it wasn't empty. Right in the middle, eight or ten feet below him, was a lone bristlecone pine tree, growing all by itself in the center of the igloo.

Ty took off his glasses, cleaned the lenses on his shirt, replaced them on his nose and studied the tree. Again, he wished he'd paid more attention in science class. But even with his limited understanding of the plant and animal kingdom, the boy knew enough to wonder how a tree could grow in there at all, how it got enough sunlight. Down in a hole like that, it couldn't have gotten more than a couple of hours a day—right around noon.

Then he noticed something else strange about it.

"That Jesus tree's not all twisted up and ugly like the others," he told P.D. "It's … pretty."

The tree was about twelve feet tall, with a straight trunk and limbs that stretched out from it in every direction as perfectly formed as an artificial Christmas tree. The limbs on the other bristlecone pine trees were all bent the same way, all pointed downhill like road signs showing the direction the wind blew.

That was it!

"This tree's not all twisted up because the rocks protect it from the wind and snow," he said, and P.D. listened attentively to every word. "Maybe they'd look like this if somebody built a wall around them."

Ty sat down, dangled his feet into the crevice and looked at the tree. He reached over then, picked up a pebble and engaged in the universal activity of little kids. One after another, he chucked pebbles into the hole and watched them disappear into the shadows. It wasn't as much fun as tossing rocks off the cliff face in front of St. Elmo's Fire. But whenever Grandpa Slappy was around, he wouldn't let Ty go anywhere near the cliff, said he'd fall off and break his neck.

While Ty sat there tossing rocks, the crevice gradually filled with light as the sun marched up the sky. Pretty soon, Ty could see dust motes in the shaft of sunlight that lit up the tree like a spotlight.

Sunlight! It must be near noon. Ty didn't realize he'd sat there so long— an hour and a half, maybe, and hadn't looked for thunder eggs at all. How had he spent that much time throwing pebbles into The Cleft?

The Cleft. Yeah, that was a good name. That's what he'd call it.

"We gotta go, P.D.," he said and looked anxiously at the blue sky he knew could turn grey and stormy in a heartbeat. As he hopped down the stairs and headed back to the chalet and the trail to the cabin, Ty felt a stab of loneliness. He had nobody to tell about finding The Cleft. It must have been wonderful to grow up like his mother had, with a twin brother to do and share everything with. No wonder she missed Uncle Garrett so much.

He turned and looked over his shoulder and determined to come back tomorrow to search for thunder eggs.

Beneath the overhang, where a rock the size of a house had been balanced all these many years, waiting for just the right moment to fall.

CHAPTER 14

Agatha Wizniuska eagerly ripped open the package forwarded from Old Boston Road in Whitehall to the house on Cedar Boulevard in Mt. Lebanon—which was coming up in the world, for sure! But she was disappointed by the contents. Wasn't a thing inside but a framed picture of a curly-haired little kid holding up a fish, and not a very big fish, neither. She stuffed the picture back into the box but didn't tape it up or anything. Let that goon put it back together when he came by to get the mail. Aggie had too much to do as it was, trying to run Bernie's whole operation until he decided to come waltzing back in here and ask her, "How yinz doin', heh?"—making fun of her Pittsburgh accent.

And when he did, she was going let that little chrome dome have it! Vanishing like he done. Here in the office on Friday moaning about all the postings on Rebecca Nightshade's fan page and nowhere on the planet the following Monday. And today was—she looked at the calendar—July 16, so he'd been gone three full weeks! Oh, she knew it had something to do with the fake disappearance of the author and her security guard, knew Bernie'd spring the stunt sooner or later and the three of them would show up with reporters all around and video-cams rolling.

But in the meantime, Aggie had to hold down the fort.

She glanced over at the framed picture on the wall of Bernie with his arm around Garrett Griffith of Withered Soul.

"Would it have killed yinz to throw a girl a warning, heh?" she asked the image.

The office door opened and in walked the suit-and-tie goon. He was all nicey nice, of course, but any fool could see his shoulders straining at his shirt and the bulge of a holster under his coat. Agatha Wizniuska didn't fall off a turnip truck yesterday.

"No bills or nothing like that," Aggie told him. "Just this." She held out the picture. "I don't s'pose yinz know when they're coming back. I need to talk to Bernie about—"

As soon as he got a good look at the picture, the man snatched it out of her hand, turned on his heel and practically ran out of the office. Him so polite and all—didn't even close the door behind him.

* * * *

Theo didn't even realize what he'd said until the words were already out there in the air and he couldn't call them back.

It was Cornelius's fault. Had to be. That danged tumor messed with his life more every day. It made him so dizzy sometimes he had to hold onto the furniture to keep from falling down. Gabriella'd noticed a couple of times and he'd explained it away, said it was the thin mountain air everybody harped about all the time. But the headaches that stabbed into his skull without warning hurt so bad they actually blinded him, couldn't see his hand in front of his face for hours at a time! He had one yesterday morning. Ty had come into his room but he didn't think the boy had noticed. If he had, Theo sure couldn't claim *that* was caused by the altitude.

And Cornelius was stealing his hearing, too, what little he had left. He'd lost every speck of it in his left ear 'fore he left Pittsburgh and now it came and went in his right ear, blinked on and off like a Joe's Beer Joint sign. And that was something he couldn't lay off on the thin air, neither. Sometimes, he'd lie awake at night wondering if losing his hearing meant that soon's he closed his eyes it'd be all over and he'd wake up in Heaven. And he'd wonder if he ought to leave. There might still be time to serve that eviction notice. He figured "good as new" was a stretch, but being able to continue breathing in and out on a regular basis for a few more years wasn't too shabby.

Couldn't do that, though. Seemed like that boy needed him more every day. He'd just have to put up with Cornelius being ornery and hope his number wasn't ready to be punched just yet.

There was one symptom, though, that had just come on recent, a new way Cornelius was messing with him. That rascal had given him a loose mouth, had somehow broke down walls that'd been securely in place for years, caused him to say things he couldn't believe'd ever fall off his own tongue.

THE LAST SAFE PLACE

This was one of those times.

He was sitting on a tree stump a few feet from the bank of Piddley Creek—*facing* the creek, of course, with his back to the cabin and The Huge. That's what he'd named the empty space out there in front of the cabin that was too big and deep to get his mind around. He wasn't any more used to it now than he'd been that first day when he climbed out of the jeep about to wet himself from scared. But he'd figured out how to cope. He didn't look at it, pretended the cabin was a thumbtack that stuck a National Geographic poster of a mountain to the sky.

Over the course of the weeks they'd spent up here, Theo had witnessed a couple of significant transformations. For starters, he'd watched his shiny bald head begin to fuzz over with a crinkly mat of nappy curls. But more important, he'd watched a glorious change take place in the hollow-eyed little boy who'd cowered in the backseat of the car the night they ran for they lives. Theo had about decided that he'd been wrong, that there wasn't something tormenting the child—something that didn't have a thing to do with that nutcase triple dipped in psycho who was after them. Until Ty woke up screaming in the middle of the night last night, that is, so loud even Theo could hear him. His bedroom was up on the second floor and by the time Theo hobbled up the steps to see to him Gabriella was already in there comforting him. She'd come out shaking her head.

"I guess he's dreaming about Yesheb coming after him," she said. "But maybe not. He started having nightmares after … you know, my face. And they really got bad after his father … died. He won't tell me about the dreams." She paused. "Maybe he'd tell you, though. Would you see if you can find out what's wrong?"

He said he'd try to get something out of the boy when they went on what had become their daily trip to the stream together. It took Theo something like a hundred years to make the journey. All them folks talking about thin air was like having a flock of birds twittering around your head—nice birds, robins and sparrows and the like—but maddening. Trouble was, them birds was right. Sometimes he had to stop two or three times to catch his breath before he made it to the creek.

Once he finally got there, though, he could sit on a log and watch Ty and P.D., talk to the boy, tease him, teach him one-liners and sort of warm himself on the little boy's smile.

He wondered if Smokey'd ever smiled like that. If he had, Theo'd missed it. But he wasn't missing this.

Only Ty wasn't smiling today.

Lord, they's something ugly eating at this boy. I don't know what it is but you sure enough do. And you know he need to get it out of the dark where it's in there festering. I'm here to listen if you'd be willing to give him a little shove.

Theo sat quiet and watched Ty try to catch a trout. The boy's face was all pinched up in concentration and those round glasses made him look all eyes—like he was a baby squirrel. But them trout was wily critters. Other than the one he'd caught with Pedro's help, Ty hadn't been able to snag a single one. Theo suspected there wasn't many fish of any kind in this piddly little creek. 'Course there could be walruses and whales in it for all he knew—the only moving water he was up close and personal with swirled around and around in a white bowl when he pushed a little silver handle.

Or water out a fire hydrant on the streets of Pittsburgh on hot summer days.

He'd intended to make some kind of remark to that effect when he opened his mouth and the wrong words fell out. What he'd meant to say was, "When I's a kid, I played in the water on Towne Street." What he did say was, "When I's a kid, I prayed the water wouldn't drown Skeet."

What'd you let me say a thing like that for, Lord?

Surely, God wasn't prodding him to go *there*. Had to be the work of that rascal Cornelius. Only the why or who wasn't near as important right this minute as the what. What was Theo going to say now?

Ty turned and looked up at him. "Who's Skeet?"

"He was my cousin. And my best friend." It was like Theo'd been injected with truth serum. He'd ought to come up with a convenient lie to end the conversation right here.

"Did he drown?"

"Yes, he did for a fact. He drowned."

Ty put his fly fishing pole down on the creek bank and walked over to stand beside him. He'd picked up on something in Theo's voice. That was another thing Cornelius was messing with. Theo couldn't keep up his Teflon front now good as he used to, couldn't be glib. Or maybe it wasn't Cornelius at all, maybe the purity in a little boy's eyes was burning away what didn't really matter anymore.

"Were you there when he drowned, Grandpa Slappy?" He pushed his glasses up on his nose and put his hand on Theo's boney shoulder. "Did you see?"

Theo couldn't find a convenient lie laying around anywhere.

"He got throwed off a bridge into the river and he couldn't swim. His head went down into that dark water and never come back up."

Some part of Theo had gone down into the water with Skeet. He was coming up now for the first time since the day more than sixty years ago when the white boys caught him and Skeet on that country road where wasn't no help in sight.

The family is in Mississippi for Granny May Belle Washington's funeral. Mama says she died of the wall-eyed epizootic. Started twitching and then her eyes rolled back in her head and she was dead.

It's hot here like Theo has never felt heat. He and Skeet sneak away from Granny's house where all the grown-ups sit and sweat, fan themselves and tell lies about how much they loved Granny. Mama always said the woman was a witch—and she used a b instead of a w—who beat her and her sisters with a belt even when they hadn't done nothing wrong at all.

The two boys strip off their white shirts buttoned up too tight at the neck. They leave them folded neat in the backseat of Uncle Rupert's coupe along with their shoes and then head toward the river down a road covered in red dust. It'll be cooler in the shade of the big bridge. They can sit there with their feet in the water, squishing red mud up between their toes.

A car drives by, stirs up the dust and it sticks to the sweat on their scrawny, bare chests in a sticky film. The car stops down the road in front of them, just sits there.

"What them fools doin'?" Theo asks Skeet.

Skeet's lower lip is fat, sticks out like he's pouting even when he's not. He's two years older than Theo, but small, still looks twelve. He lives two doors down from Theo on Towne Street in Pittsburgh and can make a saxophone sing.

Skeet slows down, then stops. Theo keeps walking until Skeet reaches out and grabs his arm.

"Them's white boys in that car," Skeet says. "We hadn't ought to walk by it. Let's take to the woods."

The two boys turn off the road and start toward the trees about fifty yards away. All at once, the four doors of the parked car open and teenage boys pile out hollering, "Let's git us some niggers."

Theo paused in the telling, knew it wasn't a story he'd ought to share with his grandson. Not sixty years later. Not now, with things different, changed. Oh, lots of white people still hated. Scratch deep enough and you'd find that almost all of them thought they was better than you. But they covered it up these days, had to, so most times you didn't have to see it, glazing over they faces like slime on a rotten tomato.

Mixed like he was, Ty didn't need to hear this.

So why was Theo telling it?

"Grandpa Slappy, what happened to you and Skeet?"

"We run, but I was faster. I made it to the trees. Skeet didn't."

"And then?"

"I hid in the woods and watched. Them boys took Skeet to the bridge and dangled him over the river upside down. He was yelling, begging them to let him be and they was hooting and laughing. And then … he was falling."

It seemed to take forever for Skeet to hit the water. He was flailing his arms and legs the whole way down, like maybe he could spin fast enough to curdle the air and it'd hold him up.

"He landed in that dark water and he was gone. He never come back up. And them boys up on the bridge, they stopped laughing then. Got real quiet, stood there looking, waiting for him to bob up to the top of the water and swim over to the shore. Or walk over. The river was deep under that bridge, but downstream there was places you could wade across it. When he didn't come up, they started hollering at each other, yelling 'What'd you let him go for?' and 'I thought you had him!' Then they took off running for the car like the devil himself was after them."

Theo remembered the looks on their faces as they ran.

"I was standing in the edge of the woods when they come streaking by but they didn't see me, was so hell-bent on getting in that car and getting out of there. But there was one, a fat kid couldn't run fast as the others. He was huffing and puffing and sweating. He saw me and he stopped dead in the dirt in front of me, just looking. There was tears in his eyes and streaming down his fat cheeks. And I knew he didn't mean nothing, hadn't intended no harm and now he'd gone and killed somebody and he was gonna have to live with that the rest of his life."

"What did you do, Grandpa Slappy? Did you call the police?"

Wasn't no sense in trying to explain to a boy like Ty that the police wouldn't have done anything if he'd told. Which he didn't.

"This is the honest truth. I never told a single living soul what I saw that day until right now, this minute."

Ty didn't ask him why not, but he told him anyway. "I was too scared, thought it was my fault it happened 'cause I's the one talked Skeet into sneaking off. All these years, Skeet's people thought he walked out on that bridge all by himself, fell off it and drowned. And I never told 'em no different."

He didn't say the rest of it out loud. Couldn't. So he whispered. Told Ty about the nightmares, the images that haunted him, how it had all took root inside and grew into tangled, poisonous vines that had wrapped themselves tight around his soul and held him prisoner for all these many years. Wouldn't let him ride in a boat or go swimming or climb trees.

"What about the boys who did it? What … happened to them?" Ty's voice was small, sounded scared plum to death.

"I don't have no idea, son. No idea at all."

* * * *

When Yesheb returned to Chicago from New Hampshire, he went into seclusion. He saw no one, ate almost nothing, was tormented in body and soul night and day. His being walked jagged paths of unimaginable pain and impenetrable darkness; he knew an agony unparalleled in human existence.

His caretakers see only that he lies in the dark on the floor of a filthy room, unwashed, unshaven, catatonic. He knows they fear for his sanity, but they do not realize that far more than his sanity is at stake here. The futures of kingdoms/worlds/universes rest on his shoulders.

When he finally returns to his body, and his body returns to the world, he is not the same man who left. His focus is different. He has clarity, now, determination and confidence.

His hair is different, too. It has turned pure white.

For the next week, he pours over the book of prophesy, the words that had awakened in him an understanding of what his destiny demanded. He studies *The Bride of the Beast* page by page, line by line—and confirms what was brought to his mind during his torment. He understands now that his plans have been thwarted for a reason—they were doomed to failure from the beginning because his approach was all wrong. When he finds her, and he is certain now that he will find her in time, he must *not* frighten her. Though he desires her fear above all other things in life, he must hide his desire. There will be time later for fear. Now, he must overwhelm her with his charm, woo her with his gentleness, be everything she ever wanted in a man. The prophesy foretells that she will fall under his spell and eagerly give up her soul to be with him. But he cannot *demand* it of her, cannot force her to wed him. The decision must be *hers* and everything he has done since the first moment he saw her has been counterproductive to that end. He has been a fool and he has paid dearly for his foolishness. He has a lot of ground to make up in a short period of time. But he is supremely confident. He has yet to meet a woman who did not fall for him. Zara would be no different.

He is not at all surprised when he receives an urgent call from the head of his investigation team. Not surprised by the news the man brings. He knew it would happen like this. It was destined to be.

While Yesheb examines the photograph of Zara's son, the operative speaks in succinct sentences, no elaboration. Yesheb has taught his men to get to the point quickly.

"The picture was emailed to the photography studio by Rev. James Benninger. Rev. Benninger got it from a man named Pedro Rodriguez."

The investigator pauses for effect, sees no reaction on Yesheb's face and continues.

"Here are full reports on both of them. I've marked in red what is most significant to our search." The highlighted description of the minister's mountainside cabin and the town of St. Elmo plants a rueful smile on Yesheb's lips.

So Zara really is in the mountains … but not in New Hampshire. The smarmy little agent at the bottom of the Monongahela River beside the security guard and his mutt wasn't completely wrong after all.

THE LAST SAFE PLACE

"It took some digging to find their connection to the subject …" Yesheb detects a need for validation here, a bloodhound angling for a pat on the head for finding a lost child. "… but we determined that it's possible she spent time in that cabin when she was eight years old. Her older brother died in 1982 and the death certificate was issued in Chaffee County, Colorado."

Yesheb says nothing because his mind is whirring, but the operative takes his silence as an indication that he should elaborate.

"I have a full extraction plan mapped out, sir. We could land a helicopter within fifty yards of—"

"You are not to go anywhere near that cabin!" Yesheb says. "Is that understood?"

"Yes sir."

"The only thing I want from you is confirmation that she's there, positive identification. That's *all*. When I'm certain, *I* will make plans."

Once the prophesies are fulfilled, Yesheb can summon the assistance of legions of demons, of his human operatives, of an army of servants and underlings. But in the beginning, he must succeed or fail under his own power and strength.

He glances at the clock on his desk with the date and time. "There is no hurry. We have five days, plenty of time to develop a foolproof strategy."

He tosses the Rev. Benninger report on the desktop and opens the one on Pedro Rodriguez, which he is certain contains everything the man has ever done, where he lived and worked, who he slept with, married or cheated on, everything down to what's tattooed on his backside. The person who took the picture of Zara's son is likely her ally. Knowledge is power and it is always wise to know more about your adversary than he knows about you.

Yesheb realizes the operative is still standing in front of his desk. He looks up at the man questioningly.

"Sir … about the reward …"

"*Reward?* You think you bumbling morons earned a reward? You didn't find her; she found you. I'll let you know when I require your services again. Leave me."

"Yes sir."

Yesheb is surprised he doesn't salute, but he does pivot on his heel and march out of the room with military precision. Yesheb sits alone with the framed photograph of Zara's son and a trout. He stares at it, studies it, and a smile creeps up to his mouth and soon captures his whole face.

This is it; this really is it. He makes a Tiger Woods fist-pumping motion and hisses a single word under his breath.

"Gotcha!"

CHAPTER 15

Pedro picked up Angelina's right hand and gently cleaned it with the sea sponge full of sweet-scented soap. He'd tried lots of things over the years looking for the softest possible material, before he happened upon a sea sponge. Who would have thought something as rough and scratchy when it was dry could be so incredibly soft wet? He squeezed the soapy sponge in the basin of water and smiled. When he and Ty had gone fishing, the boy had commented, "Imagine how deep the ocean would be if it wasn't full of sponges." Had to be one of Theo's lines.

Ty's humor was only surface, though. Underneath the smile was a lonely little boy who needed a father, someone to—

Whoa, there, hold your horses. That position may be vacant, but nobody's asked you *to apply for the job.*

Pedro needed to tread lightly here. He was definitely in a mine field and any wrong step could set off an emotional explosion. He had not felt anything for a woman in ... okay, way too long. Just like Angelina's fingers had drawn up into something like fists because she never moved them, his emotions had atrophied from disuse. Until Gabriella walked into the Mercantile trying to act calm and self-assured when he could see the pain beneath the façade as clear as trout in a mountain stream. He had discovered that day that his emotions had a lot more life in them than he'd imagined. But Gabriella had been so traumatized, how could she ever trust a man again, how ...?

Just let it go. Back off and let it go.

He picked up a fluffy towel to dry Angelina's hand. As he did, he tried hard not to imagine her hand holding a fishing pole, sunshine sparkling in her black hair. She probably would not have wanted to go fishing, though. Anza had been a girly-girl even as a toddler, liked pretty dresses and dolls, turned up her nose when Joaquin came in from outside dirty and sweaty.

But maybe not. Maybe Angelina would have been—

Don't! Would-have-beens were dangerous waters. Swim out far in them and a riptide picks you up and carries you out to sea.

The ventilator puffed and sighed, puffed and sighed and the chest of the china doll lying perfectly still on the bed rose and fell each time it did. That was the only sign of life in her. Every couple of days, he'd disconnect the breathing tube and watch her chest rise and fall on its own for a while. Five minutes. Ten, sometimes. But she tired quickly, grew weak. As soon as she began to have trouble breathing, he hooked her back up to the machine. The doctors said it might be possible to wean her off the ventilator, let her gradually build up strength breathing on her own. They also said her heart might stop from the effort.

The bell on the door of the post office/laundromat side of the Mercantile jingled when someone stepped inside.

"I'm in here," he called out to the customer. Whoever it was would have to wait until he was finished getting Angelina ready for the day. He had to take care of the child and run the cash register in the store at the same time because Anza had gone to a dentist's appointment.

If Anza leaves, this will be the new normal.

He had wallowed the whole thing around in his head over and over until all the arguments had worn so thin he could not even donate them to Goodwill. Once he had calmed down, he had been forced to admit that his screwy ex-wife had been right about one thing—Anza had no future in St. Elmo. But she was so devoted to Angelina it would break her heart to leave. Should he … *force* her to broaden her horizons, experience more of the world than a little town on a mountainside? Better question: *Could* he force her to go? Could he *make* her leave … and could he make himself demand it?

Reality check: How on earth could he do life without Anza to help him care for her little sister? Oh, his mother lived down the street and she always helped when she could. But she was seventy years old and had her own medical issues. The neighbors always pitched in whenever there was an emergency. But on a day-in, day-out basis, Pedro and Anza were the ones who kept the wheels on the bus. Without Anza, how—?

The saloon doors that separated his home from the store swung inward and Gabriella took an uncertain step through them. His heart ramped into a gallop at the sight of her and a wide smile spread across his face. So much for *back off and let it go.*

He could tell she was instantly ill-at-ease at the sight of Angelina. He had forgotten about that part, how seeing the little girl so helpless made some people feel awkward at first. No one in St. Elmo was uncomfortable with Angelina anymore; almost all outsiders were.

"I don't need anything right now," Gabriella said. "You can go ahead with … I can get my laundry started before I get supplies."

"I will not be long. Come back when you get the machines loaded and running. The coffee ees not out of a fancy rocket engine but it ees fresh."

"Okay, thanks," she said and hurried out.

That woman was as twisted up inside as last year's Christmas lights, had so much hurt down in the depths of her hazel eyes, so much sadness. Pedro supposed it was what drew him to her—the pain. He had been down that road. And if what he suspected about her was true, her pain had driven her to the place where the Wild Things are.

She came back a few minutes later with a smile on her face that never reached her eyes. He knew she had screwed up her courage to come through the door chatty and cheerful, pretending Angelina was not there.

Pedro was not okay with that.

"Tell me where the cups are and I'll pour us both some coffee," she said.

"I already have a cup." He gestured toward the hospital bed tray that stretched across the end of Angelina's bed. "You can warm it up though. Get a cup for yourself in that cabinet beside the fireplace."

She poured coffee for herself then brought the pot over to pour him some. She did not look at Angelina.

"It ees all right," he said. She looked a question at him that he answered before she wrapped it in words. "It ees hard to know how to act." He nodded toward Angelina. "Hard to know what to say. I understand."

He could feel it coming then, the way you can feel something hurling at you in the dark. *The question.* He knew he had left himself open for it, practically invited it. But it had been a long time since he had had to answer it and he had forgotten how hard it was.

She didn't ask. She did look at Angelina, though, almost caressed the child's face with her eyes.

« 209 »

Pedro put the towel down on the tray and crossed to the table and stood with his back to Gabriella. He felt the words leave his mouth without consciously willing them to go.

"I left her in the car, strapped into her car seat when she was six months old. Forgot about her." A heartbeat pause. "Eet was July, a hot day."

He turned around. Gabriella's face was white. She lifted her hands to cover her mouth as tears welled in her eyes. Slowly shaking her head back and forth, she whispered, "Oh, Pedro, no …"

He could explain what happened.

How his only two employees had *both* called in sick, left him busier than a one-armed paperhanger.

How Adriana always dropped Anza and Joaquin off at their aunt's house in Buena Vista on the days she worked as a part time nurse in the infirmary at the prison.

How *she* always took the baby to day care.

How that morning Adriana had gone in early so he had to make the kid run.

Adriana had strapped Angelina into her car seat. Anza and Joaquin had argued and bickered nonstop all the way to their aunt's house and the car was blessedly quiet after they got out. Angelina had fallen asleep.

He could explain how … but he didn't. It was hard to breathe. It still hurt so bad to go there it literally took his breath away. His mouth went dry, his heart thudded with a pedantic clumping sound in his chest. Sweat popped out on his brow. He sank down on the bench beside the table, facing Gabriella. He stared at the floor, couldn't look at her.

Finish it!

The words were made of daggers and razor blades and broken glass.

"I parked in front of the store. I deed not find her until … about noon."

A line has stretched out in front of the cash register five deep all morning, even before the tour bus arrived. Now a herd of large women wearing uniformly ugly flowered dresses crowds the narrow aisles of the Mercantile babbling about everything and nothing in unpleasant, nasal voices he is trying hard to ignore. But one voice rises above the others. It belongs to a frazzled woman, her face a bad-sunburn red, fanning herself with an ugly pink sun visor.

THE LAST SAFE PLACE

"... *and I said to Edna, 'Edna, I just think it's awful to leave that little baby out there in a car like that with the windows rolled up. It's too hot—'"*

Realization slams into Pedro's chest with the force of a hundred-ton wrecking ball. He drops the gallon of milk he is placing in a customer's sack and it bounces twice before the plastic container splits open and splashes milk all over the wooden floor. He shrieks an inarticulate, yearning wail of denial and terror and slogs through air as thick as quicksand.

Everything has cranked down into slow motion.

He is at the door, shoves a camera-laden tourist out of the way.

He races down the porch steps at a crawl.

The car is locked; the keys are in the cash register drawer.

He slams his elbow into the driver's door window. Hits it again and again until it shatters, and all the time he hears someone screaming and the someone is Pedro. The blood on his fingers makes it hard to pull up the button on the back door.

Angelina is limp, not sweating.

He whispers her name.

Calls her name.

Shrieks her name.

But she doesn't open her eyes.

After that, reality breaks into shards of jagged glass that shift like the colors in a kaleidoscope to form the images and moments he remembers. The space in between those moments is blank.

At times, Pedro seems to be on a dark stage in front of a large audience and he wanders around the stage until he happens to step into the beam of a spotlight and is momentarily illuminated before he steps out again. Other times, he is standing on some tall white cliff somewhere overlooking the sea and at regular intervals the beam of a distant lighthouse shines on him for a moment and then passes on.

When Pedro is in the light, he is aware of and can relate to people, events and life. When he is in the darkness, he is as cold and dead as he prays to be with every breath he takes.

At some point in the telling of the story, Gabriella had left Angelina's bedside and now sat next to Pedro on the bench. He couldn't look up, couldn't meet her eyes.

Go ahead. Tell her the rest, all of it.

"I served a year in prison for first degree assault and endangering the welfare of a minor. The remainder of the sentence was probated." He was surprised that his voice was steady, marveled at the body's ability to level the ship in the midst of a storm. "And St. Elmo, the whole town … they took it hard. Some of them walked by the car that morning, came into the store, bought their groceries, mailed their letters, did their laundry and walked back by the car when they left. But everybody was caught up in their own lives, doing their own thing. Nobody noticed her. That is why they all feel so … protective now." He let out a long breath. "Communal guilt."

He had not meant to say that last part.

Gabriella reached out and touched his arm.

"I … know about guilt," she said.

She wanted to say more. He watched her wrestle with it, then spared her from having to ask.

"You want to know how I do it," he said. "How I live with what I did."

"I've seen you, *watched* you. How did you get there, on the other side of it?"

"The God-forgiveness is the easy part. You only have to ask. But forgiving yourself … that is a get-up-every-morning-and-do-it-again thing. Some days I manage, other days … not so much."

"I can't." The defeat in her voice was heartbreaking.

"Your older brother's death, that was not your—"

"Yes, it was. And so was Garrett's."

G‌ABRIELLA WONDERED IF the look she'd seen on Pedro's face as he told his story was what other people saw on hers sometimes but didn't know why. Didn't know a movie was playing in her head and she was the star. A horror movie.

Pedro had spent every speck of emotional energy he had to lift up that horrible weight out of his heart and lay it before her, steaming and stinking in the sun. She understood that he believed what he'd done was an act so heinous nobody could possibly empathize with it. But he was wrong.

"I talk to him even now sometimes," she said. "Garrett. He's the other half of me that's always missing. He left a huge hole in my world and I still stumble into it if I don't look where I'm going. It's hard to crawl out." She took a deep breath. "In the beginning, I didn't. Crawl out. I stayed there, down in the dark pit. Lived there. Died there, but kept breathing."

She suspected she was babbling. She didn't know for sure except that Pedro wasn't saying anything. But he probably had no air or words left to speak even if she weren't rattling on and on.

"When we were little, I'd have a fever when Garrett got sick and he'd throw up when I had the flu. After Grant died, we had no one, only each other. Nobody else. Being that close you just *know* … One day on my way home from the studio, I got this sudden scared, sick feeling in my stomach. I knew it was what Garrett was feeling, too."

She told Pedro how she'd called Garrett on her cell phone as she drove to his house, about the deadness of his voice, how it was like he was reading the instructions for assembling a barbeque grill instead of explaining why he was going to kill himself.

Pedro flinched.

"I have been where your brother was. I was planning to … if it had not been for Jim Benninger, I … he stopped me."

"I tried to stop Garrett. He was drunk and high. But it wasn't the booze and the drugs talking. It was Garrett's soul. I told you how neither of us remembered everything about the day Grant was killed. Only pieces. That day when we were twelve and found the picture of Grant, Garrett told me what our mother had said about wishing she'd gotten an abortion and never had us. But that wasn't all she'd said."

Gabriella's hands are shaking so violently she can barely hold the cell phone to her ear and the car on the road. It's rush hour; she is only inching forward. At one point she screams, just screams—so loud that the driver in the next car turns and looks at her.

"You don't know what Mother said to me that day—"

"Yes, I do. You told—"

"*I told you what she said to us. Not what she said to me. She screamed at me that it was all my fault. She dragged me over to Grant's body, and the smell … I gagged and she grabbed my neck and pushed my face down until it was just inches from Grant's, the skin was … black.*" Gabriella hears him make a *grunting, guttural sound deep in his throat, the dying cry of an antelope being ripped apart by jackals.* "And she said, 'Look what you did! You killed him!'"

Then their mother yanked Garrett upright and spit words into his face, told him she knew it had been his idea to leave the chalet when they weren't supposed to because he was always the instigator, the rebellious one, the evil one and Gabriella was a pathetic little mouse with no mind of her own.

"She said I might as well have put a gun to his head and pulled the trigger." Garrett paused then and continued in a monotone, a dead voice. "She said, 'You killed your only brother. You killed my only son. You're a murderer. That's what you are—a murderer!"

And in a sudden flash, Gabriella sees down a tunnel of memory. She and Garrett in the chalet. He's shaking his head, doesn't want to go with her. He has a stomachache.

"No, Garrett!" she cries into the phone. "You're wrong. Listen to me. You didn't do it; I did."

She has pulled off the highway onto the street where they'd lived as children—before the end of the world. She can see the house halfway down the block. But it seems to be moving away from her. Like in a nightmare, she drives faster and faster toward it, but can't seem to get any closer.

And time snaps back into place and she is in his driveway, wailing into the phone as she lurches out of the car.

"Garrett, no. You were sick that day! Don't you remember? You wanted to stay in the chalet. I was the one. I wanted to—"

"Drumma du, Gabriella."

"Garrett—!"

She is on the front porch, reaching for the doorknob when she hears the stereo sound—in her phone and in the house—of a gun going off inside.

She didn't cry when she told Pedro that she opened the door and saw what was left of her brother after he put a shotgun into his mouth and pulled the trigger.

And some part of her understood that telling a story like that without tears was like dumping a motorcycle and sliding across the pavement without protective leathers. Your soul's contact with the surface of that kind of horror would rip the skin off all the way down to the bone.

"Both my brothers died because of me. I killed them."

Pedro reached out and took her chin and turned her face toward him. "You know that ees not true."

"No, actually, I don't."

"Gabriella, it was an accident! You were only seven years old!" His Spanish accent hijacked his speech and his words ran together. "If Ty had accidentally hurt somebody when he was seven, would you hold that against him? Would you want him to suffer for it for the rest of his life?"

"How do you forgive yourself? It doesn't help to know you *should*. It isn't about what you know in your head. It's bigger than that. Uglier. Meaner."

"Ees that what you meant when you said you had created a monster?"

The mention of Yesheb was like running into a brick wall at a dead run. She staggered back from it, dazed.

"No … I didn't … the monster's real. He's flesh and blood. And he's out there right now searching for me." She heard her next words drop out of her mouth but had no memory of forming them in her head. "I'm Rebecca Nightshade. I wrote …" She realized all at once what she'd said.

"*The Bride of the Beast*," Pedro finished for her. "I know. At least, I suspected."

Her head snapped up. "You do? But how …?" Then it hit her. "Does *everybody* know?"

"No. Well, I cannot swear to that, but nobody has mentioned it to me. And if *anybody* had figured it out, *everybody* would know it. Small town—hundredth monkey."

She had no idea what he meant and her confusion showed on her face.

"You know, the theory that if ninety-nine monkeys know something the hundredth will know, too, just because the others do. These people live in each other's pockets. There are no secrets in St. Elmo."

"How did you figure it out?"

"From your picture on the back jacket of the book." Before she could react, he continued. "But I am good at that, at faces, at recognizing people from pictures even when details—hair, beards, things like that—are different. I missed a real career opportunity in airport security."

He didn't say anything about the scar, how it was a dead giveaway. She appreciated that.

"And you won't …?"

"Tell anybody? Of course not." He paused. "But I do not get it. The monster in the book is made up. How could he be plotting to kill you?"

She sighed. In for a penny, in for a pound.

"Not kill me, kidnap me. A fan has been stalking me. He believes he has opened up a door in night itself, crossed over from the Endless Black Beyond for a purpose and I'm the purpose."

"That does not make sense."

"Crazy people don't make sense. He's … evil."

"And he is stalking you because—what? He thinks *you are* Zara?"

Her eyes grew wide in surprise.

"Sí, I have read the book. I found it on top of a dryer after some tourists were here doing laundry. I have … trouble sleeping at night sometimes. The writing's excellent. God gave you an incredible gift."

Gabriella was suddenly deadly cold.

"Is that it? Is that why all this is happening? I used a … gift from God to create evil and now—"

"Do you honestly think God sent some lunatic gunning for you because he did not like the book you wrote?"

"If you read the book, you know the stalker only has two days. This is the third full moon. If he can't find me in two days …"

"I do not believe you are at St. Elmo's Fire by accident. Unless you left a trail of bread crumbs behind you, The Beast of Babylon will not find you there. Hang on." He paused, struggled to smile and actually managed it. "In the words of that great theologian Dory the Fish, 'just keep swimming, just keep swimming, just keep swimming …'"

She looked down and realized she was still clutching her coffee cup in her hand. She hadn't taken a single drink. It was cold now.

"Let me warm that up for you," Pedro said. She caught herself before she blurted out, "You warm up everything for me, Pedro."

A little over an hour later, Gabriella carried a laundry basket full of clean clothes down the steps of the Mercantile and loaded it into the back of her jeep. Pedro brought out a box of supplies and she was ready to head back up the mountain. As she got in behind the wheel, she noticed a gawking tourist across the street snapping pictures with his phone—of everything he saw—the buildings, the trees, the mountains, the flowers. The sight made her smile. She'd only been here a little less than two months, but St. Elmo had come to feel like home.

She pulled out of her parking space and before she drove away she called out to the tourist what the bag lady had said to her a lifetime ago, "I hope you enjoy our mountains."

T*he tourist smiled* and nodded, then stood in the street and watched the blonde woman in the jeep drive out of town. As soon as she was gone, he emailed the photographs he'd taken of her to his boss. He'd used a phone to look less conspicuous, but his was an iPhone 4, the latest model, with a five-megapixel camera. Even had a zoom. Four clear, close-up shots of her face—in good light. Paid special attention to her right cheek. You could see a scar there even with heavy makeup covering it. Got two really good shots of that. His boss wanted verification of the woman's identity and the pictures he'd sent would leave no doubt. They'd either confirm that she was, or make it clear that she wasn't who his boss was looking for, some woman named Zara.

* * * *

Oblivious to the storm, Yesheb crosses the empty street slowly. Partly because without his cane he still has a slight limp. But mostly because he is savoring this moment, his moment. He wants to remember every detail of the day he and Zara become one.

The storm sprang up shortly after midnight. Just as he knew it would! He had stood out in the parking lot of the motel in Buena Vista with his arms spread wide, his face lifted to the torrential rain, welcoming it, feeling the wind lash its approval and blessing on his quest. Then he returned to his room and went over with his team the timing of their two-pronged assault one final time. Rainwater ran out of his white hair and dripped off his face onto the pile of aerial photos of Chaffee County, Colorado, two of them with locations circled in bright red. One of those locations was a small hanging valley 2, 600 feet below the 14,269-foot summit of Mount Antero.

The chopper pilot pointed out, as if it were new information to Yesheb, that the "extraction" would be dangerous if it was still storming when Yesheb activated his call signal—and the forecast called for scattered thunderstorms all day.

"Even if the storm's on the back side of the mountain, wind gusts on the mountaintop could reach 80 miles per hour, with wind shears that—"

"The storm will not be a problem. I'll take care of it."

And he would! He had been infused with such power since his time of seclusion that there was nothing he couldn't do. The wind and rain would obey his commands. The dog, the growling beast at the airport, would yelp at his merest glance, tuck his tail between his legs and slink away. The old man would be struck dumb in awe. And Zara, his beloved Zara, would swoon into his arms, willingly offering her son's life to seal their union. Yesheb's time was so near his two worlds almost overlapped. He could sense the presence of legions of demons awaiting his command. His blue eyes sparkled with the reflected flames from the other realm.

He feels strength pulse through his veins with every heartbeat as he reaches the wooden sidewalk that runs the length of the pathetic cluster of buildings, deserted now as rain pelts them and puddles in potholes in the street. Yesheb has glided through the torrent between the raindrops and now stands perfectly dry before the door of the St. Elmo's Mercantile.

CHAPTER 16

The bell on the door jingled and Pedro looked up to see a lone man drenched to the skin, dripping water in a pool around him as if he had made no effort at all to stay dry.

He was the first customer Pedro had had all day. No fun hiking mountain trails in the rain—particularly not a cold rain like this one. His friend Dan, who managed the Mount Princeton Hot Springs resort, always had the opposite problem. The tourists staying there loved to sit out in the hot springs when it was pouring. Had to drag them inside to keep the lot of them from being struck by lightning.

"Good morning," Pedro said.

"Yes," the man said and stepped out of the shadows into the glow of the front set of fluorescent bulbs hanging from the store's ceiling.

His hair, plastered down to his skull, was either white or a pale shade of blonde. Hard to tell in the yellow fluorescent light. What was impossible to miss was his striking good looks. He had the perfect features of a male model, and maybe that's what he was. He was outfitted right out of an L.L.Bean catalogue—windbreaker, cargo pants, hiking boots, the works. All appeared to be brand new.

"You look like a man who could use some coffee. I lit a fire in the fireplace this morning to knock the chill out of the air if you would like to warm up."

"I'd like that." Then he added, "Please." He turned and walked toward the swinging saloon doors into Pedro's kitchen.

How does he know where the fireplace is?

Pedro followed the stranger as he stepped through the doors, but the man didn't go anywhere near the crackling fire in the fireplace on the wall. Instead, he walked purposefully across the room and stopped beside Angelina's bed, though he paid her no attention, merely stood with his back to her, facing the door.

Something was wrong here, way wrong. Pedro's heart began to rattle in his chest. He never should have invited the stranger into his home. Instinctively, he fell back on Marine Corps training, sized the man up and considered how he would take him down if he had to.

Anza came into the room from the back hallway, saw the man and flashed him a radiant smile.

Pedro casually stepped in front of the table so that he was between the man and his daughter, though the visitor gave no sign that he had even noticed her. And that right there told Pedro there was definitely something wrong with the guy.

"I will get you some coffee and you can take it with you into the store while you do your shopping," Pedro said, and turned to the table for a cup.

"Actually, I didn't come here to shop." The man's tone was almost pleasant, but not quite. And Pedro had the strange, momentary impression that there were too many teeth in the man's smile. "What I need from you, Pedro, is the key to the gate on the trail up to St. Elmo's Fire."

Y<small>ESHEB WATCHES THE</small> man's jaw drop and almost laughs out loud.

"It is honorable of you to place yourself in front of Anza, but do you really think you could protect her?" Then he glances pointedly toward the motionless child on the hospital bed. "Either one of them, if I chose to do them harm? Which I won't if you cooperate."

Anza looked confused. "Papa …?"

Yesheb doesn't quite know how to read the look on Pedro's face. Clearly, it isn't fear, though. It might have been recognition. Perhaps Zara told this man about him. After all, he is the caretaker of the cabin where she is staying, had been providing her groceries twice a week. And she must surely be lonely up there on the mountainside with nobody but an old man and a little kid to talk to. Yesheb feels a stab of jealousy. His carefully devised plan calls for the elimination of Pedro and his family—leave no witnesses. But now that task has taken on an added delight.

"The man who owns that cabin left strict instructions that I was to give a key only to his *invited* guests. You're not one of them. Sorry."

There is a calm in the Hispanic man's response that unnerves Yesheb.

"Oh, but I am a guest. Not of Rev. Benninger's but of the lovely lady who is staying there now. As a matter of fact, we're engaged to be married. Very soon."

Yesheb sees the man's eyes widen slightly and his jaw clench. He *does* know. Oh, Yesheb will very much enjoy killing this man! He might even take his time doing so, inhale the intoxicating aroma of his screams. But first things first. He needs the key. His men could simply have picked the lock, of course, or blown it up. But the gate is a barrier between him and Zara and prophesies are clear that *he* must overcome every obstacle in his path on his own. And he will.

Turning casually, he picks up the electric cord that stretches from Angelina's ventilator to an outlet on the wall. The moment he touches it, Pedro tenses to spring at him.

"Don't!" Yesheb warns, "unless you want me to unplug this."

"Go ahead." Pedro's voice is cold. "Pull the plug. See what happens."

What an odd thing to say.

"Come now, let's have that key so things don't have to get ... unpleasant."

Anza squeaks out a little scream. "Papa, who is ...?" She turns to Yesheb, her eyes pleading. "Sir, you don't understand what will happen if you unplug Angelina's ventilator."

"Oh, yes, I do. The little girl here, Angelina—what a lovely name—will stop breathing. That's what happens to a person in a permanent vegetative state without a ventilator." His voice becomes hard, brittle. He drops the next words individually into the dead air that stretches out like a dark pool between them.

Four plops. "Give. Me. That. Key."

"No."

The simple act of calm defiance shakes Yesheb to his core. When he yanks on the ventilator cord and the plug leaps out of the wall socket, the action is almost as much in surprise at the man's denial as in retaliation for it.

He expects the child to sigh out a breath and stop breathing altogether. She doesn't.

He doesn't expect the whole world to erupt in a hoarse, honking cry. It does.

If an air raid siren married a smoke alarm, their firstborn would be the sound that now blasts out a loudspeaker mounted somewhere on the front porch of the building. With a revving-up, grinding-toward-a-crescendo quality, the wailing cry gets louder and louder until it threatens to burst Yesheb's eardrums.

Before he has time to recover from his surprise, the bell on the front door of the store dings, he hears running footsteps and a man bursts through the saloon doors into the room. He is huge, has a full, bushy beard and long hair that's soaked. Following in his footsteps is a woman with tattoos covering her arms and legs and close behind her is a woman in a paint-splattered suit jacket and long skirt. An old Indian man hobbles into the room from a back entrance, followed by a bald man with some kind of red mark splattered on the top of his wet head and a fat Hispanic woman with a herd of small, rain-drenched children.

It takes less than a minute from the time he pulled the plug out of the wall for the room to fill with people—maybe two dozen of them. All of them look at him, surprised and confused, and he realizes he still has the ventilator cord in his hand. Instinctively, he drops it. Pedro takes two steps to the outlet, plugs the cord back into the socket and the screeching sound stops abruptly in mid-squall.

Into the silence that follows, Pedro says, "I warned you," his tone surprisingly mild-mannered.

Yesheb's eyes dart from one face to another around the room. It isn't supposed to go down like this! He is in charge. How could this have happened? Oh, not just the people, the *opposition*. A powerful force has been set against him. He can almost see it, in fact, and the light makes him squint. He can certainly feel it, incredibly strong. The copper taste of fear fills his mouth and makes him instantly nauseous.

A woman's voice purrs with derision in his ear. *Are you some cowardly dog that tucks its tail between its legs and slinks away?*

Surely you're not ... afraid. Are you? A man's voice, speaking Arabic.

Then The Voice roars in his head with a volume ten times that of the siren.

You will stand!

Yesheb is far more frightened of The Voice than of any fate this world could deal him. The crowd's shock is wearing off.

"What'd you set the alarm off for, Pedro?" the tattooed woman asks. "Why'd—"

That moment of distraction gives Yesheb the edge he needs. He reaches into his shoulder holster and withdraws his Glock 22 and points it at Pedro. The crowd gasps. Pedro steps back in surprise.

Yesheb is in charge again.

"Give me that key—now!"

Still, the Hispanic man doesn't respond with the fear Yesheb expects—*needs*. He merely looks around and asks, "You planning on shooting all of us?"

The fat Hispanic woman makes a strangled, squealing sound and crosses herself.

"There are only fifteen rounds in that Glock. You cannot kill everybody."

"No, but I can kill …" he turns and shoves the barrel of the gun up against the temple of the little girl in the bed, "… *her!*"

Pedro's face turns white and Yesheb knows he has him. "But perhaps you'd like for me to kill her. You poached her brain like an egg in the backseat of a car eight years ago. Maybe it would be better for everybody if I blew what little gray matter she has left all over that wall."

"*No!* Please …" Pedro's face is a twisted mask of fear and indecision.

"I will count to three. One. Two. Th—"

"Okay! Just don't … okay. I will give it to you." He sticks his hand into his pocket and withdraws a key ring and begins to thumb through the keys on it.

"Don't bother trying to switch keys on me; I know they're all labeled." Pedro looks genuinely shaken. Yesheb relaxes. Yes, he is running the show now.

When Pedro locates the key, Yesheb tells him to place it on the foot of the bed and step back. Then Yesheb plucks it off the starched white sheet like a frog snatching a fly.

He flashes a beautiful smile, his most engaging.

THE MAN GRINNED, ugly and crooked, and Pedro measured the distance between them again. If the guy—the *stalker*—gave him the slightest opening, he'd lunge. But the intruder was careful to stay just out of Pedro's reach. He was sharp. And absolutely devoid of humanity. No wonder Gabriella was terrified!

"You're pathetic, you know that, don't you," the man said. He stepped away from the bed after he put the key into his pocket, but kept the gun carefully aimed at Angelina. "You think you're such a hero." Without turning away from Pedro, he spoke to the crowd. His voice dripped sarcasm. "You think he's a hero, too, don't you? The way he has stood up under such a load of pain in his life. The way he loves his children, sacrifices for them, takes such good care of them." Yesheb made a humph sound in his throat. "You're such fools."

He turned slightly, didn't move the pistol but caught Pedro's gaze and locked on.

"I know you, the *real* you." He literally hissed the words. "The you who holds his own daughter hostage, won't let her leave home to get an education because *you* need her here."

Pedro stared into eyes such a stark, arresting blue he could distinguish the color even from where he stood. It was the color of polar ice, frozen and lifeless.

The man nodded toward Angelina. "You took this little girl's life and so you have given her yours in exchange. You've sacrificed everything for her—isn't that right?" He lowered his voice in a mockery of the intimate way one friend addresses another. "Only it's not for her at all. None of it's about her or her future. She *has* no future and everybody knows it."

He leaned forward and spit words at Pedro the way cowboys spit tobacco juice on the ground. "You do everything you can—pump air into her lungs and food into her stomach—focus your whole life and your kids' lives on keeping Angelina alive so your great sacrifice will make *you* feel better. That's not love, my stupid little friend, that's guilt—the ultimate self-absorption. All of this …" He gestured toward the hospital bed and medical paraphernalia. "… is about *you, not Angelina*—as much now as it was the day you were too busy, too caught up in what was going on in *your* world to notice that your baby was roasting like a Thanksgiving turkey less than fifty yards away."

Pedro was so staggered by the man's words, he could not move, could not breathe. And that was exactly what the guy intended. Like throwing a stun grenade into a crowd, the stalker used the shock he had produced to take three steps and grab the arm of the closest child—six-year-old Serena Sanchez, who was standing beside her wide-eyed mother. Julia Sanchez cried out and reached for Serena, but the man yelled at her to shut up and stand back and held the gun to the little girl's temple. Julia clamped her hands over her mouth and didn't move.

"I don't want this kid. I have no reason to take her with me; she'd only get in my way. I'll let her go when I get to my jeep *if* you all move aside and let me walk out of here. If you don't … well, I'll blow the brains out of a little girl who actually has some."

The crowd parted like the Red Sea. The man shoved Serena ahead of him through the doors into the store. Pedro heard the jingle of the bell on the front door when it opened and when it closed. The sound released the crowd like the opening bell of a horse race and they all rushed into the store to look out the front windows.

Pedro did not move. It seemed that he stood motionless for a long time, but it was probably less than thirty seconds before he heard the commotion out front that freed his paralyzed legs. He got to the saloon doors as Serena burst through the front door of the store and into her mother's arms.

Then there was pandemonium all around him. His neighbors surged back into his kitchen babbling. Anza rushed to Angelina, threw herself across the child and sobbed. Voices assaulted him, people wanting to know what had happened, who the man was, why—

Pedro ignored the questions and fumbled in his pocket for his cell phone, his hands shaking. He pulled it out and dialed 911. The voice of the dispatcher who answered sounded as rattled and frantic as he did.

"I want to report a …" What? What had it been? "… a man with a gun threatened a bunch of people in St. Elmo and he ees on his way up to St. Elmo's Fire to—"

"Is this about the escaped convicts?"

"What?"

"There was a prison break half an hour ago. Men with automatic weapons blew a hole in the perimeter fence—is that what you're calling about?"

"No, but—"

"Sir, I'm sorry. I can only deal with life-and-death emergencies right now."

"This *is* a life-and-death emergency!"

"I will take your name and phone number and somebody will get back to you as soon as possible."

Pedro hung up. The police would not come to Gabriella's aid in time to do her any good. A prison break. How convenient. Surely … He let the thought go, turned, pushed his way back through the crowd to the gun rack above the fireplace and grabbed the .30-06 hunting rifle. He snatched his rain jacket and hat off the hook by the swinging doors as he headed into the Mercantile. There was a box of shells for the rifle under the cash register.

THE STORM ABATED while Yesheb was in the store, but the sky is pregnant with more rain and threatens to give birth any minute.

Yesheb should be elated as he drives along Chalk Creek Canyon Road to the turnoff that will take him to the jeep trail up the mountainside to St. Elmo's Fire. He has the key in his pocket! He is on his way.

But he isn't elated. The voices have been berating him ever since he shoved the little girl back toward the store, leapt into the jeep and sped away.

Yesheb couldn't even execute his own plan, they say. Things went terribly wrong. The shopkeeper is still alive. The man who helped Zara defy him, her friend, her confidant and maybe even her … *lover* escaped the retribution he deserved.

And there were witnesses! Oh, minions like that could be paid off; he could purchase their silence with pocket change. That wasn't the point. They had *seen,* watched Yesheb come close to losing in a battle of wills.

Yesheb had not shown well. Not well at all.

While the other voices rail at him, The Voice remains silent. Yesheb knows why. The Voice understands. The Voice recognized the forces that stood against Yesheb in that place, the power the mustached fool didn't even know he possessed. Yesheb should have displayed his own strength. He should have overpowered the Opposition, annihilated it.

Why hadn't he?

Was he … *afraid?*

While the other voices attack him like a thousand screaming harpies, The Voice says nothing. That silence is deafening.

Yesheb endures the squalling in his head all the way up the road to the turn-off beside a complex of red stone buildings. It continues as he struggles to maneuver his way up a trail strewn with rocks, pitted by huge potholes and knobby with exposed tree roots. When he gets to the first switchback, the noise stops in mid-babble like somebody hit the mute button. Yesheb is instantly alone, abandoned. Trembling and demoralized, he struggles to pull it together for his assault on the cabin. His gentle assault. His "kind" invasion.

Then he lifts his eyes and actually looks at the switchback and gate. His stomach heaves. He had not expected anything like this! His men had warned him, of course, but he'd dismissed their concerns.

Yesheb sets the emergency brake on the idling vehicle and steps down out of it, scrambles up the wet trail to the gate, unlocks it and shoves it open. He sinks down on the edge of the concrete gate footer for a few moments looking at the almost vertical hairpin turn carved out of the rock. How can he possibly—

Then he hears the loud rumble of an engine. Someone is coming up the trail behind him!

He jumps up, loses his footing on the slippery rocks and slides back down to the trail below. Scrambling to his feet, he leaps into the jeep, fumbles to disengage the emergency brake, then panics and slams the accelerator all the way to the floorboard. The tires spin and catch and the jeep leaps forward into the switchback.

His fear saves him. He'd never have taken the curve that fast—and he needed the speed to make the turn. He roars through the switchback, bounces heavily over a rock at the top of the trail and skids to a stop. For a moment, he sits panting, then jumps out of the jeep and locks the gate behind him. As he charges up the rutted trail to face more switchbacks— aerial photographs showed seven of them—he clings to the knowledge that he only has to make it *up* the trail to the cabin. He won't have to come back down. He will be taking a much more comfortable mode of transportation when he whisks his bride off the mountaintop and away into their future.

The thought of his beloved Zara both calms him and pumps adrenaline into his veins. He feels his resolve return. He will win. He will prevail. Yesheb Al Tobbanoft *is* The Beast of Babylon. It is a destiny that was laid out for him the moment he first displayed his power. The day he devoured his twin brother in their mother's womb, he began the journey that will end in victory on this mountaintop today!

Pedro pulled to a stop short of the first switchback and banged his fists on his steering wheel in frustration. The gate was locked. Of course, there had only been the slightest possibility that it would not be, that the man—Pedro did not even know his name!—who had taken the key was so arrogant he did not believe anybody would follow him. Or knew the police would be too occupied with the prison break to respond, which opened up another whole can of worms Pedro was not prepared to fish with right now.

The night of Anza's birthday party Gabriella had asked him if he believed in evil.

"The kind of man who delights in hurting other people—is he crazy or evil?" she had asked.

He had responded, "Both!"

Certainly the look in that man's eyes was the very definition of madness, but was that all? Or was there something bigger than insanity driving him? The stalker had actually felt … cold. Sure, the man had been soaked to the skin, but Pedro would have sworn he radiated a chill into the air around him that had nothing to do with being wet.

And the things he knew. Not just information but Pedro's *soul*, what he wrestled with in the darkest ditch of the night when no one was there to see. Almost like—

Pedro shook it off. It did not really matter at this point whether the man was a who or a *what* … a distinction without a difference. What did matter was that he was roaring up the mountain right this minute to *kidnap Gabriella!* The terror that thought struck in Pedro's heart knocked down the fortifications denial had so carefully erected and scattered the last vestiges of protest and doubt like a flock of startled chickens. His feelings for Gabriella were real and deep and he was nauseous at the thought of what that man would do to her.

And Gabriella was not the only one whose life was in danger. The madman needed "innocent blood" to offer as a sacrifice on their nuptial altar. Pedro had read the book! And the innocent blood on that mountain was Ty's.

He switched off the ignition, jumped out of the jeep, reached back in, grabbed the rifle off the backseat floorboard and emptied the box of

THE LAST SAFE PLACE

shells into his pocket. He would have to make his way up the mountain to St. Elmo's Fire on foot and he took off running—strained to outdistance his fear that whatever horror the stalker intended to inflict on Gabriella and her family would be over before he could get there to protect them.

✳ ✳ ✳ ✳

Gabriella sat propped up with pillows on her bed with her computer on her lap. It was an exercise in futility and she knew it. How could she possibly write when her mind was fuzzy from lack of sleep, her gut was tied in a knot and her hands were trembling?

Maybe if I put my fingers on the keyboard they'll hop around and write without me.

Couldn't be a whole lot worse than the tortured verse she had composed with her mind fully engaged. But she was coming along; bit by bit it was coming back to her.

She sighed, then reached out her hand to the .38 on the bedside table. Her security blanket. And she'd use it, too, she told herself fiercely. If that maniac came anywhere near her, she'd ... She didn't pick the gun up, merely touched it, felt the gun barrel as cold as a stone.

Except not all stones were cold. She looked up at the geode sparking on the dresser on the other side of the room. That stone had been warm. Even though it had been lying in the shade with all the other rocks, it had been—

The memory downloaded into her mind like a file off the internet. Between one heartbeat and the next, she *knew*.

Gabriella jumped up off the bed and raced down the stairs to the big fireplace that covered the wall between the family room and the kitchen. She scooted aside the pile of kindling and inspected a spot where the bottom of the hearth connected to the bricks going up the wall. She reached out and pushed on a brick on the bottom, wiggled it back and forth like a little kid's tooth to loosen it. Then she tugged on it and it slid out into her hand with a grating sound, revealing a small cavity behind it. Gabriella reached into the opening and her fingers felt something round and hard. She drew it out of the hole into the light and stared at it in wonder. Though the crystals were dirty, it was still incredibly beautiful—bleeg. Just like the other half of the geode on her dresser upstairs.

Getting slowly up off her knees, Gabriella went into the kitchen and turned on the water in the sink. When the accumulated dust of years inside the hearth was washed away, the crystals in the geode sparkled. All the ones in this half of the rock were the same size and shape, about as big around as the end of her little finger and multicolored like the prism of colors in the other half. They made a solid carpet of crystal that would have formed a canopy over the large, clear, center crystal before the rock was broken in half. No, not a canopy. A sky. The colored crystals were arranged in rows—red, orange, yellow, green, blue, indigo and violet. A rainbow.

T‍y sat in the deck chair on the balcony outside his room with P.D. stretched out on the damp wood decking beside him. The rain had stopped—for now—but he could hear thunder growl higher up on the mountain. He took his glasses off and cleaned them on his shirt—the mist kept fogging them up.

The lightning that sparkled in the clouds above Antero looked like Christmas lights blinking in a gray cotton ball. Ty was watching, waiting to see a bolt actually strike the peak. He shouldn't have to wait long. He'd already seen two strike the mountain near the wash above the tree line. But he was waiting for a single bolt to snake down from the clouds to the highest tip of rock—so he could draw a picture of it while the image was still fresh in his mind.

Ty's mother had purchased all manner of art supplies—colored pencils, pastel chalks, acrylics, oils, brushes and paper—for him to use to entertain himself on rainy days—said she'd had to "make do" when she was here as a little girl and didn't want him to suffer the same fate. Of course, that was before video games. Like in the Stone Age.

But even Ty had eventually tired of playing with his Nintendo. Grandpa Slappy had taught him how to play blackjack, but his grandfather had gone into his room to take a nap after lunch, so Ty had settled himself on the back deck to capture a storm over the mountain. He'd done a painting with watercolors of the view from the front porch right after breakfast—the valley and mountains on the other side. Mom had stuck it with magnets onto the refrigerator door. He wanted to paint something more dramatic this time.

Only another scene kept getting in the way. Whenever he tried to concentrate on the image of lightning striking the mountain to sketch it on the art tablet, his mind's eye saw something else—teenagers dangling a boy off a bridge over a river.

The story Grandpa Slappy had told Ty haunted him. It was like a movie where he was inserted into the action. Sometimes he was Skeet, dangling there above the river. Sometimes he was Grandpa Slappy, watching in horror from the woods. But usually he was the fat kid, the one with tears on his cheeks who paused in his escape to stare into Grandpa Slappy's eyes. The kid who hadn't meant any harm and ended up killing someone, and who had to live with the guilt of what he'd done for the rest of his life. Ty hadn't meant to hurt anybody either, but he'd gotten his own father killed.

They're fighting. Again. They're always fighting. No matter what his mother says or does, his father yells at her for it. The coffee's too hot. The music's too loud or too soft or not what he wants to hear.

And Ty is terrified. That's nothing new, either. He's always frightened when they fight, so scared he goes into his room and closes the door and puts the pillow over his head so he can't hear it. But tonight the yelling wakes him up. It's so loud he can't go back to sleep, even with the pillow over his head. There's an edge to Daddy's voice he hasn't heard before. Mommy's voice is different, too. More scared than usual. So he gets out of bed and sneaks down the stairs. His parents are fighting in the family room; they can't see him watching from the shadows of the bottom step.

Daddy has just gotten home. He still has his jacket on. And he's drunk. He usually is when they fight. But tonight he is so drunk he can barely stand up. He's sort of swaying, has to hold onto the back of a chair for balance. His words are so slurred Ty can't make out what he's saying. It is something about the book Mommy wrote.

Daddy says he knows why the book's so good, because it's a—then he uses a big word Ty doesn't understand. Sounds like "auto buggy." Daddy shouts that she's a witch, a demon.

He has a jar in his hand and he holds it out toward her and she backs up from it like it's a snake. But there's a wall behind her so she can't get away. Daddy says he's going to make the outside of her match the inside.

And then he lets go of the chair and—

P.D. began to growl. The dog was standing up, his body rigid, his teeth barred, making a sound that Ty had only heard one time before. That time in the airport when …

Ty followed Puppy Dog's gaze and saw a jeep materialize out of the mist, inching along the winding trail through the last of the grove of aspen trees. He couldn't see the face of the man who was driving it, but he didn't have to.

It was the Boogie Man. He had found them and had come to take Ty away to hurt him really bad, maybe even … kill him.

Ty's mouth was instantly so dry he couldn't swallow. How could it get dry like that so fast? His heart banged in his chest so hard he could see the front of his shirt move with every beat.

Hide!

He dived out of the chair, spilling the sketch pad and pencils on the floor, then hunkered down below the level of the railing so the man couldn't see when he got closer.

"Hush!" he commanded P.D. in a whisper just as the dog was about to bark.

Ty peeked through the slats of the railing. The jeep was coming slowly, sneaking up on the cabin. Ty had to warn—

No, wait. Think!

The man had threatened Mom and Grandpa Slappy—even hurt Mom!—the last time he came looking for Ty. He'd do the same now. They'd try to protect Ty and end up getting hurt.

Ty had to run, get away. As long as Ty wasn't around, the man would leave Mom and Grandpa Slappy alone. There wasn't any reason to hurt them when it was Ty he wanted.

The boy turned and crawled back into his room, made a hand motion and P.D. followed. Then he grabbed his jacket off the bedpost, slid his arms into it and sneaked a look out the deck door. The jeep had cleared the aspen grove and was silently approaching the cabin.

"I gotta run away, boy," he told P.D. His voice quavered but he managed not to cry. "And you gotta stay here." A plan had formed in Ty's mind, and where he was going, P.D. couldn't go with him.

"Down," he said. P.D. dropped to the floor. "Stay."

THE LAST SAFE PLACE

Then Ty crept out onto the deck below the railing and crossed to the steps on the far side that led down to the porch. He peered through the slats and as soon as the jeep was close enough that the cabin blocked it from view, Ty raced down the steps. To stay out of the jeep's sight line, Ty cut directly across the meadow on the south side of the cabin to the creek and the trees. Then he crossed the creek and plunged into the woods. Once in the trees, he turned and started running toward the mountain.

Back in Ty's room, P.D. lay on the floor, his hackles raised, his teeth barred, growling quietly. But he didn't bark because he'd been instructed not to. He didn't move, either. Placed on "down stay," he wouldn't budge from that spot until somebody summoned him.

CHAPTER 17

Theo was sitting on the foot of the bed putting on his shoes after his nap when movement outside his window caught his attention. It was Ty running dead out toward the woods south of the cabin. Several things about that stuck Theo as odd and he watched the boy until he disappeared into the trees.

Why had Ty decided to go outside right now? Any fool could see the storm wasn't finished with them yet. If his mama knew he was out there, she'd likely wring the boy's neck, nervous as she got about lightning. And as on-edge as she was today, she'd grab that boy and snatch him bald-headed. Couldn't blame her for being jumpy, though. Today was it. The full moon. That madman's last shot at her. She probably didn't even close her eyes to blink last night and hadn't been able to sit still all morning. Didn't help that it was storming.

Which brought his mind full circle to Ty. What was that boy doing out there in a storm? When he crossed the creek into the trees on the other side, he'd been looking back over his shoulder as he ran, then he turned and headed upstream. That didn't make a lick of sense. Why had the boy run straight toward the woods like a bat out of hell when the place he always played was Notmuchuva Waterfall, in the back left corner of the bowl-shaped valley? To get there, you cut diagonally across the meadow behind the cabin.

Last but by no means least in Theo's list of confusions was the dog, or rather the absence of the beast. It was never more than a step behind Ty no matter where he went—even to the bathroom. Where was P.D.?

Theo slid his foot into his other shoe, tied it, picked up his coffee cup and saucer from the bedside table as he passed and headed into the family room. He noticed that the pile of kindling had been scattered on the floor and a brick was missing from the hearth.

He found Gabriella in the kitchen washing something in the sink. He had to speak up so she could hear him over the water running, or maybe he needed to talk louder so he could hear himself.

"Ty and that dog is just about joined at the hip, but that walking fur machine's not with him now—and he's playing outside in the rain."

Gabriella shut off the water in the sink under the window and turned to face Theo, who was complaining about something P.D. had done.

"Theo, look at this!" She held out the dripping geode. "I found it—"

Then she heard a sound the running water had masked. The sound of tires crunching on the gravel beside the cabin.

Theo's eyes got huge. The coffee cup and saucer he was holding clattered to the floor and shattered, the sound gobbled up by the sudden hammering of her heart in her ears. She turned slowly, agonizingly slowly to see what Theo could see out the window over her shoulder. But she knew. Before she saw the black jeep and the man stepping quickly out of it, she knew. Yesheb had found her. She'd always known he would.

Which meant he had gotten the gate key from Pedro. A sob started in her throat but died there from lack of air. Pedro wouldn't have given the key up willingly. What had Yesheb done to him to get it? The thought of Pedro hurt, maybe even … dead … *no! Oh, please, no!* Her protests melted away then like fog on a warm morning and she faced how much Pedro meant to her. Not that it mattered anymore.

The gun! It was upstairs on the bedside table. Maybe she could get to it before … but she couldn't move. Her legs wouldn't obey her command to run and she stood rooted to the spot. Her fingers turned numb and the geode tumbled out of them and turned over and over in slow motion as it fell.

A part of her mind registered a random impression before panic exploded in it, obliterating all thought.

Yesheb's hair … it's white!

Theo understood now why Ty had run away, looking over his shoulder like the devil himself was chasing him. He *was!* A devil who intended to—*No!* Not Ty, not that precious little boy! But what could Theo do about it? Wasn't a way in the world a useless old man could help the boy, or Gabriella either.

Lord, please! Tell me what to do!

And it came to him instantly. He wasn't useless. In fact, if he played his cards right, he might be able to give Ty a gift that would save his life—*time*. Time to hide real good in the woods where that fruit loop would never find him.

Gabriella was frozen, a marble statue, but he could hear her gasping, drawing in great gulps of air like she was drowning. She must have felt like she was, having to face down a madman, must be scared out of her wits. Theo wasn't scared, though. He thought the same thing he did the first night they ran away from the Looney Tune through the streets of Pittsburgh: Scared would wear you out, and right now Theo didn't have a speck of energy to spare.

In much less time than it should have taken him to get from the jeep to the house, Yesheb materialized in the doorway leading to the mudroom.

What's wrong with you people? Don't never lock yo cars or yo houses! Might as well hang up a neon sign, flashing "Here I is; mess me over."

Must have been some trick of his screwed-up senses, but Theo could have sworn a wash of cold air preceded the man into the room, like what hits you when you open the freezer door on a hot day. And it wasn't no breeze from outside; he'd closed the outside door behind him.

Yesheb had obviously been out in the rain without an umbrella. His clothes were soaked, his hair—it was *white!*—was wild, must have partially dried in the wind as he drove. He didn't have a weapon, at least not one you could see, but Theo knew the man was too smart to come here unarmed. He had a gun or a knife on him somewhere. And Theo was likely to make the close personal acquaintance of one or both of them in the next few minutes. But he would put off that introduction as long as he possibly could.

"I was wondering when you was gone turn up," Theo said, looked the man right in the eyes. They were a blue as pale as ice on a bird bath. "It being a full moon and stormy, we been expecting you."

"Stay out of my way, old man," Yesheb said and took a step toward Gabriella.

"Not planning on getting in your way, wouldn't think of doing a thing like that. Ole Slappy got better sense than to mess with a man like yourself, strong and powerful as you is."

A little flattery goes a long way with some people.

"But I do got a question for you. You being a smart fellow—maybe you know the answer. Tell me … if you was to try to fail and you succeeded, which did you do?"

Yesheb stared at him, dumbfounded, like *he* was the lunatic. And that was fine. Theo didn't care if the fool thought he was a cross-eyed aardvark. There was a clock going tick, tick, tick, and every second that passed Ty was getting farther and farther away from the cabin.

"Leave us alone, you crazy old fool," Yesheb said. "I have no quarrel with you. Don't make me hurt you. My business is with … Zara."

He pronounced the name with a thousand shades of aching and longing.

"Nobody named Zara here," Theo said. "Your GPS must have brought you to the wrong house. Happens up here all the time. We get folks who took a wrong turn in Poughkeepsie and boom, they're on our doorstep." Theo cocked his head to the side. "Shhhh. Listen." He paused. "You hear it? That little shrunk-up Englishwoman out there in your jeep is hollering, 'recalculating … recalculating … re—'"

"Shut up! Stop your prattling. Sit down at the table and don't make another sound. I won't tell you again."

"You think I'm afraid of you?"

"You should be afraid."

"What for? What's the worst thing you can do—kill me? And that would be a bad thing because …?"

Yesheb shoved him toward the table but Theo was so unsteady on his feet, he went down in a heap on the floor, banging his knee painfully. Gabriella gasped, took a step toward him but he held up his hand. He looked at Yesheb and smiled. "Don't get your feelings hurt that you don't scare me. Don't nothing else scare me, neither. I got me a brain tumor that should have planted ole Slappy under the daisies a long time ago." He heard a stifled sob from Gabriella and was touched by it. Oh, how he'd hate it if something bad happened to her. "So you see, if you want to send me over the River Jordan right now, I'm good with that. The Archangel Gabriel probably gone put me in time-out for being late at the Pearly Gates as it is."

Yesheb reached down and grabbed Theo's collar, pulled it so tight around his neck he couldn't get his breath. With one arm, he yanked Theo up off the floor to a kneeling position and ground out words into his face.

"I am holding my temper for Zara's sake. I want to be gentle with her, not upset her. But you will leave me no choice—"

"Okay, okay, I'm sorry. I'll be quiet, won't say another word." Theo made a little-kid zipper motion across his mouth.

Yesheb let go of his collar and he slumped back onto his heels. Then the white-haired man turned to Gabriella. "My dear Z—"

"Just … one more itty bitty question, and this is the last one, I promise."

"I'm warning you …"

"If a turtle loses his shell, is he naked … or homeless?"

With the speed of a striking rattlesnake, Yesheb slipped his hand into his jacket, withdrew a pistol from his shoulder holster and slammed the gun into Theo's face. He felt no pain, only pressure—like what you feel when the dentist pulls a tooth and your gums is so numb you got spit drooling down your chin. He could hear the bones breaking, though, and teeth shattering. He could also hear Gabriella's high, wailing, "Nooooo!" but it came from a great distance, from some place on a high peak where the wind whistled and wailed with the voices of lost children.

Then Theodosius X. Carmichael's lights went out.

GABRIELLA'S THOUGHTS WERE bats, diving at her in a darkened room where they could see and she couldn't, water spiders racing across the surface of a pond without puncturing the delicate tension of the water.

Yesheb was in the room and she had no memory of him coming here. And no memory of any time that he wasn't here—the forever now of her horror obliterated the past and the future alike.

She heard Theo talking to him in a normal tone of voice, like he was discussing the Dow Jones Industrial Average or bowling balls or crop circles. There was no fear in Theo. He was fighting with what little he had, waving a red flag in front of the bull.

The old man's bravery splashed cold water into Gabriella's face, slapped her into reality so abruptly her head actually snapped back. Yesheb shoved Theo toward the table and the old man stumbled and fell. She moved to help him but he waved her away.

"… got me a brain tumor that should have planted ole Slappy under the daisies a long time ago."

A sob hitched out of her throat. He *was* sick. He was going to die.

Earth to Gabriella: So are you and Ty!

Ty! The boy was upstairs painting a picture like the one that hung now on the refrigerator with the watercolors still wet. A little-kid drawing of the view from the front porch—at least that's what he'd said it was. But the proportions were all wrong so the valley looked like it was taller than the mountain range on the other side of it. There was something unrecognizable in the foreground—a squirrel or a bear, maybe. Perhaps just a rock. The colors were nice, though. Ty probably didn't even know yet there was any danger. That a man in his mom's kitchen intended to plunge a dagger into his heart to offer his blood as a sacrifice to seal an unholy union.

No!

She had to do something. *Think!*

Nothing. Her mind was as blank as an empty plate.

Wait a minute ... Yesheb planned to sacrifice Ty as a part of their wedding ceremony, right? But there'd be no need for a sacrifice if there was no wedding, no union to dedicate. There'd be no reason to kill Ty if she refused to marry Yesheb!

Was it possible that she could save her son's life with a single word—*no?* Better question, could she actually stand up to this monster in a human being suit? She'd have to *defy* him, refuse to allow the all-consuming terror he ignited in her soul to control her.

That maddeningly rational voice in her brain spoke up then, like it always did when she least wanted to hear from it: If you refuse to do what this man wants, he'll kill you. He has no reason to keep you alive if you won't marry him and fulfill his monstrous delusion.

I die, Ty lives.

She took a deep, shaky breath.

Okay ... *I die, Ty lives.*

The rational Gabriella stuck its nose into her business one final time: Reality check. What makes you think he'll let Ty live, let any of you live, if you defy him?

That was reality, alright. It wasn't likely any of them were going to get out of this alive. *But she had to try.* She had to face down the evil she had created out of the depths of her own despair. The Beast of Babylon's story had to end here, now. Today.

She heard Theo say something about a turtle's shell and Yesheb reached into his jacket pocket and drew out a gun. With savage brutality, he slammed the pistol into Theo's face and the old man collapsed in a bloody heap in the floor.

"Nooo!" Gabriella cried.

Then Yesheb aimed the pistol at Theo's head.

"I warned you, old man."

Before he could pull the trigger, Gabriella lunged at his gun hand, threw her whole body at it. He wasn't expecting a blow, wasn't braced for it, and she knocked him off balance into the kitchen chairs. The gun spun out of his hand, hit the hardwood floor, slid all the way across it and vanished under the loveseat in the family room. She and Yesheb fell together in a tangled heap beside Theo.

Yesheb was as quick as a cat. Before Gabriella even thought to struggle, he rolled over on top of her and pinned her beneath him. He raised up to his knees, then, straddling her chest, stared down at her with a look of such naked lust it made her nauseous.

"Oh, my beloved Zara, how good your body feels beneath me."

"Get off me," she demanded. At least in her head, she demanded. But the words came out barely louder than a whisper—not defiance, just a pleading whimper.

He didn't move, just sat there staring down at her, twin flames burning in his eyes like pilot lights. Then, as he had done when he cornered her in the hallway outside her bedroom in Pittsburgh, he retreated, grabbed hold of his runaway emotions and held them in check. She actually heard his teeth grind together. He took a deep breath and let it out.

"I didn't mean to hurt you, my Sweet," he said, his voice syrupy with feigned kindness. "I mean you no harm, ever. Surely, you know that. I want nothing in life more than to give you everything you ever dreamed of, to grant you a life free of care, a life where no desire of the heart is denied, no want unfulfilled."

"Then get off me … please."

"Of course, my beloved."

He didn't get to his feet, just lifted his body off hers and sat down on the floor beside her. She sat up and made to stand but he put a restraining hand on her shoulder. Just gentle pressure.

"We need to talk," he said.

"Yes, we do." She scooted away from him until her back connected with a cabinet and she leaned against it. She kept her focus on him, didn't let her eye drift to Theo's body, lying in a puddle of blood.

Her willingness to cooperate seemed to cheer him and he smiled. "Our future lies before us and we have so many plans to make."

The eagerness in his voice was almost pathetic. Incipient hysteria threatened to burst out—not in tears but in laughter.

Does he want to pick out wedding invitations and register our silver pattern?

She coughed, averted a peal of laughter and struggled to corral the stampede of thoughts in her mind and direct them out in a neat stream of words.

"No, Yesheb, we don't have plans to make." Her voice was barely above a whisper, but it was all the volume she could generate. "At least not plans ... *together*."

The look on his face was alarm, confusion. There was no anger. Yet.

"I want to make this as clear and uncomplicated as I possibly can." Despite her best efforts to keep her voice steady, it trembled and quaked with every word. "I need for you to listen carefully and believe me."

She took a deep breath, dived off the high board and began to fall, down ... down ...

"I am *not* Zara. I am Gabriella Carmichael. I wrote a book called *The Bride of the Beast* under the pen name Rebecca Nightshade. It was a novel. Fiction. Made up! Nothing in it was real."

His hand shot out like a striking cobra and grabbed her wrist. His grip instantly cut off the circulation to her hand.

"I am not amused, Zara. The time for playfulness has passed. We are to be one today and we must—"

"No."

"What do you mean, no?"

The cork finally popped off the top of Gabriella's bottled up emotions and she spewed out words she wasn't conscious of formatting into language.

"How many things can no mean? No, I am *not* Zara. No, we are *not* going to be one. No, I will *not* marry you. You need me to draw you a picture?"

The foundations of the earth shift, rumble, and a mighty plume of fire licks up out of a crack in Yesheb's other realm. The heat of it sears the back of his neck; blisters pop out on his skin.

"*This. Cannot. Be!*" roars The Voice in his head and the volume, force and pressure make blood squirt out of his nose and run down his upper lip.

"You do not mean that, Zara!" Yesheb's voice sounds hollow in his own ears, airy and without strength or force. Almost … pleading.

"I do mean it."

He can't hear her voice over the rumble in his head, but he can read her lips. And every word is an individual dagger that stabs deep into his bowels, impales him so his blood issues forth from a dozen different wounds.

"I will not be your bride. In the story *I made up,* Zara has to come to the Beast *willingly.* I'm not willing. And you can't force me."

The world begins to slide into the flaming crack. He can see it happening as an overlaid image, like looking at a double-exposed photograph. Zara sits before him, so achingly beautiful he can barely breathe and in a filmy image in front of her, his universe is disintegrating.

"It is over," says The Voice. Not shouting but dismissive. As if The Voice has better things to do than waste its time with a lowly ruler wannabe unable to control a single, powerless woman. Then The Voice booms, like the sounding of a great gong three times: "You. Have. Failed."

Yesheb tilts his head back and emits a cry that is more feral than human, a cry huge and Jurassic that is ripped from the dark, fetid depths of his shattered soul.

He is hollow.

And then rage begins to seep into the hollow space like the sea through cracks in the hull of a mighty ship. It gains force, sprays into the emptiness in streams, begins to fill it up from the bottom, rising, rising. The deluge picks up momentum and rips out pieces of him, seawater chewing away hunks of the ship's hull until finally the metal sides give way, the hull ruptures, and the sea rushes in to sink it to the bottom.

Yesheb Al Tobbanoft is no more. He exists only as the shell of a man filled to overflowing with a cataclysmic rage.

He leaps at Zara, actually growls, knocks her to the floor, fastens her slender neck in his hands and begins to squeeze the life out of her.

THE LAST SAFE PLACE

When Gabriella told Yesheb that she would not marry him she entertained the wild, irrational hope that he would simply get up and leave, a broken man, and never bother her again.

Then he leaned his head back and howled, the guttural cry of a dying wolf. The sound raised the hair on her arms, set her teeth on edge. It was not a human cry, not a sound that could possibly have come from a human throat.

When his outcry was over, he slowly lowered his head and she gasped at the sight of his face. His features were twisted in a tortured mask of blind fury, his eyes wells of bottomless hate. The Yesheb she had spoken to, who had chased her across the country, who had demanded she become a party to his delusional madness, was gone. In his place was rage in human form.

He leapt at her and grabbed her in a stranglehold.

"I will squeeze through the skin of your neck until your head comes off in my hands."

Gabriella instantly saw black spots in the air, the sudden pressure forced blood up into her cheeks and she flushed bright red. She knew she would be dead in seconds.

Then he released the crushing force but kept his hands around her throat while she gasped in huge gulps of air.

"Oh, but you must not die before you know the fate of the others. Just as I promised that day in the airport, I will stomp the old man, break every bone until he is an unrecognizable, bloody pulp. And the boy ..." He skinned his lips back in a bloodthirsty smile. "While your son squeals, 'Mommy!' I will cut his beating heart out of his chest, hold it quivering in my hand ... and *crush* it!"

Gabriella wanted to scream, to cry, to claw his eyes out. But he began to squeeze her neck again and she knew she would not be able to save Ty.

Or Theo.

Or Pedro.

The three people she loved.

Theo awoke with the worst hangover of his life. He hurt everywhere, like he'd been hit by a truck. He couldn't remember where he'd been or who he'd been drinking with, but he must have—

"… will cut his beating heart out of his chest, hold it—"

Theo opened his eyes. He was on his back on the floor and he could see Gabriella lying nearby. Yesheb was strangling her, his face twisted in maniacal hatred like Theo had never seen before.

Theo tried to move. Nothing worked.

You're stronger than he is, Lord. Help me!

Two images appeared in his mind as clear as summer vacation slides projected on a wall. The first one was P.D. at the airport, his teeth bared, snarling into Yesheb's face. The second was Ty running across the meadow toward the trees. *Alone.*

Theo understood. He summoned every ounce of strength he possessed and yelled with a commanding voice he could hardly believe was his own.

Just two words.

"P.D., come!"

There was a thundering sound on the stairs, a blur of blond fur shot through his vision and Yesheb flew backward into the kitchen chairs with eighty-five pounds of savage beast ripping at him. He hit the floor with P.D. on top of him, his muzzle already blood-stained from the hunk of flesh he had torn out of Yesheb's arm. Yesheb screamed, writhed on the floor, tried to beat P.D. off. The dog emitted a rumbling growl as he clamped down on Yesheb's wrist, fighting his way toward the man's neck.

M<small>UFFLED SOUNDS</small>. G<small>ROWLING</small>. Screaming.

Animal Planet, a lion attack with the volume turned down low.

Gabriella opened her eyes, saw spots, closed them again. Thoughts and disconnected images spun around in her head but she could make no sense of any of them. And her throat hurt; every time she swallowed shards of pain shot down her neck.

The volume on the attack gradually grew louder until it sounded like it was right beside—

She opened her eyes again. She lay on her back on the floor, her head turned to the side. In her direct line of sight, maybe fifteen feet away, a savage beast she hardly recognized as P.D. was eating Yesheb alive.

Understanding hit her so hard it almost knocked her unconscious again. She turned her head slightly and jagged glass ripped open the inside of her neck. There lay Theo. His eyes were open.

Theo wasn't dead! She couldn't stand, but she managed to slide on her back across the floor to where he lay. His face was next to hers. She started to speak but discovered her voice was gone, her larynx too swollen to make a sound. Theo's mouth was a mass of blood and broken teeth, but he was able to say all he needed to.

"Ty … ran away." He sucked in a bubbling breath. "Find him …" Then his eyes slowly closed again. For good. Theo was gone.

Ty!

With a strength she didn't know she possessed, Gabriella pulled herself to a sitting position, then lurched to her feet, the pain in her neck excruciating. P.D. and Yesheb fought violently a few feet away. Both were covered in blood. P.D. had obviously bitten into something vital. Yesheb would quickly bleed out at that rate. But she couldn't think about that now. She couldn't think … period. Gratefully she didn't have to; she knew everything she needed to know. She had to find Ty.

She staggered toward the back door. She could hear the rain, could see through the window on the door that it was coming down hard. The sensible part of her mind was only connected to the rest of it by a thin thread, like a balloon on the end of a string. But it methodically produced a rational thought that told her she needed a raincoat, so she reached up and lifted hers off the hook by the door.

Bright flashes of lightning made iridescent shadows that fluttered like dream fire across the floor. Thunder rumbled on top of it. The storm was attacking the mountain again and Ty was out there somewhere!

She pulled the door open and stumbled out into the rain, dangling her jacket on the wet ground behind her like a sleepy child dragging a security blanket.

Yesheb doesn't know at first what has hit him. Something huge crashes into his side, knocks him off Gabriella and sends him sprawling into the kitchen chairs. Then there are teeth and claws and pain. He cries out, tries to knock the monster dog away, but it clamps its teeth into his left forearm and rips out a piece of it. Yesheb howls in agony, flails at the animal. They tumble over and over. He kicks it, hits it, but it is all over him, biting and clawing, its teeth reaching up, seeking his neck.

The life-and-death struggle goes on and on; the world is a growling, savage beast with teeth that dig into his flesh. He screams, horrible, death-rattle shrieks and tries to roll away from the dog but it sinks its teeth into his shoulder and drags him back. His kicks and pummeling fists have absolutely no effect on the animal. It will not stop until it kills him.

He is dimly aware that Zara is gone. He manages to half stand, gets his feet knocked out from under him again and falls into the living room, goes down in a heap, drags a table down with him, scattering a lamp, bowls. He scrambles on his back, tries to beat the dog off when his hand lands on something long. A pipe! No, an umbrella. But it is the only weapon he has so he whacks the dog over the head with it. The beast yelps, grabs the umbrella in its teeth and yanks it out of Yesheb's hand. Now, he has no weapon at …

Yes, he does! The dagger is in a sheath at his waist. But it is on the back of his belt and his jacket is buttoned on top of it. He can't get at it and he is getting tired, so tired.

You're going to die now. Die a pathetic failure, your disgrace unavenged, your honor gone.

It is not The Voice who speaks now. The place The Voice dwelt is a dark, empty hole where a cold wind whistles. This is Yesheb's own voice.

You have only one chance to survive. Play dead. Curl into a ball, renounce pain and do not move no matter what the animal does.

Yesheb obeys. He scoots his back against the cabinet, buries his chin in his chest, wraps his arms around his knees and stops fighting. The dog keeps at him, rakes his claws down Yesheb's thigh, sinks its teeth into his shoulder and shakes. Yesheb doesn't respond. He feels the dog's nose near his cheek right before it bites down on his ear, shakes back and forth and Yesheb feels his ear rip off. The dog steps back, barks. He steps forward again, bites Yesheb's upper arm and pulls backward, growling. Yesheb doesn't move.

He can hear the dog panting, looks out through a tiny slit and a forest of eyelashes. All he can see is a section of blood-smeared floor. And his own severed ear.

In the silence, they both hear it.

THE LAST SAFE PLACE

"Ty! Where are you? Ty, answer me. Ty!"

At the sound of her voice, the dog lifts his head, turns and bolts out of the room and out the door into the rain.

Yesheb remains rigid, fears the dog is waiting there, out of sight, ready to pounce at the first sign of life. And Yesheb knows he will not survive another attack. He has lost too much strength, too much blood.

He forces himself to count to three hundred slowly. Then he inches his eyes open, looks around without moving his head. He can see out the open back door into the gloom below the gray overcast. It is raining again now, but not as hard as before. Through the film of rain, he sees two figures in the distance. He lifts his head to get a better look. Yes. It's the dog running out ahead and the woman behind it.

Yesheb uncoils, moans and tries to assess his injuries. He pulls himself to his feet, looks around the kitchen, finds a towel and shoves it over the gaping wound in his forearm. He must bind up his wounds as quickly as possible. And he must find something, a mop or broom handle, to knock his gun out from under the loveseat.

CHAPTER 18

A pain in Gabriella's temples fired agony in heartbeat bursts into her head. Her neck hurt with every movement.

Ty! Where's Ty?

She understood on some level that she was staggering around in the rain too disoriented to form an intent and then act on it. But another part of her had gone on autopilot. Like the "danger, danger, danger, Will Robinson" robot, it kept repeating, find Ty, find Ty.

"Ty!" The cry savaged her from her collarbone to her sinuses. But she shouted out anyway, ignored the pain. "Ty. Where are you? Answer me. Ty!"

Wherever he was, she knew he must be terrified. Obviously, he'd seen Yesheb and run from him. If he'd been there, Yesheb would have hurt him, too, like he did—

Theo!

Gabriella began to cry. Each sob dragged steel wool across the inside of her throat. How could she tell Ty about his grandfather. And Pedro! What had happened to—?

She heard something approaching behind her, turned in terror to see … P.D.! He must have heard her calling Ty. The dog raced up to her, tail wagging. His wet coat was splotched with blood that his run through the rain hadn't washed away. His muzzle was bright red, as were his teeth. Yesheb's blood. *Good!*

She wanted to bellow some yell of triumph, wanted to stand over the homicidal lunatic's dead body and … Instead, she collapsed to one knee and hugged the dog that had saved her life and killed the madman who had terrorized the whole family.

"Good dog, good dog, P.D. Good boy!" The dog licked her face, smeared some of Yesheb's blood on it, but she didn't care. "Oh, Puppy Dog, I can't find Ty."

THE LAST SAFE PLACE

The dog barked and wagged his tail furiously.

Duh! Of course. P.D.! She got painfully to her feet.

"Find Ty!" she commanded and the dog instantly took off at a run toward the back right corner of the valley. That was crazy. Why would Ty …? She started after the dog, then realized she was dragging her nylon jacket on the ground behind her. She picked it up and shoved her arms into the sleeves as she followed along behind P.D..

Theo swam back up to the surface of the water from some deep, dark, cold place. He had dangled beneath the bridge, fallen into the depths and now he was struggling to—

His eyes opened and he saw an expanse of bloody kitchen floor. And brand new black hiking boots. Yesheb stood a few feet away with his back to Theo.

Somehow the madman had survived P.D.'s attack!

Always said that mutt was useless as a rubber beak on a woodpecker.

As the black boots turned and started out of the kitchen, Theo realized Yesheb thought he was dead. All he had to do was lie still and …

Instead, he reached out and grabbed Yesheb's ankle. The slick blood did the rest and Yesheb fell forward, slammed hard into the oak floor, groaned in pain. P.D. must have messed him up pretty bad; Theo forgave him.

Yesheb managed to roll as he hit so the fall didn't cause any real damage, but when he lifted his head and looked at Theo, the old man wanted to cheer. Yep, P.D. messed him up real bad! *Good dog.*

"Here's one more nut for your trail mix," Theo said, his words garbled by blood and broken teeth. "A horse walks into a bar and the bartender says, 'Why the long face?'"

The bloodied figure got to his feet and wordlessly placed the barrel of his pistol to Theo's forehead—he could feel it; the metal seemed particularly cold.

Cornelius, you about to get evicted!

"What do you call a boomerang that doesn't come back to you?"

"A stick," Yesheb replies, and pulls the trigger.

He pauses for a moment above the old man's lifeless body, sorry he'd administered such a painless death. He would have liked … but there is no time.

He turns and staggers out of the kitchen through the mudroom and pauses at the back door of the cabin before stepping out into what is now a light drizzle. He has a decision to make. He can activate the signal from the paging device in his pocket and summon the helicopter to come for him. The brunt of the storm has passed over the peak and is now assaulting the other side of the mountain. The chopper can land, rescue him and get him medical attention before he bleeds to death. But he hardly even toys with the idea. His own survival matters nothing to him. What is of paramount importance is that they die tonight! All of them. At his hand. He will not suffer them to see another sunrise.

He struggles out into the meadow, trying to keep the woman and dog in sight ahead of him. They are not moving fast, don't appear to realize they are being pursued. Soon he will have her in his sights. He will merely wound her, bring her down. Gabriella. *Not* Zara. She isn't his beloved bride, just an imposter, a fake. He will make her pay for deluding him, tricking him. He will make them all pay for what they have done to Yesheb Al Tobbanoft.

He is profoundly grateful that he did not choke her to death. Now he can kill her slowly, make her suffer delicious torment. He will inflict on her an agony like no other human being has ever felt. He knows how. He has studied the art of torture, practiced it, honed and refined it the way other men fine-tune their golf swing. Many from the worthless dregs of humanity have died agonizing deaths as he perfected his skill. The torture and death of Gabriella Carmichael will be a work of art, his virtuoso performance.

First, he will dispatch the dog with a bullet in the skull. Then in a magnificent two-act play, he will ravage her mind, force her to watch the long, agonizing torture of her son. By the time the child gasps out his final breath, she'll be begging for her own death. And he will have only just begun!

His rage is the white hot fuel that propels him forward. It is wrath alone that keeps him going. He no longer notices pain. The bandages he crafted from hand towels won't hold long. Soon, he will begin to pour out his life blood again and he has none to spare. His recently healed foot had been reinjured in his fight with the dog—perhaps even re-broken. The best pace he can set is a shambling limp. And then there is the air. He gasps and has to stop often to catch his breath. The others are accustomed to the altitude. He is not.

But none of that matters. Pain and injury are totally irrelevant. He will do what he has to do no matter how much it hurts, no matter what the cost. Nothing, absolutely nothing short of death can stop him now.

When P.D. began to scramble up the slope on the barely visible trail leading to the chalet, Gabriella finally had to admit to herself that's where he was going. How could Ty possibly have known about the place?

How often had he gone there? Did he sneak away every day to play in the bristlecone pine forest like she and Garrett did that summer thirty years ago? The flood of memories, happy and painful, temporarily blinded her as she climbed and she lost her footing, went down on one knee.

Something whizzed past her arm and slapped into the dirt beside her. *What in the worl—?"*

She turned and saw death itself on the slope behind them.

Like a black, hairy-legged spider, Yesheb was crawling up the trail below, lurching forward, limping and holding his left arm against his body with his right.

But he was alive!

She'd have screamed if she'd had the voice and the air. Instead she stood stunned, stupefied, rooted to the ground in terror. He lifted his hand and pointed at her and she realized what he was doing just in time to dive aside as a bullet went pinging off a rock at her feet. She heard no gunshot; the wind carried the sound away back down the mountain.

P.D. emitted a vicious growl and with hackles raised, started toward Yesheb.

"No," she said and P.D. stopped in his tracks. Yesheb would shoot the dog if it got anywhere near him. "Find Ty."

P.D. turned and continued up the rock trail toward the forest of bristlecone pine trees. Jesus trees. She followed close behind, zigzagged and hopped abruptly from rock to rock to present a moving target. The hair on the back of her neck stood up and she cringed away from the agony she would feel any second from a bullet ripping into her back. He fired twice more; the bullets dug up dirt beside and behind her. At first, she thought he was a lousy shot. Then she realized he wasn't aiming at her back at all but at her legs. He wanted to wound her, not kill her outright. She knew why, knew what he would do to her if he caught her.

But she wasn't helpless anymore. She had the advantage this time. Once she made it to the trees, she could lose him. She knew this forest; he didn't. It'd been here 4,000 years so it hadn't likely changed a whole lot in the past 30. And though she stood up taller now than the trees, the labyrinth of passageways between them would provide excellent cover. She'd go to the chalet for Ty and then the two of them and P.D. would vanish into the trees. She could find her way through the forest by moonlight. Yesheb would quickly become hopelessly lost. She doubted he'd thought to bring a flashlight.

She stumbled in the gravel and slid backward a few steps, then staggered forward the final few feet up the trail to the crest. The slope had shielded her from the worst of the whistling wind, but it hit her full force now, a cold, wet fist that almost knocked her off balance. It pummeled and battered her, whipped her jacket around her, lashed her face with her hair and took her breath away.

P.D. had already disappeared into the trees and she had to hurry. Once Yesheb made the crest, he could follow along behind her down the trail. It was indistinct from lack of use, but if you looked closely, you could see it. She had to get to Ty and get him out of the chalet and into the forest where there was no trail to lead Yesheb to them.

As she plunged into the trees, she looked back over her shoulder. The black spider was still there—his shadow actually looked like a spider, humped over, using his hands as well as his feet to climb. He was farther back; they'd gained on him. And now that she could run standing up, she'd put even more distance between them. She knew where they were going and he didn't. That was another edge.

She'd outwit him. Outlast him.

Lightning flashed. Though the storm was on the other side of the mountain, the lightning near the crest lit the mountainside like a neon sign. She didn't have time to be frightened of it, though. She had only so much currency in her terror account and right now she was spending every dime of it on Yesheb.

Once she was among the trees, they protected her from the brunt of the wind. But she found it more difficult to follow the trail than she'd thought. It was hard to see in the odd half-light. P.D. was in front of her, waiting patiently at the first bend in the trail. Then he turned and headed deeper into the woods, but this time he stayed close, only a few feet ahead. As

THE LAST SAFE PLACE

they wound deeper into the forest, she heard a sound she hadn't heard in decades, the mournful wailing of the wind around the crags of the peak two thousand feet above their heads. For the first time, Gabriella realized how cold she was, chilled to the bone, she had her jaws clamped together to keep her teeth from chattering and could not feel her fingers at all.

Did Ty bring a coat?

The absurdity of that thought forced a semi-hysterical giggle from her raw throat. The boy was on a mountainside in an electrical storm running for his life from a madman who wanted to cut out his heart and she was worried that he'd catch a cold!

She noticed that her breath frosted, made little white puffs in the air in front of her as she ran. Then they rounded a corner past a rock outcrop and there it was—the chalet. It was much more like she remembered it than the cabin had been. The chalet's changes had come from disuse, not renovation. As she drew closer, she saw the hole in the roof, the missing porch pillar and the crooked front door. The sight made her unexpectedly sad.

P.D. raced up to the spot where the trail connected with the rock porch of the chalet—and kept on running! What was that dog doing? She stopped in front of the chalet, gasping and called out, "P.D., come." Softly—she knew the wind would bear the sound instantly away down the mountain toward Yesheb. For a moment, she feared P.D. didn't even hear. But then he appeared from behind a Jesus tree. He stopped, looked at her, then turned and ran back the way he'd come.

Gabriella yanked open the chalet door and called out, "Ty!" though it was clear he wasn't there. The single room with no furniture offered no place to hide. But if he wasn't in the chalet, then where …?

Gabriella's heart took up a staccato rhythm and she couldn't seem to draw a breath, like the wind had been knocked out of her. Neither had anything to do with exertion or thin air.

She turned from the door and raced after P.D., but she no longer needed him to lead her. She knew where they were going.

RATHER THAN FOLLOWING the winding trail through the aspen grove, Pedro cut through the trees in a straight line toward the cabin. He had done the same thing coming up the trail. Wherever he could, he climbed the space between the lower and upper trails, rather than going all the way down and back the long traverses. He'd fallen twice scrambling up the wet rocks. Lost his rifle the last time and had to climb back down to retrieve it.

As he clambered up the last switchback before the trail to the cabin, he heard gunfire. He'd heard what he thought was a lone gunshot earlier but the wind carried sound a long way in the mountains and it could have been distant thunder. This time he was sure and the adrenaline boost gave him the renewed energy he needed to run the rest of the way.

He could see the cabin through the trees in the fading light. A black jeep sat next to Gabriella's in the gravel beside it, lights shone out every window and the back door was standing open.

Pedro instantly became again the Marine he had been years ago. He slowed, approached the cabin at a crouch, rifle ready. Keeping the jeeps between him and the cabin, he dodged from one to the other, then to the back corner of the house. He stood listening. Not a sound.

Slowly, he peeked around the doorframe and could see through the mudroom into the kitchen. Even with only a small swath of the kitchen visible, what he saw there momentarily took his breath away. Blood was all over the floor, dripped, in puddles and smeared. An overturned chair lay next to a lampshade, broken cups and bowls were scattered on the floor. And it looked like … there was a piece of bloody … was that a *human ear* lying in a puddle of blood?

Pedro had been in combat in Somalia and had seen enough battle scenes to know this was a place where a life-and-death struggle had been staged. But who had fought? Who had won? And where were they?

He eased slowly through the door, crossed the mudroom silently. Theo lay in a puddle of blood on the floor by the sink with a bullet hole in the center of his forehead. It had been a gunshot he'd heard. Pedro groaned without making a sound, but stayed focused. He stepped quickly into the room and swept the perimeters of it and the family room with his rifle. No one.

He crossed to the stairs and eased up them, urban warfare in Mogadishu, street by street, house by house.

As soon as he was certain the cabin was empty, he raced back downstairs and tried to puzzle out what had happened here. Theo had been shot at close range. Executed. Pedro felt rage meld with the fear that had been building in his chest as he raced up the jeep trail to the cabin. Paw prints in the blood. And human footprints—large and small. Gabriella and the stalker. Where was Ty and where—?

Another gunshot! The sound came from the mountain. Pedro remembered Gabriella's description of the chalet in the bristlecone pine forest and he took off at a dead run across the meadow.

Gabriella stood stock still at the edge of the clearing, staring in awe and wonder. Thunder rumbled and lightning flashed on the other side of the peak. P.D. had run ahead, leapt up the steps and stood on the top stone, flashing his golden retriever smile. But Gabriella couldn't move, merely gawked at the apparition from her dream come to life before her.

The igloo-shaped rock formation. The stair-step stones leading at an angle around and up the side of it like a spiral staircase. All of it resting squarely beneath the ominous overhang—the diving-board rock with boulders piled on the other end of it.

The sight detonated a bomb in her head and the concussion blew open all the locked doors that held her memories captive, imprisoned for so long they'd sneaked out as dreams and fantasies. Now they were a stampeding herd, thundering past her so fast she hardly had time to examine them.

She and Garrett had found this place, came here often.

This is where they'd sat on the day before their birthday almost thirty years ago, where they'd dangled their feet as they tossed in pebbles.

And … this is where the piece of granite hit the dirt and rolled out through an opening at the bottom, the rock that didn't look like a geode, the one that contained an inner treasure of impossible quartz.

All of those thoughts fired through her mind with the speed of a comet, lit up her brain inside with light.

Just like the light shining up from the pile of boulders.

No, not just like it. The light in her head was the fierce white of the halogen bulbs in a stadium that illuminated a football field so bright you could perform surgery on the fifty-yard line. The light coming from the boulders was golden. Not shining, really. A golden glow.

This couldn't be real. She had to be imagining it. It must be like the ghost images you see after the ophthalmologist dilates your eyes.

P.D. barked, a single yap, and suddenly Gabriella was running, couldn't cross the clearing fast enough, couldn't scramble up the stone steps quickly enough. She peered down through the opening at the top of the boulders at a single, perfect Jesus tree below.

Ty was sitting on the ground next to it, a golden glow sparkling in his round glasses.

But for the space of a single heartbeat, the boy wasn't Ty. He was Garrett.

"I've got a secret. I've got a secret," Gabriella chants in a sing-song voice.

"I don't care," Garrett says. He's grumpy today; his stomach hurts. He didn't want to leave the chalet, didn't want to come with her to The Cleft after Grant and their parents left to search for aquamarine near the mountain peak.

Oh, how she wants to show him the rock! She has his half of it in her pocket and it is like an itch she can hardly stand not to scratch. She has to wait until their birthday party later today, though. She has *to.*

But the rock is a hard secret to keep. Because of it, she can't tell him the real reason she is so determined they go to The Cleft today—so she can search for more rocks like it!

Instead, she tells him she needs his help with the pole. After Grant told them about St. Elmo's fire—they call it firesies—they found a broken fishing pole and decided to stick it in the ground above The Cleft to get firesies to land there—like the sugar water Mom sets out in those little glass things on the porch attracts hummingbirds.

Once they've made their way through the forest to the special pile of boulders, Garrett helps her find a spot and then jam the fire stick down into a crack between two big rocks. But then he sits on the edge dangling his feet, won't help her look for thunder eggs. She has to do it all by herself. All the rocks she finds are granite. But the special rock was like that, too, didn't look like a geode at all. She'd been certain it was just another hunk of granite when she tossed it in yesterday, but now she remembers that when she picked it up after it had rolled out the opening in the bottom of The Cleft, it felt warm, like it'd been lying out in the blazing sun. Only it hadn't. She'd found it in the shade up next to the boulders along with all the pebbles she'd chucked into the opening—and they'd all felt cold.

THE LAST SAFE PLACE

And the rock with the amazing crystals had felt ... heavier, too, but that's crazy. Well, she'll just have to gather up a whole sack full of them and take them back to the cabin and hit them with a hammer and see—

There is a sudden crack and boom of thunder so close to them both children jump and cry out.

Gabriella had been focused on finding rocks; Garrett on his stomachache. Neither of them noticed the storm. They do now. It's not noon, probably not even eleven o'clock yet, but dark, bubbling clouds are gathered around the peak of Mount Antero and are spreading out toward them, reaching out monster fingers in the sky.

Cold wind that smells of rain lifts Gabriella's long curls and tosses them into her face; Garrett's Pirates baseball cap flies off and disappears on the other side of The Cleft.

"Come on!" Garrett says, leaps up and runs down the stair-step rocks with Gabriella right behind him. Before the two of them hit the bottom rock, lightning rips out of the sky and snakes down in a blurred white flash and incinerates a pine tree in the forest—between them and the chalet.

The boom of thunder that follows in its wake is deafening. Like an invisible breaker hitting a beach, a wave of air knocks the children backward a step.

Both of them squeal in terror and then start to cry. Since the day they arrived at the cabin, they have never been outside during a storm. Certainly not way up on the mountainside in the boulder field! They have seen one, though. From the window of the cabin, they watched in awe as lightning danced around the mountaintop, so many bolts of it at once it looked like the mountain had grown white fuzzy hair that was attached to the clouds the way their hair stuck to a balloon that time Grant rubbed one back and forth on the carpet and then held it above their heads.

They can't go through the trees back to the chalet! It's too far. But they can't stand here out in the open, either.

That's when Gabriella remembers the opening in the base of The Cleft that the rock rolled out of yesterday.

"This way!" she says, turns and dashes around the bottom of the boulders to the far side, gets down on her hands and knees and starts to crawl into the opening.

"What are you doing?"

"This goes all the way through. Come on!"

Gabriella drops down on her belly and squeezes through the tunnel formed by the rocks. It is a tight fit. If she'd been much bigger, she couldn't have made it, but within seconds she is through, in the empty space formed by the overhanging boulders. Empty except for the lone bristlecone pine tree in the center, where the sun would be shining if there'd been a sun to shine.

She turns and urges Garrett on. He is taller than she is, but only a little bit larger. Even so, he has to grunt and strain to make it through. When he crawls out into the opening with her, he has a large scratch on his cheek.

But he doesn't mention it. Neither does she. They'd been so terrified; it had been so noisy, windy and dangerous out there. But in here, it is quiet. No, more than quiet. Hushed.

Gray storm light streams in a pallid beam through the opening above them, and it has begun to rain. Hard. The drops fall through the opening and pummel the tree. But the rocks overhang—they hadn't realized how much, looking at it from above. From down here, it looks like the picture Grant showed them in a National Geographic *of a house made out of ice where Eskimos live. It was called an igloo. Smoke went out the hole in the igloo; rain falls in the hole of their boulder igloo. But only what is directly beneath the hole gets wet and that's the pine tree.*

Maybe it is just her eyes adjusting to the darkness here. Because it doesn't seem nearly as dark as it had looked from above. In fact …

She turns to Garrett and he's grinning, the first time he's smiled all day. She can see the gap between his teeth where he has already pulled out the two top ones in the front. Hers are loose, but she's afraid to pull them.

And it seems like … no, it is. Garrett's face is glowing.

He says nothing, just points behind her at the tree. She turns to look and realizes Garrett's face isn't really glowing. It's reflecting the glow from the tree. The glow shifts through amber, caramel and yellow and turns her brother's pale face the color of a brown-toast suntan.

Is this real?

They can hear the rumble of thunder out there in the world. It sounds a little like being in a bowling alley. But the sound doesn't really come in here. Nothing from the outside does. The air is different, the light is different, the sound is different.

Gabriella lets out a shaky breath she didn't realize she'd been holding. It's okay now. They're safe. The lightning won't get to them here. In fact, she's pretty sure that nothing bad can get to them here.

She turns and looks at Garrett. She knows he's thinking the same things she is. He reaches out and squeezes her hand.

"Drumma du, Gabriella," *he says. Or maybe he doesn't say the words. Maybe she hears them without him having to say them.*

"Drumma du, too, Garrett."

"Mom!" Ty leapt to his feet. "How did you fi—?" He saw P.D. and didn't finish the question. "You can't stay here, you have to run. That man is looking for me and—"

"How did you get down there?" She knew he hadn't crawled through the opening she and Garrett had used. They'd barely fit and they'd been younger and much smaller than Ty.

"I jumped. Sort of. See over there, on the back side, where that rock juts out over The Cleft like a little shelf?"

The Cleft? How did Ty know …?

Gabriella looked where he pointed. A piece of the back boulder extended out past the other boulders on the top portion of the igloo. It was about the thickness of a shelf in a closet.

"I scooted down off that on my belly, let my legs dangle below, scooted farther and farther until I was just holding on with my hands. Then I let go."

That was still a long drop. He could have broken … She realized she was about to scold him for doing something dangerous!

Without another word, Gabriella got down on her hands and knees on the shelf with her back to the hollow space between the boulders—nose to nose with P.D. What about Puppy Dog? There was no way to get him down into The Cleft with them and Yesheb would shoot him on sight.

Then Ty called out, "P.D.—Hide!"

The dog turned instantly, raced down the rock steps and disappeared into the trees. She turned and looked a question over her shoulder. "It's a new game I taught him," he said. "He won't come out until I find him or call him. We play it here all the time."

Play it here all the time?

Gabriella flattened out on her belly on the shelf overhang with her legs dangling into the hole and slowly eased herself backward until she'd slid all the way off the shelf and was hanging from it into the hole. She didn't have much strength in her hands and arms.

« 259 »

"Out of the way," she cried, let go and fell down through the years into the shelter of The Cleft, the only place she had ever felt perfectly safe.

She understood now what she'd really known all along. The Cleft was the reason she had come to Colorado.

Gabriella landed without much dignity on her backside in the dirt and Ty leapt into her arms, held on so tight it shot bolts of pain through her injured neck. But she didn't care, squeezed him just as tight, realized she was rocking him back and forth in her arms, crooning the universal mother song,

"Shhhh. It's okay. Mama's here. Mama's gotcha. Shhhh."

He wasn't crying, but he was trembling violently. It seemed to take a long time for him to stop shaking, but she knew it was actually only a minute or two.

"He's coming, isn't he?" he finally whispered into her shoulder.

"He won't find us here."

"He's not looking for us. He's looking for *me*."

Children always thought everything was about them.

"I ran away because I didn't want him to hurt you and Grandpa Slappy."

Theo! How could she possibly tell Ty that his grandfather was dead? And … no, she couldn't think about Pedro now. If she did … With a great effort of will, Gabriella banished the images from her mind.

She eased the boy gently back out of her arms and looked into his face.

"You don't understand, Ty, Honey. He's stalking *me* because he's crazy. He thinks he's—"

"No, Mom. *You* don't understand. He's come to punish me for …" Then he did start to cry. Softly though, not great gulping sobs. More the worn-out tears of a child who has been crying for hours.

"Do you know Grandpa Slappy saw his best friend drown?"

Where did *that* come from?

"No. When?"

"But they didn't mean to do it. It was an accident. And one of them, the fat kid. He's felt guilty about it for sixty years."

She had no idea what he was talking about.

"I don't want to do that." He looked up into her eyes. "I don't want to carry it around for sixty years. I think … it'd kill me if I did."

"Carry what around?"

THE LAST SAFE PLACE

He grew quiet then, turned and looked at the tree. There was no denying it now. It was no trick of the light, no optical illusion. The tree really was glowing. Like a firefly, light from within. And tiny golden sparkles floated in the air all around it. There had to be a reasonable explanation, of course. Maybe it was … pollen, and up here so high the altitude made it … glow. Or … well, *something*.

Okay, she couldn't explain it. Or the fact that it was warm in here, had to be twenty degrees warmer than the windswept mountainside on the other side of the rocks.

And she certainly couldn't understand why the instant she dropped into The Cleft, all fear had left her. Yesheb was still out there, as dangerous as a wounded lion. He was still intent on murdering them both. The storm was dropping lightning bolts on the other side of the mountain like Santa tossing candy to the children along a parade route. She should have been terrified, but she wasn't. No reason, she just wasn't.

Ty didn't seem to be frightened, either. But terribly *burdened*. She didn't push him, just waited. He'd tell her in his own time. Finally, he let out a long sigh and scooted away from her, looked at the tree, warmed himself on it the way you warm yourself on a campfire.

Still not looking at her, he said. "The bad man is after me because I have to be punished for what I did." He turned slowly, resolutely from the tree to look at her. His voice was steady, but so terribly, terribly sad. "I did it, Mom. Not Daddy. I burned your face with acid."

CHAPTER 19

Yesheb stands in front of the chalet turning slowly around, three hundred and sixty degrees. The cold wind drives the water dripping from tree limbs at him, horizontal rain, like tiny pieces of shrapnel from a grenade. He sways, unsteady on his feet. Loss of blood, lack of oxygen, pain and exhaustion are taking their toll. He understands that he can only drive this injured body so far, that even the fuel of his rage will not propel him forward if there is not enough blood in his body for his heart to pump. He steps inside the chalet to get out of the wind and to bind up half a dozen bleeding wounds.

The one on his forearm is the worst, the only one that is life threatening. The dog tore out a chunk of tissue the size of an egg there and the dish towels and napkins he shoved into the wound are soaked. He stares at it for a moment and makes a decision. He sits down on the bench of a battered picnic table and his dagger makes short work of a bloody dish towel, cutting off a foot-long strip that he wraps around his arm above his elbow. He finds a stick on the floor and uses it to make the strip into a tourniquet. Twists it tight. That will stop the flow of blood, keep him from bleeding out. But unless he gets rapid medical attention, he will likely lose his left arm. He doesn't care. He only needs one arm, one hand to destroy the woman and the boy—to cut and stab and slice them. He can picture it in his head, imagines every wound, every scream. Ah, the delicious screams! He can picture nothing beyond it, though. On the other side of ripping the two of them apart lies absolute, infinite darkness. He will not need his arm there, either.

Yesheb traces the three entwined G's carved into the tabletop with his finger as he counts slowly to three hundred again. To rest, to regain his strength and to be certain the tourniquet holds.

When he hits three hundred he looks at the wound. It is no longer bleeding, nor are the puncture wounds below it on his hand. He stands and imagines he feels strength he didn't have before. Renewed passion for the tasks ahead. For the screams. Then he steps out into the howling wind and his eyes peel away the gathering gloom. He can see like an owl, details in the trees and the rocks and he can smell the faint scent of fear clinging to the ground where she passed, the way a bloodhound can smell one scent among a thousand on a busy sidewalk. He inhales deeply, fills his lungs with it, and follows where it leads him.

PEDRO REACHED THE rocks that formed the back wall of the valley on the right side below the bristlecone pine forest. It would be quite a climb to the top of them and he was losing light, hard to see in the gray shadows. Did she really come here? Did the stalker follow—?

There on the side of a rock at his feet where the rain had not washed it away. Something dark. He wiped it onto his finger and brought it up to his nose. It was blood. Someone passed here who was bleeding. He felt his gut yank into a knot.

Ty? Gabriella? Did the stalker shoot them? No way to tell. The bloody kitchen made only one thing clear. At least one of the combatants in that blood bath was P.D. Paw prints in the blood, scratches on the floor. So it made sense that it was the stalker who was bleeding. But still … He started up the incline and saw other drips of blood in rock crevices or diluted in puddles. Someone was badly injured. Pedro had no doubt that he would come upon whoever it was, or their dead body, soon. If it was the stalker, the man would be as dangerous as a wounded bear. Pedro would not hesitate to shoot him on sight.

"WHAT DID YOU say?"

"It was me. I did it." Ty grabbed her hand, looked into her eyes with such anguish. "But it was an *accident*. I swear, I didn't mean to."

Gabriella's head began to spin.

"What are you talking about?"

Ty took a deep, trembling breath.

"I was there. The night when you were fighting. I was on the bottom step of the stairs watching."

Gabriella couldn't stifle a gasp. What a horrible thing for a seven-year-old to see!

"I was so scared for you, Mom. Daddy was so much bigger than you are and he was drunk, yelling so loud I put my hands up over my ears so I couldn't hear but I still could." Ty paused. "Then he … *hit* you."

The scene was blurred in Gabriella's memory. The doctor said that was normal with people who'd had concussions. She'd been unconscious for two days, which as it turned out was a good thing, since she was spared at least some of the agony of her burns, the part where doctors cleaned the acid out of the wound and removed the destroyed tissue.

"And I couldn't let him do that, hurt you like that. I jumped up and ran at him. Slammed into him … like to tackle him, I guess. I don't know. I just threw myself at him."

He paused. Drew a breath.

"I didn't know what he was holding in his hand." Ty began to cry then, sob. His words were strangled, but Gabriella heard them. Understood them. And understood a world of other things that happened later, things that made no sense at the time. "When I hit him from behind, it knocked him off balance, and the jar in his hand … he dropped it on the floor. You were lying there and what was in the jar, the acid, it splashed in your face."

Gabriella started to cry, too. "Oh, Ty. You poor baby."

"Daddy was so drunk, he didn't even know. He stumbled and fell down on one knee, got some of the acid on his hand and he started yelling, hollering. It scared me to death. I thought he was mad at me, that he was going to kill me. I turned around and ran as hard as I could back to my room and hid under the bed."

Smokey had actually managed to dial 911—for the burns on his hand, not for Gabriella. When the EMTs arrived, they found her on the floor. After Smokey sobered up, he couldn't remember a thing, had been in a total blackout, pleaded guilty to assault and went to prison. He was killed there, knifed by another inmate in a fight over a package of cigarettes on Christmas Eve.

Ty stopped crying, but tears still streamed down his cheeks. "I didn't tell because I *wanted* Daddy to go to prison—for being so mean and for hitting you. And because I was afraid I'd get in trouble. And I was afraid … that you'd hate me."

She grabbed him and crushed him to her chest. "I don't hate you. I could never hate you. I love you!"

"I burned your face, Mommy." He hadn't called her Mommy in years. "I got Daddy killed!"

"No you didn't!" She held him out away from her so she could look directly down into his tear-slathered face. "Now you listen to me, Tyrone Griffith Carmichael. What happened was an accident. You were only seven years old."

Pedro's words rang in her mind then.

"… *you'd forgive him and you'd want him to forgive himself.*"

"But … the bad man. He's—"

"Don't you worry about the bad man. He can't hurt us here. We're safe."

"Actually, that's not entirely true, *Gabriella.*"

The voice came from above them. A voice as cold as a polar ocean. It seemed to take a long time for Gabriella to lift her head and look, but, she already knew what she would see, who she would see. Knew he'd have a gun in his hand, pointed at her. Even knew he'd be smiling that ugly, crooked smile.

YESHEB STANDS TRIUMPHANT. The storm in this world has passed over the peak, the sky is clearing, the rising moon lights the shadowed mountainside brighter than the setting sun. The storm in the other realm is over, too. He feels no pain. He is complete, whole again. The force of his own will has healed his injuries! No longer is his life blood pouring out of him from a dozen gory wounds inflicted by vicious teeth and savage claws. His whole body is flawless, without blemish. Even his severed ear has grown back.

But far more important than the healing of his body is the healing of his mind. The scales have dropped away, the gauzy curtain raised. He sees with absolute clarity now, understands that this—all of this—has been a gauntlet he had to run to cleanse his body, mind and soul. It has been a test—that he is about to pass!

When The Voice spoke in his head as he ran—staggered—through the ugly forest of stubby, mangled trees, he had dropped to his knees in terror, surprise and wonder.

It is almost over.

The hole inside him was filled again with the presence of The Voice. And with its power. He felt it surge through him like an electric current as the other voices spoke to him. They were all there—the sultry woman's voice urged him to get up, to go on. Voices in Italian and Arabic directed him down the path. The child's voice from his boyhood revealed where his prey was hiding.

And they all speak in harmony now as he stands triumphant. They chant in concert, "Kill them! Kill them!"

That was the plan all along, the will of The Voice! She is a false prophetess; the words in her book are heresy designed to deceive and subvert the powers of darkness. She is an agent from the light. He saw it clearly when he passed through the ugly trees into the clearing—a golden radiance shown out like a beacon from the pile of boulders, led him to where she cowers in terror in a hole like a cornered rabbit. She must be eliminated and he has been chosen for the task.

But he also knows what The Voice does *not* know. Once he has completed the task, he will *become* The Voice. It was foretold before the laying of the foundation of the world. When he tastes the blood of the false prophetess, Yesheb Al Tobbanoft will become more than The Beast of Babylon. He will become the most powerful force in the universe.

He looks down into their faces, throws his head back and laughs out loud, a full, roaring, glorious laugh that echoes the maelstrom of the storm rumbling on the other side of the mountain peak.

"You will die in agony. Slowly. I will make you *scream*." He tosses his gun aside and withdraws the dagger from its sheath. "You will beg me for death."

He crouches to leap into the branches of the tree to break his fall. It is perfect. His prey will have nowhere to run.

G<small>ABRIELLA STARED AT</small> the apparition above her, a character out of a slasher horror movie. Yesheb was drenched in his own blood. His clothes were torn, his left arm dangled useless at his side, most of his right ear had been ripped off. But the maniacal twisting of his perfect features into a mask of hatred and evil was the most horrifying sight of all—one last, apocalyptic celebration of madness.

He lifted his dagger and cried out that he would make her beg for death.

THE LAST SAFE PLACE

"I'm not afraid of you anymore, Yesheb," she said and only became aware of the truth of the words as she spoke them. "You can't hurt me here."

She suddenly understood that he had been feeding off her fear like a maggot off rotting meat. He *needed* her to be afraid.

"You're not The Beast of Babylon. You're a pathetic psychopath with delusions of grandeur. Now, get off this mountain and leave me and my family alone!"

Yesheb stood with his dagger raised, a quizzical look on his face. He seemed to shrink before her eyes, out of the grandiose proportions her terror had granted him, down, down into reality—a mortally injured man who'd be dead inside half an hour. Oh, he was still as dangerous as a pit viper. But he couldn't touch her or Ty. They were safe here.

"You'll be sorry you ever—" he began.

"No, you're the one who's about to be sorry."

Rage washed anew over his face and he crouched to jump into the opening.

"Leave now, Yesheb. I'm warning you."

Where did that come from?

He tensed to spring, but an instant before he leapt down on them a flame appeared on the end of Yesheb's dagger. Bright blue, shimmering into violet, the tiny blaze danced on the point of the dagger like the flame on the end of a cigarette lighter. Slowly the flame spread. Up his arm to his head. Down his body to his feet. She clutched Ty tight against her and started in fascination at the bloody horror lit in blue-violet flame. Tiny sparks appeared, popped in the air all around him, and she could hear a humming, crackling sound.

St. Elmo's fire!

Y ESHEB FEELS THE power of the universe flow through his body, a force of such incredible strength that it sparks and pops off him in flickering blue fire. He is the Anointed One! All the elements in time and space bow to him and obey his will. He controls the sun and moon, stars and constellations. The earth rotates at his pleasure; life exists by his divine design.

He is invincible!

The full moon rising as the sun set left the shadowed mountainside awash in an odd half-light, neither day nor night, that made it hard for Pedro to see. He had followed the trail of blood in the growing dusk until he reached a slight rise that looked down on a conical pile of boulders. Light glowed out a crack between the boulders. From a small fire? But there was no smoke. A lantern, then.

A dark shadow hulked above the light. When the shadow leaned over the opening, the light illuminated it like the face of a man looking out of the darkness into a campfire. Except the golden glow was steady, not flickering.

The shadow was a man, the stalker. Gabriella and Ty, one or both of them, must be hidden down between the boulders. Pedro saw the stalker toss something away, then he drew a knife, a long thin knife, a dagger, and held it above his head.

In a single, fluid motion, Pedro lifted the rifle and fit the stock tight against his shoulder. A hundred yards; he could make the shot. Through the telescopic sight, he could see the man clearly and knew whose blood had been smeared all over the kitchen floor in the cabin and dripped on the trail to lead him here. An image from a movie flashed into his mind—Carrie, covered in blood, her face distorted in rage and evil intent. That was the man in his gun sight. Any second, he would leap into the crevice. Pedro didn't hesitate. He fit the crosshairs on the center of the man's chest.

Then a light appeared on the tip of the man's dagger, a blue-violet flame. It spread slowly over him until it outlined his whole body. Pedro lifted his head, looked out over the sight to be sure it wasn't a reflection of some kind on the glass. The man's body was bathed in blue flame.

St. Elmo's fire!

Pedro returned his eye to the sight, breathed in slowly and held it. Then he squeezed the trigger to send a bullet hurtling across the clearing into the heart of the figure outlined in blue flame.

The rifle recoiled, kicked Pedro's shoulder like a mule and knocked him backwards. His hat flew off his head and the gun flew out of his hands, its barrel puffed out in the middle like a golf ball had been stuffed down it. Pedro landed on his back, the wind knocked out of him.

What in the …?

THE LAST SAFE PLACE

The barrel was jammed! When he fell climbing up the mountain and dropped the rifle, something must have gotten stuck in the barrel. He was lucky it hadn't exploded like a hand grenade in his face.

He staggered to his feet and began to run toward the boulder pile. Weaponless now, he would rip the stalker apart with his bare hands! But he knew he would be too late. In seconds, the stalker would leap into the crevice. Gabriella would be dead before Pedro could save her.

A sob exploded out of his chest as he ran.

"No!" he cried.

God, please, don't let—

A flash of white ripped the world open, so bright it wiped out every image in an explosion of light.

Crack!

Boom!

A mighty fist of sound and pressure and hot wind hammered Pedro backward into a bristlecone pine, jammed broken limbs into his back and arms, slashed a jagged cut across the side of his face. He couldn't hear. A roar like a pounding surf filled his head. He couldn't see, just bright spots of brilliance, sparkling explosions of white.

He gasped in air that smelled like cordite and ozone, slid down out of the branches of the gnarled tree to the ground, shook his head.

Lightning!

From the storm on the other side of the mountain!

Pedro staggered to his feet again and stumbled toward the pile of boulders. He still could see fiery rings of light, flashbulbs popped all around him and he could hear the rumbling surf pounding in his ears.

Rocks on the side of the pile of boulders made a natural staircase leading to the top. When he stepped on the bottom one and looked up, he saw it. It was clear even with his distorted vision. A huge slab of rock above the boulders—that looked like a diving board over a swimming pool—was *moving*, beginning to tilt slightly downward. Rocks and boulders on the far end of it were sliding away.

W HITE LIGHT.
A mighty roar.
Then Pedro's face.

One, two, three.

It was like there had been no time between them. But it also seemed like an eternity had passed between the brilliance of the sun above her and the face that looked down at her. A face lit by a golden glow from below.

Pedro! He was *alive!* She wanted to laugh and cry and sing and—.

Pedro's lips moved. He was saying something, but she couldn't hear it, could hear nothing at all, in fact, but a buzz like a million bees had built a hive in her head. And his face ... his cheek was bleeding.

"... get out now ..."

The voice seemed to come from a great distance, sounded hollow.

"Rock slide ..." The words were muffled.

Ty leapt up out of her lap.

"Mom get up!" He yanked on her arm. "The overhang ... it's falling!"

For some reason, that didn't surprise Gabriella. Though she felt a sense of urgency, a need to hurry, she still was unafraid.

"... get you out of there!" Pedro called.

Out of here? She looked around. She had not given a nanosecond of thought to how she would get out of The Cleft once she'd gotten into it. There was no way to climb out; the roof hung out over the walls. The hole was too far above their heads to jump up and grab hold of the rock where she'd slid in.

"... your jacket. Take off your jacket," Pedro yelled.

She slipped out of her nylon rain jacket because he told her to, but she had no idea why.

Ty understood, though. He yanked off his own jacket and began to tie the arm of his jacket to the arm of hers. She looked up and Pedro was leaned into the opening from the waist, dangling his jacket above them. It was too high for her to reach.

"Hold me up, Mom, on your shoulders."

Gabriella crouched down. Ty climbed up on her shoulders and she staggered to her feet, swaying from his weight. She couldn't look up with him there, but in a moment, he jumped down and a nylon-jacket rope hung from the hole above.

Pedro pulled it out of the hole—must have been securing the knots Ty had tied—then dropped it back down into the opening. Gabriella lifted Ty up high enough for him to grab the rope and Pedro quickly hauled him to the top.

Gabriella could hear it now, the crunch of rocks grinding together.

She grabbed the jacket-rope when Pedro tossed it down to her, held on tight and rose agonizingly slowly to the edge of the hole. Ty reached out as soon as she was close and caught the collar of her shirt and pulled. Her hands connected with the rock. She held on and started to climb up. Then Pedro gripped her arm and yanked her up over the edge in one motion.

"Run!" he yelled.

She didn't look up.

There was something black, charred, lying beside the opening. She recognized the smell. But she didn't look at that either.

She leapt down the rock steps, with Ty in front of her and Pedro behind. She heard a rumbling sound, rocks peppered her back, a roar rose up with a cloud of dust and she kept running.

Pedro grabbed her arm to pull her along faster, dragged Ty almost off his feet. It all happened so fast.

She had no memory of actually crossing the clearing. Her next clear awareness was of Pedro knocking her and Ty to the ground and covering them with his body. She couldn't see, but she could feel the avalanche chew up the world behind her.

She smelled dust. Pedro lifted himself up off her and rolled over onto his back, panting. Dirt and little pieces of rock were still raining out of the sky. She sat up. Ty sat up beside her and she noticed the rims of his glasses were bent. The two of them turned around together and stared at the cloud of dirt in the moonlight, watched as the dust settled out of the air above the massive pile of boulders that lay in a heap on the other side of the clearing. A pile of boulders that had shattered The Cleft and buried the body of Yesheb Al Tobbanoft. And a single, perfect Jesus tree.

Then Pedro was kneeling in front of her. He cupped her face in his hands, gently brushed her hair back from her forehead. Tears glistened in his eyes. When he spoke, the roar in her ears muffled the sound. She could hear the thick Spanish accent, though, and she didn't need words to know what he was saying. She reached out to him, tried to wipe the blood off his cheek, but he folded her into his arms before she had a chance and held her against his chest. She closed her eyes but could still see star bursts of colored light behind her eyelids. Then she felt something warm and wet slide across her cheek and her eyes popped open. P.D.! Ty must have called him. The dog's tail was wagging so fast it was a blur and Ty was hugging the ball of fur almost as tight as Pedro was hugging her.

CHAPTER 20

Gabriella put the final pair of jeans into the suitcase, wrestled the zipper closed and carried it downstairs and out to the jeep. When she came back in, she held a box Ty'd slipped in between the suitcases—a shoebox with holes in the top.

"Whatever's in here—a tiger salamander, a green snake, a mountain lion, a sperm whale—whatever it is, take it back to Notmuchava Waterfall and let it go."

"But Mom, I—"

"Take a picture of it to prove to Joey you didn't make it up. You can catch another one next year."

That put a smile on his face. And on Pedro's, too.

"I mean, if Jim Benninger invites us."

"Oh, he will invite you," Pedro said. "I can absolutely guarantee he will invite you!"

The boy and P.D. headed out the back door and across the meadow toward the creek and Pedro held up a cup of coffee.

"Break time," he said. "I spared no trouble or expense in brewing the perfect cup of coffee, made from eleven herbs and spices—"

"That'd be fried chicken."

"Then I threw in two all-beef patties, special sauce, lettuce, cheese, pick—"

"It's instant, isn't it."

"Yep. But sit on the porch and look at the view and you will not notice."

She followed him out the front door and eased carefully down into a chair. The doctor had given her a cervical collar and instructed her to wear it on her injured neck for two weeks. She'd taken it off after ten days, but was beginning to regret that decision. The plane flight from Pittsburgh to Denver, the three-hour drive to St. Elmo and the ride up the mountain yesterday had reawakened the pain of the injury.

"Your neck hurts."

"A little, but—"

"You are not lifting anything heavier than a toothbrush! Ty and I can handle the rest of it."

Gabriella didn't even bother to protest. She had learned that when Pedro went into what she called Pancho Villa mode, resistance was futile. He was in charge ... as he had been from the moment he half-carried her down from the bristlecone pine forest, wouldn't let her or Ty go into the cabin, just whisked them off the mountain and took care of everything. It was all a blur now. Her only clear memory was that Pedro had been there through it all—the hospital, the police investigation ... and Theo's funeral.

"You figure they will sue?" Pedro asked.

She barked out a little laugh.

"Of course they will! When I tell Hampton Books there'll be no sequel to *The Bride of the Beast* and that I'm not going to make any more appearances to promote the book, they'll sue all right." She looked sideways at him without moving her head. "I'll survive. It's only money. I can live comfortably the rest of my life on the royalties from Garrett's music."

They sat together in companionable silence, looking out over the vista of the Arkansas River Valley.

"When does Adriana's flight get in?" she asked quietly.

"A couple of hours after yours leaves. The timing ees perfect."

Gabriella said nothing.

"And we will talk. All of us, as a family. I think I know where eet will go, eventually. Where it has to go. Perhaps Angelina can learn to breathe on her own without the ventilator ... but if she can't ..."

Gabriella reached out and squeezed his hand.

Ty came around the side of the cabin and up onto the porch and said he'd returned the creature to the creek.

"You got all your stuff gathered up?" Gabriella asked.

"Just one thing's left and it'll have to stay here."

"You're not leaving your rock?"

Gabriella had given Ty the half she'd hidden in the fireplace to save as a Christmas present for Grant more than thirty years ago. An ordinary rock. Except it wasn't. A chunk of granite that couldn't be a geode. Except it was.

With rainbow crystals inside that were a geologic impossibility. Just like The Cleft was an impossibility.

She and Pedro had talked and talked about it, and they always wound up at the same place. And that was nowhere at all. There was no explanation, not for any of it.

They wondered what they'd find if they dug farther down in the rock slide than the authorities had dug to recover Yesheb's body. If they dug out where The Cleft had been—would every pebble she and Garrett had tossed into it that summer be changed on the inside, too? Be just as beautiful as—?

"The impossible rock—no way!" Ty said. "It's the best present I ever got! I'll keep it my whole life."

Her eyes were suddenly moist.

"Then what …?"

"I painted a picture last night with the oil paints. I didn't know it'd still be wet this morning. We can't take it with us."

"Put it on the refrigerator."

Ty grinned. "And we can get it when we come back next summer."

She nodded, then made a shooing motion. "Go on now, go get it. We've got a plane to catch."

They went back into the cabin and Ty bounded up the stairs with P.D. a step behind him.

Gabriella turned to Pedro.

"Pedro, I've been trying to think of a way to say—"

"Shhhh."

"But—"

He pulled her into his arms. "Call me when you get back to Pittsburgh." He held her tight and she breathed in the soap smell of him as he whispered into her hair. "We have many things to talk about."

They heard Ty's footsteps like the rumble of a stampede down the wooden stairs. He held a piece of paper from the art tablet in his hand, 12 × 16 inches. He went to the refrigerator, pulled off four magnets and carefully affixed them to the unpainted edges of the paper and positioned it below the watercolor he'd done of the view from the front porch of the cabin the day Yesheb—

The room went airless. Gabriella looked at the piece of art paper and the world slowed down and stopped. Didn't move on its axis. For a breathless, eternal moment nothing in the universe stirred.

Below the little-kid-drawn watercolor of the valley was an oil *painting* of a single, perfect bristlecone pine tree—a tree that glowed. Somehow, Ty had captured the incandescence, the light from within. Each needle on every branch was a golden firefly. Around the tree were hundreds of points of light, sparkling, each a star, a universe of its own. The glow spread out into the shadows; the rock walls curved protectively around it.

It was stunning, a work of art!

Gabriella dragged her eyes from it to the picture above it—a child's scrawl on a refrigerator door with the Mona Lisa. She looked at Pedro, saw his eyes go from one picture to the other, watched him make the same comparison, reach the same conclusion. He turned his eyes toward her, opened his mouth, but no words came out.

Ty was completely oblivious to their response. He stepped back, adjusted his baby-owl glasses on his nose and looked it over himself.

"I wish Grandpa Slappy could have seen it," he said, his voice thick with unshed tears.

"Me, too," Gabriella managed to gasp.

Then Ty turned around and saw that his mother and Pedro were gaping at him.

"What?" he asked, looking from one to the other. "What's everybody standing around for? I thought we had a plane to catch."

THE END